THE ORIGIN OF ME

BERNARD GALLATE

THE ORIGIN OF ME

VINTAGE BOOKS
Australia

VINTAGE

UK | USA | Canada | Ireland | Australia
India | New Zealand | South Africa | China

Vintage is part of the Penguin Random House group of companies whose addresses
can be found at global.penguinrandomhouse.com

Penguin
Random House
Australia

First published by Vintage in 2020

Cover design by Alex Ross © Penguin Random House Australia Pty Ltd
Cover images: chicken © los_ojos_pardos/Getty; background © NataLT/Shutterstock,
Alted Studio/Shutterstock, Wilqkuku/Shutterstock
Illustration on page 5 © Bernard Gallate
Typeset in 11.5/15.5 pt Adobe Garamond Pro by Midland Typesetters, Australia

Printed and bound in Australia by Griffin Press, part of Ovato, an accredited
ISO AS/NZS 14001 Environmental Management Systems printer

A catalogue record for this
book is available from the
National Library of Australia

NATIONAL
LIBRARY
OF AUSTRALIA

ISBN 978 0 14378 962 8

penguin.com.au

MIX
Paper from
responsible sources
FSC® C009448

CAST OF CHARACTERS

Lincoln Locke
    Gus (dog, staffy)
Venn (older sister)
    Oscar (cat, Burmese)
Charis (mother)
    Morgan Brierly (business partner)
    Penny Button, Emma, Jules (employees)
    Vienna Voronova (model), $KiNT (designer)
Lance (father)
    Steve (business partner)
Pop Locke, Nana Locke (paternal grandparents)
    Tippi (dog, Jack Russell–Chihuahua)

Northern Beaches life
Dr Finster (GP)
Nicole Parker (ex-girlfriend)
Maëlle Beauvais (French house guest)
Valmay and Roger Harris (neighbours)
    Dougal (dog, foxhound)
Elliot Grobecker (ex-boyfriend of Venn)

Tom Nugent (best Northern Beaches friend of Lincoln)
Blake Nugent (older brother of Tom)
Coops (friend)
Maxine Partridge (best friend of Charis)

Crestfield Academy students
Tibor Mintz (orientation buddy)
Isa Mountwinter
    Dee (mum)
    Terri, Stef (housemates)
    Delilah (cat)
Phoenix Lee (best friend of Isa)
Pericles Pappas
    Con (father)
    Helena and Christina (twin sisters)
Darvin 'Nads' Naylor
Sean 'Mullows' Mulligan
Evan Starkey ('Starkey' for short)
Cheyenne Piper
Liliana and Ingrid Petersen (twins)
Heather Treadwell
David York
Byron Paget

Crestfield staff
Mr Dashwood (principal)
Mr Simmons (sportsmaster and swim coach)
Deb Gelber (assistant coach)
Ms Tarasek (art teacher)
Mr Monaro (maths teacher)
Dr Limberg (school psychologist)
Mrs Deacon (head librarian)
Mr Jespersen (caretaker)
Miss Keenan (biology teacher)
Mr Field (English teacher)

Mrs Hatcher (history teacher)
Miss Moreau (French teacher)
Nurse Nola

The city
Sergio (personal trainer)
Bert McGill (junkyard hermit)
Blue Lady, Pink Lady, Loose Pants Lenny (other eccentrics)

My One Redeeming Affliction
Edwin Stroud (author) a.k.a. Taloo, a.k.a. Harold Hopkins
Thomas (brother)
Loula (sister)
Esther Stroud, *née* Hunnicutt (mother)
   Walter Hunnicutt (Esther's father)
   Martha Hunnicutt (Esther's mother)
   Althea Beauclare (Esther's stepmother)
   Frederick, Samuel, Arthur (brothers)
   Madame Zora (employer: a milliner)
William Stroud (father)
   Hannah and Matthias Stroud (William's adoptive parents)
   Ah To, *or* Johnny, and Lin Cheong, *or* Mac (friends)
   Dimitrios (Greek fisherman in Sydney)
   George Pemberton (entrepreneur)

Edwin's Pyrmont life
Deidre 'Diddy' Budd (neighbour)
Neville Sampson (employer)
Reg McGuffin (local bully)
Dr Melvin Fletcher

Melinkoff's Astonishing Assembly of Freaks
Irving Melinkoff (showman)
Ruthie Davis a.k.a. Baby Cakes the Living Doll
Roy Lister the Human Globe

Melvina Wellington; Leopold (son): the Fully Bearded Family

Milton Banks a.k.a. the Whispering Flame

Serpentina and her diamond python Octavius

Lloyd Farbridge and leopards Samson and Delilah

Paulo Esposito a.k.a. Paulo Penguino (best friend of Edwin)

Hilda Groot a.k.a. Zerodia Nashko the Circassian Beauty,
a.k.a. mermaid princess

START HERE

According to family lore, exactly forty weeks after my father won the prestigious and fiercely contested GravyLog® Pet Food account for his advertising agency, I was born. Whether his victory had inspired the little guys to swim harder or it had more to do with the favourable new position my parents had found themselves in is a disputed element of the story. But the date of my birth is not. It was the twelfth of February, the same day that Abraham Lincoln and Charles Darwin were born. I know – incredible. Three illustrious figures sharing a birthday. My parents couldn't decide between Abe and Charlie, so they settled on Lincoln.

On the origin of the little brown spot, I'm more dubious. I'd neither seen nor felt the thing at the base of my spine before turning fifteen last year, but when I visited Dr Finster he said it was a birthmark. I wasn't about to ask my mother if it had always been there. She would've asked for a look. The doctor reassured me the matter would remain strictly confidential, and urged me to return if I noticed any changes. Over the following months, its development was gradual enough to deny . . . until late last year, when my first and only girlfriend, Nicole Parker, inadvertently touched the tiny nub. Her crushing reaction set off a series of events that resulted in me being torn from my old public school on Sydney's Northern Beaches and transplanted into a private institution in the Eastern Suburbs.

Today marks the end of my first week at

CRESTFIELD ACADEMY FOR THE EXCEEDINGLY GIFTED AND DANGEROUSLY PRIVILEGED

If Aunty Beryl filled her tank with unleaded petrol at $1.65 a litre and stopped once on her way from Sydney to Dubbo, how much would it cost Uncle Barry to reach Coonabarabran if he drove twice as fast in his V8?

Today Mr Monaro wrote that and nine other absurdly challenging questions on the board and barred us from leaving until we'd solved them. All I could think about was the fact that Uncle Barry wasn't helping to reduce global warming. I chewed my pen and waited for inspiration. Nothing came except the taste of ink, so I prayed for a small natural disaster to pull me out of the room. The answer arrived in the form of Tibor Mintz, who'd been performing the role of my personal Orientation Buddy with excessive enthusiasm all week.

He approached Monaro and whispered something behind a cupped hand. Monaro nodded and tilted his head away, obviously not enjoying Mintz's breath humidifying his ear canal. Mintz scanned the room, sucked air between his disorganised teeth and said, 'Lincoln Locke. You had an appointment with the school psychologist Dr Limberg in Student Welfare at fourteen hundred sharp. The time is currently fourteen twelve.'

The guys up the back laughed. I stashed away my junk and made a snappy exit – though not snappy enough to evade Mintz, who was waiting in the hall outside.

'Thanks for that,' I said, thrilled at having mental instability conferred on me in front of my new classmates.

'Would you like me to escort you to Student Welfare?'

'You've helped enough already.' I turned and headed off.

'Wrong way!' he called out, but I kept walking till I was out of his sight then checked the school map on my phone. Let me get this straight: Crestfield is a maze, I'm the new lab rat, and Limberg . . .? Well, you get the picture. Only problem being, this little rodent wasn't hungry for cheese.

Student Welfare was not some poky room in the admin block but an entirely separate wing accessed by the HALL OF CHAMPIONS, an inclined passageway hung with black-and-white blow-ups of students performing sporting feats. The first was a runner breaking through a finish tape; next was a back-arching high-jumper, then a Becks look-alike demonstrating his ball skills. All were blond except for the final student, a backstroker with a shaved head about to release himself from his starting block, snarling with dental perfection. Above the shots on one side was a blue banner with gold lettering that said, AUDE ALIQUID DIGNUM. And on the other, a banner with the translation: DARE SOMETHING WORTHY. Frankly it was all a bit too Leni Riefenstahl for my liking. I watched her film *Olympia* in History last year – epic but with sinister overtones.

The sound of pan pipes, rushing water and assorted bird calls greeted me at Student Welfare. The carpet and three of the walls were moss green; the fourth was papered over with an enormous rainforest print, with the word

BREATHE

superimposed on it. The receptionist sat beneath, following the instruction but not doing much else. She was wearing a natty cape and a cap with a red cross on it, the kind of gear a kid playing hospital might wear. In the centre of the room was a massive fish tank surrounded by leather sofas, one of which was occupied by a miserable squirt with a precision bowl cut.

'Lincoln Locke?' the receptionist said.

'That's me.' Approaching the counter, I realised that except for the thick-framed glasses, which curiously had no lenses, she looked very much like one of my classmates, Isa Mount-something, who'd been absent from Maths.

'You're twenty-five minutes late. Take a seat. The doctor will be with you shortly.'

Instead of sitting, I checked out the fish: three big silvers and one small pink guy hovering near the coral. Whenever the silvers approached, the pink guy took refuge in a miniature ruined castle. I tapped the glass to say hello, accidentally causing him to dart into open water. The big silvers surrounded him and nipped at his tail. I rapped the glass again and they swam away, but it was too late. Little Pinky was paralysed and started to sink.

The receptionist was throwing me a stink eye, so I sat and perused an old copy of the school magazine, *EXCELSIOR!* Crestfield's first eleven had won the cricket, and Alakazam Smallgoods was sponsoring the jazz band's trip to Tasmania. Exciting times – free cabanossi for the horn section! I pulled out my leaking pen to have a crack at the cryptic crossword.

1 Across: Brad idly arranged insect displays (8 letters). So . . . Brad's a lazy entomologist, but that has twelve letters. I read all the across clues and none of them made a lick of sense, then the sick kid next to me started rocking and whimpering, obviously in dire need of distraction from his pain. So I said, 'Pssst, kid! I think I might've killed that pink fish.'

His head sank between his knees, and he groaned.

'Please don't upset the other patient,' the receptionist said.

'I wouldn't classify myself as a patient,' I said. 'I'm just here to—'

'He killed the fish!' the kid blabbed.

'Don't worry, Byron. He's just in shock,' the receptionist said.

'Poet or parents' preferred holiday destination?' I whispered.

Kid didn't answer.

A lady in a cream suit and a powder-blue shirt came out of her room, spoke briefly to the fake nurse/receptionist then turned to me and said, 'Hello, you must be Lincoln. I'm Dr Marion Limberg. Please follow.' Rectangular glasses, shiny black bun, slight European accent – she could've been an SBS presenter.

Her room was mostly white, with monochrome farm photos and frosted windows, vast white desk, iMac, potted white orchid and a scent diffuser producing a fine mist that smelt of lavender and something woody. 'Would you like some water?' she said. 'It's filtered.'

'No, thank you. Am I in trouble?'

'Of course not.' She leant forward, steepling her pinkies. 'It's customary for new students to receive a personal introduction to our counselling services. You'll come across many exciting challenges on the road ahead, and we're here to help you. Crestfield Academy is so much more than a school, Lincoln. We're your second family.' She handed me a tissue.

'Thanks, but I won't be needing that.'

'There's ink on your face.'

I wiped my mouth and checked the stained tissue. 'Wow! It looks like a map of New Guinea.' I showed her and she almost smiled.

'Interesting observation – perceptive. Perhaps we could do a small exercise? When I hold up the image, tell me what you see – whatever pops into your mind.' She pulled a card from the drawer then checked her watch. 'I hope you don't mind me recording the session for later analysis?' I shrugged. She tapped her phone and placed it between us. 'Subject: Lincoln Locke. Visual recognition: level three. Commencing two-forty.' She flipped the card to reveal a black-and-white graphic. 'What do you see?'

'A sad Japanese princess blowing a kiss.'

'Anything else?'

'The head of a praying mantis, or maybe a space alien. A frying egg and an eight ball. Could I please hold the card?'

'Certainly . . .' She craned her head towards the phone. 'Subject now revolving card.'

'A pirate's been shot in the head. Or is that King Henry?'

'There are no correct or incorrect answers.'

'There's a rabbit and a chicken laying an egg.' I didn't mention the underpants in case it revealed some latent fetish.

'Anything else? Anything at all?'

'Underpants?'

'Thank you.' She returned the card to the drawer. 'So, your parents have separated and you're currently living with your father?'

'Did you glean that from my answers?'

'The information was in the student profile questionnaire they completed. Here at Crestfield, we take a holistic approach to our students' wellbeing. We encourage parents to be actively involved in their children's schooling.'

'My parents run their own businesses, so don't expect to see my mother making devon sandwiches in the canteen.'

'The school café doesn't use processed meat.'

'But Alakazam Smallgoods sponsors the jazz band.'

Limberg frowned and wrote something in a folder – possibly 'combative smartarse'.

'Do you ever experience feelings of animosity towards your parents?'

'Never,' I said, denial curling my top lip.

My mind raced back to midway through last year. Following months of sniping and standoffs that had culminated in the perfect shitstorm of my mother's fiftieth birthday, my parents began a trial in-house separation. Intended to foster a calmer atmosphere for my sister Venn's HSC preparation, it only made the place crackle with unresolved tension. And not wanting to exclude me from exam thrills, they made me sit the Crestfield Academy entrance test – six gruelling hours. I gave it a good shot, never thinking I could possibly make the grade.

Checking the mailbox a couple of months later, I found a bulky envelope addressed to me with AUDE ALIQUID DIGNUM in gold on the corner. I tore it open and read that I'd been offered an interview at one of the most well-equipped, academically prestigious and sportingly competitive schools in the state. Terrified at the prospect of going there, I took the letter out the back and set it on fire. Valmay Harris, our next-door neighbour, stuck her head over the fence and asked whether I was burning something.

'No,' I said, clapping the embers out. I thought I was in the clear until a few weeks later, when the school rang to find out why there'd been no response. Dad asked if I'd seen the letter and I lied.

In that moment, the bitter seed of deception embedded itself in the soft pink tissue of my heart. Till that point in my life I'd been scrupulously honest with my parents, even when they confronted me about smoking grass. And that hadn't even been pot – just lawn clippings wrapped in a banana leaf, which was more humiliating. It wasn't so much the act of lying about the letter that bothered me as my father believing the lie. Even worse, I knew that my grandfather, Pop Locke, who used to be a postie, would've been mortified that I'd tampered with the mail – a federal offence if it hadn't been addressed to me.

In August I'd been interviewed at Crestfield, and a month later was offered a place in Year 10, which surprised me more than it did my parents. They'd still have to pay full fees, but, as they constantly reminded me, they could afford it, and only seven students were being given the opportunity. The idea of being separated from my mates to go to a school on the other side of the bridge prompted an immediate no. Dad told me to mull it over. In October he moved out of the family home at Signal Bay and into his recently vacated investment apartment in the city. The actual geographic separation of my parents after twenty-five years together, though incredibly sad, palpably reduced tension in the family home.

Now to explain my ex-girlfriend's pivotal role in this chain of events: Nicole Parker was a committed Christian who, having made some sort of personal purity vow, restricted our level of physical contact to handholding and the occasional snuggle, which drove my sexual tension to unbearable levels. Over the following months I progressed from casual to excessive masturbation, judging by the level of skin irritation and, on one occasion, actual bleeding.

One night, at the height of my frustration and despondency, I went alone to a party at my best friend Tom's place behind Avalon Beach. Nicole unexpectedly showed up and, even more surprisingly, we had our first kiss. It was incredible, but in the excitement she slid her hand down my back and touched the nub, which was by then slightly hairy. Nicole's abject revulsion and swift departure propelled me into my first drinking binge with enough determination to obliterate myself.

At 2 am, my sister Venn found me facedown, unconscious and soaking wet, near the water's edge. The next morning, Mum banned me from any further association with Tom and his brother Blake, even though we'd been best friends for ten years, gone to the same schools, rode the same waves – and they'd had nothing to do with my blackout. Following a massive argument, she called Dad to settle the matter. They decided that at the beginning of the next school year I would attend Crestfield Academy and live with him during the week.

So yes, Dr Limberg was right on the money. There was a degree of residual animosity towards my parents for sending me there.

'Have your fellow students been welcoming?' she said.

'Bent over backwards.'

'According to some feedback, this week you've spent almost every recess and lunchtime alone in the library.'

'Are we under video surveillance or something?'

'Mrs Deacon, our head librarian, noticed you sitting alone on consecutive days. She logged her observations on The Owl, the faculty network and student monitoring system, which automatically sent me a Hoot. Lincoln, why do you think you've been isolating yourself?'

At that moment, a ladybird landed on Dr Limberg's lapel. I have no recollection of my reply, other than evasive rambling, because I was focused on the insect taking the scenic route towards her neck, its orange-and-black markings a dramatic contrast to the cream material. It disappeared over the lip then re-emerged on her shirt collar. I didn't warn her because I wanted to see how far the ladybird could get before she felt it.

'There's a lot going on in that head of yours. Experiencing anxiety is a natural response to all of your big changes. But I have a feeling there's something else really bothering you.'

I felt a distinct, almost electric tingle in the nub that made me flinch – as if it wanted to claim responsibility.

'Please be assured that you can tell me about anything at all and it will remain confidential.'

'There's nothing I can think of.' Again the tingle and flinch.

'I'd like to see you in a month's time, just to touch base.'

Bad choice of words. 'But I don't have to?'

'Coming under duress would be counterproductive – ooh!' This time Dr Limberg flinched. She reached to her neck and brought the tiny insect close to her face. 'Ladybird, ladybird, fly away home! Your house is on fire, your children are gone.' She blew the bug onto the white orchid.

'It's after three-thirty. Can I go now?'

'Of course.'

A ladybird is supposed to be a sign of good luck, but that nursery rhyme was hardly brimming with optimism for the little bug's future.

ACCIDENTS DON'T MAKE APPOINTMENTS

Escaping the interrogation room and the Crestfield grounds only brought partial relief because it was thirty-eight degrees outside and Edgecliff Station was closed. I stared at the sign directing commuters to the replacement bus, thinking it heralded the end of the world instead of a minor inconvenience. A rail employee with high-vis sweat patches bellowed, 'System meltdown, mate. All lines are affected.' So I walked home.

I'd been living in the city with Dad for ten days and it sucked more audibly than a Dyson – especially in this heatwave. For one, I couldn't surf with my mates after school anymore. Bondi's not far but public transport's a bitch. We'd brought my bike over on Sunday and it had been stolen outside a convenience store on Monday. Dad had spewed, saying I was stupid for leaving it unlocked.

'That's the neighbourhood for you,' I'd said.

He said I needed to start taking responsibility for myself so I stuck my hand in front of his face and said, 'Mirror!'

It didn't go down well. I now had an 8 pm curfew and had to answer Dad's constant video calls for him to make sure I was doing homework. Gold star for vigilance, Lance. Maybe there's an opening for a warden at Long Bay?

As I passed through the lobby of our apartment building, Frank the concierge said, 'Hot enough for you this afternoon?'

'Hot enough to fry an egg on my forehead.'

Frank is the gatekeeper, the concierge station his gate. T H E E Y R I E is hermetically sealed from anyone or thing that isn't welcome – probably one of the most appealing factors for the type of people living here.

I pressed my thumb to the elevator's sensor pad and exactly eight seconds later arrived at level twenty-seven. Inside my room I dumped my satchel, changed into Speedos and boardies, grabbed a towel and rode up to the unsupervised fitness centre and pool on thirty-three. Marble columns, a tiled mosaic and an enormous overflowing urn – very 'lost city of Atlantis'. There was nobody around, so I peeled off my boardies and slid into the cool water. Refreshing, but it didn't clear my mind like surfing does. The narrow twenty-five-metre strip demanded laps. Ten down, I was joined by a woman in a daisy-covered bathing cap who, despite her age, soon caught up to me. Paranoid that with goggles on she might spot the nub, I got out.

The phone was ringing back at the apartment and, assuming it was Mum checking up on me before she and Venn left for their girls' retreat in Bowral, I let it ring out and went to the balcony. Beyond the CBD, the Corporate Bandits' Domain, the Blue Mountains were turning purple beneath synthetic-looking pink clouds. My phone plinked. A text from Dad, saying he was on the verge of sealing a deal and couldn't make dinner. A second instructing me to order home delivery because it was past lockdown.

I called Big Tony's Oven™ and ordered a large Roman Holiday. Half an hour later, Frank buzzed to tell me the pizza boy was in the lobby. The pizza boy turned out to be a solid fifty-year-old dude with no discernible neck, a shaved head, gold tooth and a nose you could build a viewing platform on. 'One piping-hot Roman Holiday,' he said, pulling the box from its vinyl pouch. 'That'll be thirty bucks for you, champion.'

'I thought it was twenty-five?'

'Five for delivery.' I gave him forty bucks and the big lug said, 'Cheers!' and turned to leave.

'Hey, what about the change?'

'Don't carry any. You can have one of these instead.' He handed me a fridge magnet with a caricature of Big Tony on it.

'Is that you?' I said.

'Smartarse. Enjoy your Roman Holiday.'

'Sure, I'll send you a postcard.'

I ate the pizza on the balcony, watching the action heating up on Darlinghurst Road twenty-seven levels below. Thrillseekers arriving from the other side of town. British rugby lads singing their club anthem and getting blasted from the gridlocked cars and taxis. The wail of sirens and the parting of traffic to let a fire engine, ambos and cop car through. Exploiting their slipstream, a stretch Hummer limo pumping gangsta rap for the benefit of the street crowd. Was it Jay-Z and Beyoncé bouncing behind the smoked glass? More likely chicks from the sticks on a hen's night. Exciting either way.

The pizza made me thirsty. I had ten dollars to blow and there was a Vietnamese bakery across the road that sold Cokes® for a buck. Time to defy the curfew and walk on the wild side.

Frank's less vigilant son, Vince, was on the concierge desk and didn't look up as I passed. Waiting on the corner for the green man, I heard >MEEP! MEEP!< behind me and stepped aside. Different breed of road-runner – a bald guy on a mobility scooter. He charged past and straight into the traffic. Tyres screeched and burnt, but it wasn't enough to stop the black BMW E93 from hitting him.

>CRANG!<

The old man received a nasty jolt but his chariot remained upright. Behind reflective sunglasses the BMW driver's face was doughy, his girlfriend's crumbling. The old guy dismounted, walked to the driver's side of the BMW and kicked in the door panel with his bare heel, then remounted his thunder cart and zipped off. Two cops arrived on motorbikes. Having been the closest witness but not wanting to be questioned while breaking curfew, I skulked back to the apartment without my Coke®. Hey Joe, the wild side will have to wait.

The incident with the BMW and the scooter brought back memories of the other big event from last year that I haven't mentioned, the demise of Pop Locke. Everybody loved my grandfather, especially my dog Gus and his mate Dougal, who would trot along next to Pop's little red Honda CT110 under the delusion of being his official escort. A few years back, my grandparents had closed their bakery in Blacktown after a franchise stole all but their most loyal customers, and moved to Dee Why to be closer to us. Unable to bear the tranquil inertia of retirement, Pop Locke found his second calling delivering the mail and 'having a yarn to the good people' he met on the route. Last year, on the twelfth of February, one of those adoring customers accidentally killed him.

Distracted by her kids fighting in the back of the Pajero while reversing down the driveway, Brenda Morris didn't see Pop Locke tootling along, and knocked him over. Apparently he got up, dusted himself off and somehow managed to lift his bike, mailbags and all. Despite his protests, Brenda called the ambulance. Halfway to the hospital, Pop Locke suffered a fatal cardiac arrest. Even more devastating, he died on my fifteenth birthday. It was difficult to cop, but I told myself that accidents don't make appointments.

Pop Locke had established a tradition of posting our birthday cards and delivering them on his mail route – a ritual that transcended logic, as many rituals do, but always delighted my sister Venn and me. Though he never reached our mailbox that day, I hoped someone from the post office might find my card in his bag and deliver it. Every day I checked our box before and after school, finding only bills and junk mail. A week later I called Australia Post and they told me that everything had been delivered. There was nothing left.

In the middle of my emotional turmoil, Homunculus made himself known. Everybody has thoughts constantly running through their minds, but early last year mine started speaking to me in voices. Some were calm and reasonable, offering wisdom and encouragement. Others were sarcastic and critical, madly superstitious or seemed to possess knowledge beyond my experience. Those ones became more insistent after Pop's death and throughout the next few months amalgamated into one distinct bossy voice.

Its first directive was to continue checking the mailbox for a birthday greeting from Pop, with a promise that my vigilance would be rewarded. Obediently I checked the box every day for a month, but there was never anything addressed to me so I stopped. A week later, the voice piped up again: 'Pop Locke can't communicate from where he is, but he's severely disappointed that you've given up on him.' Regardless of whether the voice rose from a guilty conscience, my grief, or a more general anxiety around death, I feared that I was going mad. I googled 'the little man inside my head' and found my way to articles on the Homunculus. As I was reading them, the voice said, 'That's me.' And the name has stuck.

Anyway, tonight when I returned to the apartment, Homunculus was taunting me for breaking the curfew without actually buying a Coke®, so to block him out I checked the landline for messages. I expected the earlier call would be Mum apologising for leaving me stranded in the city, bravely enduring a week at my new school. But nope. Only Steve, Dad's business partner at The BrandCanyon, inviting him for tennis and a picnic tomorrow with his new girl-friend and her sister, a 'topnotch bird'. Who even uses the word 'bird' like that, or still calls on the landline? Steve, when he's being ironically retro.

ONE MAN'S JUNK

Saturday morning I woke with Ms Tarasek's 2000-word essay question on my mind. 'What is art?' she'd said, floating around the studio in a peacock kaftan. 'What is its purpose? I want you to think inside the box. Find a box and climb inside. Feel the boundaries imposed on self. Remain in darkness until an answer comes.' She squeezed my shoulder. 'Hello, new student. Don't frown. Embrace contradiction. Two thousand words.'

So this morning I crawled into an IKEA box left over from a recent mission to furnish my room and closed the flaps. The confined darkness got me speculating on whether burial or cremation would be less damaging to the environment. Then I accidentally gave myself a Dutch oven of unmitigated potency that made a mockery of my concern, demanding immediate evacuation and an alternative approach.

On my way to the art gallery I stopped across the road from the Coca-Cola® sign at a sculpture that resembled seven lumpy balls stuck on black poles. Though I'd seen them before, I'd never stopped to look properly so I sat on the steps and began sketching. Two minutes later, a woman in a grubby lime hoodie and liquorice allsorts tights came

15

and stood behind me. Ignoring her was close to impossible, especially when I heard a burst of aerosol spray followed by the smell of solvent. I turned to see she had the can in one hand and a paper bag in the other. There was blue all around her nostrils and mouth.

'What are you doing?' she said.

'I'm drawing the sculpture.'

'No shit. What for?'

'An art assignment.'

'I used to be an artist,' she said. 'They call that thing *Poosticks*.' She laughed and walked away, coughing.

I finished my sketch, labelled it *Poosticks* and walked down to Woolloomooloo, up past Brett Whiteley's giant matchsticks and into the Art Gallery of New South Wales. Thinking it might be helpful to observe people observing art, I stood near a couple who wore only black and had geometric DIY hair, botanical tatts and facial piercings, and were scrutinising one of Jeffrey Smart's urban landscapes.

'Hyperrealistic,' the woman said. 'Bleak but beautiful.'

'Just like you,' the guy said.

They turned to a huge colour field painting, an indigo rectangle, on the opposite wall. When the attendant wasn't looking, the guy ran his hand along the surface. 'That's not art,' he said. What a disrespectful nob.

Down the escalator I found my favourite thing in the entire gallery – a circle of huge smooth stones suspended from the ceiling by wires, making them appear to float just above the floor. *Suspended Stone Circle II* by Ken Unsworth. Tension and equilibrium, nature and artifice, everything being held perfectly in place. The beauty plagued by an undeniable fear that one day it all might suddenly come crashing down. It reminded me of my family and life in general.

I sat on the floor and sketched. Five minutes later, I sensed somebody watching me from behind again. I prayed it wasn't Blue Lady, and closed my book to avoid another encounter with a stranger.

'Don't stop on my account,' a familiar voice said.

I turned and saw Isa, the girl who was playing receptionist at Student Welfare yesterday, taking a phone shot of the sculpture.

I remembered her surname: Mountwinter. Evocative – picturesque, even. Though she was smiling, her expression was icy. My face burnt with the jarring embarrassment of seeing a fellow student in an unfamiliar setting.

'What are you doing?' she said.

'Drawing the sculpture for the art assignment.'

'I was going to write about the same piece.'

'You still can. By the way, my name's Lincoln.'

'We established that at Student Welfare.'

Lost for words, I said the first thing that came to mind. 'I saw a weird lady sniffing blue paint from a paper bag.'

'Raina Bramble. She used to be an artist.'

'She obviously still enjoys the smell of paint.'

'That's not funny. It's tragic. Where was she?'

'Up in the Cross, at the *Poosticks* sculpture.'

'Its correct name is *Stones Against the Sky*, and it's another piece by Ken Unsworth.'

'I'll have a second look with that in mind. Good luck with the assignment. I'm finished here. All yours.'

After having spent a night uncovered in the fridge, the last slice of Roman Holiday tasted fishy, so I ditched it and set out on a mission to scavenge something tasty from Dad's picnic. I took the scenic route, skating down Liverpool Street into a narrow lane canyoned by garage doors and, reaching a dead end, ollied the kerb and shot blind down the root-buckled concrete footpath. Ducking low to clear a lantana canopy, I emerged unscathed on a street lined mostly with old sandstone and weatherboard workers' cottages, probably all worth a few million now. On the corner was a larger two-storey house surrounded by a vine-covered wire fence that wasn't quite tall enough to hide an enormous carved eagle with outstretched wings.

Unable to resist an inspection, I climbed the fence and discovered the eagle was the top figure of a fake totem pole that must've been made for a shopping centre or minigolf course back in the seventies. Beside it were a table made from a cable spool and tractor seats shaded by a plane tree growing from a huge tyre. There were two Ampol petrol bowsers, shipping palettes and stacks of metal signs. And lying stiffly inside an enamel bathtub was an armless mannequin, smiling bravely despite her baldness – perhaps cheered by the aroma of all the surrounding rosebushes. I was about to leave when a glint of sunlight, reflecting off a curved metal bar that was poking out from coils of plastic tubing, caught my eye.

Ignoring the BEWARE VICIOUS DOG sign, I jumped down and squeezed through the wire gate, then pulled the tubing away to reveal an object of great beauty: an old-school dragster, complete with sissy bar, ape hanger handlebars and stick shift, circa 1974. A high point of style in the history of cycling. Though rusty, the paint job was fully sick, a slow burn from yellowy orange to fiery red. Attached to the handlebars was a plastic FOR SALE tag.

I knocked on the front door of the house but nobody answered, so I walked around the side. Sitting out the back on a crimson cracked-vinyl armchair was a crusty old dude in a stained singlet, with two empty VB longnecks by his feet. He was facing away from me, so his muttering was hard to decipher, but I caught parts of it: 'Big explosion down at Garden Island. Ka-boom! Next thing you know, young Johnny's off to Korea on his Pat Malone. Quack wouldn't let me go because I had a little something extra. Rained cats and dogs that year and myxomatosis on the bunnies. Rabbitohs won the premiership. Good thing ol' Bugs was a Yank. Came on with the newsreel, he did. Before the main feature, he did. Myeah! What's up, doc?'

I edged closer and saw the man was talking to a pale-yellow bird with peachy cheeks – stuffed, and perched on a little branch stuck to a wooden base. Having second thoughts about the dragster, I turned to leave. Then he sang, 'If I knew you were coming I'd have baked a cake, howdy-doo, howdy-doo, howdy-doo.'

'Excuse me?'

He turned and extended his head, squinting like a short-sighted turtle. I'd seen him before – the guy on the mobility scooter who'd kicked in the Beemer's door last night. His foot was swollen.

'Sorry,' I said. 'I didn't meant to disturb you.'

'Rack off!' he said. 'G'arn! GIT!'

'Sorry, I just saw the—'

'Nothin' here for ya. Now scram or I'll call the coppers.'

'I just wanted to know, how much for the bike?'

'Not selling it.'

'But there was a sign that said—'

'Closed on Satdee.'

'When do you open?'

'Never. So be a wise lad and bugger off.'

The old man's refusal to sell the bike made me want it more, a perverse form of determination I'd inherited from my father. I walked around the block, conjuring a sentimental story, and returned.

'Back again like a bad smell?' the old codger said. 'Don't know when to leave good enough alone.' One eye was fierce, the other dead.

'I wanted to tell you that my dad rode a Malvern Star just like that when he was the same age as me.'

'Whoopee-doo! Didn't I tell you to bugger off? Beat it, and don't come back again.'

'It was exactly the same as that one. Same colour and everything.'

'Bullshit. I painted it myself. It's a rusty piece of shit and the chain's cactus.'

'I could fix it.'

'Show me your hands.' I walked closer, then he grabbed them and turned up my palms. 'Never done a scrap of real work between 'em.' He slapped them away. 'Girly hands!' He cocked his head towards the stuffed cockatiel. 'What's that, Perce?' He put his ear against the bird's beak. 'Seventy quid, you reckon? You're a soft touch. Percy here says seventy.'

'All right then. I'll bring the money tomorrow.'

'Just what I thought. A whole lotta puff.' He spat a wad of brown phlegm directly onto my left trainer, which I ignored for the sake of the deal.

'I have to get the money from my dad. I'll bring it tomorrow.'

'Tomorrow, tomorrow, tomorrow never comes. If it does, might be gone.' He pushed himself off the chair and shuffled towards the back door.

'You said that it wasn't for sale,' I said, following him. 'Who else wants it?'

'I meant me, not the Dick Van Dyke. First and last time in a private box. Final curtain, that's all folks!' He waved me off and shut the screen door.

'If you're still around, I'll be back with the cash.'

I skated on down to the Rushcutters Bay tennis courts, where I spotted Dad and Steve with the topnotch birds on a tartan picnic rug near the café. I hid behind a trellis to observe the dynamic. Dad was delivering a semi-factual anecdote to the girls, who couldn't have been more than seven years older than my sister. The punchline earnt a polite titter from one and a loud snorty drawback from the other. While her head was tilted back, my father popped an olive into her mouth. A truly shocking act. Not just because the olive got lodged in her throat and might've been fatal if quick-thinking Steve hadn't administered four solid blows between her shoulderblades to eject it – but also because popping an olive was something my father had only ever done to my mother. Witnessing him pop an olive for another, much younger, woman rendered me incapable of joining the gathering. I left without eating.

Arriving home a couple of hours later, Dad asked how my day had gone, oblivious to the fact I'd been observing his.

'Productive. I worked on my assignment and then found a bike I like.'

'Snap! Because so have I.' He went and fetched a brochure from the living room. 'Check out the specs on this beauty. With the Bike Buddies Bonus, we'd get thirty per cent off the second one. We could start training together.'

'What for, the Tour de France?'

'Some kids would get mildly excited if their father offered them a bike like that. I get nothing but smartarse lip.'

'I don't want the responsibility of a three-grand bike.'

'Only two-and-a-half with the Buddy Bonus.'

Buying the same bike would be a bonding exercise in Dad's mind, but I didn't rate the idea of pedalling around the park on matching cycles. Next there'd be matching lycra shorts, helmets and sunglasses. So I nipped that plan in the butt [*sic*], immediately, explaining it would be much cheaper if he spotted me for the dragster. He agreed and insisted on coming along to make sure I didn't get ripped off.

The Sunday morning air was filled with the acrid waft of burning bush, a yellow haze and a pulsating cicada chorus. Walking beneath the lantana canopy, Dad shared his bargaining strategy. 'We know his starting price. We'll offer thirty-five.'

'He didn't even want to sell it.'

'Leave the talking to me.'

We squeezed through the wire gate and walked to the back of the house. The old man was sitting on his armchair, swigging another longneck.

'Well, look what the cat's dragged in, Perce. And he's brought a playmate.'

'Actually, I'm his father. Lance Locke.' He extended his hand but the old man ignored it. 'I hope Lincoln hasn't been bothering you?'

'Persistent little bugger. Chip off the old block, eh?'

'Some people think that—'

'Scorcher today. Forty-five out Penrith way. Don't mind the heat but Perce isn't too keen on it.'

Dad looked at the bird and frowned. 'Cockatiel, is he? Must be well trained. Have you clipped his wings?' Sketchy effort at pretending the bird was alive. 'Does he talk?'

'Not to idiots. Come here for the bike, have you?'

'We've got the cash,' I said.

Dad frowned again. 'Perhaps I should see it first?'

'Right you are. I've done a little tinkering and gussied her up a bit. Hold your horses and I'll fetch her.' The man doddered off to the other side of the cottage, leaving an inflated pink rubber ring on the seat.

'Looks like a severely reduced mental faculty isn't the only thing he suffers from.'

'He's just a bit eccentric.'

21

'Lincoln, he's nuttier than a fruitcake. Did you notice one of his eyes doesn't move? I think it's made of glass.'

'So what?'

'Have a little think about how that might've happened.'

'Shh! Here he comes.'

The old guy wheeled the bike around, beaming like a dentally challenged Santa Claus. 'Here she is,' he said, propping the dragster on its kickstand. It looked nothing like the bike I'd seen yesterday. He'd repaired the chain, fixed the brake and gear cables, and replaced the tyres. The chrome fixtures were gleaming. He must've worked on it all night long and, judging by the added extras, had a team of gay elves assisting. There was:

1) A white woven plastic basket with a daisy on the front
2) Spokey Dokeys on the spokes
3) A fluoro-orange flag on a bendy pole
4) A horn

'Wowee!' Dad said, and gave it a honk.

'Came up a treat, didn't she?' The man winked. 'Bet it looks just like the one you rode back in the day.'

Dad shot me a side eye and I gave him a subtle nod to play along. 'Oh yeah,' he said. 'The old Malvern Star. Same model and everything, without the fancy bits. I was a terror on that baby, fastest kid on the street.' Then he spotted the new price tag. 'A hundred and fifty dollars? You told my son seventy!'

A price dispute ensued and quickly became heated. Dad accused the old guy of swindling me, even though he'd obviously put in well over a hundred dollars' worth of parts and labour. The old guy thought he'd done me a solid by gussying it up, and my subsequent refusal to admit that I didn't actually want the extras infuriated Dad. He threatened to contact an imaginary reporter friend from *A Current Affair*. The old guy told us both to fuck off.

My father's pride was at stake, so as the guy wheeled the bike away he called out, 'I'll take it off your hands for two hundred.' The guy kept going. 'Make it two-fifty then?' No response. 'Three hundred?' The guy stopped. 'We got him,' Dad whispered.

'You can have the bloody thing!' the man growled, and let it drop. And when my father produced his wallet, the old guy snapped, 'I don't need your filthy lucre. Just piss off, the pair of you!'

'Get your bike,' Dad said.

I didn't move.

'Get it!'

I lifted the two-wheeled trophy of shame, wondering if I'd ever be able to ride it. Dad pulled a couple of hundred-dollar notes from his wallet and offered them to the man but he refused, then shuffled inside and slammed the flyscreen door.

'Stubborn old goat,' Dad said, and wedged the notes between the mannequin's fingers.

RIPPLES OF INFLUENCE

My sister Venn was born three years before me. My parents couldn't decide on a name so they drew a Venn diagram with the intersection of two circles holding the names they both liked. Unable to choose one of those, they decided to call her Venn. I'm not sure if it's connected to her naming in any way, but diagrams have continued to play an important role in Venn's life. She draws them to make sense of tricky things – to manage disruptions before they have a chance of causing chaos. Another coping mechanism of hers is to go into the bush and meditate on the natural order. But her innate sense of balance and harmony went totally whack when my parents split, and her diagrams failed to diminish the resentment she's been feeling towards Dad since he moved out. So she turned again to the healing power of nature.

Tonight, while Dad was cooking dinner, Mum called – purportedly to find out how my first week at Crestfield had gone, but really to bang on about the wellness retreat Venn had talked her into going to.

'It began with something called "beneficial deprivation",' she said. 'Which meant we weren't allowed to drink anything except a fermented kale tonic that tasted a little more fetid than swamp water. They confiscated all electronic devices for three hours of communal silence, which just made me want to scream. As soon as I got my phone back

I packed your sister into the car and almost escaped, but she talked me out of it. And I'm glad she did because the next morning, during a hot stone massage, I worked through some anger issues.'

'I didn't realise you still had them?' I said, restraining the level of sarcasm in my inflection.

'Neither did I, until Revati made the stones too hot and burnt my back. I overreacted, which made her cry, and then I cried. Even though I'd been scorched, I couldn't stop apologising. Talking it through, I realised I'd been conditioned to make other people feel better – especially men. Despite your father's significant contribution, I'd blamed myself for our marriage failing. I felt guilty for working too hard at building the business and neglecting you in the process.'

'I hardly felt neglected.'

'In hindsight, your father and I had been drifting apart for a couple of years. The surprise-party business with Maëlle was simply the final straw.'

Now is a good time to tell you about the party.

In April last year, Maëlle Beauvais – so Frenchy, so chic – had glided into Signal Bay with a joie de vivre that instantly captivated us all. Her family in Paris had hosted my sister as an exchange student a couple of years before, and we reciprocated the favour during Maëlle's gap year. Madly intelligent, politically engaged and insatiably curious about our suburban existence, she made us believe we were far more interesting than we really are. Mum was delighted to have an eager sous-chef in the kitchen; Maëlle conversed in French with Venn while shopping or drinking coffee at La Poule en Étain, helping Venn prepare for her looming final French exam while simultaneously endowing my sister with a sophisticated Parisian je ne sais quoi by osmosis.

I bonded with Maëlle by teaching her to surf, which garnered greater respect for me from the line-up, especially from Tom and Coops. Though realistically there could never be anything between Maëlle and me, I basked in the tanning lamp of false kudos that came with letting people speculate. Disconcertingly, Dad seemed to be relishing her attention as well. He and Maëlle shared a love of Scrabble, and would continue playing into the night after the rest of us had given up. Perhaps she was simply eager to please everyone, I thought.

But Mum wasn't thrilled by their late-night games and soon my parents' arguments, private but audible, flared up again. So whatever possessed Dad to enlist Maëlle's assistance in preparing a surprise dinner party for Mum's fiftieth when she'd flagged her desire to let it pass quietly is beyond my comprehension. The plan was for Mum's business partner, Morgan, to take her for Friday drinks while the rest of the team took the stealth route to our place for the ambush. It quickly backfired because she declined his invitation, pissed off that Emma, Jules and Penny had abandoned her with a stack of work. Initiating Plan B, Morgan sneaked down to the car park and deflated one of her tyres. Instead of accepting a ride, Mum called the NRMA. Unable to endure her darkening mood after waiting for almost an hour, Morgan let the cat out of the bag. Mum cancelled roadside assistance and accepted Morgan's lift, promising to act surprised on arrival.

Back at Signal Bay the guests had by now been drinking for hours and, having eaten only Maëlle's delectable but insubstantial canapés, some of them were on the looser side of tipsy. Roger Harris, our next-door neighbour, was legit shit-faced. His foxhound Dougal was barking and whimpering with canine FOMO, so he let him into our backyard. After scrapping with Gus and chasing Venn's cat Oscar up a tree, Dougal foraged about, humping anyone or anything in his path. Eventually he found his way into the unguarded kitchen, pulled Maëlle's mustard-encrusted lamb rack off the bench and wolfed down half of it before being caught. After Dad and Roger Harris debated the ethical and health ramifications of serving the salvaged remains without informing the guests, Dad ordered ribs from Jeb's Smokehouse.

Maëlle was dejected about the lamb, so Dad took her into the living room for a consolation dance. The song was 'Burn' by Usher. Wrong track – too slow. And in one of those moments of perfectly bad timing that would have you calling out 'Bullshit!' in a film, Dad dipped her at the exact moment that Mum walked through the door.

'SURPRISE!' we all yelled.

Surprise all right.

For the duration of the night Mum maintained perfect composure, faking gratitude with the fixed smile of an event professional. But during breakfast one week later, without warning she suggested to Maëlle that it might be a good time to move on and see more of Australia, especially the Northern Territory, which boasts an abundance of crocodiles. She didn't pinpoint that particular danger but the inference was there, leading me to believe that something more than the dancing had tipped her over the edge – something I'm yet to uncover. There was no chance of Maëlle staying in the house, it seemed, so she left.

Venn was naturally devastated by her friend's eviction. As the HSC approached she broke up with her boyfriend of three years, Elliot Grobecker, and hardly left the house. She refused Mum's refreshment visits, and reheated meals when it suited her. Venn had always been a top student, but I observed her confidence subsiding with each exam until she seemed like a wreck.

On the eve of her final one, her anger suddenly turned towards Dad. And when he left the family home, she began restoring her relationship with Mum. Organising the retreat was her latest effort and, judging by my phone conversation with Mum, it seemed to have worked wonders. She reeled off a list of all the therapies she'd had, culminating in a volcanic clay body mask.

'As Revati applied the cool clay I felt truly cherished for the first time in God knows how long, even though I'd paid for it. We all need to be touched, Lincoln. It's built into our DNA.'

I thought about that night at the party with Nicole Parker. The last time I was touched, it didn't end well.

'At the end of the treatment, Revati asked me what I wanted most from the universe. I said a single word: "release". And she whispered one word back: "granted".'

I wanted to ask who'd appointed Revati as Master of the Universe. Instead I also uttered a single word, 'Wow!'

'It is "wow", isn't it? But enough about me. How was your first week?'

'Great. I feel like I really belong at Crestfield. I'm cherishing the experience.'

'Darling, that's wonderful. Revati said my renewed energy would radiate in ripples of influence. How are you coping with your father?'

'He bought me a bike today.'

'You see? The circles of influence are expanding and multiplying.'

My lies were the only thing expanding and multiplying. But I didn't want to burst Mum's bubble with the truth. Her post-retreat euphoria would probably deflate of its own accord in three days max.

Hovering near the phone, trying to catch snippets of conversation, Dad had forgotten about the fish frying in the pan until the acrid smoke drew him back. Mum never wants to speak to him unless it's logistics. Whatever really went down between them, I feel sorry for him at times.

I wound up the call with Mum, promising we'd talk soon. Dad and I ate dinner watching a film about a deranged clown who goes on a killing rampage, which made swallowing the blackened kingfish even more difficult. Possibly triggered by the actor's believable perform-ance, Dad said, 'Lincoln, I don't want you going within a mile of that old crank's junkyard again. Do you understand me?'

'We already live within a mile.'

'Don't go there.'

'I wasn't planning to.'

DRAFTED

Early Monday morning I spent an hour divesting my bike of its embellishments, and rode the stripped-back beast to school. As I was chaining it to the rack, a pink bubble appeared in my periphery, then expanded and popped, releasing the odour of cherry-flavoured smoker's breath. 'Nice wheels,' the blower said, peeling gum from his sparsely haired top lip. 'Got a light?'

'I don't smoke.'

'Commendable. Where'd you score the treadly? Looks familiar.'

'Found it in a junkyard.'

'Sweet.' The kid's overbite and weak chin gave him a rodent-like appearance, something I would never say to anybody because it's cruel, but his twitching made the comparison impossible to ignore. I slung my satchel over my shoulder and started up the embankment.

'Wait up, rookie. My name's Starkey. It's Evan Starkey, but everyone calls me Starkey.'

'I'm Lincoln.'

'I know. You're Tibor Mintz's girlfriend. Do people call you Stinkin' Lincoln?'

'I get Abraham more.'

'Why?'

29

'Never mind. I'm peeling off. I have to see Simmons before first period.'

'Catch ya later, Stinkin'.' He headed back to the racks, probably to check for unlocked bikes. Funny – I thought this school was selective.

E X C E L T O D A Y is etched into the glass entrance of the Coralee Coombs Sports Centre, nicknamed The Hive for the hexagonal photochromic glass cells of its vaulted ceiling. Ground level features a fifty-metre pool with tiered seating on one side and a gymnasium, hydrotherapy facility and showers on the other. Above the gym are two classrooms and the PDHPE faculty offices. These overlook the pool, which this morning was a perfect blue mirror against the pale amber of the glass ceiling. The only thing moving, aside from the hand of the Speedo lap timer, was me on my way to see the sportsmaster.

Simmons was reclining in an orange armchair, surrounded by dusty trophies and gleaming shields. His white polo shirt was tucked into white shorts tight enough to strangle his best friend. His white trainers looked as if they'd never touched grass. My impression that he might have once come close to rugby glory was in no way diminished by the substantial girth of his stomach, which he was doing his best to increase with an egg-and-bacon roll.

'What do you want, germ?'

'I haven't enrolled in a sport yet, sir. I had to see Dr Limberg last Friday instead.'

'Name?'

'Lincoln Locke.'

He shook my hand with a super-firm grip, eyebrows challenging me to submit before he powdered my metacarpals. 'Which sport?' he said, then released.

I nominated chess, ping-pong and bowling, the three least likely to expose or aggravate the nub through physical exertion, but each option came up as blocked on his laptop.

'Unusual,' he said. 'Let me check The Owl.' He scanned my student profile, nodding and frowning. Then the electronic glockenspiel chimed, signalling the commencement of first period, which made me need to pee. 'Congratulations, Locke. You're in the pool with me.'

'What do you mean?' I said, guts now liquefying.

'Says here that you represented your previous school at zone level and your PBs for the fly aren't too shabby at all. You've already been drafted into swim squad by Assistant Coach Gelber.'

'I'm not that great at butterfly.'

'No need for false modesty.'

'But that note in my file is wrong, sir. I was struggling to finish.'

'Don't you worry about that, son. Endurance training is my speciality. Your physical dimensions were fed into an algorithm that calculated swimming to be your ideal sport – specifically butterfly. Great wingspan and size-eleven feet.'

The talk of physical dimensions provoked an extremely awkward sensation in my lower regions, as though the nub was turning in on itself – inverting. Terrified that wearing only Speedos in a lane crowded with other swimmers would inevitably result in its exposure, I pleaded to be allowed to join another sport.

'In a couple of months, if things don't work out, you can switch. But you look like a swimmer to me. And trust me, son, I can pick 'em. Ever heard of Coralee Coombs? Of course you have – this sports centre's named after her. She's on the national team and a shoo-in for the Games. I was her first coach and now I'm yours.'

'But—'

'Training starts this Wednesday morning, clinic on Friday, training again on Mondays. Off you go now – scoot, you're late for class.'

E X C E E D   T O M O R R O W was etched on The Hive's exit doors. 'Exceed what?' Homunculus said as I walked through. 'Your current low level of bladder and bowel control?' I relieved myself and then ran to catch up with my art class, who'd already set out on an architectural tour of the school.

'How kind of you to grace us with your presence,' the Crestfield old boy Nigel Lethbridge said when I arrived panting at Old Block.

His sculpted platinum hair, strangely taut skin and withering blue eyes gave him the appearance of someone who'd only recently been cryogenically defrosted – but his leather-elbowed jacket had obviously only been preserved in mothballs. The unmistakable smell of camphor discouraged me from getting any closer.

'Rightio, let's get cracking,' Lethbridge said, and led us to the original house on the property. 'Our most worthy founder, the pastoralist and cattle breeder Joseph Millington Drake, built his magnificent residence, Crestfield House, in eighteen seventy-nine. Judging Australian schools inferior to those of the motherland, he began teaching local boys in his own home.' As we crossed the threshold, he said, 'Those of you with classes here will appreciate the high ceilings and natural ventilation.'

We climbed three levels to the attic. 'Best view in the house,' Lethbridge said, waving us in. 'And it belonged to the servants. Ha!'

From my position I could only see a blue patch of harbour, but on my turn at the small dormer window I looked straight down and saw the caretaker, Mr Jespersen, grooming one of many hedges that made a pattern of lines inside a huge square. In the centre was a hexagonal pergola covered in vines. 'Wow!' I said. 'There's a maze.'

'The correct term is labyrinth, as there's only one possible route,' Lethbridge said.

Next stop was Redmayne Hall, which was completed in 1888 on the centenary of invasion, though being an old fart, Lethbridge used the term 'settlement'.

'Redmayne was designed by Justus Cobham, a proponent of the neo-Gothic style, which explains its somewhat ecclesiastical appearance. But even with its expanded capacity, Crestfield was soon overcrowded again. So Millington Drake devised a notoriously difficult entrance test based on mathematical, scientific and physical aptitude, with a vision to cultivate only the finest young men in the colony.'

'Sounds like a crank,' Phoenix Lee said.

Lethbridge showed us where the coach house and dairy once stood, then led us back to the tech workshops at New Block.

'The Ormerod Wing was constructed in nineteen seventy-four to accommodate the first female students. The exposed concrete and brown bricks, while at odds with the elegance of earlier buildings, are typical of the brutalism school of architecture. One might consider it downright ugly. It was named after Crestfield's first female librarian, Judith Ormerod – rather fitting, considering personal appearance was never her most pressing concern.'

'I have a question,' Phoenix said. 'Were you born before or after the word "misogyny" was invented?'

'I beg your pardon?'

'Please excuse the interruption!' Ms Tarasek said.

Lethbridge licked his lips and took us right back to where I'd begun my day, The Hive. 'Completed four years ago at a cost of fifteen million dollars, this glass temple of sporting excellence exemplifies our founder's vision – the development of physical perfection. Some of Australia's most notable figures and successful businessmen are Crestfield alumni. Their exceeding generosity made the construction of this superior facility possible.'

'Of course no women contributed,' Phoenix said to Isa as we entered the building.

'When I was a Crestfield lad we had no pool here, but I consider myself a small link in the chain of our proud swimming history. Please don't think me immodest by directing your gaze to the Roll of Champions behind you.'

I calculated Lethbridge must be in his nineties, and here he was, still crowing about being the junior backstroke champion. The pompous geezer fully deserved Phoenix Lee's salty comments. His tour of Crestfield was kind of fascinating, but it made me feel I belonged there less than a three-legged Shetland pony in the Melbourne Cup.

BIRTHPLACE OF CHAMPIONS

Tuesday afternoon in Biology there was only one vacant seat at the back of the lab, next to Starkey from the bike racks. As I took my place, he turned his yellowed palm for a low five. Without thinking, I slapped it.

'Sean "Mullows" Mulligan,' he said, pointing to the guy on his left with his thumb. 'And Nads.' Hair removal cream or gonads? I wasn't about to ask. He was sitting on the end opposite me. Handsome in a 'rip your balls from the sack if you cross me' sort of way. Mullows had a ranga mullony – a mullet in a ponytail. His long neck, face and lashes gave him the appearance of a docile giraffe.

'On Thursday you will perform your first rat dissection in pairs,' Miss Keenan said. 'Anybody not wishing to participate for ethical or religious reasons may articulate their concern.'

Isa Mountwinter raised her hand at the front of the room. 'A rat is a sentient being, not an object to be cut up, pulled apart and thrown in the bin. Biology is the science of life, not killing.' She turned to face the class. 'Please stand up if chopping up animals could hold any importance for your future.' Three people stood, including Tibor Mintz, who wants to be a doctor like his father. 'Everybody else is a cold-blooded animal killer.'

'Animal killers!' Phoenix Lee repeated for emphasis.

'You self-righteous hypocrites,' Nads said, raising one scarred eyebrow. 'Somebody has to slaughter the animals you eat.'

'We're vegetarians,' Isa said. 'And only buy cruelty-free cosmetics.'

'Of course you do.'

'Enough, thank you, Darvin!' Miss Keenan said. No wonder he doesn't use his real name. 'Respecting one another's opinions is part of the Crestfield Code of Conduct. Isa and Phoenix will be performing their dissection on the Cyber Rat simulator in the tech lab on Thursday. Does anybody wish to join them?' Two other students raised their hands.

'Pussies,' muttered Starkey.

When the final glockenspiel sounded, the dread of swimming at squad the next day hit me and I went to Bondi Junction and bought a pair of black Speedos. Though the fabric was smooth and thin, I prayed they'd be dark enough to fully conceal the nub and save me from humiliation. On the train home, I puzzled over how Simmons had known my measurements. Then I remembered Dad had insisted on taking them last year. He'd told me it was for my uniform.

Five forty-five Wednesday morning, new Speedos already on to avoid changing on arrival, I pedalled furiously to get to squad on time. The synthetic chafing caused the nub to swell, and I walked into The Hive like a saddle-sore cowboy.

Squad comprised the best eight swimmers from each grade, with Year 10 represented by Nads, Mullows, Starkey, a guy called Pericles Pappas, three girls and, inexplicably, me. Simmons opened with a long pep talk, ending with, 'My dream is to make Crestfield the top swimming school in the state and this pool the birthplace of tomorrow's champions!' An image of Mrs Coombs having a natural water birth popped into my head. Tiny baby Coralee, future Olympian, slithered out and wiggled like a tadpole towards the surface for her first gasp of air, umbilical cord trailing behind, clouding the pool with blood and other bodily matter.

Simmons flipped a whiteboard to reveal the lap breakdown and tally – fifty laps total, 2.5 kilometres. 'Nobody will leave until they've completed the program,' he said, then introduced the assistant coach, Deb Gelber. Her name sounded like a brand of baby food but she was all muscle, tracksuit and topknot.

'Sort yourselves out!' she barked like a drill sergeant. 'Slowest in lane one, fastest in eight. If you're tapped three times, move down.' Everybody peeled off their last piece of clothing but I kept my towel wrapped tightly around my waist.

Mullows slapped his broad shoulders then tucked his ginger pony into a blue-and-yellow racing cap. 'Best for you to start in five,' he said to me, snapping on reflective goggles.

Three things came to mind:

1) Mullows was the snarling backstroker in the Hallway of Champions photo.
2) He and Nads were both preternaturally stacked for teenagers – possibly on the juice?
3) I forgot to bring goggles.

Fifty laps without them would fry my eyeballs, but there was no time to worry about minor inconveniences like blindness. I threw my towel onto a nearby seat and stood behind Pericles Pappas in lane five, hands behind my back and head down, hoping nobody would notice the nub.

>BOY IN LANE FIVE WITHOUT GOGGLES, FIND SOME IMMEDIATELY!< Gelber bellowed through a megaphone.

'Don't worry,' Pericles said. 'I've got a spare pair.' He fetched them from his bag and gave them to me. They were super tight, and the connector carved into the bridge of my nose, but beggars don't have the luxury of a wide product range.

I dived into the pool and the coolness of the water seemed to reduce the inflammation of the nub. But after ten warm-up laps of freestyle we moved on to breaststroke and the frog kick made me feel exposed, so without being tapped, I demoted myself to lane three and swam as fast as possible to increase the distance between myself and the next swimmer. The next ten laps with a kickboard provided the relief of knowing the nub would be impossible to see through all the splashing. But then we switched to pull buoys, holding the foam peanut between our legs and using only our arms to crawl through the water.

With legs now making no splash, I used every ounce of strength in my arms to ensure the trailing swimmer made no sighting of my little abnormality. On completion I climbed out of the pool, arms aching, lungs burning, and switched to lane two with one other sorry swimmer for the warm-down laps, every stroke a battle of will through water that felt like Clag®.

'Thank God for that,' Gelber said when I finally heaved myself out of the pool and made a dash for my protective towel. 'I thought you'd never finish.'

The single consolation of being the last male swimmer to finish training was having the change room to myself. Still, you can never be too careful so I slipped into a cubicle and after drying my back, reached around to check the nub. It felt tiny – hardly even there. I walked to first period feeling tentatively euphoric on the basis of having made it through squad without anybody noticing anything, and wondered if I was just being paranoid. Maybe the thing was in fact shrinking away.

'Don't get cocky,' Homunculus said. 'It was just your first session.'

True – and the prospect of swimming endless laps, constrained by lane lines in chlorinated water, was legitimately soul-crushing to someone who was born for the ocean.

EVERY MAN NEEDS
A TALE

Walking to the science lab for the rat dissection this morning, I remembered Venn describing her experience of it in Year 10 as if it was something for me to look forward to. She'd cut up both a rat and a sheep's eye, and had thoroughly enjoyed the process. Years earlier, the first time Pop Locke had taken us out fishing on his tinnie, he was gutting a kingfish and I couldn't watch – but Venn was transfixed by the ritual. By the time she turned eight she was gutting and filleting her own fish. She would first thank the fish for giving up its life, then perform the operation swiftly, with a light but respectfully firm touch.

Not sharing her constitution, I was apprehensive about today's session.

I was partnered with Starkey, who, after ignoring Miss Keenan's demonstration, sliced through our rat's skin, membrane and rib cage in one go. He urged me to 'get stuck in' but, overwhelmed by the sight of exposed innards, I froze, convinced I was looking into something that was never meant to be opened. Starkey pushed me aside and removed the rat's organs one by one, mostly with his bare hands, and laid them around the carcass. 'First!' he announced to the class, wiping his glistening fingers on his trousers.

Then he dragged me to the front of the lab to watch Pericles and Tibor, who was wearing a green surgical gown and mask, and using instruments borrowed from his father. After cutting and separating the rat's rib cage with meticulous care, Tibor leant down – for a closer look, it seemed. But then he fainted, face first into the splayed rat. Seconds later, his head suddenly surged back with enough force to lift his body clear off the stool and sent him crashing onto the floor, where he thrashed about, having some kind of fit. Pericles moved everybody back and cleared the stools. Before anybody had raised the alarm, a woman with bright-red hair, cut in a short and practical style, arrived. She wore a badge that said 'Nurse Nola'. Her swift action added weight to my suspicion that we were under video surveillance. She took Tibor's vital signs then called an ambulance, which delivered him and Miss Keenan to the hospital.

By mid-afternoon, I was still feeling shaken up because Tibor hadn't returned for Mr Field's English class. I'd liked Mr Field from the first moment we met last week, primarily because I'm certain he had Swiss Valley Hair Pomade™ in his hair – the only styling product that Pop Locke ever used. At the end of class today, Mr Field reminded us to get cracking on our reading list, so I dashed to the library at 2.45 pm. There were three nineteenth-century books on the list, which I searched for on the shelves, but all the copies were on loan.

We were also required to read one of our own choosing and, as I made my way through the shelves, a navy-blue, leather-bound book with faded gold embossing on the spine caught my eye. As I pulled the volume from the lower shelf, it released a musty smell, asserting its vintage by making me sneeze three times before I could read the title:

My One Redeeming Affliction
The Mysterious Tale of a Runaway Prodigy
Edwin Stroud

The electronic glockenspiel sounded, followed by Mrs Deacon on the PA. >ATTENTION, STUDENTS. THE LIBRARY WILL BE

CLOSING SHORTLY. PLEASE BRING ANY ITEMS YOU WISH
TO BORROW TO THE LOANS DESK IMMEDIATELY.<

I scoped out the queue and saw Isa Mountwinter approaching me
with intent. 'Hide it!' Homunculus said, so I knelt and slid the book
back onto the shelf.

'Looking for *Jekyll and Hyde*?' she said. 'Out of luck, it's gone. So
are *Dorian Gray* and *Frankenstein*.' Her eyes narrowed. 'Did you enjoy
slaughtering rats today?'

'The experience wasn't exactly pleasurable.' I stood up.

'Pericles told me you thought it was funny that Tibor passed out
and fitted?'

'It was ironic because he wants to be a doctor.'

'He said you laughed.'

'Maybe just a nervous titter. Nads and Starkey laughed.'

'Schadenfreude.'

'I beg your pardon?'

'Google it when you get home. Why are you even friends with
those pathologically morbid creepsters?'

'They're not that bad.'

'Really?' Isa shifted her head sideways. 'Evan Starkey offered to
help clean up after Miss Keenan left in the ambulance with Tibor.
While Raymond was out in prep, he cut off the rats' tails.'

'How do you know if there was nobody else there?' I said, wincing
from a sympathetic twinge that shot up the length of my spine.

'At lunchtime he went around the playground selling them as
good-luck charms to Year 7 boys.'

'Some would call that enterprising.'

'Trust me, those boys are serious trouble and you should stay away
from them.' She raised an index finger as if about to add something,
but instead withdrew it and said, 'That's all,' and left.

Mrs Deacon announced the library's closure. I retrieved the book
from the shelf and ran my fingers over the paler blue part of the leather,
which had been softened and smoothed by more than a century of
other readers holding it. Pop Locke once told me that the best books
make you feel like they were written just for you. Without even

40

reading the first page, I had the strangest feeling – almost a certainty – that this would be one of those books. *My One Redeeming Affliction.* The oxymoron intrigued me. My nub, an affliction of my own, had resulted in both pain and harm, yet there was nothing redemptive involved. Perhaps the book could help me come to terms with it?

But the library was closing. 'Put it in your satchel and walk out,' Homunculus said. So I did.

Tonight, I had a stack of homework to get through and didn't crawl into bed till almost midnight. Too late for reading, but I could see *My One Redeeming Affliction* sitting alone on my new shelving unit, its gold lettering catching the light. In a room furnished entirely with mass-produced flat packs from IKEA, the book smelt like the promise of another world.

It was Pop Locke who got me into reading. His favourite quote was from a French dude called Balzac. 'Reading brings us unknown friends.' With the hope of meeting a couple, I took a deep breath and opened to the first page.

Untangling the mystery of how I became the man I am today would necessitate travelling back untold generations – perhaps fortunately for you, dear reader, that would be an impossible quest. I only ever met one of my grandparents, my maternal grandfather, Walter Hunnicutt, and he was far from forthcoming with the family history. But this doesn't matter a jot, because my goal is not so much to explore the origin of my affliction as to tell you the story of how I turned it to my advantage. My mother, Esther, was a committed diarist and in her advanced years was still able to recall stories from her youth with crystal clarity. So I shall begin with the early lives of my parents and the fascinating story of how they came together.

Esther, by her own account, was a precocious child, and having three brothers demanded inventive methods of competing for her father's limited attention. From the age of five she would escape her nanny and scamper down to Fernleigh's conservatorium to watch him eviscerate and stuff animals. Walter Hunnicutt, chief taxidermist at the Australian Museum, was famed for his meticulously crafted mounts, and Esther's visits were the single disturbance he tolerated. After three years of silent observation, the young acolyte began to paint watercolours of his finished pieces. Eventually she was allowed to assist and at thirteen, having mastered the fundamental skills of taxidermy, she began stuffing her own small marsupials.

Her mother, Martha, though not sharing her daughter's fondness for dead creatures, encouraged Esther's scientific curiosity, hoping an interest in more feminine pursuits would soon follow. Tragically she never witnessed the transition, for shortly after Esther's fifteenth birthday, Martha Hunnicutt was taken by consumption. Walter attempted to smother his grief beneath a show of fortitude, but it refused containment, the great oak doors of Fernleigh barely muffling his fits of rage and bouts of sobbing. Then, turning from the bottle to excessive doses of Chlorodyne and Mrs Winslow's Soothing Syrup, both containing sufficient morphine to subdue a rhinoceros, he descended into shuffling stupefaction.

Three years later, Walter, now a shadow of his former self, went to a Spiritualist meeting in Stanmore, purportedly to prove the séance nothing more than the orchestrated histrionics of charlatans preying on the desperate and easily deluded. But on entering the home of professional medium Olive Bell, he was disappointed to find the parlour well lit by gas, making the concealment of any contraption beneath the table impossible. Worse still, the other three participants all appeared respectable and of pleasant disposition.

Once they'd all settled at the table, Olive's whispered invocation to the spirit world – and specifically Martha, at Walter's request – elicited no response. There was no rapping or tapping, no disembodied moaning or clamour. Nobody was prodded. Nobody pinched.

Undaunted by the lack of evidence, Olive declared Martha's spirit to be present and encouraged Walter to pose a question for confirmation. He asked his departed wife to reveal her favourite colour. The participants placed their fingers on the planchette and waited. Slowly the wooden heart rolled on its tiny bone wheels, its pencil scribing what at first appeared to be a looping 'P' on the paper tablet, then 'u' and 'r'. Purple? No – the first letter was in fact a 'T'. It was Turquoise. Correct.

Olive asked if the spirit was dwelling in a peaceful place, and the planchette quickly spelt out 'yes'. But, remaining unconvinced, Walter accused the assembly of manipulating the planchette. Olive advised him to ask another question without vocalising and he complied. A strained minute of silence passed before Walter cleared his throat and stated his intention to leave. The medium urged him to tarry a moment longer, and Walter curbed his rising indignation.

On returning his finger to the planchette, a strange frisson passed through the group. The wooden heart wrote 'Lady', then paused before adding 'bird' – 'Ladybird!' Walter felt his lungs compress, and an invisible band tightening around his temples. His whole body trembled. He lifted his fists and brought them crashing down on the board, flipping the planchette into the air. His head dropped to the table and he wept openly for the first time since his wife's passing. The boulder had been rolled away from his entombed heart. He'd asked Martha's spirit to reveal the last word she'd heard. 'Fly away home, ladybird,' were indeed the words he'd whispered in her ear as she'd drawn her final breath.

Listening to her father recount the night's events in an uncharacteristic babble, Esther wondered who or what had persuaded him to abandon all scientific knowledge. On being told that later in the night her disembodied mother had also communicated her wish for him to remarry, Esther surmised that her father had unconsciously moved the planchette himself – the ideomotor effect. She recorded his observations and her hypotheses in her diary. But weeks later, when Walter began taking tea with the spinster Althea Beauclare, Esther's own rational thoughts were to become plagued by a fear that some dark and mysterious force was at play.

It seemed unlikely that a scientist would believe his dead wife had spoken to him, but grief does strange things to a person. After all, I'd checked the mail for a month, hoping for a message from Pop Locke from beyond the grave.

As I was starting to nod off, I dreamt of the planchette spelling out 'Ladybird', with Walter's hand subconsciously guiding it.

L-A-D-Y-B-I-R-D

Each letter appeared in my mind's eye then rearranged themselves into

B-R-A-D I-D-L-Y

and I remembered the crossword clue from last Friday, outside Dr Limberg's office.

1 Across: Brad idly arranged insect displays (8 letters).

The letters from 'Brad idly' could be rearranged to display an insect – the ladybird! AND a ladybird had landed on Dr Limberg's jacket, AND she'd quoted the same nursery rhyme as Walter Hunnicutt.

Goosebumps spread over every inch of my skin – even the nub. I lay awake for another hour, trying to persuade myself that this was all nothing more than a coincidence.

YOU ARE HERE

On Friday morning, Ms Tarasek, dressed in a black hooded poncho with dark smudges around her eyes, wheeled into the studio a paper-shredding device bearing an old-school ghetto-blaster. Without introduction, she turned on some staccato medieval lute music and performed a bizarre interpretive dance, first whirling about then striking a series of angular poses with matching facial contortions that would've traumatised a small child. On the point of exhaustion she collapsed into a writhing then spasmodic, twitching finale, reminiscent of Tibor's episode during the rat dissection.

Isa Mountwinter alone clapped enthusiastically, but Ms Tarasek remained prostrate on the floor until others joined in with their applause and the volume reached the required level for resurrection. Ms Tarasek peeled off the black poncho to reveal a green bodysuit and rose like a plant sprouting in a time-lapse film. 'The foul stench of corruption,' she said. 'The rot, the miasma. Fleas on rats spread bubonic plague, ravaging Europe. Millions perish. The Church is powerless to intervene. Then from the ashes of the Black Death comes the Renaissance – the rebirth of classical ideas and thinking.'

'Terrific,' Cheyenne Piper said. 'But what's with the shredder?'

'In this digital age we have become binary and linear. We forget that everything in nature moves in cycles. Living things perish and return to soil. From death springs new life. I've read your essays and will now destroy them. Old ways of thinking must die to make way for the new.' She turned on the shredder and fed it the first paper.

'I so cannot believe you're actually doing that,' Liliana Petersen said. 'I missed a very important party on Saturday night to finish my paper. Ingrid went without me, and we never do anything separately.'

The teacher shuffled through the papers till she found Liliana's. 'Such noble sacrifice for art!' She fed it into the slot.

'Our mother's on the school board and could have you removed from Crestfield like that.' Liliana snapped her fingers.

'No need for indignation. You've been released from the traditional form of marking.'

'Then what was the point of doing it?'

'For you, enlightenment. For me, to learn how your minds work. I've chosen pairs for the collaboration project based on discordant thinking. Friction creates the spark that lights fire. Some of you wrote about the same artwork with opposing views, for example. Those students will be working together.'

Having bumped into each other at *Suspended Stone Circle II*, Isa Mountwinter and I looked at each other at the same time, then both pretended we hadn't.

During swim clinic, Deb Gelber's PowerPoint presentation on the hydrodynamics of competitive swimming had me making connections with what Ms Tarasek had said about linear versus cyclical movements. In a swimming race, you follow a straight line. There is a start and a finish, and you're digitally timed – constrained in an artificial environment. Whereas surfing is organic and freeform: it's governed by the forces of nature, waves that come in cycles influenced by the tides, which are in turn determined by the cycles of the moon.

Walking out of The Hive, I couldn't wait to free myself from the straight lines of the city and return to the natural beauty of Signal Bay for the first time since moving out. I caught the train from Edgecliff to Town Hall station, switched to the North Shore line on platform three, then boarded a carriage packed with workers clutching their phones to their chests like privacy shields. Perhaps if they'd bothered to look out the window as we emerged from the tunnel, there might've been a collective 'Hurrah!' – but it seemed that I was the only one thrilled by the sight of the wind-chopped harbour. I alighted at North Sydney and walked to Mum's office.

NOW BE TIGERS! is the name of Mum's events company. The neon words glow orange at reception – an 'exhortation to be fierce' dreamt up by Morgan Brierly, her business partner. Penny, the English receptionist, was untying a stuffed cupid from a massive bunch of roses on the front desk when I walked in. 'Woot-woo!' she said. 'I'm liking the new look.'

'Settle. It's my new school uniform. Who are the flowers from?'

'Curtis. We met exactly one month ago. How's your love life, mister? I bet you're driving those Crestfield girls wild.'

'Not even close.'

'Come on. I'd be first in line if you were five years older.'

'There's only two and a bit years between us.'

'Not like you're counting?' She winked. 'Can I get you something to drink? Your mum's having a crisis meeting with Morgan. They might not be able to snag Vienna for the launch and he's already promised her to the client.'

'I'm good, thanks. Who's Vienna?'

'Vienna Voronova is a Russian model who's exploding in Europe right now. Some boffins on the *Scientific Beauty* website calculated the dimensions of the perfect woman and they ran a global competition to find her. Vienna won.'

'What's the problem?'

'Morgan brokered a deal with her agent months ago, but now they're asking for more. Vienna wants business flights for her full entourage, including her mother, and we can't really say no. She's just turned fifteen.'

'Why are people so obsessed with youth?'

Penny shrugged. 'Andy Warhol's fault. He said that in the future everybody world-famous would be fifteen.'

'Really? My window of opportunity's about to close.'

'Morgan's already sent out a press release saying she'll be here. So we're up shit creek in a nutshell without a paddle, basically.'

'Gee, I hope you don't capsize.'

Penny let Mum know I was there, gathered the roses and clipped the cupid to my collar on her way out. I flipped through a pile of magazines looking for Vienna, then heard Mum exploding down in the meeting room, berating Morgan, her closest ally since they'd studied set design at uni together.

I inserted my earbuds and sneaked into Mum's empty corner office to check out the view. Harbour Bridge – Opera House – Botanic Gardens – Dad's apartment building. Mum could spy on him with her binoculars if she wanted to. I trained them on a window in the nearest office tower, where I saw a worker who appeared to be looking directly at me, so I lowered the binoculars and waved. She waved back. That's never happened before.

Returning the binoculars to the bookshelf, I found my favourite photo lying facedown. The family is having a picnic at Mackerel Beach. Maëlle can be seen feeding a goanna, hair blowing across her face – which had now been crossed out with a red marker. Legit creepy, but at least Mum hadn't burnt her eyes out.

I heard heels clicking on polished concrete – meeting done. I scooted back to reception just before Morgan came in, red-faced and shiny with sweat. 'Hello, young man. Snappy outfit.'

'It's my school uniform.' I unclipped Cupid and slid him into my pocket.

'The preppy look suits you.' He picked some fluff off my lapel and said to Mum, 'Don't worry, Charis. I'll have this sorted by Monday.'

'I know you will.'

On the drive home, I asked for the lowdown.

'Nothing to be concerned about,' Mum said, removing a tiny

smear of lipstick from her teeth with the guidance of the rear-view mirror. 'I'm leaving work in the office, where it belongs. This weekend is all about you, my darling. How was your day?'

I spoke briefly about school, suppressing my lingering annoyance at being sent somewhere I didn't belong.

Halfway down Spit Hill, we got stuck in a jam.

'Looks like a storm brewing,' Mum said, and began texting.

'You're working,' I said. 'And you smell weird.'

'You don't smell so fresh yourself, mister.'

'I mean different.'

'New fragrance.' She stretched her neck towards me. '"Prescience" by Caffarelli. Do you like?'

'As long as it's not made from the civet's anal gland. Apparently they extract some pheromone from a cat's arse that can make people attracted to you.'

'Maybe a hundred years ago, but now it's synthetically replicated. Who put that nonsense into your head?'

'Nobody.' It was Isa. She'd told the whole biology class that some of the most exclusive perfumes still contain the real thing, and that ambergris isn't whale vomit, like most people think – it's whale shit. Anyway, Mum didn't smell or look like her old self. Her hair was shorter and darker and wig-like, and, knowing she'd soon ask my opinion, I turned on the radio.

I was four the first time we drove through the subtropical rainforest of the Bilgola Bends. Venn told me it was the entrance to Jurassic Park. This evening, beneath the building February storm, the area felt wild again. I stuck my head out the window and inhaled deeply.

'What are you doing?' Mum said.

'Savouring the Earth's most glorious fecundity.'

'Pull your head in! You've been with your father too long.'

'Exactly.'

Rain was bulleting the Volvo's roof by the time we got to Signal Bay and, despite her new car having hill-descent control, Mum was too scared to go down the driveway. The year before, when she'd been driving up in the rain with me, her old car had lost traction, slid backwards and knocked the side wall over. The airbags almost killed us. So tonight we walked down the steeply pitched, slimy drive, Mum clutching my arm and tottering in danger heels.

Venn's Burmese cat greeted me in the kitchen, purring loudly as he ground figure eights around my calves. 'Hello, Oscar. Nice to see you too. Now nick off!'

'Be friendly,' Venn said, walking in from the living room. 'He's just pleased to have some male company again, and so am I, little brother.' Venn had always worn her hair in a ponytail, so when she appeared in the kitchen with an asymmetrical pink hairdo I pretended not to be shocked and congratulated her on breaking free of the elastic band.

'It marks a new phase,' she said, running her fingers through her hair. 'Come here and give me a hug.' She gave me a much-tighter-than-usual embrace.

'So when does uni start?' I asked, partly to extract myself.

'It doesn't. Five years of law before doing my Master of Environmental Law would kill me. At the health retreat I realised that I want to be a naturopath instead.'

'What does Dad think of Revati's career advice?'

'I haven't told him yet.'

'Perhaps he'd like to be kept in the loop?'

Venn rolled her eyes and said, 'I think he forfeited that privilege last year.'

Mum cooked a paella for dinner, a masterpiece of fiery colours with prawns, mussels, capsicum and chorizo on crispy toasted saffron rice. Before we ate, I asked why Nana Locke hadn't come. Venn told me that she'd bought a rescue dog – a Jack Russell–Chihuahua mix that was afraid of cats and would need exposure therapy.

'Or you could lock Oscar in your room?' I said.

After wolfing down two massive helpings of delicious paella, I scraped the chewy bits from the bottom of the pan, prompting Mum to ask if Dad was feeding me enough.

'He's doing his best,' I said.

'We all know he's Gordon Ramsay without the cooking skills.'

'You *are* looking a bit undernourished,' Venn said.

'Thank you. It's all the compulsory swimming.'

After dinner, I carried my bags to my room and instantly sensed that somebody had been in there touching my things. Examining my bed, I discovered a long blond hair on the pillow and took it down-stairs to investigate its source.

Seeing the disgust on my face, Mum said, 'Lincoln, what's wrong?'

'I know beyond reasonable doubt that somebody's been sleeping in my bed.'

'What are you talking about?'

'THIS!' I drew the hair from my pocket. 'It was on my pillow.'

The women glanced at each other and Venn shrugged, her non-chalance unconvincing.

'What is this, *CSI: Northern Beaches*? It's just a piece of hair.'

'Except it's blond, and nobody in this family is.'

'Okay, Sherlock. My friend Jessie stayed over last night.'

'I knew it. Why couldn't he sleep in the spare room? That's what it's for. I suppose you wanted him closer so he could sneak into your room without Mum hearing? You never made it any secret that you and Elliot were shagging, so why start now?'

'Jessie is a girl.'

'Oh.' I was momentarily stumped by the possibility that my sister was a lesbian. But my righteous indignation kept rolling with its own momentum. 'Does she suffer from alopecia or something? You could've at least changed the sheets.'

'Good God, Lincoln, when did you become so neurotic?'

I didn't think I was, but I did walk back upstairs and give my bed a thorough hair inspection before getting in – and found three more! Lying awake, I analysed my reaction and came to the conclusion that I'd become jealous when I wrongly assumed Venn had a new boy-friend to replace Elliot.

We met Elliot six years ago at Mackerel Beach. He was staying in the cottage next to ours and we instantly became a gang of three, running wild in the bush, paddling boards to little beaches beyond the

51

safe distance set by parents, and playing games invented by Venn to test our courage or stupidity. Three years later, she and Elliot had got together. And a tiny unspoken rift had started growing between us.

Anyway, last year my sense of isolation had reached an all-time low when I was rejected by Nicole Parker and by my crew shortly after. I should probably explain why it all hit me so hard. In his retirement, Pop Locke had started attending a charismatic church called the Fire Station, but he couldn't persuade Nana to join him – she said she wasn't into all the 'happy clappy' business, so he dragged me along. Nicole was playing guitar in the worship team. She had a beautiful voice and was totally hot. I was singing praise to Jesus, but it was really Nicole I was worshipping.

After a month of flirting with her at the church's youth group, Fired Up Friday, I drummed up the courage to ask Nicole out. She said yes immediately, but from there things progressed at a glacial rate. Our physical interaction was kept in check by her rule that we only meet in groups comprising other zealous youth who'd taken an oath of purity, which didn't impress my friends. My best mate Tom, fellow surfer and generally loose unit, couldn't help taking the piss out of the Fired Up Friday crowd.

At the peak of my frustration, I broke free and went to a party without Nicole – a celebration of Tom's older brother Blake scoring a sponsorship from Thurston® surfwear. Mr and Mrs Nugent were at a real-estate conference up the Goldie, so the party was going off – completely hectic. Their house is enormous and sits just above the northern end of Avalon Beach on Marine Parade. When I walked in the front door, Blake tossed me a beer. 'Get amongst it!' he said. 'Tommy's out the back.' I dropped the can in an esky on my way through the kitchen.

Out on the back lawn, at least a hundred punters were dancing around a huge bonfire and a white guy with dreads playing an African drum. Tom and Coops spotted me from Mr Nugent's new cabana and waved me over.

'Nicole let you off the leash for the night?' Coops said, handing me a beer.

'Yeah, but I'm not drinking.'

'Want a pinger then? They're so good. I'm defo going another.'

'Blake organised them,' Tom said. 'You can have one for twenty. Family discount.'

'Let me explain,' Coops said, gripping my shoulders. 'Imagine you're lost in the car park of a giant shopping centre and you find a map. And there's an arrow on the map that says YOU ARE HERE! Well that is so true right now, eh? Because I am SO here. The arrow is pointing down at me. And I've never been more here. And it's so TOP LEVEL!'

'I am so with you,' Tom said, hugging him. 'We're on a different plane.'

'Exactly!' Coops said. 'A private jet. And you're flying Jetstar.'

'Not that sort of plane. But the metaphor was ideal.'

Witnessing my friends' chemically induced elation filled my heart with a mix of fear, sadness and jealousy. My relationship with Nicole had driven a wedge between us that would cause a gap too wide to breach if she kept refusing to associate with them. So when I turned to the ocean, she was the last person I expected to see. She beckoned me over to the back of the yard and I left the boys to their fun.

'I thought you were busy saving the world?' I said.

'Only you, by the look of things.' She took my hand and we walked to the end of the lawn, then down wooden steps to a secluded nook above the rocky shore.

'Are we really together, or just friends?' I said.

Nicole reiterated her stance on purity and its supposed rewards for the seven hundredth time as a light rain began to fall. I suggested it was time to bail.

'Why?' she said, wide-eyed in her pale-pink hoodie.

'It's getting cold and I'm only wearing a t-shirt.'

'Poor baby. You're shivering. Come over here and I'll warm you up.' I slid across and she wrapped her arms around me, then drew me so close our noses touched. Her breath was sweet from raspberry-and-cream chews, the longing in her eyes contradicting the purity spiel.

I closed my eyes and waited, afraid to make a move but praying she would. When her lips brushed mine they were incredibly soft, yet every cell of my body felt electrified. We breathed in time with each other, savouring the ecstatic agony of delayed tongueage. And when they finally did touch it was like a flickering flame to a marshmallow, and nothing less than divine. Right in that sweet moment I felt truly born again, and saved from being ordinary.

Unsure whether the kissing was a one-off or a welcome amendment to the rules of engagement, I kept my hands strictly to myself. Nicole slipped hers inside my shirt and began exploring my chest, causing me to flinch and tremble. Her hands ventured around to my back and, without warning, slid just beneath the waistband of my jeans. And then – 'Sorry!' she said, suddenly withdrawing.

'What's the matter?'

'Nothing. Nothing at all.' Her fake denial couldn't hide something worse than revulsion in her eyes. She'd touched the nub. The tiny little thing that was about to change everything in my life. 'We should stop now.'

'Definitely.' I held up my hands.

Nicole looked to the heavens then lowered her head, eyes closed, lips moving as if she was asking God for the quickest way out. Finally she took a deep breath and said, 'Lincoln, have you read the last book of the Bible, the Book of Revelation?'

'Parts of.'

'I need to ask you a very serious personal question, but I don't want to offend you.'

'Spit it out.'

'Lincoln, are you the beast?'

Being asked by my girlfriend if I was the most heinous thing ever written about in the history and future of the world was difficult to comprehend because it was so preposterous. I was pretty certain that I wasn't evil incarnate, but having a minor deformity interpreted like that certainly made me feel like the ugliest person on the planet. We argued. She said I was scaring her. I begged her not to tell anybody. She cried. I offered to see her safely home. She left. Instead of chasing her, I walked back to the cabana to find my mates. They'd gone somewhere else but had left behind a half-bottle of vodka and some Coke®. I mixed a cup and drank it. Nothing. I took a slug of straight vodka and it burnt my throat. I slid to the floor so nobody could see me and drained the bottle.

Linkin Park was booming from the balcony. Chester Bennington singing that he's tired of being what somebody else wants him to be. I could totally relate. I made my way up to the house and pushed into the centre of the crowded living room. I shouted the chorus with Chester and danced with abandon. Everybody was smiling at me, pumping their fists. And then Coops' arrow appeared.

YOU ARE HERE!

It flashed in different colours and pulsated, pointing down at me.

Yes, me

!!!

!

Ten minutes of euphoria played out before the gears shifted. A fuzzy heat rushed to my head and, desperate for air, I staggered outside. The world tilted and I lurched with it, like a sailor on a foundering ship. Up it came the other way, turf slamming face, driving grass and dirt into my nose and mouth. I pulled myself to my knees, tried to find the axis, tried to stand, but the moon split and refused to reunite. And the ground received me.

The next morning, I woke up in my own bed in a state of almost complete paralysis. The only thing I could move was the granite block that had replaced my head, and doing that induced nausea. So I lay still and focused on a crack in the ceiling. Venn walked into my room with Mum, who fired off a barrage of questions I couldn't answer because I had no memory beyond the moon's division. She huffed and left to call my friends' mothers.

Venn filled in some missing pieces. At 2 am, she'd gone to the Nugents' place to look for me. Nobody had seen me for hours.

Tom took her down to the beach and eventually they found me facedown near the water. They roused me and helped me up to the car.

'Does Mum know all this?'

'You vomited three times in her car and the smell was impossible to eradicate, so yes, Lincoln, she knows.'

The mere mention of vomit provoked an encore of such ferocity that the gastric acid burnt my nasal membranes. Luckily someone had left a bowl next to my bed. 'Please take that away from me,' I said, passing it to Venn.

'Sure,' she said. 'And while I don't expect any gratitude for saving your life or cleaning the car, I'd suggest trying to cooperate with Mum.'

Thirty minutes later, Mum returned, demanding to know if I'd taken drugs. I denied it – because I hadn't. Then I lied, telling her that in my brief time with Coops and Tom they'd appeared completely sober. But Mum had done the parental ring-around and gleaned incriminating information from Coops' mother.

She drew a deep breath and let out an exasperated whistle. 'Cooper admitted to purchasing ecstasy from Blake Nugent and said he took the drugs with you and Tom.'

'That's not true! They were already well munted when I arrived.'

'You've just contradicted yourself, mister.'

'I swear I didn't use drugs. I walked away because I didn't want to be involved.'

'Of course. You chose the high road and walked away, which means you'll find it easy to follow the course of action that I've decided on. I'm forbidding you from any further association with the Nugent boys. You are not to surf with them or visit their house. You are not to communicate with Blake or Tom in any way.'

As it turned out that measure was hardly necessary, because I turned up at school on Monday to discover myself the new Year 9 pariah. Coops said that Mum had told his parents I'd ratted on him and Tom, and they were both in deep shit. I tried to defend myself by recounting the conversation, but they wouldn't have a bar of it.

'Apparently you told your mum we were already "well munted" when you arrived,' Coops said.

Unable to explain my reason without accusing Coops of implicating me in the drug-taking session when he told his parents, I shrugged. He and Tom shook their heads and walked away.

And, as if being rejected by my crew wasn't bad enough, Nicole Parker fully ghosted me.

Tonight, unable to sleep with the rain battering my bedroom window, I ruminated over how strange it was that people who were once prominent in your life could suddenly play no role in it. I'd hardly spoken to Tom or Coops since the end of last year – but they'd probably be out surfing tomorrow if the low-pressure cell generated a decent swell. What would happen if they found me on their break?

'Don't worry,' Homunculus said. 'They'll never be your friends again.'

'What are you, a life coach with a mean streak?'

THE BURNING QUESTION

Five-thirty am Saturday I was woken by magpies cawing and a sharp pain at the base of my spine, as if one of the bedsprings had pierced the mattress and drilled into my back. I pulled off the fitted sheet and ran my hand along the mattress but detected nothing. I felt the hairy nub at my coccyx. It was tender and swollen, and a little bit larger than usual. Maybe it had been bitten or I'd banged it against something? I laid a tissue over it and traced around it with a pen, then measured with a ruler. The nub's diameter was 1.7 centimetres. Mildly alarming.

After breakfast I went down to the beach for an early, hoping to avoid any of my old friends in the water. Got out an hour later feeling devo that I hadn't seen them.

Mum was in her studio, the 'turret', when I got home. It was a cube at the top of our house with a ribbon of window all the way round. With a sofa bed, bar fridge and ensuite, you could live there independently, which Mum sort of did for the months of in-house separation before Dad finally packed his bags. This morning she was sketching at the drafting table, with Botticelli's 'Birth of Venus' open on the Mac screen beside her.

'I brought you a cup of tea.'

'How thoughtful, but I'm on a caffeine detox.'

'What are you working on?'

'Just another product launch, but it's confidential so you mustn't breathe a word.'

'Scout's honour.' I made a three-finger salute.

'My client, Sanctus Mineralis, have discovered the Holy Grail of the beauty industry – a secret ingredient that can delay the skin's ageing process.'

'That's original.'

'I knew you wouldn't be interested.'

'No, I am. What is it?'

Mum opened an image file of seaweed. 'They've bioengineered nanoparticles containing kelp spore seven hundred times smaller than a skin pore, which allows them to germinate inside the lower layers of skin and accelerate collagen production to a phenomenal rate. This will be a viable alternative to cosmetic surgery.'

'How much for a jar?'

'A seventy-five millilitre vial of the E-Radiata Serum™ will retail for around two-hundred and seventy dollars.'

'Well within the reach of your average housewife.'

Mum turned to face me with folded arms. 'Ninety per cent of the women in the trials judged their appearance five to ten years younger post-treatment.'

'Do you actually believe it?'

'I believe the cross-platform marketing campaign will make the product fly off the shelves.'

'Where do you fit in?'

'Sanctus Mineralis are planning to upstage the opening of Fashion Week with a spectacular marine-themed launch, and they've given us the budget to pull it off.'

'Cue the nude chick in shell.' I snapped my fingers.

'Yes, the Venus hero,' she said, her eyes lighting up. 'Imagine guests being served oysters and champagne inside a giant inflated pearl beside the harbour, while a choir sings something stirring by Enya.' She played a YouTube clip of Enya singing 'Only Time' while she narrated the proposed action. 'An enormous shell emerges from the sea and moves towards the shore as if blown by the wind. Ever so slowly it opens to reveal the goddess Venus. Lustrous tresses of golden hair and one hand protecting her modesty, the other holding an over-sized vial of E-Radiata Serum™, illuminated from within. Everybody takes photos.'

'And then?'

'A banner unfurls that says, "Who knows? Only time" – which we don't have the rights to use yet, but Morgan's working on it. The guests are given goodie bags filled with product samples, a small gift to reward their endorsement on social media. Hashtag perfectly beautiful.'

'Who's playing Venus?'

'Only the most divinely gorgeous creature on the planet right now.'

'Vienna Voronova?'

'Penny told you. That girl couldn't keep a secret if her life depended on it.'

Mum hadn't always been a cog in the machine relentlessly promoting extravagant consumables. Decades before I was even a concept, she'd been the resident set designer for a radical theatre company. Late in the eighties, the government cut their funding so the company sought corporate sponsorship. She met Dad at one of the meetings. They fell in love and married, then she left the theatre scene to have Venn. When I was eight, Mum returned to work, staging small events for some of Dad's clients. Four years later she formed her own events company, NOW BE TIGERS! She and Morgan had had a bumpy start, but now they were smashing it.

I hadn't brought *My One Redeeming Affliction* with me, but I found *Strange Case of Dr Jekyll and Mr Hyde* on Dad's bookshelves and spent the rest of the day reading it. Later in bed, nightmares of transforming into the maniacal Mr Hyde, and committing heinous acts, had me tossing and turning. I woke early Sunday morning with my sheet in a ball on the ground, half-believing Nicole Parker had been well within reason for asking me if I was the beast. My nub was tender but I was afraid to measure it again. At the breakfast table Mum noticed that I kept touching myself, and I told her I had a sore back.

After a hearty breakfast of French toast, Mum drove Venn and me to the Zen Gardens to help find a new backyard feature. She was immediately drawn to a granite Buddha, whose expansive stomach was being tickled by reeds. Disregarding the expense of chartering a helicopter to airlift him into our backyard, Mum began recording the Buddha's dimensions with her FatMax®. Venn and I walked to the Pool of Eternal Bliss, which turned out to be a murky pond teeming with koi and a couple of scary eels. We crossed a stone bridge onto a miniature island, and I threw a pebble into the water.

'Don't do that!' Venn pulled me back. 'You'll traumatise them.'

'Settle down. Fish love me,' I said, then thought about little Pinky losing his tail in the school's tank and left the fish alone.

'The koi symbolises perseverance in times of adversity, because it can swim upstream like salmon,' Venn said. 'It's also a charm for marital bliss.'

'Maybe we should buy one for Mum and Dad at the gift shop?'

'Too late. Mum told me she wouldn't take him back in a million years,' Venn said, extracting another Jenga block from my wobbly tower of false hope.

'I thought it was a trial separation.'

'They used that term to ease everybody into the idea that we're no longer a family unit.'

The truth hurts in different ways. Sometimes it's a slap in the face. Today it was an elephant sitting on me and sharting. And still I persisted. 'Why not?' I said. 'That's the burning question.'

'He made some mistakes that can't be fixed.'

'He didn't do anything that bad.'

Venn shrugged. 'That would be from his perspective, and I'm not going to argue against it. You have to live with him.'

'Why are you acting like fucking Switzerland when it's so obvious you hate him? You know something I don't. Tell me what it is. I beg you.'

Venn walked back over the bridge and I followed her to a little bench shaded by a Japanese maple. We sat down. She prefaced what she was about to say with a warning that it would change the way I felt about my father forever. And then she let it all out.

After Mum's fiftieth, one of the guests, who'd asked to remain anonymous, told Mum that she'd passed Dad's study on the way to the bathroom and had caught sight of Dad in there with Maëlle. Apparently it looked like they were doing something they shouldn't have been, but she couldn't be certain. Mum questioned Dad directly and at first he was affronted but then he laughed, dismissing it by saying that he'd taken Maëlle there to sign a birthday card. His response only made Mum more suspicious, so she asked Maëlle to leave. Venn knew nothing about the reported sighting and took Dad's side because she was so upset that Mum had evicted her friend for no reason. Maëlle had promised to update Venn on her travels, but the emails were brief and impersonal. The tension between Venn and Mum became close to unbearable for both of them while Venn was studying for the HSC, so Mum told her what the guest had revealed. Venn sent about ten emails to Maëlle asking if the allegations were true. Eventually she responded.

Maëlle confirmed that Dad had taken her to the study to sign the birthday card but then he'd complained of a sore neck from the tension of preparing the party. She offered to give him a massage. He accepted. One thing led to another and they'd shared a kiss. She confessed that she'd been attracted to my father from the moment he picked her up at the airport, and then felt something building between them. But the kiss was an isolated incident – a one-off. A terrible mistake that she wished she could take back and would forever feel remorse for. Maëlle said that she and Dad had made a pact never to tell anybody, and now she'd broken it. She pleaded with Venn to keep the secret. Venn showed Mum the email, and the next day Mum told my father to leave or she would.

Venn showed me Maëlle's confession on her phone. I wanted to throw it into the Pool of Eternal Bliss. Instead I said, 'That's totally fucked up.' I felt betrayed, to varying degrees, by everybody involved in the drama. 'Why didn't you tell me before?'

'We wanted to protect you from it.'

'I'm always the last to know. Don't tell anybody I do, though. I can't deal with this right now.' We walked back to the entrance and found Mum, still examining the Buddha.

'I need your help,' she said. 'I can't decide between this big guy and the water feature over there.' She pointed to a stone bowl on a plinth that was overflowing with water pouring down from a spout above it.

'Water bowl,' I said.

'I was leaning towards Buddha. We could have our own little meditation garden out the back.'

'That thing's gargantuan.'

'Darling, he'd be dwarfed by the angophora.'

'Mr Harris won't like it,' Venn said.

'Then he might stop gawking over the fence.'

Mum ordered the Buddha statue, but I doubted it would bring the serenity she hoped for.

Late in the evening, as we drove from Signal Bay back to the city, I asked Mum if Nana Locke had bought the rescue dog because she was lonely without Pop.

'I think so,' she said. 'Tippi yaps a lot but your nana adores her.'

Travelling through the harbour tunnel, I pondered my own sense of isolation and realised I was stuck in a limbo between Signal Bay and Kings Cross – and neither felt like home. It wasn't the geographic separation that made me feel lost, so much as the emotional distance between my parents.

Mum asked if I was all right as we approached the flashing Coca-Cola sign.

'I'm fine,' I said, distracted by one of its malfunctioning lights.

Mum turned into Kings Cross Road and pulled over. 'Promise you'll tell me if anything's bothering you.' The driver behind blasted his horn. 'I'll speak to you tomorrow – okay?' She leant over and kissed my cheek. 'Love you.'

'Love you too,' I said as I got out.

Standing on the footpath was an overweight guy with a comb-over, wearing a yellowed singlet and threadbare grey trackies devoid of elastic. He was staring at an illuminated rolling billboard that featured a blonde babe in a blue bikini biting into a Cornetto®, between ads for Vodafone® and home insurance. Each time the beautiful girl rolled away, he waved and his pants dropped to the pavement.

'Good evening, Master Locke,' Frank said as I walked into the lobby. 'How was your weekend?'

'Okay. Who's the guy outside?'

'You mean Leonard? He's harmless. Been around these parts for yonks. They call him Loose Pants Lenny. He's had the same pair since I've known him.'

'Why doesn't he get new ones?'

'Wouldn't have anything to keep himself busy.'

WHAT ARE THE CHANCES?

My phone alarm woke me at 5.30 am and I was glad that squad provided a legitimate excuse to avoid my father. Bolstered by the lack of pain and swelling in my nether regions, I rode my bike to school and suffered no chafing. I wasn't so worried about anybody spotting the nub – until I learnt that the swimming sets would be separated by three sessions of dry drill. Lucky I'd brought shorts, which I whipped on every time I got out of the pool.

First was straight-arm raises with hand weights, Gelber using her megaphone to blast anybody who faltered. Second was linked-arm sit-ups, which felt like military training, Nads and Starkey muttering threats of violence to anybody dragging the chain. The final session involved jogging with knees to waist in a figure-eight formation like prancing ponies in team dressage, Mullows a thoroughbred with his ginger ponytail swishing from side to side.

Alternating between wet and dry drills pushed me to the brink of my fitness level. I'd given it everything, hoping the exertion might somehow weaken the severity of anger I felt towards my father. But it only increased when I realised that I wouldn't have been stuck there doing squad if he hadn't cheated on Mum – and used my paralytic episode at the Nugents' place as a pretext for dragging me into the city to share his luxury doghouse.

In Maths, Monaro introduced the probability unit by stating that the likelihood of any particular event occurring at a given time and place could be predicted using a formula. And the more potentially havoc-wreaking the event – like a nuclear-reactor meltdown or terrorist attack – the more important for its probability to be calculated. He turned to write on the board and Tibor Mintz suddenly yelled 'FUCK!', which was probably a first. Monaro demanded an explanation, and Tibor said that he'd been stabbed in the left buttock. Starkey confessed by raising his arm, holding a pair of compasses. Monaro winced and sent Tibor to Student Welfare for a tetanus shot. Then, after rebuking Starkey for the assault, Monaro devised a formula for calculating the probability of his causing disruption in any class. Whatever variables were entered, the result was more than seventy per cent. Instead of expressing remorse, Starkey looked stoked that the chance of his acting like an arsehole could be so accurately predicted.

At lunchtime I found a spot behind Old Block that catches the cool nor'-easter blowing across the harbour, beneath a Port Jackson fig that had been roped off. The tree's trunk looked solid, its branches strong, but it was blighted by a pathogenic fungal infection that had weakened its structural integrity and could kill it. Pop Locke had been fighting fit when he'd been felled by the Pajero, but the tree reminded me of him. Probably because Venn had told me that if Pop was reincarnated as a tree, he would definitely be a Port Jackson fig. She would've hugged the diseased tree if she'd been here now. So I climbed under the rope, wrapped my arms around him and said, 'I hope you get well soon.'

With nobody else around, I took out *My One Redeeming Affliction*. I'd left off with Walter Hunnicutt possibly manipulating the planchette to communicate his dead wife's wish for him to remarry. Funny how people manufacture or interpret 'signs' to support their dubious intentions or beliefs. I wondered for a moment how Dad would justify frenching the French house guest, who was the same age as my sister, if I confronted him. Then I opened the book to get the troubling mental picture out of my head.

The following Monday, my grandfather, in a show of spontaneous benevolence, announced his decision to enrich the museum's ornithology collection with five of his prized bowerbirds. The director responded to his generosity by allowing him to employ a studio assistant. Without deliberation, Walter chose his most promising student, Enoch Fernsby.

On hearing the news, Esther was both indignant and aggrieved. Though opportunities of education and employment were usually withheld from women, there were some notable exceptions. Walter's predecessor had been Jane Tost, the first woman employed at the museum and one of their finest taxidermists. How, then, could Esther's father now spurn the only child who shared his passion for the natural world, and understood the agonisingly slow thrill of resurrecting the natural form of a creature, making it almost immortal? She knew more than all of his students combined.

One week later, Walter attempted to console her by giving the museum her bowerbird illustrations to be displayed alongside the mounts – a dire miscalculation. Instead of being delighted with the surprise, Esther wrote that she had 'gawped in utter disbelief' at being robbed by her own father. Her devastation was made complete on discovering that he'd also given away the mounting of a cockatiel called Percy, who was once the family's most treasured pet.

The old dude from the junkyard had a stuffed cockatiel called Percy. What were the odds of two stuffed cockatiels having the same name? A million to one? Or maybe the old hermit's Percy *is* the one from the book? Not even Monaro could come up with an algorithm to calculate the possibility of that.

My curiosity about the cockatiel, combined with the recent revelations of Dad's behaviour, dissolved any hesitation I felt about breaking his rule to stay away from the junkyard. I rode my bike down there after school and, pushing apart the vines that grew on the fence, saw the old dude pegging a pair of stained, blown-out grundies to a line strung between the plane tree and the fake totem pole.

'Hello,' I said, but he turned to go back inside so I yelled out and gave him a fright.

'No need to shout,' he said, approaching the fence. 'What do you want, you little punk?'

'I really like that bird of yours – the cockatiel. I was wondering where you got him?'

'Percy? Can't have him.'

'Don't worry, I don't actually want him. I just wanted to know where you found him?'

'You stole my bike and now you want the bird.'

'My dad left you two hundred dollars.'

'Poppycock!' He peered through the fence and saw my bike on its stand. 'You've stripped off the fancy parts. Ungrateful little bugger!'

'Sorry. No disrespect, but I thought all that stuff was more suitable for a girl.'

'Well, you're hardly the finest specimen of manhood.'

'Look who's talking.'

'Piss off, you little turd!'

That didn't go well.

I pushed my bike back up to T H E E Y R I E and got stuck into homework. When Dad arrived, I didn't come out.

Later he called me to join him for dinner. Spag bol is one of the few dishes he's competent at, but my simmering resentment towards him had stolen my appetite. Holed up in my room, I decided to act like Dad was a stranger who I had to be polite to. Completely consumed with his work, he didn't even seem to notice my absence.

LOST AND FOUNDLINGS

Tuesday I had History with Mrs Hatcher, who, like Ms Tarasek, has an alternative approach to teaching. She encourages free debate, and today things got a little loose.

'What do Moses, Oedipus, Hansel and Gretel, Snow White and Superman all have in common?' Mrs Hatcher said, tapping the e-board to make them appear. 'Anybody?'

'They were all abandoned children.'

'Correct, Isa. The foundling is a character type found frequently in historical narratives, mythology and popular culture. The child is often discovered and nurtured by a lowly couple, unaware of its special destiny. In other variations the child is raised by animals. For instance, Romulus and Remus were suckled by a wolf, Paris by a bear.'

'Paris Hilton?' Starkey said. 'That's hectic.'

'Not her,' Pericles said. 'Paris was a prince in Greek mythology who abducted Helen, the most beautiful woman in the world, which triggered the Trojan War.'

'The Greeks practised a form of child abandonment called exposure,' Mrs Hatcher said. 'If a child was disabled, deformed or deemed somehow imperfect by the elders, they would leave the child on a hillside to the mercy of the elements.'

'That's called murder,' Cheyenne Piper said.

'They didn't see it that way because the child still had a slim chance of surviving, which the Greeks would attribute to the intervention of the gods. Though yes, Cheyenne, most died from hypothermia – if they weren't ravaged by wild dogs.'

'Those Greeks were barbaric,' Cheyenne said.

'Hold on,' Pericles said. 'Athens was the cradle of Western civilisation, the birthplace of democracy.'

'Nice if you were male and belonged to the elite ten per cent who were citizens and owned slaves,' Liliana Petersen said.

'Yeah. You could force them to work all day and reward them with a flogging,' her twin, Ingrid, finished her thoughts. 'Now that's democracy.'

Mrs Hatcher turned to Pericles to encourage a rebuttal.

'It had to start somewhere.' He shrugged. 'That was thousands of years ago. Things evolve over time.'

'Whatever,' Cheyenne said. 'Everyone knows you Greeks are still the same. One set of rules for the guys and a different set for the girls.'

Mrs Hatcher held up her hands. 'Let's keep this civil, please.'

'Cheyenne has no idea,' Phoenix said.

'But you do?' Nads said. 'China still has child restriction policies. What happens when a couple wants a boy and gets a girl? You're lucky you were spared.'

'Darvin, please!' the teacher said. 'No personal invectives.'

Phoenix stood, hands on hips. 'I was born in Australia. So were my parents and my grandparents.'

'Big deal,' Starkey said. 'You're still a blow-in, so sit down. I can trace my family back to the First Fleet. We've been here the longest out of anyone.'

'For a white boy,' Isa said. 'And of course white men never did anything nasty, did they? No – they just massacred the first peoples, stole Aboriginal kids away from their families and tried to breed out the Aboriginal race. There's equality in action. Aboriginal and Torres Strait Islander people weren't even fully counted in the census till nineteen seventy-one. Go, white man!'

'That was ages ago,' Starkey said. 'It's got absolutely nothing at all to do with me.'

'If the past means nothing, then stop bragging about your stupid convict roots.'

Mrs Hatcher looked at her watch then ended the session. Nothing like a spirited discussion to bring out people's true colours. And it made me realise for the first time just how white Crestfield was. It's funny: dressed in my blue blazer with its golden trim I fit perfectly into the demographic, but my secret deformity means that I'll never feel I belong there. Still, it was better than Ancient Greece. If I'd been born with the nub, I would've been abandoned on a hillside to become dog food. Grecian GravyLog®.

Homunculus ridiculed me intermittently all the way home with politically incorrect names for someone who doesn't conform to the physical norm. Riding up in the lift, I slapped my forehead to shut him up. Inside the apartment, I made myself a peanut butter sandwich, contemplating all the reading I had to do for school, but the tantalising mystery of the Percy coincidence drew me back into the pages of *My One Redeeming Affliction.*

Bloody arrival to bloodier departure, my father William's life was punctuated by accidents – some grave, others fortuitous. His conception was the unintended but hardly unforeseeable result of an incautious liaison between wealthy industrialist Thaddeus Stone and his mistress Evie Griffin. Weighing nine pounds and possessing an exceptionally large head, William had to be cut from his mother's belly, a procedure only the infant survived. Thaddeus already had six grown children, so to avoid scandal he gave the child to his deceased lover's sister, Hannah, and her husband, Matthias Stroud, a Cornish tin miner. Unable to produce their own, they considered the child a blessing from Heaven, and the boy thrived in the countryside.

Shortly after William turned nineteen, Matthias declared his plan to seek his fortune on the goldfields of New South Wales. He asked William to look after his mother in his absence, but the young man's fierce desire to join his father on the adventure prevailed. William abandoned his study of philology, breaking a condition of the trust established by his birth father, and together he and Matthias set sail for the colony.

The Araluen diggings yielded mostly alluvial gold: the precious grains gleaned by hours of cradling, sluicing and panning. In a good week a miner might extract fifty or sixty ounces, fetching about four pounds on the market – ten times the average weekly wage for a factory worker. A bad week would produce nothing. Though the work was arduous, the diggers were bonded by a shared dream and, unlike at many other fields, a fair degree of harmony existed between the various nationalities.

Two Chinese fellows, Ah To (who chose the English name Johnny) and Lin Cheong (known as Mac), supplied William and Matthias with their tea, flour, sugar and fresh vegetables. In return for English lessons, Johnny introduced William to the exotic tastes of dried fish and pickled ginger, and the game of fan-tan. Along with poker and two-up, it became my father's preferred form of entertainment. Life itself was a game of chance for William, and whenever his pockets were full he went out to play. I knew nothing of his fondness for gambling nor the awful repercussions of the habit till some time after his death, when Johnny visited my family to pay his respects and, under duress from my mother, revealed all. The only gambling stories my father had ever told us involved taking chances that paid off.

One of those stories began with the decision to leave the Araluen diggings in the autumn based on the flip of a penny. William and Matthias bade farewell to Johnny and Mac and headed north to the Turon River near Bathurst, granting themselves six months to strike it rich. If the story's true, their good fortune arrived before they'd even pitched their tents. As William was digging a cesspit, his shovel hit something metallic a few feet beneath the surface. With incredulous fervour, the men dug out an enormous nugget of gold. It was officially weighed in at 132 pounds and six ounces troy, fetching £5467! Divided in half, it was still a fortune.

Only blind greed could've kept a man on the fields a day longer. The pair travelled to Sydney, where Matthias bid William a heartwrenching farewell and set sail for England. He returned to his wife Hannah a wealthy man. But, having found great fortune in New South Wales, William believed his destiny lay in the colony's bustling port.

Lodging at the Ship and Mermaid Hotel on Gloucester Street, my father struck up conversation with a Greek fisherman from the small island of Ithaca. Over copious pints of ale, Dimitrios gave a rollicking account of his odyssey around the world. William suggested they eat at one of the fried-fish-and-oyster shops but Dimitrios refused, declaring them the last resort of hungry drunkards. He shared his dream of buying a fishing boat and opening a restaurant selling only the freshest fish and oysters, then invited William to his tiny cottage on Millers Point to sample his snapper pie. One glorious bite and my father promised to make his friend's dream come true.

Six months later, with William's finance and Dimitrios's experience, the pair opened a small oyster saloon a stone's throw from their first meeting place. Selling oysters and exceptionally fresh fish, the establishment quickly became well patronised, especially by drunkards when the public houses closed.

Seven years of solid business later, William and Dimitrios sold the saloon for a handsome profit and my father took another gamble, acquiring a lease on the top level of George Pemberton's newly built Magnificent Emporium. The partners decorated their dining room with copies of classical statues, some carved from marble, most cast in plaster with a faux-marble finish. Assuming them to be authentic antiquities, Sydney's high society flocked to the Ionian Restaurant to immerse themselves in the splendour of its decor, thrilled to be surrounded by statues they assumed to be the spoils of plunder.

Wednesday afternoon, Ms Tarasek announced pairs for the collaboration project. My hunch – that I'd be partnered with Isa Mountwinter, who I hadn't spoken to since she'd cornered me in the library last Thursday – was confirmed. Obviously finding the idea of working together irksome, she requested a partner swap. Despite the feeling being mutual, my self-esteem took another dive. Awkwardly for both of us, the request was denied.

Ms Tarasek showed us a photo of a rocky landscape covered in material. 'In nineteen sixty-nine, the artists Christo and Jeanne-Claude, along with their volunteers, wrapped Little Bay in thousands of metres of synthetic fabric. It was the largest public artwork in the world. They continued working together for another forty years, until Jeanne-Claude's death. This is devotion, yes?'

Ms Tarasek directed us to sit opposite our partners and gave each pair a slab of clay and an empty bowl. 'Truly successful collaborations are rare, because egos get in the way. Today we learn to merge our creative impulses.' She filled our bowls with water. 'Without tools, you will create one piece together. No planning, no talking at all. Be guided by your intuition. Begin.'

Isa wouldn't even look at me, which made non-verbal communication challenging. Minutes passed without either of us touching the clay. Worried we'd have nothing to show, I whispered, 'What should we make?'

Isa shushed me and pinched off a small nugget for herself, then pushed the rest to me. 'That's yours,' she whispered. 'Make whatever you want.'

I looked around the studio. Everybody else was getting stuck in. Mullows and Cheyenne Piper had made their clay sloppy and were squishing it between each other's fingers. Cheyenne's eyes were shut, and she appeared to be channelling Demi Moore in the pottery scene from *Ghost*. Mullows caught me looking and winked.

Disregarding whatever plan Isa had for her clay – if there was one – I began modelling half an oyster shell, influenced, I suppose, from the previous night's reading. She shrugged a what-the-hell shrug, so I made the other half and connected them. She shook her head and frowned. I tapped my watch, so she rolled her clay into a small sphere, dipped her finger in water and smoothed it into a pearl. Ms Tarasek came over and placed Isa's pearl inside my shell.

'Here is a perfect union of minds,' she said to the whole class. 'Lincoln and Isa have trusted their instincts to create a cohesive and meaningful piece.'

'You know, a pearl is nothing more than a self-protective response to an invading irritant,' Isa said to me.

'I didn't. But thank you for sharing.'

Pericles Pappas is a nice guy, but I noticed during squad he gets edgy whenever Nads, Mullows and Starkey are around. Sometimes he seems nervous talking to me. Could be because he's buddies with Isa and Phoenix, who wouldn't piss on me if I caught fire. This afternoon I was feeling chuffed that I'd managed to stay right behind him for the entire three-kilometre training session, until we got out of the pool and he accused me of drafting.

'Don't even know what that means.'

'You slipstreamed me the whole way, which makes the swim thirty per cent easier. You should've tapped.'

'I didn't want to pass.'

'Then don't come so close. It's annoying.'

I have zero interest in competition, but Pericles obviously does. My only goal was avoiding nub detection by the swimmer behind.

Training finished later than usual, and I was ravenous when I got home. Dad had left a note saying that if he was late there were some gourmet sausages to grill and eat with pre-made slaw and mash. At seven-thirty, unable to wait any longer, I broke the seal of the sausage tray. Four gourmet bangers, translucent skins bulging with minced lamb and Middle Eastern spices. I was overcome by an intense hunger, stronger than I'd ever experienced before – an instinctual urge. Without considering the ramifications, I bit off the end of a sausage and sucked out the raw filling. It was gamey and spicy and delicious, and one was not enough. Dad walked through the door and caught me with the third sausage in my mouth, no grill on the bench, no cooking smells.

'Quickest way to give yourself salmonella, mate.'

'I couldn't wait.'

'You're an animal.'

'I desperately needed protein,' I said.

'I've been thinking exactly the same. It wouldn't hurt you to bulk up a bit now that you're right on the verge of turning sixteen, so I've booked us an introductory session with a personal trainer at BigTown Gym™.'

'Terrific,' I said, thumb-gouging my eyes at the thought of participating in another physical activity that could expose the nub.

'Lincoln, you've been acting very strangely since the weekend. It feels like you're avoiding me. Is everything okay?'

'Yeah. I'm just missing Pop Locke really badly. He died a year ago tomorrow.' It was only half the reason for my despondence, but I wasn't ready to reveal the rest.

'I know. I miss him terribly too.' Dad's voice broke, his chin crumbled. 'I didn't get the chance to say goodbye properly.' He started crying, which really threw me. Then, attempting to recompose himself, he said between sobs, 'We had some unfinished business. I disappointed him very badly.'

I'd never seen my father fall into such a broken state so suddenly, not even on the day Pop died or at his funeral. Tonight, as he wiped his nose with the back of his hand, he seemed embarrassed that his vulnerability had been exposed. 'Let's talk about it another time, eh?'

'Sure,' I said, unable to utter anything more encouraging than that, and afraid to tell him he'd disappointed me as well.

LAMPWICK'S
CIGAR

Sweet sixteen today and I've only been kissed once, by Nicole Parker. Terrific but ended badly. Regret at my lack of experience was weighing heavily on my mind as I sat in one of the fleet of minibuses taking Year 10 to see

CHARLES DARWIN:
VOYAGES AND IDEAS THAT SHOOK
THE WORLD

at the National Maritime Museum in Pyrmont.

Our first stop was a re-creation of Darwin's cabin; a flimsy hammock was strung up above a table and chairs. Having been to the exhibition twice already, Tibor Mintz assumed the role of personal guide, unaware of my personal connection to the subject.

'Darwin shared it with two others,' he said. 'Charting coastlines was the main point of the voyage, not his specimen-collecting.'

'It would've been awesome sailing around the world,' I said.

'Except that he suffered from terrible seasickness.'

'Still, what an adventure.'

Starkey poked my back. 'Why are you hanging out with T-boring? Come and check out Darwin's crabs.' He pulled me over to the display of crabs caught on the epic voyage, on loan from Oxford University. 'Do you reckon they flew over first class?'

'Sure,' Nads said, cuffing his head. 'They were served oysters and champagne on take-off, dickhead.'

I broke away to check out the drawings and watercolours of South America's flora and fauna. Who'd have the patience to record everything so meticulously? There would've been so much work in pickling all the insects, and skinning and stuffing animals. Lucky Darwin had a trusty cabin boy, Syms Covington, assisting him. I bet they had some interesting conversations as they chowed down on roast turtle.

Heather Treadwell, leader of the Crestfield Bible Study Group, and David York, staunch atheist, were having a discussion on the existence of Noah's ark beside the display of flesh-eating plants. David was arguing that the larger, more ferocious animals would've devoured the smaller ones before the first drop of rain fell. Heather countered that God can do anything because he's God – including creating man fully formed, without the involvement of evolution. Having been a member of the Fire Station Church for six months, where they preached quite a literal interpretation of scripture, I could appreciate where Heather was coming from, but evolution is a scientific fact.

'Show them your backside and win the argument for the atheist,' Homunculus said distinctly. I thought Heather and David had heard him too because they both turned and looked at me at that exact moment. I skulked away, scorched by shame.

During lunch, Starkey spread a rumour of a bikini parade at the upstairs exhibition, EXPOSED! THE STORY OF SWIMWEAR, and persuaded a group of us to sneak in and check it out. When Nads and Mullows realised he was bullshitting, they punched him and left. But three black-and-white photos on the walls caught my eye.

The first was of Australian swimmer Annette Kellermann posing in front of a painted ocean backdrop, foot resting on fake stone. She was wearing a thigh-length one-piece with tights underneath. The caption said that Harvard professor Dudley Sargent had measured thousands of students and, finding Annette's proportions closest to the Venus de Milo, he'd declared her the perfect woman. I guess she was the 1910 version of Vienna Voronova. A year later, Annette was the first woman to swim with a mermaid tail in a film and, five years after that, the first big star to do a nude scene. Serious legend.

Beneath was an 1890s shot of American performer Hilda Groot swimming with a mermaid tail in a tank at Coney Island in New York. Standing outside the tank on either side were two men poised to spear each other with tridents. One had virtually no limbs, with his hands and feet appearing to be attached directly to his torso, making him very short. The other was tall and well built. Their names, according to the caption, were Paulo Esposito and Edwin Stroud.

Holy smoke! Edwin Stroud: he was the author of *My One Redeeming Affliction*. I googled him on my phone, but the only relevant results I found directed me back to his biography, which I had at home, and the website for the EXPOSED! exhibition. My curiosity about this Stroud guy was off the charts.

The bottom photo had been taken a few years earlier than the second at Pyrmont Baths, which were once not far from the museum. Ten scrawny boys in old-fashioned vested swimming costumes are sitting on the edge of the tidal pool, arms around each other's shoulders. Another boy is sitting apart from them, and not looking at the camera. He is Edwin Stroud at sixteen. His stark isolation caused a lump of sadness to rise in my throat. I glanced back at the photo above, of him with Paulo and the mermaid. 'Don't worry,' I said. 'Things get better for you.'

At home, I went straight to the book and flicked through the pages, looking for images, but there were none. The thrilling coincidence of seeing those two photographs was still buzzing in my head, and I was impatient to discover exactly what Edwin's affliction was now that I knew he'd become some sort of aquatic performer. I wanted to jump ahead to the point where he makes an appearance in his own biography. But then I recalled Pop Locke telling me that, 'Once a person connects with their ancestry, they'll never be alone again.' Learning about Edwin's parents would help me understand him better. I would allow the story to unfold as the author had intended.

There was no time for reading, anyway. I had to write a report about what I'd learnt today at the museum, and Mum, Venn and Nana Locke were meeting us soon in the city for my birthday dinner. The first full family meeting since the separation. With Venn having spilt the beans on Dad's fateful 'indiscretion' and nobody else knowing that I knew, the awkwardness indicator was nudging catastrophic.

Dad changed his shirt twice before I got him out of the apartment. William Street was warm and sticky, heavy with the smell of an approaching storm. We walked past three campervan rentals, a pawn shop and two prestige car dealerships before stopping at a small alcove, stale with piss. There was a door with no handle, covered with scabby poster remnants advertising festivals and bands I'd never heard of. Stencilled on the manky collage was the word **V e n e e R**.

The door opened before we'd knocked, revealing a slender woman in a miniskirt almost as wide as a bandaid, holding a metal clipboard.

'Good evening, Mr Locke. The other members of your party haven't arrived yet. Perhaps you'd like to wait at the bar?'

The bar was schmick. The counter and tabletops were printed with vintage Kings Cross images embedded with twinkling LEDs. Checking out the other patrons, I realised we were the uncoolest people in one of the coolest bars in Sydney.

'Name your poison,' Dad said. 'It's your sixteenth birthday and we're toasting your grandfather tonight.'

I looked at the drinks list and chose the ale with the best name. 'Lampwick's Cigar.'

'Two Lampwick's IPAs,' Dad said to the barman, who winked and pulled the beers. We carried them to a corner table.

'To Pop Locke,' Dad said. We chinked glasses, and the first sip of a frothy cold beer with my Dad was bitterly magic. I shared a story from a couple of years ago, when Pop took me night-fishing on Pittwater. Venn's boyfriend, Elliot, had taken the tinnie out for a spin the day before without telling him, and left it almost empty of fuel. So Pop and I became stranded in the middle of the bay at midnight and started rowing back. Pop prayed that God would have mercy and rescue us and, sure enough, ten minutes later a fishing boat came by and picked us up. Pop bemoaned the diminishing number of fish in his favourite spot to the skipper, who, upon dropping us off at the wharf, appeased him with an enormous kingfish. Pop used to joke that it was the biggest fish he'd ever caught.

Tonight the beer started making me feel pretty damn fine about getting melancholic, as Dad began telling a story from when he was my age and helped Pop build an extension on their tiny fibro cottage in Blacktown. Before he could finish, three women appeared on a monitor above the bar. Nana Locke was fanning herself, Mum was checking her make-up and Venn was looking incredulous at the deceptively low-rent façade – the grungy veneer of **V e n e e R**. I skolled my beer before the miniskirted lady let them in.

'Here's a sight for sore eyes,' Dad said, and gave Venn a kiss on the cheek, which she appeared to accept with suprising equanimity. He then went for Mum but she air-kissed him as she would a colleague. Nana Locke had earlier stipulated that the evening was to be a celebration and that nobody was to become maudlin – and she'd dressed accordingly, in a floral smock and trousers. But when we hugged, I sensed the hidden depth of her grief in the tightness of her grip.

We all sat, and Venn pulled a silver package from a paper shopping bag and gave it to me. '*Joyeux anniversaire, mon frère.* It's just a book.' She beamed with anticipation as I tore off the foil.

'Brilliant. *The Picture of Dorian Gray.* It's on my reading list.'

'That's why I got it,' she said. 'Don't you like it?'

'Of course he likes it,' Dad said. 'Tell your sister you like it.'

'I already said brilliant.'

'I've written a birthday message on the inside cover, so it can't be returned.'

I opened the book to read the message and a green bill fluttered out. 'A hundgy!' I sniffed it. 'Fresh mint – mighty generous of you.'

'Actually, Nana slipped that one in.'

Nana winked at me. 'It's from Pop as well,' she said. 'And so is this.' She handed me a small box wrapped in red paper, which I removed intact. Inside the box was a mint-green jar of Swiss Valley Hair Pomade™. 'I finally began going through Pop's belongings,' Nana said. 'But I just couldn't bear to throw anything away. And I know how much you two loved your visits to the barber.'

'Thank you for the best present ever,' I said and then without warning, hiccupped.

Mum's face darkened as she examined, then sniffed, my schooner. 'You've been drinking beer?'

'It would seem that way,' Dad said.

'Have you seen the ad with the drunk teenager wobbling on a tightrope? One in three hospitalisations of young people results from alcohol consumption.'

'That PSA was one of ours. It's one in four.'

'I concede,' Mum said. 'Wrong yet again.'

'Concession noted and accepted.' Dad lifted his empty glass. 'Cheers.'

'Don't be smug, Lance. Buying alcohol for your underage son is the giddy limit of hypocrisy. Especially considering his test drive into oblivion last year. What were you thinking?'

'We were just toasting my father on the anniversary of his passing.'

'Don't use your father as a scapegoat – it's undignified. He was a lifelong teetotaller and wouldn't be at all impressed.'

Nana Locke caught my eye and gave a little shrug. Well acquainted with Bombay Sapphire and fond of an after-dinner sherry, she stayed out of the quarrel. The miniskirted woman arrived in the nick of time and escorted us by tiny elevator to an elegant underground cavern – soft, with rounded edges and dark-chocolate walls – and seated us in a booth that had a glowing orange teardrop suspended from the ceiling.

Pre–family crisis, dining had always been a communal affair, with a lot of plate-sharing. Tonight, when Mum refused to try Dad's entrée, he twirled some squid ink spaghetti on his fork and held it to her mouth. She pushed his hand away, causing three slick worms to drop onto her cream silk top. Dad dipped a napkin in water.

'Don't even,' Mum said and went to the ladies, Venn in tow.

Things settled during the mains until Dad asked if Mum had 'any interesting little projects on the boil?'

'That's a teenie bit patronising,' she said.

'I've always spoken like that.'

'The dawn of self-awareness.' Mum lifted her glass for the waitress to fill. 'I'm producing a big launch for a prestige client. But it's all a bit hush-hush right now.'

Dad touched the side of his nose. 'Mum's the word.' He steered the conversation to Venn, and she revealed that she'd chosen to study naturopathy instead of law. Dad's brow furrowed in an expression of subdued disappointment. He asked Venn a few loaded questions, which she answered with the deftness and conviction of somebody who'd practised their response.

Defeated by the rhetoric he'd trained her to use, Dad relented. 'Whatever you think's best.'

Nobody ordered dessert. There was no cake. Nobody even suggested singing 'Happy Birthday', which was a massive relief. Nana Locke looked at her wristwatch and brought proceedings to an end by announcing that it was almost ten, and that she should get home because her neighbour Glenda was dogsitting Tippi.

On the way out Mum said, 'Oh I almost forgot,' and gave me a Westfield gift card, which must've required a lot of thought.

'Wow! Thank you. I don't deserve it.'

'Nonsense.'

Despite the friction and occasional snide jabs, I wished the whole family had been walking home together. Instead, Dad and I said our awkward goodbyes to the ladies outside the restaurant and began walking up William Street. Halfway up, the storm broke, so I shoved the paper bag holding my presents under my shirt and we ran.

Back at the apartment, showered and dried off, I began reading *Dorian Gray*. He's a handsome rooster who's so full of himself and afraid of his looks fading that he sells his soul, committing his life to total pleasure-seeking without physical consequence. A portrait of him, painted by an artist called Basil, starts to bear the signs of his ageing instead, and becomes increasingly grotesque. Mr Field asked us in class to make note of how Oscar Wilde treats the notion of living a double life, and compare it with Robert Louis Stevenson's treatment in *Dr Jekyll and Mr Hyde*.

'Shouldn't be a stretch,' Homunculus said. 'You're a bit of an expert on the double life.'

'Please be quiet,' I said.

But Homunculus wouldn't shut up. 'You'll be making your screen debut on Friday the thirteenth.'

'What are you talking about?'

'Deb Gelber is filming you for stroke correction in swim clinic tomorrow. Good luck with that.'

A new level of dread gripped me at the thought of the nub not only being exposed, but also recorded and shown to the rest of the squad. Hoping that a sniff of the Swiss Valley Hair Pomade™ might alleviate my panic by transporting me to happier times, I jumped out of bed and looked for it in the paper bag. It wasn't there. It wasn't in my room, or the kitchen or the bathroom. I called the restaurant to find out if I'd left it there. Nobody answered – there was only a recorded message directing the caller to book on their website.

I returned to bed, distraught and furious at myself for losing something so precious to me. Sleep eventually arrived in the form of a tiny elevator cabin with carpeted walls like the one at **V e n e e R**. I asked the operator, a shadowy figure with his back to me, to take me down to the restaurant. He pushed a button and the cabin descended. But it continued down past that level. Deaf to my pleas, the operator kept pushing buttons, taking us lower and lower underground, faster and faster, until I shouted, 'WHO ARE YOU?'

The lift stopped with a spine-cracking thud. The operator turned around and I looked into his terrified eyes. The operator was me. The door opened and somehow it was already Friday morning.

#BOTTOMSUP

At the start of clinic, Simmons told us that the swimming carnival was fast approaching and that focusing on technique would give us the winning edge in the pool. He separated us into the four stroke groups to be filmed by overhead and underwater tracking cameras. Butterfly was first. My fear of the nub being caught on film was so intense it induced vertigo and high-frequency tinnitus simultaneously. I told Deb Gelber I felt sick.

'You're still doing it,' she said.

One by one we swam a lap of fly, then returned to have our technique scrutinised. Everybody else looked natural and fluid – born to swim. I appeared to be swimming a stroke of my own invention.

'Jerky and spasmodic,' Gelber said. 'Next time focus on minimising resistance, gliding not churning. Soften your hand entry. And stop looking for the camera.'

On our way down for a second attempt, Pericles asked where I thought my centre of energy was.

'I don't know, maybe here?' I pointed to my sternum. He pressed his palm against my chest.

'Okay, this time imagine it's a furnace, and focus on releasing a blast of fire out through your back, shoulders and arms every time you launch.' He swept his hands across my upper back then down, a little close to the nub for comfort. 'Allow the burst of power to travel down your spine and through your torso, keeping it strong all the way down your legs and out the tips of your toes. It should be a perpetual wave of energy moving through you, a cycle of tension and release – not separate stroke and kick.'

'Thanks for the tip. I'll give it a try.' I held up his goggles. 'I've still got these, by the way.'

'Keep them.'

We repeated the exercise and I followed Pericles' advice, visualising my core as a blasting furnace. I ignored the black line and the lane markers and the camera and felt no resistance or struggle, only slickness and buoyancy, as if I was swimming butterfly for the first time ever – almost like a dolphin.

Gelber and the other swimmers were astonished by the obvious difference between playbacks. I was almost feeling proud until she froze a frame in the aerial footage to talk about my alignment. My arse was sticking up out of the water, and there it was, visible even beneath my black Speedos – a bump in the topography casting a tiny crescent of shadow, vague but still damning evidence of my nub for anybody who was looking hard enough. But nobody was because they were all doubled over, laughing at my butt in the air . . . I think.

On the way to Mum's office I called the restaurant again to ask if they'd found a mint-green jar. The lady said nothing was handed in last night, which made me gloomy. And walking into NOW BE TIGERS! and seeing Penny slumped behind the reception counter failed to lift my mood. She was in a bummed-out torpor because Curtis now wanted an open relationship.

'We broke up,' she said. 'And tomorrow is Valentine's Day. Curtis is the only guy who's given me flowers, and I threw them out when they died. I don't have anything to remember him by except the seven thousand happy-couple photos I made him pose for, and the little cupid I gave you. Sorry for asking, but could I have him back?'

'Not a problem,' I lied, because last week I'd transformed him from cherub to satyr with a goatee, XXL dick and balls.

Emma and Jules came into reception, followed by Morgan. 'Your mother!' he said, making devil horns, and invited Penny to join them for a 'soothing elixir'.

Before they could escape, Mum poked her head through the door and said, 'Remember, Morgan. The word "can't" isn't in our vocabulary.' I think that's what she said.

On the trip home, Mum told me that the cost of having the Venus shell move through the sea was beyond their budget, so they'd settled for a stationary shell. But Morgan had failed to get approval to stage anything in the water. 'There'll be no wow factor without water,' she said.

'I thought "can't" wasn't in your vocabulary?'

'Don't throw my words back in my face.' She put music on and neither of us spoke till the Wakehurst Parkway.

'I've got an idea, but it might be a bit gay.'

'That's perfect for a cosmetic launch, because every single man there will be homosexual.'

'You know what I meant.'

'No, I don't, actually. Did you mean "excessively flamboyant" or "feeble and insipid"? You know I don't like the word being used in a pejorative fashion.'

'Have you just figured out that you're a lesbian or something? Because if you are, I don't have a problem with it.'

'I won't legitimise that with a response.' Mum turned the music off and we drove through Oxford Falls, both simmering in silence. I apologised at Mona Vale.

'Apology accepted,' Mum said. 'Now tell me your idea. Anything would be appreciated.'

'Well, you could still have the launch beside the sea, but have the shell floating in a giant inflatable pool on the grass.'

'Interesting . . . We could have a bar in the pool that the guests wade out to. Perfect for social media. Hashtag wetbar. Hashtag bottomsup. Yes, and inflated balls with the product inside, like bubbles floating on the surface. Yes, yes. I have to call Morgan right now.' She pulled the car over and told him my idea over speakerphone.

'Love, love, love!' Morgan gushed. 'That son of yours is an absolute genius!'

'Careful, he can hear you.'

'It's obviously genetic.'

'You don't think the idea's a bit gay, do you?' She winked at me.

'Absolutely,' Morgan said. 'Beyond fabulous!'

'Maintain your enthusiasm. We need to nut this thing out ASAP. Are you available tomorrow morning?'

'Of course, El Capitane.'

On Saturday morning, Mum left for the office before seven. I was sitting in the kitchen considering an early surf when Venn came in, took a peach and scored the furry skin with a knife. 'Happy Valentine's Day,' she said. 'Four months without Elliot.'

'You're way better off without him.'

'I know that now.'

'You changed so much when you got together.'

'It's funny, because at the start he said he was attracted to my free spirit. But then pretty soon he started trying to change me and contain me. He used to tell me that I was "too much" but could never explain what he meant.'

'Too interesting, too smart, too fun?'

'I think probably too strange.' Venn frowned.

'Remember all the games you invented for us to play on Mackerel when we were younger, all the rituals you made up? Elliot made you think they were stupid and childish.'

'Hmm.' Venn peeled the fuzz off the peach and then ate it anyway.

'Isn't that defeating the purpose?'

'I can't stand eating the fruit covered in fuzz. Separately they're fine. That's probably a metaphor for something.' She paused for a moment then turned to face me. 'Elliot schmelliot,' she said. 'Why did Nicole break up with you? You've never really told me.'

'She thought I was the embodiment of evil.'

'Is that all?' Venn laughed. She cut up the peach and gave me a slice. I was reminded of when Mum first returned to paid work. Venn used to prepare health snacks like almond and chia spread on apple slices for me after school, then would take me out catching crabs or exploring the bush with my dog Gus instead of making me do homework.

'Aside from telling Dad about your change of direction, you hardly spoke to him at my birthday dinner,' I said, to deflect from Nicole.

'Do you blame me?'

'I haven't been able to bring that stuff up with him yet. Do you think things will ever return to normal?'

'Lincoln, there is no normal and there probably never was. Things will eventually settle and improve, but they'll never be the same. "Normal" is a construct anyway – like Valentine's Day. Speaking of, I've thought of a little ceremony we could perform, something to prove to you that Elliot Grobecker failed to make me conform to his idea of normal. A Solemn Relinquishment.'

Venn took a large sheet of origami paper and wrote NEED FOR ROMANTIC LOVE on the plain side, then instructed me to write whatever I thought I most needed or wished for in secret on another sheet. I wrote NEED FOR A FRIEND and WISH TO BE ANYBODY BUT ME. We folded our squares into little boats and took them down to the shore.

'By solemnly relinquishing your need for something, you'll be freed from the power it holds over you. And one day that very thing might return of its own accord.'

'Reminds me of Pop Locke's advice to cast your bread on the water.'

'My inspiration comes from a variety of sources.'

We launched our boats from the end of the jetty. A gentle offshore breeze blew them twenty metres out and left them bobbing merrily. Then the whiny roar of a speedboat split the air as it rounded the point and ploughed right through them.

'Nothing solemn about that,' Venn said.

'Definitely won't be returning.'

I envied and admired Venn's ability to attach significance or meaning to something one day then let go of it the next, while I tended to get stuck on things. She'd become intensely serious and seriously intense last year – understandable, given everything that had happened, but it was good to see her recovering her independence. I just hoped her decision to steer away from environmental law was what she really wanted.

We walked home, and I joined Oscar the Burmese out on the deck to read *My One Redeeming Affliction*.

Performing the role of a respectable lady in polite society held no appeal for a young woman of infinite capability like my mother. Not only had she been overlooked for the role of taxidermy assistant by her father, she was also forbidden from pursuing any form of paid work or formal study. Her prescribed lot was nurturing her younger brothers, Samuel and Arthur, in the sanctuary of the family home – a duty made insufferable by the jealousy her elder brother Frederick's departure for England had aroused. Unwilling to continue practising the accomplishments of singing, dancing and deportment under her sharp-nosed governess, Esther secretly responded to a milliner's advertisement for an assistant with taxidermy skills. Her knowledge of hat-making was negligible, but being the only applicant with the required ability to skin and stuff animals, she won the position. Walter, though perplexed by his daughter's caprice, allowed her to accept the role, declaring it a 'self-inflicted punishment commensurate with her defiance'.

Coming from a good family won Esther no special attention from her employer, Madame Zora, who vacillated between extreme irritability and crippling shyness, the legacy of mercury poisoning from years working in a pelting factory. Suffering frequent tremors and dizzy spells, she relied heavily on her employees Henriette and Maude to cover for her. Both from humble beginnings, they'd endured unpaid apprenticeships for the sake of eventual remuneration and assumed the new girl, having no financial imperative, would be gone before Friday.

But Esther was driven by a stubborn determination to prove her father wrong. Apart from the aching back and raw-boned fingers, she preferred labouring in the cramped and stuffy studio to the supposed reward of serving on the floor. There she found it galling when customers from her genteel suburb, on discovering her in a position of servitude, affected an air of superiority. Her most frequently recounted incident involved one particularly haughty neighbour, Mildred Babbington.

The Vice President of the Hospital Spring Gala Organising Committee had ordered a hat for the event, which Esther had spent every night of the prior week constructing. A magnificently verdant study in the cycles of nature, it featured on one side a leaf-chewing caterpillar, a chrysalis suspended from a pink orchid and an iridescent blue-winged Ulysses butterfly. The other boasted a worm peeking from a crabapple beneath a swooping lark. Dipping the poor bird in molten silver had been the most irksome task for Esther, who considered it a distasteful indulgence.

Mrs Babbington was delighted with the assemblage and spent fifteen minutes before the looking glass, gazing at the exotic garden sprouting from her head. Finally yielding the hat for boxing, she asked if Esther was attending the gala.

'Unfortunately, circumstances prevent me,' Esther said.

'Come now. The Gardens are already in full bloom and all of Sydney's most eligible men will be there.' She paused. 'Why the look of vexation? You've turned the colour of a plum.'

A handsome moustached fellow on the other side of the window was stealing glances at Esther while feigning an interest in the display. It was my father's third such appearance. Hoping to send him on his way before Mrs Babbington turned and caught sight of him, Esther said loudly, 'My Aunt Harriet has insisted on introducing a Melburnian to me, and my father has forbidden me from any other social occasion until I comply.'

Mrs Babbington clucked her tongue. 'A peach not picked in due season will soon overripen and fall of its own accord.'

The hat's elaborate architecture was preventing it from fitting into the box, so Esther forced it down and gave the lid a decisive tap, causing Mrs Babbington to scowl. 'One must treat Madame Zora's work with the utmost delicacy,' she said. The woman's misattribution of the hat's creator, and her comparison of Esther to rotting fruit, sparked a small angry flame in Esther's chest. Wishing the woman gone, she tied the package with string instead of ribbon. Apropos of nothing save her penchant for gossip, Mildred Babbington said, 'I understand that Althea Beauclare has been showing uncommon kindness to your family lately. The spinster's charity must be a welcome relief to your father.'

Esther was overcome with prickly heat, fiercer than a company of ants biting at her neck and sides. She glared at my father till he left, then, abandoning all concern for etiquette, scratched at her arms and neck, and tugged and twisted her corset to prevent further aggravation. Mrs Babbington, appalled by Esther's lack of decorum, smacked the service bell repeatedly, demanding to see Madame Zora.

'That won't be possible,' Esther said. 'She's taken ill.'

Suffering a bout of anxiety, Zora Blatchford had taken refuge behind the two-way mirror and nothing had gone unnoticed. Her hands trembled as she scrawled a rebuke, inserted it into a wooden ball and set it on the cash railway. It rolled through to the other side, then down a switchback before dropping onto a red velvet cushion in a basket.

'Troublesome thing,' Esther said, making a performance of unscrewing the two halves. She turned her back on the customer to read the scrawled message:

Insolence will not be tolerated!

Venn came out and caught me reading the end of the passage aloud to Oscar. 'He's very intelligent,' she said, 'but he only has a vocabulary of thirty-seven words. What's the book about?'

I told her about Esther's lack of opportunity in the world, and said how much better it was for women today.

'Yes, things have improved dramatically,' Venn said. 'But there's still a long way to go.' And then she delivered a short but assertive lecture on the perpetuation of rich, white, heteronormative male privilege.

Neither Oscar nor I had a leg to stand on. We were two ostensibly straight guys sunbaking on a third-level deck with uninterrupted water views. And I was soaking in as much as I could before returning to the grinding city.

JUST FOR THE
SMELL OF IT

Monday was the final squad session before the swimming carnival. I bought a new pair of goggles and returned the oldies to Pericles, who slung them into the bin. Swimming in lane five, free of cranial pressure and goggle fog, I managed to stay just far enough behind him to avoid accusations of drafting.

At the end of training, Simmons rallied us for a pep talk. 'Everybody who wants to win on Wednesday, raise your hands.' Everybody did. 'Keep them up if you have what it takes.' Keenly aware that lowering my hand would demonstrate a conspicuous lack of esprit de corps, I stiffened my arm. 'Look up there at the Roll of Champions,' Simmons said, pointing to the wooden shield that I'd seen on the school tour. 'If any of you break a Crestfield record on Wednesday, your name will be recorded alongside those legends.'

My eyes were drawn back to Nigel Lethbridge, Junior Backstroke Champion in 1942. Simply reading the old boy's name triggered the smell memory of his mothballed leather-elbowed jacket. Merely imagining the odour of camphor made me gag.

*

During English, Mr Field read a passage from *The Picture of Dorian Gray* where Dorian studies the psychological effect of perfumes. Oscar Wilde wrote about ambergris, the whale poo Isa had mentioned, stirring passion, and the scent of musk troubling the mind. Aloes cure your melancholy and hovenia, the Japanese raisin tree, sends you mad.

He then called on Isa to read a passage from Marcel Proust's *In Search of Lost Time* about a guy who dips a madeleine, a small shell-shaped sponge cake, in his tea. The taste summons a flashback to happier days.

'Well read,' he said. 'You seem familiar with the text.'

'I read all seven volumes last year,' Isa said.

'Congratulations. That's no small undertaking. Would anybody like to share their experience of an involuntary memory triggered by smell?'

'The stuff in your hair,' I said. 'It's Swiss Valley Hair Pomade™, sir.' Mr Field touched his head. 'It reminds me of going to the barber with my grandfather.' The class laughed. It was supposed to be a compliment but it backfired, so I didn't tell them the rest.

I really missed having my hair cut with Pop Locke at Joe and Vic's Continental Hairstylists. No matter what style I requested, Giuseppe always gave me a short back and sides, matching Vittorio snip-for-snip as he worked on Pop. The climax of the sacred ritual was the liberal application of Swiss Valley Hair Pomade™. Giuseppe never asked if I wanted it, and I never refused. Pop used to say it would've been like preventing Michelangelo from making the finishing touches to the Sistine Chapel. On completion, Pop Locke always purchased a mint-green jar from the pyramid stacked behind the counter, and emulated the pomade styling every day till our next visit. It smelt floral and minty and antiseptic all at once.

In Biology, we explored triggered memory from a scientific perspective. Raymond, the lab assistant, arranged thirty plastic cups, each containing a different essence, on the benches running along the wall, with a small picture card in front of each. In turn we moved down the line, sniffing the cups while looking at their accompanying pictures. Each time I smelt something pleasant, like peppermint, strawberry or eucalyptus, I experienced a peculiar sensation: the nub tingled. But not every odour was pleasant. When Starkey sniffed the cup behind an image of a boat, he called out, 'That's fucking cat piss!'

'Vulgar language will not be tolerated,' Miss Keenan said. 'Evan, take yourself down to The Labyrinth immediately. Sit there and have a think about your behaviour. Mr Jespersen will be waiting for you.'

'This school fully sucks arse,' Starkey said on the way out. Crestfield seems to be rigorously monitored and yet I've noticed that punishment here seems strangely lenient. When I smelt the cup that had caused Starkey's outburst, it made the nub prickle and itch, and I realised that he was on the money – it was definitely cat piss.

During Art, Ms Tarasek announced that our collaborative works were to be loosely themed around life in our local or school community, and would be exhibited in a show called YOU ARE HERE! She then played us a doco on French sculptor Camille Claudel, who wasn't just Auguste Rodin's pupil, and later his lover and collaborator, but was also a talented artist and innovator in her own right and had to fight for a place in an art world controlled by men. The doco featured a recurring photo of Camille taken when she was nineteen. Aside from the dark hair falling on her face, she bore a striking resemblance to Isa Mountwinter. At the part where Camille separated from Rodin to establish her individuality, I noticed Isa fidgeting with her pencil. When we heard of Camille becoming overwhelmed with paranoia and destroying her artworks, Isa snapped the pencil in half. And at the point where Camille was committed to a mental asylum and prevented from receiving letters from anyone except her brother, Isa herself looked to be at breaking point.

Tonight at home, still unable to broach the Maëlle incident with Dad but not wanting to continue living in self-imposed isolation, I initiated a conversation with him about the psychology of smell. Dad told me that neural marketing was becoming a large part of his business at The BrandCanyon, and the 'first-sniff principle' was key to its success.

'We've partnered with Tschoppe Shibata, who've created a gaming console with scent pods,' he said. 'Imagine a game designed around a female hero who's beautiful, strong and confident. One of our clients, say a clothing company, pay for their signature scent to be associated with that character. During game play, the signature scent is released whenever she performs well. Sometime later in real life, the player walks into a clothing store equipped with scent diffusers that release an identical aroma. The customer will experience the same emotion they felt playing the game, increasing the levels of serotonin and oxytocin in their brain. Their dwell-time will be extended, increasing the likelihood of purchase.'

'It's a brave new world,' I said, getting up from the table. I went to fetch my wallet from my satchel then came back through the dining room.

'Where are you going?'

'Coles.' I wanted to find out if they stocked Swiss Valley Hair Pomade™, and hoped that a sniff would instantly transport me back to the barbershop with Pop.

Scoping out the haircare section, I saw an old lady dressed in a pink heart-patterned skirt with a pink blouse and pink ribbons in her pink plaited hair, the same shade as Venn's, reaching for a packet of dye. She even smelt pink – like a musk stick. She turned to me and said, 'Excuse me young man, could you reach the L'Oréal box up there for me, the pink one?' Her lipstick had strayed well beyond the creases of her lips, and two distinct circles of blush highlighted the lack of flesh remaining on her cheekbones. I grabbed a box of the L'Oréal Dirty Pink. 'You're a true gentleman,' she said as I handed her the box. 'Your mother must be very proud of you.'

I left without finding the Swiss Valley.

Lying in bed tonight, I thought about how much effort the Pink Lady must put into maintaining her look. When you're young like Venn, it's called individuality. But when you're old, the refusal to slip into elastic-sided obscurity – to fade away without screaming that you want to keep dancing forever on this Earth – is assumed to be madness. Camille Claudel; Raina Bramble, the Blue Lady; the Pink Lady; Loose Pants Lenny; and the old junkyard guy.

An idea for the collaborative assignment I was working on with Isa began swirling in my head, but I needed a good sleep before the carnival. Just as I was about to drop off, Homunculus said, 'Tomorrow you stand virtually naked before the entire school. Perhaps you want to check what's been going on down the back? Ignoring it won't make it go away.'

I crawled out of bed and assessed my backside in the main bathroom's full-length mirror. The nub had neither shrunk nor grown, which gave me mild relief, until I noticed eleven dark hairs had sprouted between my shoulderblades.

CRACKED EGGS

Walking through The Hive's glass doors exhorting me to excel, I was smacked with the ammonial funk of superchlorination, evidence that today would be all swimming and no carnival. Every student was expected to enter at least one event unless they'd lodged an exemption request on The Owlet and had it approved by Simmons, who believes a lack of enthusiasm for swimming is un-Austraaayan. Competing in the carnival had nothing to do with some misguided notion of patriotism for students like Amber Briggs and Tibor Mintz who, occupying opposite ends of the weight spectrum and seats on the back bleacher, probably had no desire to walk past the rest of the school in a wet swimming costume. Having an extra feature of my own to conceal, I could fully empathise.

Conversely, Nads and Mullows were all about maximum exposure. They'd entered as many events as they could manage. Nads peeled off his shirt and began stretching to impress his imaginary fan club. The striations in his deltoids heightened my earlier suspicion that he was on the juice. His shoulders weren't just big – they were grooved and ridged with tightly strung fibres. Mullows was more modest. Though he was equally ripped and taller than Nads, his skin was milky white, and covered with hundreds of freckles and a smattering of moles.

Runty in comparison, Starkey was taking a shot of them with his phone, and noticed Pericles and me walking past in the background.

'Better watch your arse, Pappas!' he called out. 'Nads and Mullows are down for the fly.' Pericles and I left them in their poolside posing pen for a spot high at the far end of the bleachers, intending to save our energy for the hundred fly, which was scheduled for mid-afternoon. I thought the absence of Isa and Phoenix might give me a chance of bonding with Pericles, but he hardly spoke until the racing began. Then he fired up and assumed the role of commentator, outlining the strengths and weaknesses of every contender he knew from squad and telling me the Crestfield record before it appeared on the board.

Four hours later, the hundred fly was finally announced. Pericles' bag vibrated with a danger alert ringtone.

'Aren't you going to answer?'

'It's my father. I don't want to speak to him.'

On the way to the marshalling area he kept his head down, slapping and rubbing his shoulders, so I did the same. Nads, Mullows and Starkey joined us at the blocks along with three other swimmers, making it a straight final. Stepping onto my block, I ignited the furnace in my chest, as Pericles had instructed me, and felt the fire spread to my extremities.

>SWIMMERS, TAKE YOUR MARKS!<

I assumed the position.

>BEEP!<

I timed my dive perfectly and streamlined for ten metres.

>FWOOSH!<

I resurfaced and stormed the lane, pouncing and plunging, more leopard than butterfly.

>fwOOshka fwOOshka fwOOshka<

I hit the touchpad and a switch flicked inside my head, illuminating three words that had become lodged there from Simmons' constant repetition.

POSSIBILITY. INTENT. BELIEF.

100

I swam the return lap, leaping from the water with wide sweeping arms, feeling faster than before and sensing that I was on a negative split.

>fwoOshka fwoOshka fwoOshka<

My lungs were burning.

Every fibre of my body screaming.

One mighty final lunge, and >BANG!< I smacked the touchpad.

Totally spent, I turned to see Pericles beside me with exhausted disbelief in his eyes. We looked up at the timeboard and waited. My name appeared on top.

L. LOCKE 1.07.07

'Congratulations,' he said. 'You won.' The look of utter dejection on his face drained the flavour of victory before I'd even tasted it. Nads and Mullows swam into my lane and hooked their muscled arms over my shoulders, submerging me in their excessive – and puzzling – jubilation.

We climbed out of the pool. Pericles lurched and collapsed, body heaving as he vomited over the tiles. I went to help but Nads and Mullows pulled me away.

'It's not the first time,' Nads said. 'And won't be the last. He can't fucking handle it. Forget about him and come to mine for pizza.'

Walking away was a betrayal, and Nurse Nola's timely arrival hardly alleviated my guilt. The stupid thing is that I didn't even want to go with them, but I was afraid of saying no.

Nads took us by taxi to his place near the end of Darling Point. We got out and he tapped a code into a security console and the gate slid away to reveal a nineteenth-century sandstone mansion fronted by an oval of fine grass and a waterlily-filled pond with a bubbling fountain. We followed Nads up the path, passing geometrically pruned shrubs spaced evenly around the pond.

'Impressive shack,' I said to Starkey.

'They've got a bigger place in Moss Vale and a property in the Territory,' he said. 'The old man's in mining.' He ran his hand over one of the miniature trees. 'Do you like the way Mrs Naylor has her bush trimmed?'

French doors opened to a kitchen fitted out with industrial-sized whitegoods that were all black, including a fridge that looked big enough to walk into and three identical ovens. A short woman wearing a plastic cap slid into the room on polishing scuffs. 'Good afternoon, Mister Darvin,' she said. 'Would your guests like afternoon tea?'

'No thank you, Minnie. Has the games room been restocked?'

'Yes, and the man has fixed the ice.'

'You can go home then.'

'First I'll do the floors.'

'Don't bother. Mum wants you to take the afternoon off.'

Minnie frowned. 'If you say so.' She skated a lap around the island bench and slid out of the room.

Nads phone-ordered three large Roman Holidays from Big Tony's™, gave them the address and then turned to us and said, 'Best pizza in Sydney.'

'He should know,' Starkey said to me. 'He gets the same thing every time.'

'Can I hear an ungrateful arsehole talking?'

Starkey obliged with a volley of obscenely slick armpit farts.

Nads took us down to the games room in an elevator. 'Welcome to the man cave,' he said as the doors opened. Starkey made a dash for a game controller on the sofa's armrest and challenged Mullows to a game of *Super Smash Bros. Ultimate:* Jigglypuff vs Pikachu.

'Loser gets blackballed,' Nads said.

Starkey physically punched Mullows every time Jigglypuff landed a blow on Pikachu, but Mullows swatted him away like he was an annoying fly. Eventually Pikachu killed Jigglypuff.

Without hesitation, Starkey sat on the floor and spread his legs.

'Do we really have to do this?' Mullows said, flicking his ginger ponytail.

'Of course we do,' Nads said. 'House rule.'

Mullows reluctantly knelt behind Starkey and held back his arms. Nads took the eight ball from the pool table and slid it with full force into Starkey's scrotum. He yelped and folded into the foetal position, cradling his cracked eggs. Nads then retrieved the eight ball and challenged me to a game of pool, raising his scarred eyebrow in a way that prompted me to ask if there was a penalty involved for the loser.

'Only Starkey gets blackballed,' he said.

'Isn't his father a urologist?' I muttered. 'He'd be horrified.'

'Especially if he found out his numbnut son invented the rule. You break.'

I did as ordered, and Nads followed by sinking three solids in succession. Chalking his stick, he said, 'There's something about you that's been bothering me.' I silently prayed it wasn't something to do with the nub. 'You've been sniffing around Isa Mountwinter.'

'Nah.' I frowned. 'A hundred per cent not.'

'Good, because she's been blacklisted by the Brotherhood.'

'What's wrong with her?'

'She acts like an avenger for justice but she's a meddling bitch.'

'Thinks her shit don't stink,' Starkey clarified from the sofa, lighting a cigarette.

'Outside, dickhead!' Nads threw the chalk cube at him. Starkey skulked out, lit cigarette in mouth, blue dust on forehead. Mullows followed him.

'Where are you going?' Nads said.

'To make sure he doesn't scoff the pizza when it arrives.'

'Good call.' Nads handed him a wad of twenties and, when he was out of earshot said, 'Mullows' parents are farmers. Struggling to keep him at Crestfield.' He sank another ball. 'Lives with his brother. Do you reckon he's good-looking?'

'Is this a trick question?'

'Yeah, I'm checking to see if you're a filthy homo.' He patted my back. 'Chill, bruh. He could have whoever he wanted but last year he hooked up with Phoenix Lee at a party. No big deal for a one-off, but then they started hanging out, going to the beach and the movies.

She sat next to him in every class and wouldn't let him out of her sight at lunch. She went the full limpet.'

'Sounds serious?' I said.

Without explanation Nads abandoned the game. He went to the bar and made two bourbon and Cokes®. I have no idea why I accepted the drink, other than some craven need to impress somebody who didn't impress me at all.

Nads told me a story about Phoenix turning up to their rugby grand final dressed as a cheerleader and prancing around the sidelines with pompoms. Starkey filmed her and posted it on a site called Most Meddling Mingas.

'That little bitch Pappas found out about it and squealed to Isa and Phoenix. Phoenix lost her shit and gave Mullows an ultimatum – her or us. Mullows, the faithful carrot top, chose us. Isa stormed the principal's office and told him about the post. Dashwood made us write a thousand words on respecting sluts.'

'Your word, not his?'

'Whose side are you on?'

'Nobody's.'

'Wrong. You're on ours now. Here's to you winning the fly and teaching that slippery wog a lesson,' he said, holding up his glass.

'I beat him by a fraction of a second. It was lucky.'

'Luck played no part. It's all about preparation and training. You could be a contender if you bulked up.'

'I'm not the type.'

'Type's just one factor,' Nads said.

Without prompting or warning, he peeled his shirt off and went through a series of Mr Universe–style poses. The narcissistic nature of the display turned a bit homoerotic when he flexed his bicep into a sphere approaching the size of a grapefruit, barely contained by the stretched skin, and kissed it while looking directly into my eyes. 'You could have guns like that,' he said. 'And I could help you get them.' He went to the fridge, reached to the back of the bottom shelf and returned with a small plastic bottle. He lifted my hand and poured two green-and-white capsules into it.

'What are they?' I said. 'Steroids?'

'Don't be stupid,' he said. 'Just amino acids and other natural shit that helps your body produce more of the hormone that grows muscle – not the hormone itself. Over-the-counter stuff. Go on then, down the hatch.'

Against my better judgement, I swallowed the capsules with a swig of the bourbon and Coke®. 'How long will it take?' I said, imagining myself bursting from my shirt Hulk-style on the way home.

'Nothing will happen without serious training. Take two before every session.' Nads poured half the bottle into a baggie and pushed it into my hand. 'First cycle's on me. Make sure you finish it. Doctor's instructions.'

'I thought you said it was over-the-counter?'

'Yeah, well, just finish them.'

The aroma of onion, garlic and spicy-sausage pizza heralded the return of Starkey and Mullows. I pocketed the baggie. The boys each claimed a box and forfeited one of their slices to me, which I wasn't in a position to complain about.

'I bet you've never tasted anything like this before?' Mullows said.

I took a bite. 'You're right.' Yet another lie.

The evening was cool on my walk home. Thank God, because my head was overheating trying to process everything. Had I just become a member of their group? Belonging made me feel apprehensive. And it came at the cost of turning my back on Pericles in his moment of need. I pulled out my phone to text him and realised we'd never swapped numbers.

Loose Pants Lenny was shadow-boxing the rolling billboard outside T H E E Y R I E. The Cornetto® girl had been replaced by the image of a boxer advertising boxer shorts. I wonder how much the creative genius was paid for coming up with that idea?

'C'mon, pretty boy,' Leonard said to the boxer. 'Put up your dukes!' He delivered a series of jabs and uppercuts, letting his dirty trackies slide to his knees. Then he pulled his right arm way back and held it there for a moment. And just as the boxer began to slide away, Leonard drove his fist through the glass with a mighty roar and a crash. A thousand crystal shards caught the streetlights and went skittering over the pavement. Leonard doubled over, wailing. There was so much blood. Blood everywhere.

Frank the concierge ran out.

'I'll call the ambulance,' he said. 'Go inside now.'

I rode the lift to level twenty-seven. Dad asked about the carnival and when I told him I'd won the fly, he whapped my head with a cushion. 'I knew you could do it,' he said.

'How's that possible when I didn't?'

'I know what you're able to achieve when you're challenged. That's why we invested more into your education. Doesn't winning feel awesome?'

'For about a minute.' I wondered why Dad was more excited about my victory than I was, and decided to ask him the question that had plagued me since I'd started at Crestfield. 'Did you lie on my student profile?'

'What?' He touched his nose.

'Did you make up my personal best times on the Crestfield application?'

'You weren't around when I filled it out, so I wrote down what I knew you'd be capable of.'

'I was drafted into squad because you made up my PBs. And I probably only got accepted into the school for that reason.'

Dad gripped my shoulders. 'And now your victory has vindicated me. Everything in life revolves around competition, Lincoln. Sport, business, relationships, survival. I just want you to have the best chance.' He gave me a shake then released me. 'Don't worry about it. It's not like you took somebody else's place. We're paying full fees, unless you reach state level, and then—'

'Please don't go there, because it's not going to happen.'

'You can achieve anything if you want it badly enough.'

'All I want is to go to bed now. I'm exhausted.'

'Okay, champion. We can talk about it another time.'

Even if life does revolve around competition, what if you don't want to compete? Maybe I did, though. Why had I swum so hard at the carnival? Was I just trying my best or was I afraid of losing? The only reason I managed to beat Pericles was because he'd explained how to swim the stroke in a way I could understand. And I'd thanked him by leaving him vomiting by the side of the pool and going off to celebrate with his enemies.

I climbed into bed with *My One Redeeming Affliction*, hoping there'd be no mention of competition – I'd had enough of that for one day. I was defeated by the first sentence.

If the greatest fight we face is the struggle for life itself, the second most hard-fought competition – the one that leaves the most wounded in its wake – must surely be the quest for a suitable partner. A battle royale, wherein one man's self-belief and determination might be vanquished by the ingenuity and charm of his adversary.

Following weeks of her father's attempts to convince her to meet Newland Beale, Esther finally capitulated and was introduced to the Melburnian barrister by her Aunt Harriet in the fernery of Pemberton's Magnificent Emporium. Beale was perfectly average, his otherwise benign appearance saved by dark side whiskers that extended almost to the chin. My mother, who possessed an uncommonly keen sense of smell, identified on his person the scents of bergamot, Bulgarian rose and cedar. Assuming that the exotic combination indicated a depth of character, she consented to her aunt's departure with a pre-arranged signal.

The pair ascended to the Ionian Restaurant on the third floor. Fronted with fifteen-foot columns bearing a frieze of Odysseus's return to Ithaca, it was the crowning glory of the Emporium. The decor and head chef were Greek, the bill of fare incongruously French, and the maître d'hôtel English. Esther instantly recognised him: the man she'd caught lingering outside Madame Zora's shop. His moustache, a distinct circumflex, provoked a thrilling repulsion that she stifled by focusing on the panoply of statues as he led her and Beale to their table: nymphs on plinths, satyrs dancing in alcoves and Theseus slaying the minotaur. The couple's table was in a corner, guarded by a leonine creature with a goat's head growing from its back and a serpentine tail.

'He looks set to devour us,' Beale said.

'*She* is the Chimera,' Esther said. 'Isn't she marvellous?'

The meal began with mock-turtle soup, accompanied by the barrister's lengthy account of defending a poulterer whose lad had absconded after regular beatings and had been forced to sleep where the fowl were strangulated. The deathly silence that followed gave William a chance to intervene and take their order for the mains. Beale selected ragout of lobster, and Esther chose William's suggestion of oysters au naturel. 'I promise you won't be disappointed,' he said. 'They were harvested only this morning by my partner, Dimitrios.'

Waiting for the food to arrive, the pair's conversation turned to Esther's interest in taxidermy and her current employment, both of which confounded Beale. 'The true art of millinery is making an ugly face look pretty,' he said. 'Your Madame Zora is an astute businesswoman, employing such lovely shopgirls to sell her wares to those not so blessed.'

A second glass of champagne made the barrister exceedingly delighted with his own cleverness as he delivered a lecture on the desired attributes of a good wife, finishing with the declaration, 'She should possess only sufficient knowledge to ensure the home is a place of rest and joy for her husband after his daily travail.' Mercifully, at that point William arrived with the ragout and six oysters on a mound of crushed ice. He drew a silver shucking knife from his apron and, with consummate skill, prised one open and laid it on a gold-rimmed plate before Esther.

'This can't possibly be!' she said on seeing a pearl inside. 'It's the most delicate shade of pink.' She lifted the plate to show the men.

'I'd lay the odds at a million to one,' William said. 'A most propitious omen.'

'Indeed,' Beale said, removing the oyster from the plate for a closer inspection of the pearl.

'It must be immediately returned to Dimitrios,' Esther said. She folded a napkin on the plate and slid it across the table to Beale.

'His neck is fat and brown,' William said. 'This pearl was destined for a neck as slender and pale as yours.'

'That's quite enough!' Beale said. He dropped the pearl on the napkin and thrust the plate at William. 'Have it cleaned and placed in a suitable box.'

Evidently, the barrister was unaware that the pink pearl grows only in the conch. Esther knew of its natural provenance, however, and correctly assumed that William had artificially transplanted it into the oyster shell. Feigning ignorance to avoid the embarrassment of two stags locking horns, she resolved to accept the pearl and return it to William as soon as Beale boarded his train back to Melbourne.

The rest of the meal was a chore as Esther struggled to conceal her annoyance at my father's audacity and her diminishing appetite for Newland Beale's company. Refusing to accept defeat, he ordered pigeon pie, beef à la jardinière and eggs à la neige. When William returned to deliver the boxed pearl, Beale leapt to his feet to intercept him, but his excessive consumption of champagne had compromised his balance and, stumbling backwards into the Chimera, he snapped off her tail.

I became sleepy, with my thoughts travelling from the pink pearl to Mum's Venus shell launch to the day I'd made an oyster shell from clay and Isa had made the pearl. Which reminded me: we hadn't discussed our collaboration project since then, and Ms Tarasek was expecting our proposals tomorrow. I drifted off, dreaming of Isa being annoyed as our art teacher took her clay pearl and placed it inside my shell. I heard Isa say, 'A pearl is nothing more than a self-protective response to an invading irritant.' Then she transformed into Esther Hunnicutt, who, instead of 'feigning ignorance' as she had in the book, called out the hoax, igniting a punch-up between Newland Beale and William Stroud. Every sculpture in the restaurant was smashed to smithereens, leaving no identifiable piece except for the Chimera's tail, which William seized and held high like a sceptre.

THE DOG TURD MANDALA

After French on Thursday, I followed Isa along the catwalk, down the stairs and across the quadrangle to Old Block, where she suddenly spun around and accused me of stalking. I explained the need to discuss our proposal before class and she gave me two minutes.

I told her about an episode of *Extreme Medical Intervention* that had featured a teenager suffering a severe headache whose mum rushed him to the hospital. The doctors diagnosed a disease that affected his brain and spine, and spread through his bloodstream.

'Sounds like meningitis,' Isa said.

'That's the one. He suffered organ damage and fell into a coma for a week. They gave him a five per cent chance of survival. Miraculously he pulled through, but had both legs amputated below the knee. They actually showed the procedure.'

'Gruesome hospital stories don't thrill me. My mother's a nurse.' She checked her watch. 'What does this have to do with our project?'

'*Extreme Medical Intervention* is the modern equivalent of a nineteenth-century freak show. Last week some surgeons separated conjoined twins. A hundred and fifty years ago an entrepreneur would've stuck them in a tent and charged people to see them. Same thing – people put on display for profit.'

'I'm still not seeing the connection?'

'Our work is supposed to relate to our local environment, and there are stacks of weird people in my hood.' I reminded Isa of the Blue Lady and told her about the toothless car-kicker with the stuffed bird, the Pink Lady, and Loose Pants Lenny punching out the sign last night. 'I thought we could create images of them, like bill posters for sideshow acts, and hang them in a row. The last one would be a gold-framed mirror with a sign above that says YOU.'

'That's incredibly offensive,' Isa said, and turned to leave.

'Wait, I didn't mean you. I mean whoever's looking in the mirror. It would be social commentary on how we perceive those sorts of people.'

'That's not just condescending, it's cruel. How do you think "those sorts of people" would feel about being depicted like that? Perhaps you could find out by inviting them to the opening.'

'You don't get it. It's about challenging people's notion of what constitutes a freak. Maybe in our own way we're all a bit freaky?'

'Speak for yourself.'

'That's all I've got.'

'Good, because you've used up all our time. So you'll have to trust that Ms Tarasek will like my idea.'

In the studio, Isa explained her vision to the class: we would 'yarn-bomb' the school grounds by hanging pieces of knitting in seemingly random locations. It was irritating to hear her use the word 'we', as if I'd contributed to the proposal in any way. Even more annoying was Ms Tarasek's enthusiastic response. 'A reinterpretation of the school's structures,' she said. 'This I like very much.'

I left the studio with a cracking headache, stars fizzling in my peripheral vision. On my way to the bike racks, I kicked a recycling bin.

'Hey, dog!' Starkey had materialised from nowhere, like the Cheshire cat with bad teeth. 'Has the bug up your arse got a name?'

'Isa Mountwinter.'

'What'd we tell you?' With yellow-tipped fingers he pinched a pellet of gum from a shrivelled packet and dropped it into the palm of my hand.

'Thanks. I'll save that special treat for later.'

111

*

This afternoon I threw down a couple of the capsules Nads gave me with some water and met Dad at BigTown Gym™ for our introductory training session. The gym was large, but what made it look enormous were the mirrored walls that multiplied the arsenal of high- and low-tech torture devices. Dad pointed out Sergio, our personal trainer, whose upper back was three times the width of his waist. He was saying goodbye to his earlier appointment, the ex-reality-show contestant Kimberly Romaine, who'd extended her fifteen seconds after she'd had an extreme allergic reaction to breast enhancement surgery by ending up on *Extreme Medical Intervention.*

Sergio walked over to us. 'This body, one hundred per cent natural,' he said by way of introduction, performing an independent pectoral flex.

'Well done,' Dad said. 'I'd be happy with half that.'

'There is only one Sergio. You cannot be Sergio. But Sergio will give you the tools to make the most of what you have. Yes?'

'Yes,' Dad and I said in unison.

'Today we work on chest and triceps. We start easy and build slowly. Sergio is all about technique and discipline.'

We began with the bench press and progressed through a series of free weights and machines. Dad's well built for an old fart, but next to Sergio he looked like your average office worker. He insisted on adding a few extra plates for his sets, as if he could possibly impress our herculean trainer or any of the other cavemen in the gym whose lats prevented them from walking with their arms by their sides. Tempering Dad's enthusiasm, I came up with excuses to avoid any machine or exercise that might put the nub in a compromising position – which was quite a few. Sergio was very touchy-feely when pointing out which muscles were being worked so I stepped back each time, allowing Dad to be the happy recipient of his attention.

At the end of the session we went to the change rooms to grab our bags, and Dad started untying the laces on his trainers.

'What are you doing?' I said.

'What does it look like?'

'Can't you shower when we get home?'

'Buddy, I'm soaking with sweat.' He peeled off his singlet. 'You should jump in too. You're a bit whiffy.'

'The showers are communal.'

'So what? You haven't got anything I haven't seen before.'

Instead of contradicting him, I turned and opened my locker. 'I'm so not hanging out with a bunch of other nude men,' I said and pulled out my gym bag. 'It's fully weird.'

'What's wrong with you? It's completely natural.'

'About as natural as Sergio's ripped physique.' I closed my locker. 'See you in reception.'

On Friday in Biology we carried out part two of the olfaction and memory experiment. Miss Keenan and Raymond set out the thirty cups again, this time without their corresponding pictures. Our challenge was to sniff and identify each odour, and recall its associated image. Basil, shoe polish, aniseed – easy. Number twenty-nine unmistakably the cat-piss concentrate and I instantly remembered a boat on the card next to it, so I wrote that down. We swapped papers and Miss Keenan read out the correct answers.

When we got to the end, Liliana Petersen, who was marking mine, called out, 'Ohmygod!'

Her twin Ingrid snatched the paper, and they said in unison, 'Lincoln Locke got all thirty correct!'

'Extraordinary,' Miss Keenan said. 'I've never had a student score over twenty-five.'

'Maybe Lincoln has an unusually high number of receptor cells in his olfactory bulb?' Tibor said.

'His honker's big enough to fit them in,' Starkey said, then leant in close to me and whispered, 'Maybe you're part bloodhound?' Then he shouted 'WOOF!' so loudly I fell off my stool.

*

113

Waiting on platform three at Town Hall Station for the train to North Sydney, I conducted further experimentation to validate my lab results. Closing my eyes, I inhaled deeply and concentrated on identifying the random odours of the transit environment. Buttery croissant, dry-cleaning, bubblegum, coffee and tunnel grime borne on the column of air being pushed forward by an arriving train. Then I smelt my mother's perfume and opened my eyes, fully expecting to see her. She wasn't there but somebody was wearing her scent, Prescience. I walked along the platform, sniffing like a rabbit. Right down the end, as I pointed my nose towards a young woman in a high-waisted skirt who was talking on her phone, the strength increased exponentially. I moved closer and inhaled deeply. She turned and glared at me, then said to the person on the phone, 'You won't believe this. A creepy schoolkid just came up and sniffed me!'

Telling her that I was conducting an experiment, or that she smelt exactly like my mother, wouldn't have rectified the situation, so I returned to the other end of the platform.

'Howdy!' Morgan Brierly said as I walked in to NOW BE TIGERS! 'Congrats on your blue ribbon for breaststroke. Wear it with pride.'

'Butterfly.'

'Even better.'

'Does Mum tell you everything?'

'Ever since our university days.'

'What was she like back then? Was she a massive swot or did she party?'

'She was studious with an experimental edge. In second and third year we shared a warehouse in Surry Hills with an artist.'

'Dad's mentioned Luis the crazy Spaniard once or twice.'

'He chain-smoked Ducados and drank red wine on the roof while listening to Jacques Brel. Having both grown up in Conformia, we thought he was so very bohemian.'

'Was Mum his girlfriend?'

'One of his muses. She modelled for him.'

'Please don't say nude?'

'Always tastefully. She had long hair back then.'

'Did you have parties at the warehouse?'

'Monthly happenings where people did their thing. Music, spoken word, burlesque, the occasional drag performance by yours truly. Live piercings and suspensions. Later, when people were trying to outdo each other, there was a contortionist called Mona who stretched the limits of decency further than she stretched herself. It all turned into a bit of a freak show.'

'That's hectic.'

'A guy called Pebbles, who wore a bone in his hair, collected dried-up dog turds for a year and painted them in day-glo colours. One night he arranged them into a huge mandala that he illuminated with black light. It was strangely beautiful.'

'Is it still there?'

'The dog turd mandala?'

'The warehouse.'

'It was converted into a trendy apartment complex a year after we left. Sad.'

'Why did you leave?'

'One night Charis and I returned from a party and found Luis on a bender, singing along to his favourite Brel song, "Amsterdam". He was totally fried, and painting the walls with drunken sailors and prostitutes. The landlord turned up for an impromptu inspection a week later and didn't appreciate the artistic merit of his mural.'

'Were you evicted?'

'Not for that. But shortly after, we found out Luis hadn't paid the rent for three months. He confessed to spending it on feeding his drug habit. The next morning he was gone – vanished. After graduating, your mother travelled alone across Europe. She'd never admit it, but she was searching for Luis. Never found him. Nobody did.'

We heard Mum's heels clacking on the polished concrete floor.

Morgan whispered, 'I think that's why she chose your father – the complete opposite. Solid and dependable. Turns out nobody's perfect, eh?'

Well, that half-explained her freak-out last year when she thought I'd taken drugs. Funny how people change.

After Mum had smashed her car into the wall last year, she'd bought a Volvo XC70 – safest car on the road. It had a heartbeat sensor to warn you if there was a serial killer hiding in the back before you got in. There was no homicidal psychopath in the car as she drove down Military Road this arvo, though – just two bottles of Moët, a roll of purple satin and three handbags.

'You came first in the breaststroke,' Mum said.

'Dad told you?'

'He's proud of you, and at least he's showing an interest in your progress.'

'It was butterfly, not breaststroke,' I said with a degree of irritation.

'Same difference. I made a mistake.'

A driver cut in front without indicating, which triggered the Volvo's collision avoidance warning. Mum palmed the horn. 'How much more of the road do you want, you FUCKING ARSEHOLE!' She attacked the S-bends of Spit Road with unprecedented aggression, making the tyres squeal – an impressive feat in a Volvo.

I flicked Starkey's gum into my mouth. The pellet was imbued with the stale pungency of his tobacco-stained fingers, so I spat it into my hand.

'That's disgusting!' Mum said.

'Tell me about it.'

She handed me a tissue from the dash. 'In here, please.'

On arrival at Signal Bay, she poured herself a gin and tonic, and called me out to the Buddha garden to apologise for being snippy. 'I've had the week from hell, darling. But I want to assure you I'm interested in everything happening in your life. Fine if you don't want to talk about school, as long as we keep the channels of communication open.'

'Tell me about your week, then?'

'Wednesday we launched Neroni's new accessory collection. Emma and Jules did a superb job and the client was delighted. But Lucy Seymour, the social media influencer, gave the event two thumbs down. She said the first was for running out of champagne, which was a lie. The second because she missed out on a freebie handbag – true.'

'I saw three on the back seat.'

'Emma and Jules deserve their perks. The third is a present for Maxine, who I haven't seen much of lately.'

Early Saturday morning, woken by tender swelling. The nub seemed to have grown. I measured its diameter at an even two centimetres. An increase of three millimetres, possibly triggered by the pills Nads gave me. I was afraid to stop taking them, though, because he'd said it could have adverse effects. Nads wasn't a real friend – nor were Mullows or Starkey. Not like Tom and Coops. Despite Nicole driving a wedge between us last year, and despite the fallout from the party at the Nugents', and despite Mum barring me from hanging out with Tom – which basically ruled out Coops as well – I still believed they were the friends who most got me. And I missed them badly.

I recovered my old esky lid and fins from under the house, scraped off the mouldy fuzz and went for an early. The surf was less than average but Coops was arsing around on his dad's mal, so I paddled over in an attempt to patch things up.

'You've turned into a sponge kook,' he said.

'Looks that way.'

'I've forgiven you for ratting us out last year,' he said, which was mighty gracious considering that I hadn't. 'But Tom's still dark at you. Blake's been charged with supply, so I'd maintain a low profile if I were you.' And he took off on the next wave. Just like that another aspect of my future had been decided without my involvement, and it felt completely shitful. The very small part of me that considered going after him was strangled by Homunculus.

'Don't bother trying to explain yourself to that dumbarse,' he said. 'He has no respect for you and doesn't deserve it.'

I got out of the water and dragged my board along the sand ridge, collapsing sections with each step until it looked like a bombed coastline. At the end of the crescent was a dead, mottled brown-and-grey Port Jackson shark. Its tail was buried in the sand, and its big blunt head was pointing out to sea as if still hoping to escape. No eyes – just empty sockets. Maybe pecked out by a bird? Poor bastard.

'Would you like to try my Bircher muesli?' Venn said when I got home.

'I'll stick to Coco Pops.'

'Gone,' she said. 'I've eliminated all high-sugar and high-sodium products.'

'Well, I'm stoked that your college has turned you into a health crusader, but I want you to know that I still need comfort food occasionally. In the meantime, lay some of the birdshit on me.'

Venn obliged. It was surprisingly tasty.

'Not bad,' I said. 'Hey, have you heard of yarn-bombing?'

'I saw some recently on Macquarie Street in the city. Multicoloured stripes stitched onto a light pole, and exactly the same pattern on the other side of the road.'

'What's the point of it?'

'The point is there is no point. Maybe the creator's just taking the piss and sharing the joke with us. Or it could be a way of feminising a sterile space. I don't know. Possibly it's about subverting the traditionally masculine street-art scene.'

'You sound like Maxine.'

'She used to be really into it.'

Maxine Partridge was a sculptor, and my mother's best friend. She worked a lot with 'found objects', often ones that Venn had found washed up on Mackerel Beach. We used to spend a lot of time at the Partridges' beach house over there till about six months ago.

'Why are you asking?' Venn said.

'One of my classmates has roped me into yarn-bombing the school.'

'That's exciting.'

'I think it sucks. It reminds me of the lame macramé owl I made for Mother's Day.'

'I loved Professor Hoot.'

'Yeah, anyway, I don't know how to knit.'

'I can but I'm crap. Nana Locke would love to teach you.'

Even though she'd recently adopted Tippi, I figured Nana was probably eager for some human company. After Pop died, my parents had urged her to come and live with us, at least for a while, but she'd refused to leave the Seabreeze unit she and Pop had shared. Teaching me to knit probably wouldn't provide her with a new purpose in life, but it might help make her feel important to somebody again.

FREAKING
DORIAN

In lieu of having friends of my own to hang out with, I was invited to 'Chick Flick Night' with Mum, Maxine, Venn and Jessie – the girl who'd slept in my bed. I already knew she was blonde from the evidence she'd left behind, but when she walked through the front door I was stunned by the luminescence of her eyes, bluer than Plax® mouthwash. She was super fit and tanned – the Northern Beaches ideal of female beauty. I couldn't wipe the goofy grin off my face, so Venn did it for me.

'Lincoln, this is my friend Jessie,' she said. 'She's not a boy and she doesn't suffer from alopecia. Jessie, meet my little brother Lincoln. He has a unique hobby of collecting hair.'

Jessie laughed. 'Thanks for letting me sleep in your bed.'

'Anytime.' It was meant to sound hospitable but came out lech.

The night was balmy so we sat out on the deck. The women drank chilled rosé and I drank tap water, listening to Mum's more embellished, juicier account of the launch incident wherein Lucy Seymour, society blogger, had got bollocked on champagne and was refused service for groping a waiter. Mum gave Maxine the Neroni handbag and said, 'You can thank Lucy Lushington for that one.'

A gentle onshore breeze stirred, tickling the yachts' rigging and carrying the heady scent of Valmay Harris's monstera deliciosa up to our gathering. A ribbon of burning copper light broke through the western clouds, turning strands of Jessie's hair into glowing filaments. For a brief moment, life was perfect. Then Roger Harris shattered the serenity by revving his outboard motor in Dougal's washtub. Dougal went totally apeshit, barking and trying to catch the spray in his mouth. I visualised him getting too close and having his snout butchered by the spinning blades, and had to shake my head to get the resulting carnage out of my mind.

We moved inside to eat. After dinner I was keen on extending my time in Jessie's presence, so I let the girls think they'd persuaded me into watching *The Devil Wears Prada*. Mum clucked with recognition at various scenes, saying things like, 'Hello – that is so Morgan!', but failed to identify Miranda Priestly's megalomaniacal tendencies in herself.

Halfway through the movie, I left to refill my glass. A minute later, Jessie followed.

'I'm not really into the girly stuff,' she said.

'Neither.' I poured her a glass. 'Venn told me you surf. What's your favourite break?'

'Definitely P-Pass at Pohnpei in Micronesia, north of New Guinea.' She told me about her recent trip – the perfect barrels wrapping around the reef, her expedition to the island's ancient ruins and snorkelling at Ant Atoll.

'That's my ultimate dream.'

Jessie crinkled her perfectly freckled nose. 'You should come next time.'

I couldn't believe my ears. 'That would be hectic!'

'Nate's already planning our next trip.'

'Sorry?'

'My boyfriend Nate is planning our next trip to the islands.'

'Oh, cool.' But absolutely not, because of course you have a boyfriend and you're three years older than me and what was I even thinking? And I have this strange growth that you'd probably be repelled by, which recently expanded by three millimetres and is currently tingling to remind me that it's still there.

'Yeah, we actually met searching for coconut crabs, then we got talking and discovered we live only one kilometre apart and know lots of the same people.'

'Six degrees and all that? I'd better get stuck into my homework.'

'Aren't you going to watch *Beaches* with us?'

'You know it's not a surf film, right?'

I went up to my room. Instead of reading *My One Redeeming Affliction*, because my own affliction was doing my head in, I continued with Dorian Gray. And though his unfailing beauty and eternal youth opened a world of untold thrills for him, I realised I didn't need Jessie to take me surfing at Pohnpei. I didn't even need Tom and Coops. Because one day I would escape from everything and go there on my own.

On Sunday morning I asked Mum if I could get a new surfboard, citing the difficulty of transporting my oldie from the city just for weekends. She immediately nixed the request and told me I should be more focused on homework than the beach.

'First you drove away my friends,' I said. 'And now you're treating me like a prisoner in my own home.'

'Nonsense. I'm simply setting a few boundaries. Remember the time you jumped off the Warriewood Blowhole with Tom and Cooper, and the boy who followed you had to be airlifted out because he had spinal damage?'

'Is that what all of this is about? That guy was a stupid tourist who'd never jumped before.'

'I'm afraid that if you keep going along with the reckless choices they're making, you'll be the next one to end up in serious trouble. Your friends up here treat every day like it's a beach holiday. They were exerting too much influence on you.'

'So you sent me to Kings Cross, with its bars and strip clubs and brothels and junkies and dealers. Though Frank the concierge reckons the supervised injecting rooms have made it a much safer place now.'

'Stop it, please,' Mum said.

'The other week yet another guy was punched in the head by a random, and he's still in hospital. I really love living there.'

'I'm sorry that you feel stuck between a rock and a hard place.'

'The hard thing about this place is that I've got no friends here and I'm not allowed to surf. It's barely worth making the two-hour journey to come over anymore.'

I saw a twitch in Mum's face. 'I think you're being a bit melodramatic.'

'I'm saying exactly what I think.'

'Then I suggest you have a think about whether you want to keep coming over or not.'

'There's no need for that. I've already decided not to.'

'The arrangement that your father and I have established isn't negotiable.'

'You should've considered that before offering me a choice.'

'Lincoln, I don't think you have any real understanding how difficult these past few months have been for me.' She tucked some hair behind her ear, revealing white roots.

'Or you me.'

'Where are you going?'

'To pack my stuff. I'm going back to the city.'

I went to my room and began stuffing clothes into my backpack. Mum stood in the doorway, looking almost desperate. Even in that moment I knew that I was taking all my frustration out on her because I couldn't confront Dad. But now that I'd decided to act like a dick I was committed to the performance.

'Leave those here,' she said. 'I'll wash them for you.'

'Thanks, but I've been managing on my own.'

I said goodbye and headed for the bus stop, expecting Mum to jump in the Volvo and drive alongside me until I surrendered – but she didn't.

Riding home on the L90, I realised the Locke family had reached our lowest trough. We'd never been so divided. I tried to think of my happiest family memory and the clear winner was the first time we'd all walked from Mackerel to West Head. Venn, who was ten, spotted a magnificent red gum with twisting boughs reaching up to the sky. She told us it was the 'Mother Tree' and had us all take off our shoes, hold hands around her and recite an ad-libbed oath to respect and protect Mother Nature. Further on, at the Aboriginal rock carvings, she was mesmerised by the human and animal figures, and insisted we read all of the information panels before proceeding.

Remembering the knack Venn used to have for bringing the family together, I decided it was time to clear the air with Dad.

By the time I arrived back at T H E   E Y R I E, I'd formulated my opening sentence: *I think we need to have a conversation about Maëlle.* But I walked into the kitchen and found Steve packing an esky with beers. 'How's it hanging, champ?' He winked.

'Where's Dad?'

'Showing Sophie and Mandy the view. We're taking *Foxy Lady* out. Why don't you come with?'

'Nah, but thanks.'

'Perfect afternoon for it. We'll find a beach, drop anchor, catch some rays.'

'I've got a reading assignment. *The Picture of Dorian Gray* by Oscar Wilde.'

'What's it about?'

'Refusing to grow up.' Now that my plan to speak to Dad had been thwarted, I detoured through the living room to avoid him, but one of the topnotch birds caught me as she came in from the balcony.

'Ooh! You gave me a fright.' She had pigtails, was wearing a singlet and cut-offs and smelt of coconut lotion.

'What are you doing home already?' Dad said from behind her.

'I live here sometimes.'

He introduced the women then I excused myself to finish the book.

'*Dorian Gray*,' Steve said, and winked again.

Dad returned late that evening sunburnt and testy, demanding to know why I'd left Signal Bay earlier than usual. I told him about the argument with Mum and my decision to remain in the city on weekends. His response was all about respecting her wishes, making it clear he didn't want me impinging on the new-found freedom he'd been enjoying, but I stood my ground. Despite having told me earlier that he had no interest in Mandy, you'd still think my father would have had a smidge of remorse after the Maëlle incident, and enough discretion to avoid socialising with women in their twenties. I could've used his merry jaunt on the high seas with the topnotch birds as a way into that conversation, but I was far too angry. I didn't want to be the one telling *him* to start behaving himself. He was too old to be acting like freaking Dorian Gray.

CATCHING
STITCHES

On Monday morning, the situation with Pericles didn't improve. At squad I was behind him in lane five and he was swimming dead slow, trying to force me to overtake. So I stayed behind him. At the end of the sixth lap, he stopped and stood up.

'What's going on?' I said.

'Stitch. Just go.'

'No, you just go.' We stood with our arms folded, backing up the next three swimmers.

Simmons spotted the stand-off and bellowed at us through his megaphone, >THOSE TWO WOMEN HAVING A MOTHER'S CLUB MEETING IN LANE FIVE, GET MOVING NOW!<

'Go!' Pericles shoved me. 'You're the big champion now.'

'Whatever.'

Simmons was striding our way, so I ducked underwater and pushed off.

*

126

SOHCAHTOA. Shit Often Happens, Causing Arse Holes To Operate Automatically.

It's all you need to know about trigonometry, gastroenterology and my life.

At the start of Maths I sat near Pericles, but he stood up and moved to the vacant spot next to David York. Whatever. Tibor was sitting next to Nads, which was unusual. Then Monaro sprang a surprise trig test on us. Five minutes later I caught Tibor surreptitiously sliding his paper across to show Nads his answers. How had Nads known there was going to be a test today when it was supposed to be a surprise?

At lunch I found Pericles sitting under a tree with his girlfriends. Phoenix Lee was applying a fake mermaid tattoo to Isa Mountwinter's forearm.

'Is licking absolutely necessary?' Isa said.

'If you want it to stick properly,' Phoenix said, then looked up as I approached. 'Hello, stalker. You here to get inked?'

'I want to talk to Pericles.'

'Go ahead, then.'

'Preferably without you two tuning in.'

'You can say whatever you need to in front of them,' Pericles said.

'Okay. The carnival – when I started squad, I couldn't swim butter-fly to save myself. You gave me goggles and some good advice, which I followed, and to everyone's surprise I won.'

'Bravo,' he said, and the three of them clapped.

'You're totally pissed off at me and I can understand why, but—'

'The world doesn't revolve around you, mate. I'm pissed off at myself for losing my place in the relay team – nothing more.'

'That's the thing, Pericles. I don't even want to be in the relay team. I don't want to be in squad.'

'And that's supposed to make me feel better?'

'Sorry for whatever it is that you think I've done wrong.'

'I think you should go now.'

I hate things festering, but as I couldn't force a resolution, I left.

*

127

After school, when I was unchaining my bike from the rack, Pericles came and stood next to me without talking. I couldn't be arsed trying to initiate another conversation, so I started to wheel my bike away.

'Hold up!' he yelled. 'Your back tyre's flat.'

'Shit.'

'Odds-on it was Byron Paget. Year 8 turd who's been busted with tacks before. Serial puncture artist.'

'The dingus with a bowl cut?' I said, and Pericles nodded. 'We met in Student Welfare.' I re-chained my bike while Pericles stood there not speaking. When I turned to face him he was massaging his temples, preparing to release some hefty burden.

'I was devo about losing the race,' he said. 'But my reaction was more from a fear of how my father would react. Winning's all that matters to him.'

'My dad's the same. All about the competition.'

'He couldn't be as bad as mine. Last year I scored ninety-nine in the maths final, equal top with Tibor. Dad wanted to know why I hadn't extinguished myself.'

'He meant "distinguished".'

'He hit me for correcting him.'

I didn't know what to say. Pericles took a couple of deep breaths, pressing his temples again. He told me that when his father rang him before the race, he was actually calling from the pool, despite the fact that parents weren't allowed to be there. Pericles saw him on the way to the marshalling area and it totally spooked him. Standing on the starting blocks, he had a full-on panic attack, and missed the start by a couple of seconds.

'It was a miracle you came so close to winning,' I said.

'I've never swum so hard in my life.'

'I saw you throwing up after.'

'Yeah? Well, you left before the main act. My father came storming down and chewed my head off in front of Gelber while I was still hurling. Not my proudest moment.' His train of thought was interrupted by two mynas bothering a sparrow. 'Don't know what drives him. Has to be more than the school-fee incentive.'

'What's that?'

'If you represent Crestfield at regionals, they take a grand off your school fees. If you swim at state level, your parents pay nothing the next year.'

'What happens if you make nationals? Do they dip your Speedos in gold and display them in the trophy cabinet?'

'With you still in them.' Pericles almost smiled, then his face darkened. 'At least I won't have to deal with the goon squad anymore. Nads, Mullows and Starkey hate me. Dad's constant interference last year gave them and Simmons the streaming shits.' He stared at me, unflinching, jaw tensing then sliding to chew on the words that couldn't quite make their way out. He blinked hard then said, 'Was deserting me to follow them a sign of your allegiance?'

'I try not to take sides.'

'Come back and talk to me when you say no to the brotherhood of bullshit.' He walked away, and I felt weak as piss for not simply apologising.

On Wednesday, before training commenced, Simmons announced the team for the Crestfield Invitational with St Eugene's and Clovelly College. Both Pericles and I had qualified for the individual butter-fly, but I was named on the medley relay team. Nads, Mullows and Starkey walked over to congratulate me.

'Welcome to the Brotherhood,' Mullows said, patting my back with his big hand.

'Not so fast,' Nads said. 'Initiation's on Friday.'

'What initiation?'

'Yours,' Starkey said. 'Piece of piss really – no need to freak.'

>ATTENTION ALL SWIMMERS!< Deb Gelber's megaphone cut through the banter. >SERIOUS TRAINING BEGINS TODAY.< She flipped the whiteboard to reveal the program. >IN ADDITION TO THE BREAKDOWN, EVERYBODY WHO MADE THE TEAM FOR THE INVITATIONAL WILL BE REWARDED WITH AN EXTRA FIVE HUNDRED.<

I followed Pericles to lane five. After he dived in, Nads grabbed my arm and jerked me around.

'Leave that choking fag in the loser's lane,' he said. 'You belong with us in seven.'

I turned my back on Pericles a second time.

After school, I rode the B-Line bus to Nana Locke's flat in Dee Why for a knitting lesson. I knocked on the door and Tippi started yapping on the other side. Nana Locke let me in and the Jack Russell–Chihuahua went ballistic, running around me, barking and whimpering.

'Don't be afraid, little one,' Nana said and put her hand on my shoulder. 'This is Lincoln. He's a nice, kind man.'

Tippi growled and nipped at my ankle.

'That's quite enough now,' Nana said to her. 'Go to your cushion!' Tippi looked confused, so Nana pointed to the sofa and snapped her fingers. Tippi jumped onto the sofa, circled her designated cushion three times, then lay down. 'I hope she didn't hurt you, dear?'

'I'm fine,' I said, showing her my ankle. 'I thought she was afraid of cats?'

'And men, when she first meets them. Her first owner was a very cruel fellow apparently.'

I looked over at Tippi. Her plaintive eyes, a little too big for her head, almost melted my heart. 'She's lucky to have you now,' I said and sat on the recliner. 'You've had your hair done since I saw you on my birthday.' It was short and fire-engine red like Nurse Nola's.

'Too bright?' Nana said, primping it.

'It's hectic.'

'I had such a lovely time at your birthday dinner, but I forgot to give you this.' She handed me an envelope and for a moment I thought it might be last year's card from Pop. But then I opened it and saw a picture of two elderly nudists driving a golf buggy. 'Life begins at eighty!' the caption said.

'Oh dear.' Nana took the card from me. 'Glenda will be wondering why I wished her a sweet sixteenth.' She put it on the sideboard and went into the kitchen, followed by Tippi. We chatted as she made us both a cup of tea, then returned and put a plate of lemon slice on the coffee table. Tippi leapt up, delicately removed one of the slices between her teeth and went back to her cushion to eat it. 'Naughty little thing,' Nana said with a chuckle and picked up the crumbs with a napkin. Then she turned back to me and said, 'Now, tell me what this knitting business is all about.'

I explained the project, thinking she'd agree that it was pointless to knit something to wrap around a pole, but like Venn she was intrigued by the idea. Eager to begin, she fetched a Spotlight bag and a vintage Arnott's red parrot tin from the cupboard.

'What's the frown for, sourpuss?'

'Knitting's traditionally for girls.'

'Phooey. Your pop couldn't knit but he darned all his own socks. And he baked a much better sponge than I ever could. You won't learn diddly squat if you don't try new things. Glenda and I are learning salsa at the community centre with a Colombian instructor called Ernesto. The way he moves gives us both the palpitations.'

'Way too much information.'

'Old chooks cluck the loudest – don't you worry about that. Choose a colour while I sort out my bibs and bobs.' I ferreted through the bag and chose a ball of atomic orange. 'Casting on is a bit tricky, so I'll do that for you.' Using her fingers, she magically created a row of stitches on one of the needles.

'Now we're set. Watch carefully – needle through, yarn around, pull it down, slide it off. Easy as pie.' She made me repeat the instructions as she knitted a row. 'You take over now,' she said and handed me the needles. But before I could begin, Tippi jumped off her cushion and came and sat on my lap, which wasn't exactly helpful.

I grasped the needles firmly and pulled the yarn too tightly, stitching a row of mean little knots. 'I can't do this.'

'Don't get huffy. You're doing well for a first-timer.' She put her hands over mine and guided me through a second row. 'Keep going now, and you'll find your rhythm.' She fished around in the Spotlight bag and pulled out a blue-and-yellow scarf. She brushed it against the side of her face with her eyes closed. 'I was knitting this for Pop. Ten years living here and he never wavered in his allegiance to the Eels. I might finish it for your father instead.'

'Dad backs the Roosters now.'

'Oh well, I'll give it to Clarry up at six-oh-five. He'll think all of his Christmases have come at once.'

We knitted together and chatted, the repetition soothing my mind, melting away the frustration. Every time I dropped a stitch, Nana Locke retrieved it and told me there was no mistake that couldn't be mended. It was slow going but satisfying to see something grow beneath my hands. And Tippi stayed on my lap the whole time.

'Somebody's got a new friend,' Nana said. 'I hope you're staying for dinner? I've got some nice lamb cutlets from the meat tray I won at the club.'

'Dad wants me home by eight.'

'It's only half-six.'

'I'd better get going.' I lifted Tippi off and said, 'You be a good girl – and take care of my grandmother.'

Nana took my face in her bony hands and her smile betrayed the weary solitude of her grief. 'Don't leave it so long before your next visit. And bring that father of yours along next time.'

'Okay. Thank you so much for teaching me to knit.'

She put my knitting and an extra ball of atomic-orange yarn in a plastic bag. 'Take these with you and keep at it. Next time I'll teach you to purl.'

THE NANG-NANG

Friday morning I slept through my alarm, waking at 8.48 am. Dad had gone. My bike was locked up at school. Telling head office that my late arrival was the result of anxiety-induced insomnia would have incurred another session with Dr Limberg, so I jigged History and arrived in time for second period – English. While Mr Field was talking about a theme commonly explored in Victorian Gothic novels – the descent into madness – Starkey passed me a piece of paper that accelerated my own decline. It bore a crudely drawn picture of a plucked chicken that could've easily been mistaken for a penis, being strangled over a boiling cauldron. Below it was the note, *BUK BUK BEGEEEEERK! We thought you'd chickened out.*

Later, in Biology, Nads kept leering at me with his scarred eyebrow raised, probably nutting out the final details of my impending humiliation. The lesson progressed about as fast as a crushed snail towards a pile of salt. When the glockenspiel finally sounded I made a controlled dash for a study room in the library and hid behind an old copy of *Scientific American*. Ten minutes later, Heather Treadwell tapped the glass. 'R3 is booked for a prayer meeting,' she said.

'Send one up for me. I'm in desperate need of a miracle.'

During French, my guts surrendered to the nerves, demanding

I request permission to use the toilet on threat of letting loose in the classroom. Miss Moreau asked me to repeat it in French. Luckily it was the first phrase I'd ever learnt.

Down at Rushcutters Bay Park in the afternoon for PE, Mullows and Nathan Trammel were chosen to be softball captains. Mullows picked Nads then Starkey, me and Cheyenne Piper, who was now his girlfriend. Afraid to pick anybody Mullows might want, Nathan chose all girls and Pericles. Simmons didn't care about the gender loading – he revelled in watching his boys trouncing the girls.

Towards the end of the final innings we were smashing them 22–3 and Cheyenne was our last batter. With the bases loaded, she belted the third pitch well past the outfielders, over the trees and into the sea. Pericles pulled off his trainers and began climbing over the seawall.

'Leave it!' Simmons yelled. 'You'll cut your feet to ribbons on the oysters.' Cheyenne strutted the diamond, picking up Nads, Mullows and Starkey on the way.

Our teams lined up to shake each other's hands.

'Congratulations,' Pericles said to me. 'You beat me again, champion.'

'Please don't call me that.'

'Joking. I know I've been a bit shitty lately, but I was wondering . . . if you maybe wanted to hang out?'

There was nothing I wanted or needed more than a solid friend – but the arsehole behind me had two fingers pointed in the small of my back like a gun. 'Yeah yeah,' I said. 'But I can't right now.'

'Move!' Starkey shoved me.

'I'll explain later.'

'No need to.'

I half-expected a rooster to crow my third denial of Pericles, but there was nothing so epically poignant. Only the imagined 'Begeerk!' of Starkey's plucked chicken to condemn my cowardice.

Nads and Mullows helped Simmons load the equipment into his egg-yolk MGB GT. When his back was turned, Nads stole a bat and passed it to Starkey, who left the group and went behind the change shed. Simmons squeezed himself into the tiny car and tooted farewell to the golden boys.

Everyone was leaving the park except Cheyenne Piper and Liliana Petersen, who were lingering on a bench.

'Bros before hos,' Nads said to Mullows.

Mullows took the hint and asked them to go. They had a small discussion among themselves I couldn't hear then stood up and left, Cheyenne shaking her head as they passed Mullows – obviously annoyed that he'd complied with Nads. When they were out of sight, Nads said to me, 'You're about to become a fully-fledged member of the Brotherhood.'

'I'm honestly fine with having a sister.'

'Don't speak.'

'Sorry.'

'If you ever reveal any of this to anyone, you'll suffer painful and long-lasting consequences. Understand?'

Starkey's reappearance with the bat sent shivers down my spine – all the way to the nub, the exclamation mark of my worst fears. I scanned the park and saw Pericles, Isa and Phoenix still standing on the bridge over the stormwater canal. Nobody else from school was around. I attempted to send a message telepathically, asking them to remain as witnesses from a safe distance, but only Nads read my mind – or the direction of my gaze. He turned and spotted the trio. 'Sorry, no spectators,' he said as if they could hear him from so far away. 'Move along, nothing to see.' He waved them off.

Phoenix returned a single finger and the three of them headed towards Edgecliff Station without looking back.

'Time for us to pay a visit to the Nang-Nang,' Nads said.

Starkey started a chant: 'Nang-nang-nang-nang-nang-nang.'

'What's the Nang-Nang?'

'All of your most hellacious nightmares in subhuman form,' Nads said. 'The local lolly-baiter.'

'What do you mean?'

'He's a paedo. A registered sex offender.'

'The filthy old bastard pisses his pants and stinks like shit,' Starkey said.

'Why's he called the Nang-Nang?'

'Years ago he spilt the beans on some big drug lord – blabbed to the cops,' Nads said. 'Mr Big got thrown into the slammer. His heavies hunted down the Nang-Nang for payback. Cut off his tongue for squealing.'

'Can't talk anymore,' Starkey said with bulging eyes. 'All he can say is "nangnangnangnang".' He waved his arms above his head, bumping me along with his chest.

Walking up the backstreets of Darlinghurst, fear trickled cold down my sides. I wasn't scared of the Nang-Nang – I was scared for him. Starkey was tapping the fat end of the bat in the palm of his hand, again murmuring 'nangnangnang'.

'Why do we have to go and see him?' I said, stopping.

'It's part of the relocation plan,' Nads said. 'We're providing him with some gentle encouragement to move away from the hood.'

'He's too close to Crestfield,' Starkey said.

'What's the bat for?'

'You'll find out soon enough.'

The street we were walking along was empty except for five or six cockatoos perched on poles. I slid my phone from my pocket, hoping to find a message requesting my immediate presence elsewhere. Starkey snatched it away before I had a chance.

'No photos,' he said, and put it in his bag. We continued past the workers' cottages towards the old man's property on the corner, confirming my hunch that the 'Nang-Nang' was the old guy who'd sold me the bike.

'I don't want to do this.'

'Tough shit!' Starkey clawed the neck of my shirt and twisted it till it bit into my skin. Then, mock-soothingly, as if pacifying a crippled pigeon whose neck he was about to snap, he said, 'Calm down and don't ask questions. Do exactly what we say and nobody'll get hurt.' We stopped at the junkyard.

'Keep watch,' Nads said. He pressed his shoulder into the wire gate and pushed, causing the unlifted bolt below to grind a screeching arc into the concrete. He squeezed through the gap and reached back for the softball bat.

There were six rosebushes in bloom. Nads crouched beneath the window line of the cottage and crept to the closest one. Twisting his shoulders and lowering the bat, he lined up his shot then swung the bat skywards, hitting the top rose with such force it exploded silently into a hundred pieces that fell to Earth like the dying red sparks of a firecracker. Starkey cackled, hands bearing down on my shoulders, pinning me to the spot.

Nads passed the bat to Mullows, who performed the same act of violation on the second rosebush with clinical precision, expressionless, merely executing his duty. Starkey, unable to wait his turn, let go of me and pushed through the gate, snatching the bat before letting Mullows out. He strutted past the windows to the third bush, oblivious to the possibility that the old man was home. He cranked the bat way back then snapped it forward with such uncontrolled aggression he missed the bush completely, performing a clumsy pirouette.

'Just warming up,' he said, and proceeded to smash every one of the seven flowers, counting as he struck them from their stems. He turned to us, lifting the bat above his head, and took a bow. Nobody applauded.

'Hurry up!' Nads snarled, but Starkey ignored him. He slid the bat under his arm and hefted the shop mannequin from the dumpster, held her from behind and pumped his hips against her.

'C'mon baby! C'mon, c'mon! Tell me you want it.' Two green hundred-dollar bills, dislodged from the mannequin's fingers by Starkey's violent jerking, fluttered to the ground.

'Get out now!' Nads said.

In one fluid movement Starkey laid down the mannequin, picked up the notes and pocketed them. I was dumbstruck, unable to tell them that the cash had been the payment for my bike – and in doing so reveal I knew the old man. One of the cockatoos swooped low, splitting the thick air with a furious squawk.

Starkey rammed the bat into my gut and said, 'Your turn.' My head was mushy with panic as I squeezed through the gate, devoid of escape options. I'd asked Heather Treadwell to pray for a miracle and I think she must have taken me seriously because at that exact moment Pop

Locke appeared in my mind's eye. His hair was slick from a visit to Joe and Vic's. I could smell the Swiss Valley Hair Pomade™ – maybe that was just the shredded rose petals? He looked pleased to see me, but when I held up the bat his smile dropped. And I clearly heard him say, 'Lincoln, what are you doing?'

'What the uck-fay are you doing?' Nads said. 'Smash it up!'

I lowered the bat and shook my head.

Starkey shut the gate, trapping me in the yard. 'NANGNANG-NANG!' he yelled. He pushed the bolt into its hole and stood on it. Nads jumped onto the wire fence and shook it like a rioting prisoner. 'NANGNANGNANGNANGNANGNANGNANG!'

I froze. The bat fell from my hand.

I imagined myself melting, liquefying, running down the drain and flowing like filthy sullage through the stormwater pipe to the canal under the bridge that Pericles, Isa and Phoenix had been standing on, floating out to the harbour – way out, to be absorbed by the deep blue ocean.

The >SMACK!< of a rickety screen door returned me to my senses like a slap in the face. The old man came lurching around the side of the house. Nads, Mullows and Starkey fled.

'Johnny-come-lately. Run rabbit run! Johnny shot the buggers with an elephant gun.' He sounded like Dr Seuss on a bender.

I raised trembling hands. 'Good afternoon, sir. You probably don't remember me. I'm the kid who bought the Malvern Star.' I was seconds away from soiling my shorts.

'Ruby Rose. Turned-up toes. Long black car. Off she goes.' He registered the torn petals scattered on the concrete. 'The hooligans came back, Rube.' Fixing me with his one good Bombay Sapphire eye as he backed me up against the wire fence, he said, 'You're one of them, aren't ya, Finnegan Beginagain?'

'They're not my friends.'

'Billy Liar!' he shouted at my face, the fence pressing diamonds into the back of my head, the thin air between us souring from his fermented breath. 'Get out of here.'

I picked up the bat.

'NOW!' he yelled.

I dropped the bat, pushed the gate open and ran.

Ten metres shy of the corner, something hit the back of my leg and felled me. I'd been shot by Johnny's elephant gun, whoever Johnny was. Rocking and groaning on the nature strip, I felt the liquid warmth of blood seeping from the bullet wound in my hamstring. My life flashed before me, and it was a short and disappointing movie. The thought that I may never experience anything more exciting than pashing Nicole Parker distressed me. I wanted to live some more.

I was dizzy and possibly going into shock. Starkey still had my phone, so I couldn't call an ambulance. What would Bear Grylls do? Staunch the flow with a tourniquet made from his t-shirt. But when I reached around to assess my potentially fatal injury, I discovered my leg was bone dry. Sore and tender but there was no blood, not even a drop. My life had been spared.

I looked back down the street and saw that the crazy old git had gone. The projectile was in the gutter – a wooden ball the size of a grapefruit, too large to pass through the drain's iron grate. Dividing the two hemispheres of the ball was a metal equator engraved with the word 'Pemberton's.' I unscrewed them and found inside a small metal cylinder, which was empty.

The Nang-Nang may have been a cantankerous and mad old fart with a volatile temper, but he'd been acting in self-defence. He'd found me in his property with a softball bat. As much as it hurt, I didn't blame him for pegging the wooden ball at me.

Remembering the bat was still behind his fence and I'd been the last to hold it, I limped back to the junkyard to retrieve it. I heard him around the back giving a rambling account of the incident – hopefully to Percy, not the police. I slid through the gate, switched ball for bat and left.

'Sport today, was it champ?' Frank the concierge said when I walked into the lobby with the bat. He frowned. 'Are you limping?'

'I got hit by a ball. Any mail?' I said to block further enquiry.

'Afraid not.' As I passed Frank's desk he added, 'Nasty bruise you've got there. I'd get some ice onto that quick smart.'

Safely back in the apartment, I checked out my bruise in the mirror. It was the size of a bread plate, a yellow-grey circle with a dark purple circumference, parts of it almost black. The graphic nature of my injury vindicated me for thinking I'd been shot by an elephant gun. But I also saw something more disturbing. The nub appeared to have the same diameter as before, but it was definitely protruding more. Maybe I could ice it as well as the bruise?

No ice in the freezer. Phone gone. I called my mobile from the landline and Starkey answered.

'Hello?' he said in a fake voice. 'Stinkin' Lincoln's phone.'

'It's me.'

'Hey, piker! I was waiting for your call. Did the Nang-Nang get you?'

I gave him a condensed version of the assault.

'That bentarsesonofabitch fully nailed you.'

'Can you bring my phone to school tomorrow?'

'Sorry but it's closed on Saturday, dickhead.'

'Monday then. Please don't forget.'

'Wait. You got a message. Some hot chick's cooking dinner on Sunday and she wants you to go. She's begging for it, man. Her name was something stupid like Venn.'

'That's my sister.'

'What's it short for – Vendetta?'

'Please just turn off my phone and bring it on Monday.'

He hung up. Fifteen minutes later the landline rung. It was Starkey. 'Just got a message from your dad. He's entertaining clients tonight. What is he – a hustler?'

'Advertising.'

'Does he sell Coke or snort it?'

'Just bring my phone on Monday,' I said, and hung up.

I sat on the balcony, knitting as the sinking sun turned the sky atomic orange, like the colour of my wool and probably the end of the world. The afternoon's drama played through my mind on continuous loop until I finally twigged. I'd read about a wooden ball like the one that had hit me. I ran through the books on my reading list – *Jekyll and Hyde*, *Dorian Gray*, *Frankenstein*. It featured in none of them. And then I remembered – *My One Redeeming Affliction*. I found the passage:

It rolled through to the other side, then down a switchback before dropping onto a red velvet cushion in a basket.

'Troublesome thing,' Esther said, making a performance of unscrewing the two halves. She turned her back on the customer to read the scrawled message:

Insolence will not be tolerated!

My ball also had two halves that could unscrew. And it had something engraved on the metal seam – what was it? Perkins? Peabody's? Pennington's?

Pemberton's! I scanned the book again and discovered the hatmaker was located in Pemberton's Magnificent Emporium.

FLUSHED WITH SUCCESS

Saturday morning Dad burst into my room singing 'Good Morning Starshine' from the musical *Hair*. When he hit the 'Sabba sibby sabba' part in falsetto, I begged him to stop.

'Get your trainers on,' he said. 'We're going in five.'

'It's Saturday. I'm going to sleep in.'

'You already have. It's eight-thirty. Quick sticks!'

The bruise had expanded and darkened overnight, so I wore long boardies to hide it. In the kitchen I took a box of Nutri-Grain® from the cupboard but Dad snatched it away mid-pour. 'No time for breakfast,' he said. It dawned on me that he was playing hardarse so that I'd want to return to Signal Bay on weekends.

'Bugger that,' Homunculus said. 'Keep up with him and pretend to enjoy it.'

We trotted down the McElhone Stairs en route to Garden Island, where a gargantuan American aircraft carrier was docked. Its crew, all short and broad with buzz cuts, were joining the tourists for a Harry's pie. Crossing over to the Botanic Gardens, we ran past Boy Charlton Pool and got trapped behind a troop of weekend warriors wearing nothing but Speedos and trainers, every foot strike rippling their back fat.

I stayed with Dad all the way to Farm Cove – a.k.a. Woccanmagully, as I'd learnt in Aboriginal Studies. There on Gadigal land, men had once gathered to perform Yoo-long Erah-ba-diang – a ceremony where boys sat on the shoulders of male relatives and had one of their upper teeth knocked out. An initiation where boys became men. All about respect for elders. The opposite of my initiation, in which an elderly man had been tormented by juvenile delinquents. The opposite of Mum's impending launch here, where people would gather to marvel at a product formulated to make you look younger.

We ran up and down the Fleet Steps two at a time until my leg cramped and I collapsed. 'What's wrong with you?' Dad said, still jogging on the spot. 'Kenny Wallis, my rugby coach back in the day, made us do burpees if we lagged behind.' He dropped, kicked out his legs, tucked them in and jumped. 'C'mon! Let's see what you're made of. What's wrong with you, pussy?'

'This small thing,' I said, hitching up my boardies to show him the bruise. 'I got hit by a ball yesterday.'

He looked concerned, and thankfully changed tack. 'Ooh, looks sore. We need to get ice onto that. Let's walk back.'

Without mentioning anything to do with 'the Brotherhood,' I asked Dad if they'd had initiation ceremonies in his rugby days.

'Mandatory dunny flushing for all new players,' he said. 'After my first training session, six of the bigger guys jumped me and dragged me into the change shed.'

'Did you fight back?'

'They'd just done Trev Pullitt and he'd lost a front tooth – smashed it on the side of the shitter. So I stopped struggling once I got near. They lifted me upside down, shoved my head into the bowl and flushed. Thought I was going to drown on piss. Bastards flushed it three more times.'

'Brutal. Then what?'

'I ran home, gargled Listerine and stood under the shower for half an hour.' He laughed. 'Pop Locke clipped me over the ear for using all the hot water. He was different back then. Really hard on me. Did I ever tell you that before and after school I had to work in the bakery, right through to the end of Year 12? It was no small miracle that I got into university, but he was disappointed that I didn't want to take over the business. As you know, it had been in his family for three generations. Anyway, he softened when you kids came along. Transformed into a different person. You were his little prince,' he said, with what sounded like a tinge of jealousy.

We climbed the McElhone Stairs in silence and I thought again about Pop telling me that when a person knows their ancestors they'll never be alone. Reaching the top of the stairs, I asked Dad why he had no siblings.

'Let's go and sit down over there,' he said. We walked into Embarkation Park and sat on a bench facing the city skyline, gold with the still-rising sun. 'I did have some foster brothers and sisters at different times. But Nana and Pop couldn't have children.'

'They had you, though?'

'Well, not really. I've got a bit of a story to tell you.' He took a deep breath. 'Pop Locke found me. I was abandoned on the steps of St John's, where he was church warden. Pop and Nana were allowed to foster me after I'd been a week in the hospital. And some time later they were granted permission to officially adopt me.'

I remained silent.

'It's okay, mate. I know it's a lot to take in all at once. I was ten when they told me.'

'But why? Why didn't you ever tell us?'

'It knocked me for six. Because unless my birth parents identified themselves, I'd never be able to find them. They never came. Nana and Pop constantly told me that I was a gift from God, which was a tough gig to live up to. I went through a pretty rough rebellion stage. Anyway, your and Venn's relationship with Pop was something really special. Probably closer than mine ever was. And it just felt wrong to make him seem anything less than your true grandfather. Because he was – he is.'

We stayed on the bench for over an hour. We talked about Dad's early identity crisis, and his years of speculating that his mother or father could've been watching his life from afar without identifying themselves. I thought back to the History lesson a couple of weeks ago.

144

My dad was a foundling, like Moses and Snow White and Superman. He'd been raised by a humble couple who ran a bakery and he'd made a huge success of his life in advertising. But he admitted, with tears in his eyes, that Pop had never been happy with his chosen career path.

'What was the unfinished business with Pop that you mentioned on the night before my birthday?'

'I'd just told him that we'd won the Rising Loaf account, the big breads and cereals company. I thought he'd finally be impressed, but—' Dad shook his head, unable to continue. He whimpered and struggled for breath and it was almost unbearable to witness him breaking. 'Fuck it all!' he said, and recomposed himself. 'He told me that I'd sacrificed my family in the process. And that was our last conversation.' He exhaled loudly, shaking himself out. 'Let's get some ice onto that bruise of yours, eh?'

On Sunday, Dad worked from home and I wrote an essay on *Dorian Gray* comparing the treatment of the external and internal self in the book with the same in contemporary life. Dorian's signs of ageing and corruption appeared on his portrait, which was hidden away from public view. Conversely, my newsfeeds were filled with people posting digitally perfected images of themselves, hoping to be gratified by the likes. I proposed that in both instances this compulsion to maintain our self-image eventually has a detrimental effect on the soul.

This afternoon Dad and I hovered around each other, tentative after his confession and the new understanding it had brought between us. But still the unspoken Maëlle thing lingered in the air. When he flagged the idea of calling Venn to tell her the story of his origin, I said that she probably wouldn't take the call. So he used the landline, which didn't have caller ID, and Mum answered.

From the lounge room I could hear Dad's side of an argument that, for reasons unknown, seemed to be about me. The call lasted less than three minutes and he didn't get through to Venn.

Dad came out and warned me that I was squarely in the doghouse with him. Then he asked if I'd sent Mum an offensive text message.

'Of course not. I lost my phone on Friday, remember?'

'Well, you're going to have to sort this one out on your own when you get it back. Nobody over there wants to talk to me.'

Starkey must've sent my mother a message. I dreaded what it could have been.

On Monday morning, I walked to school super early carrying the softball bat in a postal tube, hoping nobody would see me returning it. My plan backfired on arrival, when I discovered The Hive was locked. I could smell Mr Jespersen's Indonesian clove cigarette in the air. Dressed in paint-splashed grey coveralls and a tatty Greek fisherman's cap, the caretaker came around the corner of the building pushing an equipment cart made from a repurposed golf buggy that made him look like the lone survivor of the apocalypse. I told him I was returning some equipment for Mr Simmons. He shrugged, unhitched a key ring the size of a basketball hoop from his belt, chose one of the 738 keys and opened the main doors of The Hive. I sneaked down to the storeroom and replaced the bat, prematurely congratulating myself on the reverse heist. On my way back to the front, however, I heard someone coming through the doors. I pulled my towel from my bag and slung it over my shoulder.

'What are you doing here so early, germ?' Simmons said.

'I came to warm up before squad, sir.'

'You know that's forbidden without a staff member present. There'd be sweet hell to pay if you injured yourself or, God forbid, drowned. Not that you'd care because you'd be dead. I should report this on The Owl – but I won't. Let's both hope you weren't caught on camera. Now get out and let me eat in peace.'

Nads and Mullows arrived together and wanted a firsthand account of what had happened after they scarpered on Friday. I gave them an embellished version and showed them the bruise.

'Meaty,' Nads said. 'Did you bring the bat?'

'It's back in the storeroom.'

'Anybody see you?' Mullows said.

146

'Nobody.'

'Strictly speaking, you didn't pass the initiation,' Nads said. 'But, taking into account the hammering you copped from the Nang-Nang and your successful mission with the bat, I forward the motion that you be accepted into the Brotherhood.'

'Here, here,' Mullows said, rolling his eyes.

'Motion passed.' Nads thumped me.

After training, Starkey returned my phone with a dead battery. 'I called a few of your friends,' he said.

'You're joking?' I said.

'Nothing funny about it.'

The electronic glockenspiel chimed in an unfamiliar way.

'Special assembly,' Starkey said. 'Rumour has it that Tibor Mintz is being awarded the Crestfield Medal for Brownnosing.'

In ascending years we filed into the Joseph Millington Drake Auditorium. Assisting with the pointlessly regimental procedure were Tibor and Isa, who both seemed to perform an inordinate amount of school service.

The lights dimmed, the chatter died down. Someone wolf-whistled, another impersonated a ghost and a third arm-farted, causing the entire assembly to erupt in laughter. Silence returned when Dashwood strode onto the stage. He could've been the handsome, silver-haired commander of a Tactical Operations Unit, except for his occasional lip-licking.

He adjusted his tie and tapped the microphone. 'Good morning, student body and members of staff. Before I address a most serious matter, Mrs Hammond will lead us in the school anthem to remind us of the values our school was founded on.'

The anthem lasted forever. This was the final verse:

> Live a life of virtue.
> Uphold the Golden Rule.
> Community ambassadors,
> bring glory to your school.

'Fine words indeed,' Dashwood said, and licked his lips. 'But amongst us are students who have not behaved as community ambassadors.' A shock of adrenaline surged through my veins. 'Boys who have behaved like hooligans and heaped burning coals of shame onto our beloved school.' He double-side-licked. Sweat dripped from my pits. 'Ruffians who've vandalised the property of an elderly member of the community. To say I'm appalled by their disgraceful behaviour would be a gross understatement. Would the boys whose names I call join me onstage? Darvin Naylor . . . Evan Starkey . . . Hurry up, lad! And Sean Mulligan.'

I rocked forward, preparing to stand, but my name wasn't called. Relief washed over me like a wave of raw sewage.

Dashwood announced to the entire school their four-day suspension and five hours of community service every weekend till the end of term. From centre stage, Nads gave me the death stare of an outlaw betrayed by his own gang member. The assembly was dismissed, and the condemned trio were led away by Dashwood.

'You were so lucky,' Pericles said on our way to Maths.

'How so?'

'I'm not stupid. I saw the bruise on your leg at training.'

'I got hit by the softball.'

'Bullshit.'

Considering that Pericles, Isa and Phoenix had all seen me with them, there was no point in keeping the details of the initiation secret – and I still desperately needed a friend. So I told him the whole story.

'That's brutal,' he said. 'They must think you squealed.'

'Exactly.'

'They'll be planning retribution. What are we going to do?'

'We?'

'I'm fully in,' Pericles said. 'A hundred per cent.'

'Suggestions?'

'You could hire after-school protection. My cousin Angelo's a night-club bouncer – massive unit, all muscle. I could organise mate's rates.'

'Terrific.'

*

148

At lunchtime Pericles helped fix my tyre with a puncture-repair kit and a bucket borrowed from Mr Jespersen. When I held the inflated innertube underwater to locate the holes, it fizzled in five places.

'Byron Paget is such a little sphincter,' Pericles said. 'You'd think once was enough.'

'At least it wasn't stolen.'

'The bike's a bit old for that.'

'Old things have greater value. They've stood the test of time. More people might've used them, but that gives them a history. Imagine all the adventures this bike has taken people on in its thirty years of service.'

'All the sweaty arses that have sat on the seat.'

'Anyway, I'm not fully anti-consumerist. I want a new surfboard, but my finances are low and I'm not in a good position for mooching.'

'So get a job.'

'I would if Maccas wasn't the only option.'

'You serious about wanting a job?'

'Hundred per cent.'

'I might be able to help.' Pericles pulled out his phone, called his Uncle Manos and handed it to me. Uncle Manos gave me a two-minute interview then asked if an avocado was a vegetable or a fruit. When I answered correctly he said, 'I like you, Lincoln. A friend of Perilakimu is a friend of his Uncle Manos. You're a good boy. You've got the job.'

So that was settled. I'd be working 5 to 9 pm on Thursdays, and maybe some Fridays, at Give Me the Juice at Bondi Junction with Perilakimu. Aside from the very real possibility of those three goons seeking revenge, it seemed like things might be improving.

DESTRUCTIVE AND
HABITUAL BEHAVIOURS

I arrived home, plugged my phone into the charger and checked all the messages I'd missed while Starkey had it. All two of them. One from Venn and one from Mum, both saying they'd missed me and urging me to go over for dinner yesterday. I felt sick when I read Starkey's malevolent response to my mother:

BACK OFF YOU STUPID COW! I'D RATHER EAT MY OWN SHIT!!!

No wonder she'd cracked it on the phone with Dad. I called her to explain that it wasn't me, but she didn't believe me.

'We all have our moments of irrational anger and sometimes fail to think before we act,' she said. 'But that doesn't excuse your destructive behaviour. Your remark was highly offensive and deeply upsetting, and I expect an apology.'

I couldn't take the blame for something I hadn't done. Evan Starkey was obviously a nutjob and I had no desire to protect him, but I didn't want Mum knowing what had really happened, so I said he was a friend playing a practical joke.

'Sixteen's a bit old for imaginary friends, Lincoln.'

'Believe me – he's very real.'

'Only a sociopath would text something like that.'

'I absolutely agree.'

'Heaven help us all! We send you to a school that attracts some of the best and brightest students in the state, but when it comes to finding friends you still manage to scrape the bottom of the barrel.' That pretty much ended the conversation.

I should've begun reading *Frankenstein*, my third book on the list for English, but in my agitated state I could almost hear the voice of Edwin Stroud cutting through the mental static, calling me back into the pages of *My One Redeeming Affliction*. I turned to where I'd left Esther planning to send back the pearl to William after his oyster hoax.

Esther returned to the Ionian during morning-tea service, hoping William would be too busy to engage her in conversation. When he finally appeared at reception he went one better by pretending not to recognise her. 'The dining room has reached its full capacity,' he said. 'May I suggest the fernery? They have a butterfly cake so light it's been known to fly away.'

'I've no time for any more of your foolish tricks,' she said. 'The ruse with the pearl was quite enough, and I've come only to return it.'

'Would your procrastination in doing so betray a degree of reluctance?'

'No, sir. Only the unpleasant nature of the task.' The conversation developed into something of a tennis match, Esther returning each of William's shots with interest until finally he agreed to take the pearl, on the condition she accept his invitation to join him for a stroll the following Saturday. Conscious of the line forming behind her, she capitulated.

Independence, boldness and determination: these three qualities Esther hoped to convey with her choice of dress for the walk. The bodice featured five gold-buttoned navy bands down its centre, from which rose wide diagonal mulberry stripes. William was rendered speechless when they met at the grand staircase of the Emporium. Whether by the militaristic nature of her attire or the presence of her brother Samuel is a contested element of the story. But if my father was disappointed by the prospect of a young chaperone, he disguised it by making the boy feel most welcome, asking if he'd visited the Market Carnival.

'Never,' Samuel said.

'Very well. Our destination has been decided. We shall descend to the lower reaches, where a thousand earthly delights await.'

Esther had earlier imagined they would be listening to a ten-piece German band or promenading through the Botanic Gardens, and was irked that William had not sought her approval to visit the markets. Though she figured at least she'd be less likely to encounter one of her friends there. And, as the trio descended the spiralling stairwell of oxblood-and-duck-egg tiles into the swelling laughter and chatter of the masses, the dreadfully delicious excitement of venturing somewhere slightly dangerous coursed through her being.

Millions of tiny particles from hessian sacks, corn husks and animal hides were made visible by the almost horizontal beams of golden light piercing the western windows. The dying sun, like Midas, anointed the captain and coal lumper, refined lady and sugar-refinery worker, rogue, dandy and dowager without favour, turning them all into gold. Tales of larrikins, pickpockets and gap-toothed prostitutes frequenting the Market Carnival had done little to hinder its success. Leading Esther and Samuel on a snaking route between the fruit and vegetable stalls on a carpet of pulped cabbage leaves, William nodded at two of the Chinese vendors, Ah To and Lin Cheong, the men he'd met a decade earlier on the goldfields.

'I see you're acquainted with the stallholders,' Esther said.

'Johnny and Mac are my best suppliers. Their tomatoes are without peer.'

Passing through the flower market, Esther's arm was snapped at by two geese in a wicker cage held aloft by their new owner.

'Don't mind me beauties,' the unravelling woman cackled. 'They'll be stuffin' me pillers soon as I get 'em 'ome.'

Eventually the trio reached the other end of the carnival, where spruikers and hawkers were vying for custom.

'Sav-a-deloys! Sav-a-deloys! Come try, come buy sav-a-deloys!'

'Yes, please!' Samuel said to his sister.

'It might upset your stomach.'

'Nonsense,' William said, laughing. 'A carnival is hardly a carnival without taking your chance on a mystery bag.'

The sausage man snapped his tongs in the air like a crab with metal pincers then retrieved two savs from the boiler, dropped them in a bun and smeared them with butter and mustard. The man and boy made a race of their consumption, William claiming first place with a gob of yellow mustard still on his moustache.

'One of the lesser dangers of eating from a stall,' he said, and removed the offending morsel with his tongue. 'Now that we've been fortified, it's time to put your marksmanship to the test, young man.' He steered Samuel to the shooting gallery.

Having never used a real rifle before, the boy was unprepared for the kickback, which near dislocated his shoulder. William showed Samuel the correct way of handling, and on his third shot he managed to hit the corner of a playing card. Selecting a duelling pistol for himself, William shot out the heart, diamond and spade at the centre of three aces. The operator pulled a sovereign from the leather pouch tucked beneath his overhanging belly. 'Don't hurry back,' he said. 'You'll send me and the family to the poorhouse.'

Further along, a crowd had gathered around a raised platform where a white-bearded man was promoting the benefits of a shilling shock from Lady Volta. 'Reanimate torpid limbs!' he hollered. 'Improve circulation! What about you, sir?' He pointed his cane at William.

'A shilling shock may be just the thing I need,' he said and started for the stage, but Esther caught his elbow.

'To think you'd pay to be electrocuted in public,' she said. 'You need to have your head read.'

Unwilling to have his prized catch so easily stolen, the spruiker said, 'Has virility abandoned you in the hour of need, sir?' The outstretched cane magically lost its rigidity and drooped to the floor, causing the crowd to convulse with laughter.

'Bawdy scoundrel,' William said, raising a fist. 'I'll knock your block right off!'

'Please, Mr Stroud,' Esther said. 'Not in front of the boy.'

'You're absolutely right.' They walked away from the spruiker's platform, then William pulled the sovereign from his pocket and asked Samuel, 'Head or tails?'

The boy called tails and won the coin.

'Spend it however you choose,' William said. 'On the proviso that you stay well away from Lady Volta and any other attraction that may place your soul in mortal danger. Meet us at the main entrance in thirty minutes.' His wink, like a starter's pistol, sent the boy dashing.

'I wish you hadn't,' Esther said, trying to see over the crowd. 'That was an extravagance disproportionate to his sense. He's only fourteen.'

'An age when men go to sea.'

'Others reach thirty and still behave like boys.'

'Marvellous, isn't it?' He smiled, then raised a brow. 'Did you really mean what you said about my need for cranial examination? Because I've been toying with the idea of visiting Dr Eisler for some time.'

'Who is Dr Eisler?'

'A professor of phrenology. Apparently he's very accurate and highly esteemed.'

'Who says?'

'Well, he does,' William said, pointing to the sign.

DR MARTIN EISLER
PROFESSOR OF PHRENOLOGY AND MESMERISM
VERY ACCURATE AND HIGHLY ESTEEMED
DESTRUCTIVE AND HABITUAL BEHAVIOURS INSTANTLY ALLEVIATED

Reminded of my session with Dr Limberg at the end of my first week at Crestfield, I closed the book. Online I calculated that a gold sovereign in the late nineteenth century would've been worth about $170 in today's currency. William sure paid a hefty price to make Samuel scram so that he could crack on to his sister. The kid was obviously destined for serious trouble with that kind of coin in his pocket.

CLAWED NEON

On Tuesday afternoon, Ms Tarasek asked us to write an essay comparing the depiction of the female form in a sculpture (the Venus of Willendorf), a painting (Botticelli's *The Birth of Venus*) and a photograph (*Madonna Flexing Muscles in Conical Bra* by Jean-Paul Gaultier). On completion, we discussed our thoughts with our collaboration partners.

'Madonna's photo conveys a provocative duality,' Isa said. 'Wearing underwear on the outside, she appears simultaneously vulnerable and powerful. It's soft and pink but structured and protective, like armour. The pointy bra is weapon-like. She's flaunting her sexuality, but making sure you know that she's in control. It was a revolutionary feminist statement that effected a shift in popular culture thirty years ago.'

'Before we were born.'

'I've been thinking about the project,' Isa said. 'I was dismissive of your idea because I'd decided we were doing mine. Now I've realised you can't force your vision on someone.'

'Exactly.'

'They'd only sulk and become resentful, and might even sabotage it. There's no point proceeding if somebody turns into Grouchy McGrouch.'

'Am I Grouchy McGrouch?'

'You don't have to be, because I'm willing to drop my idea and go with yours.'

'That's considerate but unnecessary, because I'm fully committed to your idea now.'

'Typical male strategy. You fight to get your own way and when it happens, you pretend you never wanted it.'

'Sorry, I don't remember the fighting part?'

'You're so contrary,' Isa said.

'Okay, hold that thought.' I fetched the atomic-orange knitting from my bag and laid it in front of her. 'It's not great because I've never knitted before. My nana taught me.'

Isa picked it up and wiggled her finger through one of the holes. 'It's amazing,' she said.

'I know it's not. I dropped a lot of stitches.'

'I meant it's amazing that you learnt to knit from your nana and proved me wrong.'

'It was just for practice.' I rolled up the knitting.

'No way. We're putting it up tomorrow morning, before there's anybody around. Let's meet for a coffee at International Velvet and figure out what to tag.'

'I don't drink coffee.'

'Now's the time to start. Bring your knitting and I'll bring everything to attach it. All we need is a name for our crew.'

'Our crew? There's only two of us.'

'Well, think up an alias for yourself.' Isa shot a smile at me and a light switched on behind her eyes, revealing their colour properly for the first time. They're not just green – hazel lines radiate from the pupils like trees.

'What are you staring at?' she said.

'It's like standing in the middle of a forest – your eyes, I mean.'

'It's called central heterochromia, according to Tibor. But I prefer your description.'

*

Wednesday morning at seven, I chained my bike to a pole outside International Velvet. Isa was sitting in a corner booth wearing a black t-shirt and dark sunglasses. She gave me the subtle two-finger wave preferred by secret agents. I slid into the booth beside her.

'You're in school uniform,' she said. 'I thought we should dress incognito in case we get sprung. Have you got an alias?'

'Working from the craft angle I came up with Mammoth Woolly, which I think is kind of funny.' I paused, noticing her frown. 'But you don't?'

'It's okay.' Isa was already onto a cappuccino, so I ordered a macchiato because it sounded like the serious shit.

'What about Clawed Neon?'

'Aren't they sign-makers?'

'Clawed with a "w".'

'Clawed Neon. It's got a punk vibe – I like it. I'm Dawn Sparrowfart.'

'*The* Dawn Sparrowfart – Vice President of the Country Women's Association?'

'Exactly.'

The waitress delivered a miniature cup of coffee crowned with a tiny pad of froth. 'Macchiato?' she said. It was super strong and bitter but I drank it without sugar, hoping to appear hardcore.

'Coffee moustache,' Isa said, and handed me a napkin.

We split the bill and went to scope out our first target. Isa found a pole near the back entrance of the teachers' car park and measured the circumference. 'Perfect,' she said.

'Couldn't we find somewhere less prominent?'

'That defeats the purpose. Pass me the knitting.' She wrapped it around the pole and, starting from the top, began to sew the edges together. 'This pole has been signless for years. Today we're reactivating it with a new message for everybody who passes.'

'What will it say?'

'Good morning, teachers and pupils of Crestfield Academy. Welcome to a new day of mutual enlightenment. Dare something worthy!' A Land Rover tooted, kids waving from the back window as

158

it passed. 'Shit, Lincoln! You're supposed to be on lookout. Give me some warning next time.'

'What are you going to do – jump behind the fence?'

'It's seven-thirty. Teachers will be arriving soon.'

'Sew faster.'

'Would you like to take over?'

'You're doing fine.'

'Go and keep watch on the corner.'

Despite my initial reluctance to go along with Isa's idea, I was enjoying the slightly subversive nature of the mission. The possibility of being caught was giving me a thrilling tingle not unlike tonguing the terminals of a nine-volt battery. I went down to the corner and called out every car that turned into our street. Isa finished before any teacher arrived.

'That looks hectic,' I said, inspecting her work.

'Well done, you.' She took a selfie of us in front of the pole with her phone then, while I was taking one with mine, I spotted a car coming up the street.

'White Econovan at three o'clock!'

'It's Maintenance. Act normal!' The car turned into the entrance and the driver's window slid down.

'Early again?' Jespersen said to me. 'What's this?'

I told him it was an art project and asked him to keep our identity secret. He touched the side of his nose then pointed to a security camera mounted beneath the eave of New Block.

'We're toast,' I said as Jespersen drove into the car park.

'Relax. Tibor told me it doesn't work.' Isa waved to the camera then curtsied.

With time to kill, we sat in the seniors' area planning our next hit. Isa randomly asked if I was scared of Nads.

'Of course not,' I said.

'I used to be scared of him.'

'Why?'

'Middle of last year he started following me around a lot. He'd come up really close to talk and it made my skin crawl.'

'He has no concept of personal space.'

'This was something different. He'd put his hand on me and pat me like I was an animal. It was creepy and intimidating. Has he ever spoken about me?'

'Not really,' I lied. 'Why?'

'Last year, when Phoenix and Mullows got together, Nads arrogantly assumed I'd be interested and the four of us could hang out. Cosy. I knocked him back three times. Then, one day after school, he caught my train to Erskineville. Thank God I was with Pericles. He lives at Marrickville but got off early to ensure I was safe. Nads followed us all the way to my street without speaking, so Pez turned around and told him to piss off.'

'Was there a fight?'

'Nads started ranting like a maniac, insanely jealous of Pez even though there was nothing between us. He needed a reason to explain my rejection other than his ugly personality. He kept shoving Pez in the chest, but Pez stood his ground. Nads punched him in the stomach then kneed him in the groin. Pez collapsed onto the footpath and Nads walked off laughing.'

That was a completely different version from the one Nads had told. And, after having witnessed his brutal treatment of Starkey with the billiard ball and their violation of the old man's rose garden, Isa's story was infinitely more believable. This new development tripled my anxiety about what might happen when they returned from their suspension.

When I got home from school I finally started reading *Frankenstein*, and though the story within a story was a little confusing at first, I became totally engrossed. Late at night I reached the passage where the monster sees his reflection in a pool of water for the first time. His realisation that he looked a bit worse than grotesque broke my heart. The poor bastard was made up of scraps from the slaughter yards.

SLIPPING THE TONGUE

After school on Thursday I had my first shift at Give Me the Juice. Pericles' Uncle Manos was short and barrel-chested, with massive guns from lifting melons. He never stopped smiling. His eldest son, Sam, was tall and serious and bore no resemblance to him. Pericles' twin sisters, Helena and Christina, weren't identical but their liberal application of dark eye make-up was. All of them wore a shirt with a different fruit design. I was given the banana shirt, still heavy with the odour of its previous wearer Stavros, whose badge Manos asked me to keep pinned on until I got my own. After my induction he said goodbye, leaving Sam in charge.

The first two hours were hectic. Sam and Pericles made juices and smoothies while the twins worked the counter. I wiped surfaces and rinsed containers with a high-pressure-hose gun. When service slowed, Pericles taught me how to make the drinks. It wasn't rocket science, but the ingredients had to be measured and added in the correct order. 'It might be stating the obvious,' Pericles said, 'but don't forget to secure the lid before blending.' He started untying his apron. 'I'm taking my break now. Will you be okay on your own?'

'A hundred per cent.'

The first three smoothies went smoothly. But making the fourth, a Boomberrytastic, I got distracted by the customer banging on about her nut allergy and pushed SURGE before securing the lid. >FWOOSH!< A crimson geyser hit the ceiling and splattered my shirt in pulped berries and frozen yoghurt.

'Berries go boom!' the twins said in unison. The customer looked like she'd witnessed a drive-by shooting.

I was still mopping up when Pericles returned and said, 'I leave you for ten minutes and you've destroyed the joint.'

'I forgot to secure the lid.'

'Obviously, malaka!' He cuffed the back of my head.

Despite the spill, Pericles was more chill than he was at school. When Sam took his extended break and left Pericles and me to make the drinks, we fell into a rhythm. The last two hours flew by. At 8.45, Sam told me I wasn't required for close but I offered to stay and help anyway.

'You won't be paid for it,' he said.

'Not a problem,' I said, and winked at Pericles. It was the least I owed him.

Dad had gone to bed by the time I arrived home, exhausted. Unusually, he'd left a message on a post-it note, saying that he was proud of my initiative and Pop Locke would've been too. Brushing and flossing my teeth, I felt a sense of relief that things might be settling at last.

I climbed into bed and felt a heavy drowsiness, the reward for performing physical labour. Then, right on the threshold of sleep, Homunculus whispered, 'Your shirt needs to be washed, Stavros.' I dragged my arse out of bed and carried my satchel to the laundry. Reaching in for the shirt, I felt something soft and fleshy. I tipped over the satchel. A mottled pink-and-grey thing resembling the bastard spawn of Alien dropped onto the tiles with a >THWAP<.

The sight and not-exactly-fresh smell of the amorphous, hairless creature instantly triggered dry-retching, propelling me to the balcony for fresh air. While out there recovering, I became concerned that the creature, though it lacked any obvious means of ambulation, might slither away and conceal itself somewhere in the apartment

162

like an air-conditioning duct. Recalling that a liberal sprinkling of salt can kill a leech, I armed myself with a box of pink Himalayan crystals and returned to the laundry. But the thing hadn't moved. It was still there, stuck to my shirt on the tiles. I prodded it with a mop handle and there was no response. Thinking it was dead, I knelt for a closer inspection.

It looked like a tongue – definitely not human, possibly bovine. I googled 'cow tongue' and it matched the images. Identification brought no relief. Fearing it might've come from a mad cow, I washed my hands with soap then antiseptic gel. How long had I been toting it around for? And how the hell had it entered my bag? I needed somebody to help me deal with it. I could hear Dad snoring. Maybe Pericles was still up? I turned my phone back on and found an SMS from an unknown number:

THIS IS WHAT WE DO TO INFORMERS!

My life had turned into a psychological thriller. Who'd sent the message? Probably Nads, or Starkey following his orders. He's like a trained dog that occasionally bites its master. But how had he slipped the tongue in without being seen? Everybody knows he's suspended. There's no way he'd been anywhere near Crestfield. And I'd had my satchel with me all day.

The message was sent at 7.47 pm. I thought back over my shift. At 7.30 I'd gone for my break at Hungry Jack's and later left my satchel under the table to refill my drink. I remembered it feeling heavier when I left. Where did he get the tongue? It was too big for a can. Do butchers sell fresh cow tongue? Maybe they're back in fashion because of a *MasterChef* challenge? Who do those three think they are – the Crestfield fricking mafia? They were probably at Nads' place now, having a laugh about it.

'Or maybe Starkey followed you home?' Homunculus said.

'There's no way Vince would let him in, and the lift wouldn't work if he did.'

'So stop panicking.'

163

'Fear can only survive if you feed it.'

'Correct. It must be confronted and destroyed,' he said. 'Go down-stairs and check if there's anybody lurking outside the building.'

I took the lift down to the lobby. Vince was on night shift. He asked why I was heading out so late and I told him I was buying milk. As I walked around the block, I saw nothing more antisocial than a businessman pissing against a wall in Pennys Lane, which hardly qual-ifies as unusual behaviour in this hood.

'You forgot the milk,' Vince said with a wink.

'All out,' I said and took the lift back up.

Defying my squeamishness I picked up the tongue, which was surpris-ingly rough, wrapped it in the real-estate section of the *Sydney Morning Herald* then dropped it down the garbage chute. I calmed myself with a breathing exercise and remembered that I still hadn't washed the shirt. I returned to the apartment's laundry, threw my shirt in the machine and selected HEAVY DUTY to kill any residual bacteria.

I got back into bed about 1 am. Three seconds after my head hit the pillow, Homunculus piped up yet again. 'How dare that slimy little nicotine-stained-fingered shady shithole try to intimidate you with a cow tongue! Get up and call that number and don't listen to any bullshit alibi.'

Without fully considering the wisdom of doing so, I called the number. It rang and rang. I was just about to cancel when somebody answered.

'HELLO?' he said.

'I KNOW YOU PUT THE TONGUE IN MY BAG.'

'WHAT THE FUCK? WHO IS THIS?'

'DROP THE FAKE VOICE – I KNOW IT'S YOU. IT'S NOT MY FAULT YOU GOT BUSTED. I DIDN'T TELL ANYBODY.'

'WHO IS THIS?'

'WHO IS THIS?' I mimicked his deep, gravelly tone. 'WHO DO YOU THINK IT IS? MARY FRICKIN' POPPINS? YOUR SCARE TACTICS HAVE FAILED AND IF YOU EVER PULL ANOTHER STUNT LIKE THAT, I'LL CALL THE POLICE.'

'DON'T THREATEN ME YOU LITTLE ****!' He called me a name that wasn't Chester Hunt but started with a C and ended with U-N-T. 'I DON'T KNOW WHO THE HELL YOU ARE, TALKING CRAZY SHIT AND WAKING UP MY WIFE. NEVER CALL THIS NUMBER AGAIN. DO YOU UNDERSTAND ME, CHESTER HUNT?'

'Yes.'

'SO HELP ME, IF YOU DO I'LL TRACK YOU DOWN AND RIP BOTH YOUR BALLS OUT OF THEIR BAG AND FEED THEM TO THE DUCKS. CHESTER HUNT!'

He hung up.

That hot-head needed anger management counselling, pronto. It definitely wasn't Starkey on the other end – so who was it? Maybe Starkey had swiped someone else's phone so that I couldn't trace him? It wouldn't be his first crack at phone theft.

At 1.30 am, still in a state of high-alert paralysis, I watched a televangelist called Benny Hinn banging on about the end of the world, and even though I agreed that it did indeed seem nigh, I didn't give him any money. If Armageddon really is that close, my meagre financial assistance won't help reverse it.

Friday was the last day of the goons' suspension so I didn't have to deal with them at swim clinic. To practise executing efficient tumble turns, we spent an hour in the pool doing forward rolls over the lane dividers.

Afterwards, Pericles and I headed to the Westfield food hall to eat before our shift. The massive videowall suspended in the atrium was showing footage of beautiful girls in flowing dresses running through a forest in slow motion. The leader turned back and smiled with perfect gleaming teeth, her dewy face taking up the entire screen. She held up her fingers in a peace sign, and the words appeared:

V: THE PRIVATE COLLECTION, BY VIENNA VORONOVA

Pericles was mesmerised. 'Vienna Voronova!' he said. 'The world's most perfect woman.'

'I know. Mum's bringing her out for a launch.'

'Shut your mouth right now! Do you think she could get us in?'

'Maybe,' I said.

We bought some Turkish food and found seats outside. Famished after clinic, Pericles scoffed his kebab then eyed my half-eaten pide. 'What's up?' he said. 'You're looking all around the place like some-body's after you.'

'It's nothing,' I said. Then, realising that the mere threat of having my tongue cut off had effectively silenced me, I told him about my grisly discovery last night and the ensuing phone call.

'Ohmygod, that's fully sick in the most literal sense. You have to report them.'

'They put a tongue in my bag on the assumption that I'd blabbed. Imagine what would happen if I actually reported them and they found out.'

'Maybe a horse's head?' He looked again at my plate. 'Can I have your pide?'

'It's yours.'

Pericles took a massive bite and with his mouth full said, 'We've got to beat them at their own game – intimidation. My cousin Angelo could have a little man-to-man talk with Starkey. Advise him to back off.'

'Don't tell anybody about the tongue. I'm going to act like it never happened and deprive them of knowing it got to me.'

'It's too late.' He wiped the sauce from his mouth. 'You made that mad-arse phone call last night.'

I remained on edge for the entire shift, imagining that I was being observed by one of the goons or maybe a stranger. Instead of offering to help Sam to close again, I left as soon as the clock hit 8.45. I didn't want to stay a second longer than necessary.

I got the train back to Kings Cross Station and warily made my way back home. It was only a minute's walk from there, but a lot can happen in a minute.

166

THE OTHER
BROWN SPOT

Swallowing my last minuscule portion of pride, I returned to Signal Bay on Saturday morning and apologised to Mum for my erratic behaviour and stubbornness. She was still simmering about Starkey's offensive text, so I placated her with the news that I hadn't seen him for a week – conveniently neglecting to mention that it was because he'd been suspended for terrorising a senior citizen. She said I could demonstrate my remorse by mowing the lawn. Out of all possible chores, it was my most dreaded.

Last year when my beloved staffy, Gus, died of heart failure, I pleaded to have him buried in the backyard. Dad eventually gave in and helped me to dig a grave, and I rested my little buddy there in a pillowcase. Watching Dad cover him with earth and tamp it down, while Dougal, the Harrises' foxhound, was crying on the other side of the fence, tore my heart open. Venn had to read my eulogy because I couldn't speak.

The grass now grows brown in a circle above Gus's resting place, and whenever I reach that spot with the mower, Dougal starts howling again. Today I first mowed alongside the decking and then around the Buddha statue. I mowed in straight lines across the yard, avoiding the brown circle – leaving it till last. And the very second that the mower's wheels crossed the demarcation line, Dougal started crying. Today the keening was so loud and high-pitched I couldn't bear it. I cut the engine and finished the job with secateurs. It took me over an hour.

Venn, appreciating the degree of trauma I'd just gone through, poured me an ice-cold glass of organic ginger-and-lemon kombucha. I took it up to my room, thinking that perhaps a little stress-relief session was in order. But before I could even get started, the words from the phrenologist's booth that William and Esther had visited at the Market Carnival appeared in my mind's eye:

DESTRUCTIVE AND HABITUAL BEHAVIOURS INSTANTLY ALLEVIATED

I didn't think rubbing one out was destructive – maybe habitual, but definitely not something I wanted alleviated. Nevertheless, I put it on hold and began reading the next chapter of the book instead.

Dr Eisler was reading a newspaper and smoking a pipe behind an olive gauze curtain. His silhouette revealed a pate as bald as the ceramic bust he used for consultations. 'Shall we rescue him from indolence?' William said. 'Employ his scientific expertise to delve into the workings of my mind?'

'Phrenology is a carnival act performed by tricksters obliged to give glowing assessments of the fools who line their purses. What would you do if he told the truth and exposed some deficiency in your character?' Esther said.

'I'd relieve you of my company immediately and attempt no further contact. Granted, that would be a most disagreeable outcome.'

The curtain was suddenly whipped away.

'Please step inside for a professional consultation,' Eisler said. 'All will be revealed for the modest fee of a shilling, fully refunded if the customer isn't satisfied.'

William removed his hat and reclined on the chaise. Eisler rubbed his hands and performed a preliminary palpation of the patient's cranium. 'I'll now take measurements with my callipers,' he said, opening the steel arms of the instrument to form a teardrop shape and positioning the points above William's ears, causing Esther to laugh.

'Excuse me, but the patient looks utterly ridiculous,' she said.

'The young lady has a point, but please hold still, sir. Accuracy is of the utmost importance.' Eisler measured the twenty-seven regions of William's skull matching those marked on the ceramic bust. He wiped his hands and said, 'Sir, you have a prominent brow, indicating an appreciation of fine art and an aptitude for mathematics.' Working his way from the front of the skull, Eisler gave a positive evaluation of each sector, finally reaching the back. 'The organ of amativeness lies here beneath the occipital bone, and as it is highly pronounced, indicates proficiency in the art of love.'

'Is there any field in which the patient may not excel?' Esther said. 'If those regions are all so prominent, he must have an exceedingly large head.'

'There is one anomaly I haven't mentioned for fear of causing alarm.'

'Fear not,' William said. 'You must reveal all as promised.'

'Very well. The patient's head is long relative to its width. His skull is dolichocephalic, bearing a closer relation to the hound's head than the average man's would.'

'You're not suggesting my ancestors were dogs?'

'Not I, but your own bone structure. Let me demonstrate.' As Eisler reached out to touch his face, William suddenly barked, snapping at the man's hand. Esther cried out in fright.

'Mr Eisler, your science is at best unsound,' William said. 'Nevertheless, I shall forfeit my shilling for an entertaining diversion.' He deposited the coin in the phrenologist's palm and guided Esther out of the booth, checking his fob watch. 'What a dreadful waste of time that was. Your poor brother will be wondering where in the blazes we are.'

Back then my mother gave no credence to the possible scientific merit of phrenology. But years later, during her search for the origin of my affliction, she recalled this story to me. And in a rare instance of wild conjecture, she expressed regret for not having heeded what she suggested might've have been a warning of some bestial peculiarity in my father's form.

So William, the author's father, apparently had a head with similar proportions to that of a dog. I would've asked the phrenologist to specify a breed, because there's a huge difference between the heads of a whippet and a bulldog. And what exactly was Edwin's own affliction? Why was he dragging it out? I remembered nothing dog-like about his appearance in the photographs I saw at the exhibition on my birthday.

Later, in the afternoon, Mum told me that she was heading out at seven and there was zucchini frittata in the fridge.

'Where are you going?' I said.

'Your gorgeous mother is going on her first date.'

'Mother's don't go on dates.'

'Apparently we do.'

'If it's some random meatball you met online, I hope you've worked out a signal to identify each other because he won't look anything like the pictures he's posted – they never do.'

'Thanks for your advice but I've known Grant for eight years. He'll find that amusing.'

'You won't be laughing when that con artist steals your money and you end up talking to Tracy Grimshaw on *A Current Affair* with his seven other victims.'

'Grant doesn't need my money. He's a banker.'

'Of course he is.'

On Sunday night Nana Locke came over for dinner with Tippi. Aside from some whimpering and nervous yaps, Tippi and Oscar both behaved themselves, maintaining a wary distance from one another. I showed Nana the photo of my first foray into yarn-bombing.

'It's lovely,' she said. 'You must've used every ball I gave you.' She squinted at the photo. 'And who's the pretty thing on the other side of the pole? Is she your girlfriend?'

'Definitely not.' I took the phone before she could pass it on to Venn, who had her hand out. 'It's Isa Mountwinter. We're collaborating on the project, and for the record she really annoys me sometimes.'

'The right ones always do, darling. Pop Locke drove me around the bend, God bless him.'

Over crab cakes and scallops I got the impression that Nana Locke knew nothing about Mum's date the night before, so naturally I couldn't resist the urge to drop a few oblique references. 'They say the bank's latest interest-rate hike could mean hard times for struggling families. Possibly even tear them apart.'

Venn glared. 'Since when have you had an interest in finance?'

'Oh, I'm not the one showing interest, am I?'

'Darling, come out and help me in the kitchen for a moment,' Mum said. Out of view, she pincered my cheeks, her manicured nails almost piercing the flesh. 'Button up right now, mister!' Not quite the calibre of a slap in the face, but still highly effective. I didn't speak for the rest of the meal. And it was a long bus ride back to the city, with nothing on my phone capable of distracting me from the dread I felt about Nads, Mullows and Starkey's impending return to Crestfield.

MUSIC TO BLEED TO

On my way to school I imagined the various methods the Brotherhood might employ to remove my tongue. Strangely enough, though, they kept their distance all morning, acting as if I was invisible, which was unnerving in its own way. As if their mind games weren't enough to deal with, at lunchtime Tibor Mintz cornered me in the café queue and asked me point blank why I didn't like him.

'I don't not like you,' I said.

'Since being orientation buddies, you've avoided me. Is that because I'm a nerd-nerd and not a cool nerd like David York? Or is it something like body odour or halitosis? That's bad breath.'

'I hadn't noticed.'

'That's reassuring. I only asked because your sense of smell has been scientifically verified as exceptional.' He walked away. But now that he'd opened a conversation about friendship, I wanted to find out why he let Nads cheat off him in the maths test. So I surrendered my place in the line to follow him to the far side of Old Block, where he sat against the wall and unwrapped a sandwich. 'This area is strictly out of bounds,' he said.

'I know that but I have a question for you, outlaw.' I sat next to him and asked why he and Isa did so much school service. He told me it was a condition of the Millington Drake Scholarship he'd won. Isa was on the Judith Ormerod Scholarship for girls.

'I don't mind the actual work but it does make us stick out.' He took a bite of his curried-egg sandwich. 'People call me Poindexter and Brainiac, which are okay, but I don't like Suck-arse. Evan wrote that on my satchel.' He rewrapped his sandwich and put it away. 'I'm sorry you were stuck with me for an orientation buddy when I don't even fit in to this school.'

'I don't fit in here either.'

'But you're friends with Pericles Pappas and Darvin Naylor and Sean Mulligan and Evan Starkey.'

'Only Pericles. The others are total douchebags.'

Tibor laughed like it was the first time he'd heard the word.

'Why did Nads sit next to you for the maths test?' I said. 'Is there some sort of arrangement between you?'

'He got into Crestfield on sporting ability alone and requires academic assistance. I'm supposed to be his maths mentor, but he only ever shows up to our tutoring sessions before a test.'

'How does he know when they're coming if they're supposed to be a surprise?'

Leaning in close, which was overkill because there was nobody in sight, Tibor whispered, 'Mr Monaro is buddy-buddy with Mr Simmons.'

'So Monaro allows Nads to copy your answers? But why do you let him?'

'I'm afraid not to.'

'Don't worry about Nads and his stooges. They're just bullies.' My attitude was all bravado, though, because I was still terrified they were out to get me. Sure enough, on Tuesday afternoon my fears were realised.

*

I was walking around Rushcutters Bay, enjoying the cool breeze coming off the water, when I saw Starkey leaning against the wall of the Cruising Yacht Club, his slouch unmistakable. I turned to head home, but a hundred metres from the stormwater canal I spotted Mullows sitting on an exercise bench. I veered towards the road but Nads emerged from the roots of a giant Port Jackson fig, rocking with folded arms, in a dodgy imitation of a hip-hop gangster. I aimed for the gap between him and Mullows, but the goons converged. Pretending I'd just noticed them, I waved.

'Where do you think you're going?' Nads said.

'Home.'

'We've got a meeting of the Brotherhood.'

'I'm more of a lone wolf, really. I want out.'

'Not your decision. We trusted you and you blabbed to the Dash – told him we scared the old codger. I don't give a rat's tight arsehole about my reputation, but my parents do.'

I shrugged. Nads clutched my collar, the other two standing back, Mullows with jutting chin, Starkey narrowing his eyes and looking mean as hell.

'The thing that really pisses me off is you've fucked up our weekends till the end of term,' Nads said.

I tried to protest my innocence, but he roared in my face.

'You don't scare me,' I squeaked.

'Liar,' Starkey said. 'You're one fart away from crapping yourself.'

'I kn-kn-know it was you that put the tongue in my bag.'

Starkey flickered his tongue between the V of his fingers. 'Ba-la-la-la-la. You're tripping, mate.'

'Enough,' Nads said. 'The time has come to throw you out officially.'

A cork to the back of my knee from a fourth, unseen assailant dropped me to the ground. He and Starkey grabbed my arms, Nads and Mullows my legs, and they carried me up the embankment. Twisting my head, I saw that their apprentice thug was Byron Paget, the tyre-puncturing expert. The four of them dropped me on the hard, barely grassed earth, and a surge of defiance rose in me.

'If you're going to do it, then do it,' I said.

Starkey replied with a kick to my waist that winded me.

'Take it easy,' Mullows said. And I hated him for the pathetic degree of mercy he showed without having a second ball in his bag to stop them.

They picked me up and swung me in time to their count. 'ONE! . . . TWO! . . .' I relaxed all of the muscles in my body. 'THREE!' They released me and I flew up, up into the sky. In the moment before gravity reclaimed me, I lost my resolve and stiffened. Then I dropped.

And one point.

A pin –

Pricked a balloon.

A dart –

Hit a bullseye.

A stone –

Struck a windscreen.

The tip –

Of my tailbone met the flat, hard earth.

A full stop.

My body was shattered.

Delirious with pack violence, the thugs came lolloping down the slope, Nads ruffling Paget's bowl cut, Starkey filming on his phone. Mullows reached me first.

'Run!' he said. And I did, like an antelope that was wounded but thankfully still faster than the lions.

Over the bridge, around the cricket ground, past Reg Bartley's grandstand and the tennis courts, up the lane, past St Luke's. Terrace houses, cafés, shoppers blurred. I tripped on a poodle's leash, knocked over stools, apologised. Dashed up a side lane and emerged in familiar territory: red wall, substation, car park, pay-toilet panic-room – two dollars' entry. Thank God for the gold coin in my pocket. I kissed Her Majesty and dropped her into the slot. Open sesame.

>WELCOME TO ROBOLOO,
YOUR PREMIUM AUTOMATED
HYGIENE SOLUTION.
TO LOCK DOOR, PUSH THE RED BUTTON.
TO OPEN DOOR, PUSH THE GREEN BUTTON.
TOILET FLUSHES AUTOMATICALLY.<

I smashed the red and sat on the can, chest burning. The acute-stabbing, dull-throbbing pain in my tailbone brought me close to vomiting. I held back, fearing my lungs would rise on the surge of chunky acid, fall out and slap onto the tiles, still trying to breathe on their own.

Then there was elevator music. A soothing electronic melody from the easy-listening album *Songs to Bleed to*. 'What the world needs now is love, sweet love.' Never more true.

The cabin revolved. My mouth tasted metallic. My ears burnt. My vision shimmered and faded to black.

>BANG! BANG! BANG!<

I came to.

>BANG! BANG! BANG!<

A voice on the other side – Starkey.

'We know how much you like hanging out in public toilets, but when you come out we're going to smash the living shit out of you.'

I stood and the toilet flushed itself. I drank water from the nozzle in the wall recess then read the sign: WATER NOT POTABLE. DO NOT DRINK!

With my ear against the door, I could hear my assailants talking outside but couldn't make out what they were saying. Then I heard a horn tooting.

>peep!<
>PEEP! PEEP!<
>PEEP! PEEP! PEEP!<

A red light began flashing. The writing beneath it said

MAXIMUM TIME LIMIT: 15 MINUTES
AUTOMATIC CLEANING CYCLE
WILL COMMENCE 1 MINUTE AFTER
RED LIGHT FLASHES
PLEASE VACATE IMMEDIATELY

Time flies when you're unconscious.

I couldn't decide whether to push green and run, or take my chance with the cleaning cycle.

The beep was piercing and continuous.

>WARNING! MAXIMUM TIME LIMIT HAS BEEN EXCEEDED. CLEANING CYCLE WILL NOW COMMENCE.<

Steel panels on the walls receded. Fifty or sixty small but menacing nozzles telescoped from the gaps. I assumed the brace position, covering my face.

>FWISHHHHHHHHH!<

Jets of hot water, focused and high-pressured, tattooed every inch of my exposed skin. Thirty seconds of industrial-grade excoriation later, they stopped.

ROBOloo had said cleaning *cycle*, so I kept my head down and waited. The nozzles buzzed, shifted angle and sprayed disinfectant, stinging my already stinging arms and legs. A cold rinse followed, then the jets puckered and shrank like metal cunje. Momentary silence, then clicking and whirring that built to a cyclonic howl as every droplet of water was sucked through the floor grate.

I was saturated, skin burning, ears ringing, knee bleeding worse than before. I checked my reflection in the metal mirror. Dulled by scratches, it made me look soft-edged, as if I was disappearing. Above the mirror was graffiti scrawled in black marker:

and beneath it in blue:

SO ARE YOU!

>CLICK!<
>THANK YOU FOR VISITING ROBOLOO, YOUR PREMIUM AUTOMATED HYGIENE SOLUTION. PLEASE VISIT AGAIN SOON. DOOR OPENING.<

I stepped back into the world, half-expecting to discover it had changed in my absence – but it hadn't, except for the appearance of the crazy old hermit, sitting on his electric chariot right outside the ROBOloo doors.

'You're wet,' he chuckled through a wheeze. Turns out he'd seen the goons chasing me and followed them to the automatic dunny. 'Figured they'd corralled you in that newfangled lav,' he said.

'Not my proudest moment.'

'Bad eggs, that lot. You should steer clear.'

'It's not that easy.'

'Bunkum!' He swatted the air. 'They'll stop making mischief soon enough, believe you me. I reported them to the school principal.'

'Well, that certainly helped the situation.'

'Didn't report you, though,' he said, holding up a finger. 'Figured you weren't one of 'em. Cut from a different cloth, you are. Shouldn't be knocking round with 'em. Bad eggs, that lot.'

'I'd better get home now. See ya.' I turned and started walking.

'Hold your horses!' he said, and scooted up to me. 'You're bleeding like the buggery.'

'I'll be right, thanks.'

'Come here!' He pulled a crumpled handkerchief from his pocket. 'Don't screw up your nose. I washed it Monday. Hold still now.' He tied it around my knee. 'There you go. Right as rain.' Blood darkened the pale, yellowed cloth in seconds.

'Your hanky's ruined.'

'Never mind about that, boyo. Just make sure to untie it when you get home, put some antiseptic on your leg. Don't want it dropping off.'

I inspected the hanky more closely. 'What does the B. M. stand for?'

'Bert McGill. Ruby's handiwork. She was my better half. Sewed it on so I wouldn't forget.' He clears his throat. 'Miss Daisy can give you a ride. Hop on the back and hold tight.'

'No thanks. I can walk.'

'Suit yourself then.' He pulled a tight one-eighty and rolled off, yelling, 'Stay away from those hooligans! They're bad eggs.'

Safely back at the apartment, I rinsed my knee, applied Betadine© to it and the nub, put long loose pants on and soaked Bert's hanky. Dad came home and cooked Mum's fettuccine alfredo and served me an enormous plateful. It was bland and stodgy – depressingly unlike the original.

'What's the matter with you?' he said.

'Nothing.'

'Sit still and eat then, instead of pushing your food around.'

I couldn't sit still, though, because the nub must've swollen to twice its size and demanded constant repositioning to minimise the agonising throb that was making me wince.

'I emailed your mother for the recipe specially, because I know you like it. But the look on your face is telling me something else.'

'It's great,' I said, and forced myself to eat the entire load.

After dinner I went to my room and read an account of an assault on Esther's kid brother, Samuel, nineteenth-century style. Synchronicity through the ages.

Esther and William found Samuel crouched against a stone lion at the bottom of the entrance stairs, blood from his swollen nose pooling between his feet. He told them that three Ultimo larrikins had clobbered him. William insisted on reporting the matter to the police, but the boy assured him that his injuries were minor and he still had the sovereign.

'Here it is,' he said, smiling through blood-stained teeth as he proffered the coin.

'Put that away,' William said. 'You deserve ten more for resisting those brutes.'

In fact, there had been only one assailant. Samuel had met him while waiting in line for Monsieur LaSalle's Enchanting Tableaux Vivants, a titillating show featuring famous artworks recreated by groupings of scantily clad artist's models and dancers – all required by law to remain perfectly still, on threat of the attraction's closure. The larrikin had convinced Samuel he looked too young for admission, and offered to swap boots for his higher heels. As Samuel was untying his laces behind the calliope, however, he'd lunged for his back pocket. A scuffle ensued, with Samuel copping most of the blows, his cries muffled by the jaunty tune from the steam organ.

Dora Hinkley, Fernleigh's housekeeper, had been visiting the Waxworks on her monthly afternoon off. Overcome by the grotesque displays in the Chamber of Horrors, she'd sought refuge on a chair near the calliope, hoping the gay music would expunge the scenes from her mind. Instead, she was shocked to see her young master in conversation with a larrikin. When the hooligan leapt upon him, she felt powerless to intervene and so remained hidden behind a palm until the assailant left. On returning home she reported the incident to Professor Hunnicutt, stopping short of revealing what Samuel had been lining up for.

The following day Hunnicutt pressed his son to give a full confession. In complying, Samuel revealed that William Stroud – a man whom his father had heard of, but never in connection to his daughter – had given him a sovereign to make himself scarce. Hunnicutt's anger was hardly assuaged by Samuel's confession that he'd been waiting in line for such a dubious spectacle. Hunnicutt called Esther to his study and condemned her for failure of moral obligation. And he forbade her from ever seeing William again.

Esther wrote in her diary that, up until the night of her father's chastisement, she'd been ambivalent about her feelings towards William. But the injunction had the effect of making him seem irresistibly attractive, igniting a passion that would not be easily extinguished.

I continued reading till I fell into a restless sleep. Unable to remain on my back or side for any length of time, I lay on my stomach but found it difficult to breathe. Throughout the night I was woken, frantic and soaked in sweat, by a recurring dream of my assault seamlessly merged with Samuel's beating.

SARAH BELLUM

This morning, my nub was so swollen I couldn't ride my bike to school. I tried to act normally, but between periods Cheyenne Piper asked me why I was walking with a carrot up my arse.

'I've just been to Woolworths and forgot to take a bag.'

'Freak.'

I couldn't sit still in Geography, and was constantly shifting from left to right butt cheek.

'What's up, man?' Pericles said. 'The goons get you?'

'Goons got me good. But swear on your life you won't tell anybody. I don't want this coming back around to bite me.'

At lunchtime I went to the library toilets to check the lump. The swelling had increased again. The nub had become an arsey knoll, with a disturbing new topography – an elevation of perhaps seven or eight millimetres. There was absolutely no way I could get in the pool now that the risk of it being spotted had doubled. I found Pericles and asked him to tell Simmons I was unwell, then went to the sick bay. Nurse Nola gave me a dubious look when I said I had a migraine.

'Don't they all?' She applied a plastic strip thermometer to my forehead and read the temperature. 'A wee bit high. What's happened to your knee, love?'

'I grazed it climbing a wall yesterday.'

'It's weeping.' She cleaned the wound, applied a dressing and led me to a room with a plastic-sheeted bed. 'Take off your shoes and rest now.' The lights dimmed and, facedown, I drifted off to sleep, carried by Enya singing 'Orinoco Flow'. *Sail away . . .*

I dreamt of six lovely ladies in almost see-through dresses dancing through a forest filled with butterflies, joined by Vienna Voronova. The advertisement on the Westfield videowall had come to life and I became a part of it. I tried following the girls but my feet were blocks of concrete and the girls drifted away from me in slow motion, Vienna's lustrous hair rippling in golden waves. 'Stop!' I yelled. Vienna turned and gazed into my eyes. Euphoria bloomed like a time-lapse rose, releasing an intoxicating scent that drew me closer. I couldn't stop sniffing, deeper and deeper. The corners of her mouth stretched impossibly wide, then her lips parted to reveal her two front teeth were missing. The image shocked me out of my slumber.

'It's all right,' a female voice said from somewhere above me. I was still lying facedown.

'Is that you, Vienna?'

'No, it's Isa. You were groaning so I came in to check on you. It's almost home time and Nurse Nola said you can leave if you're feeling better.'

I was annoyed that Isa had replaced Vienna. I wiped the drool from my mouth, turned onto my side and pushed myself up onto my elbows. The pressure on the nub was beyond excruciating.

'What's the matter?'

'Nothing. I'm just a bit tender.'

'Good news – I've figured out our next yarn-bombing mission.'

'Can you text me later? I've got something really important to do.'

'Sure,' she said, a little miffed, and left me alone.

Despite having soaked Bert's hanky overnight, it still had a rusty taint. I walked down to the junkyard and found him around the back, sitting on his blow-up ring on the armchair, drinking a longneck. Beside him was a metal plant stand holding two ceramic bowls, one containing walnuts and one full of shells.

'Here's the young lad that was trapped in the gents,' he said to Percy, then turned to me. 'What brings you to my neck of the woods, squire, or should that be squirrel if it's nuts you're gathering?'

'I came to return your hanky.'

'Ruby would be pleased. She sewed the monogram. A stitch in time saves nine in the event of losing your handkerchief – so thank you, chief.'

'Was Ruby your wife?'

'Thought we'd established that? Ruby was my wife but I drove her away. Carnival's over well and good now.'

'Is she not alive?'

'What is this, an interrogation? No kid, she's not alive. She's singing with the angels.'

'Sorry . . .' I said, then, to dispel the awkwardness, 'Um, I brought your hanky back.'

'Where'd you find that, then?'

'You tied it around my knee.'

''Course I did.' He tossed me a walnut from the bowl and handed me a miniature silver dagger. I stuck it into the crack but couldn't prise the shell apart.

'Twist it,' he said.

I pressed so hard the knife slipped from the dimpled shell and jabbed my left palm. 'Ow! Are you sure this was made for opening walnuts?'

'Oysters,' he said, snatching the knife. He stuck it into the walnut's seam and flicked the top off, leaving the meat sitting neatly in its cup. He held it up to me. 'What does that look like to you? Tell me, lad, what does it resemble? First thing that comes into your *mind*. That's a clue, boy – a clue.'

'A brain, I suppose?'

'Once a girl called Sarah Bellum, wrote her will on fancy vellum, guillotined in February, lost her head but didn't tell 'em.'

'One of your own?' I said.

184

'Course not, duffer. Read this.' He handed me the bowl of shells. The rhyme was written in fancy lettering around the rim. 'Tip out the shrapnel,' he said. I did as instructed, and saw on the base an image of a girl with rosy cheeks and blue-ribboned hair. She'd been decapitated.

'Who was Sarah Bellum?' I said.

'What do they teach you young ones at that institution? Hold here for a minute. I've got something to show you.'

In his absence I examined the oyster-shucking knife. The handle was engraved with tiny sea creatures and the word 'Ionian'. Right away I recalled that Edwin Stroud's father William had owned a Greek restaurant of that name. *And* he'd used a silver shucking knife to open the oyster shell that concealed the pink pearl.

'Could this be the actual knife he used?' I said to Percy. No response from the stuffed bird. Then, as if the coincidence of Bert owning the knife wasn't enough to freak me right out, he reappeared carrying a white ceramic head.

'Who were you talking to?' he said.

'Just the bird.' I pointed at the head. 'What's that?'

'Something a phrenologist used to measure your noggin.' He pointed to a region above the ear labelled 'Destructiveness'. 'For instance, that section of a hooligan's bonce would be larger than your average Joe's.'

'Does it work?'

'Mumbo jumbo. Brought it out to show you something else. The top bit, called the cerebrum – it's made of four lobes.' He turned the head around. 'Tucked under there at the back is the cerebellum. Sarah Bellum. Do you get it now?'

'Yeah, I get it.' I inspected the back of the head more closely, remembering William and Esther's visit to Dr Eisler. 'It says "Amativeness" there. What does that mean?'

'Don't know everything.' He touched the corresponding section of his own head just behind his ear and rubbed it. 'Nothing there anymore. Now, stop asking me questions and get on your way.'

*

Dad was held back at work with a GravyLog® executive, so I made us a vegetarian salad. An hour later, when he'd come home and we were eating in front of the television, he said, 'Nice entrée, but what's for the main course? My body needs protein and so does yours. You've been hobbling around like a cripple again. We need to build you up.'

He went out and bought two Scotch fillets from Coles, fried them and served them bleeding on a plate with nothing but a slathering of horseradish cream. I gave silent thanks to the cow for giving me its flesh involuntarily, then contradicted my reverence by consuming it shamefully fast.

At 11 pm, Isa messaged me.

ISA   Hey clawed neon!
ME   Hey dawn sparrowfart!
ISA   Sorry for disturbing you
ME   Not disturbed, sup?
ISA   Delilah was on the bench licking our dinner. Mum threw a birkenstock at her. Missed and smashed the plate, dinner on floor, cat ran outside hours ago hasn't come back. Mum's out looking distraught, thinks she's been run over.
ME   She'll come back
ISA   Hope so
        Why were you in sick bay today?
ME   Headache
ISA   Nothing else?
ME   No
ISA   . . . cross your heart?
ME   x heart
ISA   You're lying. Cheyenne told me what happened
ME   Like you'd trust ANYTHING she said!
ISA   She showed me the video Starkey took
ME   @#$%!!!
ISA   Are you okay?
ME   Never better
ISA   You have to report them!

ME NOT. A. BIG. DEAL.

ISA YES! BIG! DEAL! Tell dashwood – there's evidence!

ME It won't help. PLEASE don't tell anybody! Have you told anybody?

ISA Only Phoenix . . . sorry

ME More effective than announcing it at assembly

ISA The cat came back!

ME My favourite song

ISA I gotta go

ME Wait! What was your idea for the project?

ISA ●●●

I stared at the message bubbles until they dropped off the screen.

The communication with Isa reminded me of the graffiti about Pericles I'd seen during my fugitive experience in the automatic toilet yesterday. I found a packet of Chux® Magic Erasers® and sneaked out of the apartment to remove it. Vince, son of Frank, was on night watch again.

'Run out of milk already?' he said. 'You should try UHT – lasts forever.'

'Just getting some fresh air.'

The ROBOloo was occupied, so I waited on a park bench. Eventually an old man in tattered flannelette pyjamas emerged, both feet swollen purple and barely wrapped in filthy bandages. His shoes were styrofoam platforms attached to his feet with callipers made of coathanger wire, string and masking tape. He was the living definition of resilience – but when I stepped into the metal box, I had a terrible feeling that he wouldn't last as long as the smell he'd left behind. I pinched my nose and erased the graffiti with five Magic Erasers® without taking a second breath, then returned to T H E   E Y R I E.

'That was a lot of fresh air you got,' Vince said. But no, it really wasn't.

On Thursday morning, Miss Moreau brought a box of macarons into French – sweet rewards for anybody scoring a perfect ten in a spot quiz. I was heading for glory as she read out the answer to the eighth question.

'*Numéro huit. Je n'aime pas les œufs.* I don't like eggs.'

I do like eggs, though, and was counting mine before they'd hatched, imagining the macaron's shell crumbling between my teeth, dissolving on my tongue. The sheer anticipation made my tailbone twitch. The twitch travelled up my spine, making me shudder.

'*Numéro neuf. Je n'ai pas peur des chats noirs.* I'm not afraid of black cats.'

Nine out of nine! I felt the twitch again, more forcefully, and it made me giggle.

'*Arrêtez de rire!*' Miss Moreau said. 'Stop laughing.'

I pinched my leg under the table.

'*Dernière* question,' she said, eyeballing me. '*Numéro dix. Pas tous les singes ont des queues.* Not all monkeys have tails.'

Too much resonance for the nub to tolerate. No degree of mental resistance could stop the thing twitching to the point of fibrillation. I gripped the sides of my chair and pulled myself down hard, trying to smother the vibration. It fought back by shooting a surge of pure, almost agonising elation up my spine to the crown of my head.

>FWOOSH!<

A hundred billion neurons exploded simultaneously.

My vision blurred, then sharpened and sparkled. The >ZING< travelled back down to my pelvis then divided and shot down each leg, making them judder, before shooting out my toes. The stunned expression on Pericles' face made me LMHAO.

'*Quoi de si drôle?*' Miss Moreau said.

'I don't know,' I said through tears. 'Na-ha-ha-ha-nothing.'

'*Eh bien*, that's exactly what you'll receive – nothing.'

Miss Moreau gave everybody else a macaron regardless of their result.

At lunchtime, charging along the catwalk to beat the café queue, I bumped into Dr Limberg exiting the stairwell. She dropped her folder, spilling papers over the ground.

'Sorry,' I said, chasing the escapees.

'We can't have confidential notes blowing around the playground willy-nilly, can we?' she said, sliding them into the folder. 'Actually, I'm glad we ran into each other. I wanted to organise a follow-up session with you, Lincoln. Nothing serious – just a fifteen-minute chat. Tomorrow afternoon, perhaps?'

'Mr Simmons won't let me skip clinic. I missed training yesterday.'

'I've already cleared it with him.'

'Okay,' I said reluctantly. Moreau must've logged my strange behaviour during French on The Owl.

'I'll see you in my office at three-thirty.'

Later, in English, Mr Field returned our *Dorian Gray* essays. I got nineteen out of twenty, which was the equal-highest mark, so I was pretty stoked and forgot about missing out on a crappy macaron. He'd written on my paper, 'Your proposition that someone who undergoes excessive cosmetic surgery is the modern-day equivalent of Dorian Gray is hardly original. But you've argued your point with rare insight and clarity. Keep up the good work!'

On Friday we checked out each other's collaborative works in the art studio. Some of the pieces had an element of provocative ingenuity that made our knitting seem lame in comparison. Ashleigh Robinson and Vanessa Andrews had shot paint from Super Soakers® onto ten double-sided canvases, then stencilled lettering on top that read on one side:

MY KID COULD PAINT THAT

and on the other:

I AM YOUR KID

Cain Seibold and Nathan Trammel were constructing a massive sculpture from scrap metal and calling it *Scraposaurus*. Mr Faber was helping them in the tech studio. I wish I'd thought of that. The only metal I got to use was my knitting needles, which Isa today replaced with a wooden pair, almost as thick as pool cues, to get the job done faster. She unfolded a sheet of graph paper covered in a pattern of dots and dashes and said, 'Here's the master plan for art-world domination. Tibor helped me chart my new idea in Design Mathematics.'

'Great. But what is it?'

'All will be revealed as you follow it stitch-by-stitch.'

'Am I your guinea pig?'

'Exactly.'

'Oink!'

'They don't oink.'

Ms Tarasek let us go outside to work, so we sat under the old fig tree and knitted in relative silence, Isa shushing me whenever I tried to ask a question. Ten minutes in, I caught her looking at me with a furrowed brow and asked what the matter was.

'I bet you have sisters but no brother.'

'Why, because I'm so skilled at handicrafts? I've got one sister.' I told her about my parents' separation and explained our living arrangements.

'What's your father like?'

'Super smart, competitive, loves his work more than just about anything. Bossy at times but mega-generous. Argues a point more aggressively when he knows it's wrong. Thinks he knows me better than I know myself.'

'He probably does.'

'How is that even possible?'

Isa laid down her knitting. 'He's known you for your entire life. You've only witnessed a third of his, and that's been through a child's eyes. The only thing you know about your mother and father before they became parents is what they've chosen to tell, which is highly selective.'

'So what's your family like? I know you have a cat called Delilah and your mother wears Birkenstocks. What about your dad?'

'I don't have one.'

'Everybody has a father. Even if he was an anonymous sperm donor, you still have one.'

Isa pointed her needles at me. 'Don't even go there.'

'Sorry.'

We resumed knitting in silence and soon I got the hang of it, hardly needing the chart. Then a pattern emerged that made the knitting curl in on itself. 'I think I stuffed this up.'

'Give me a look,' Isa said.

'Show me yours first.' We counted to three and laid down our knitting. Isa's was twice as long but otherwise almost the same as mine, which was gratifying.

'It worked!' she said. 'Tibor is a genius and Phoenix will be blown away.'

'Why Phoenix?'

'She told me something disturbingly fascinating that inspired this design.'

'What?' I said, twisting my knitting between my fingers.

'I'll let her tell you herself. Meet us at International Velvet after school.'

'Keeping me in suspense?' I said with a smile. 'I still have no idea what it's supposed to be.'

'They go together,' she said, taking my knitting. 'Watch.' She held it up next to hers, and almost magically, the two lengths coiled around each other. 'They'll be connected by a series of small links in different colours.'

'Like a spiralling ladder?'

'Getting warm.'

'A double helix?'

'Boiling hot.'

'A DNA molecule?'

'Give the man a cigar!'

BUILDING
TOMORROW'S MAN

Walking into Dr Limberg's office later today, the first thing I noticed was a zingy citrus aroma, the second her lime-green dress. The third was the horse photo.

'Please take a seat,' she said.

'You've changed the print on the wall. There were two horses before, a mare and her foal. Now there's just the mare.'

'Are you sure about that?'

'I'm not sure about anything.'

She wrote something in her folder. 'Apparently you were being disruptive in French? Miss Moreau logged a Hoot, reporting that you guffawed for no reason. Were you trying to draw attention to yourself?'

'I just started laughing and couldn't stop.'

'Miss Moreau specifically used the word "guffawed".'

'She's French.'

'Does that have any bearing on the matter?'

'Okay. I specifically guffawed.'

'Would it be reasonable to suggest you have an issue with maintaining self-control?'

'My issue is a personal problem that I wish I had more control over. It's affecting my self-confidence more than anything else. You could probably solve everything for me right now by asking Coach Simmons to release me from squad.'

'If you tell me your reason then we can talk about it. Would you be able to share it with me? Nobody else needs to know.'

Besides Nicole Parker, Dr Finster was the only person who knew about the nub. He'd told me to report any growth and I hadn't. Instead I'd tried to ignore it – pretend it wasn't there. But sitting in Dr Limberg's office, I realised how much the nub had come to affect my life. She poured me a glass of filtered water and I seriously considered telling her everything. As I tried to form my opening sentence in my head, the thought of communicating the location of my problem was enough to stump me.

Homunculus said, 'Just tell her it's at the beginning of your anal cleft.'

I was flushed with shame and the thing contracted, just as it had at my first meeting with Simmons, making me giggle with nerves. 'Sorry,' I said. 'But I just can't get it out.'

'That's probably beneficial for everybody,' Homunculus said.

'Lincoln, three members of squad, Darvin Naylor, Evan Starkey and Sean Mulligan, were suspended last week. Is your problem connected with them in any way?'

I shook my head.

'Perhaps it would be helpful spending some time processing your own thoughts in The Labyrinth? Maybe think of how you can resolve your reluctance to continue swimming? Walk along the path, contemplating the question with an open mind. On reaching the centre, remain still, breathing deeply, until you attain a sense of calm. When you feel ready to leave, return along the same path. I'll call Mr Jespersen to let him know you're coming.'

'Okay.' I stood up, and looked at the horse picture. 'Is that the same photo or not?'

'The imagination is a powerful thing. Sometimes it reconstructs our memories.'

Jespersen was waiting by the entrance gate in his paint-stained coveralls, holding a pair of industrial hedge trimmers. 'Come to discover the meaning of life?' he said, unlit rollie stuck to his bottom lip. 'Don't get lost searching.'

'There's only one way to go.'

He unlocked the gate and pushed it open. 'Through here,' he said, then held up the trimmers. 'Perhaps take these with you and do a little trimming on the way?' No hint of a smile.

I stepped inside and whispered, 'Oh, mysterious Labyrinth, please show me the way out of squad.' I walked only a few metres before a camphoraceous scent from the hedge caught in my throat and panic instantly constricted my airway muscles. A memory was pushing its way into my consciousness – something worse than Nigel Lethbridge's mothballed jacket.

I coughed and spat then continued the walk, breathing only through my mouth to avoid the smell. The path kept turning back on itself in a curving zigzag. Eventually I got close to the centre and tried to separate the hedge to see what lay on the other side. The foliage was too dense, though, and made the back of my hands and forearms itchy. The next turn led me directly back to the perimeter and the smell of Jespersen's clove cigarette. I could see its smoky tendril on the other side being drawn up into the attic window of Crestfield House.

Recalling the view I'd taken in from the servants' bedroom during Lethbridge's tour, I figured The Labyrinth was a circle divided into quadrants by avenues radiating from the centre. I'd completed only one section, so I began jogging through the second. As my breathing quickened, the smell of the hedge overwhelmed me. I tried to outrun it but was overcome by vertigo, which sent me scraping and crashing into the leafy walls, arms prickling every time I made contact. I scratched at the itchy weals until the skin broke. And then it struck me – my first memory of that camphoraceous smell. Pop Locke's funeral. I froze, captive to a cinematic viewing of my memory.

Pop Locke was displayed in an open coffin for those wanting one last look and for the morbidly curious. Neither category included me – I'd never seen a dead person and had no desire to – but, after the service, everyone in the family slid out of the pew to have a look and I didn't want to be alone. Glancing into the casket, I received a terrible shock. Someone had stolen my grandfather and replaced him with a waxwork replicant. The brown trousers and diamond-patterned vest were definitely his, but not the waxy yellow skin or the weird expression on his face. Somebody who'd never met my pop when he was alive had been paid to make him smile, but they'd given him a smirk, and Pop Locke never smirked. His eyes were now glassy and devoid of light, like Gus when he died.

'He looks so peaceful,' Mum said. But I think 'spooky' would've been more apt. The worst thing was the smell. The familiar scent of Pop's Swiss Valley Hair Pomade™ had been overpowered by something that caught in my throat like lantana.

'It's one of the chemicals in the embalming fluid,' Dad said. I was offended by how clinical his explanation was, and how he'd seemed so removed from everything, as if flying above it. Now I knew his grief must have been churned up with his regret at arguing with Pop just before he died. Dad was running on autopilot that day, keeping his shit firm for the sake of everybody else he had to deal with. And now, a year later, that smell had paralysed me in The Labyrinth.

I had to move on. My life would be hell if I didn't get myself out of squad by Monday. But the hope of discovering a solution only diminished as I resumed my miserable journey towards the centre. When I turned the final corner, I was stunned to see a sculpture beneath the gazebo: a bronze statue of a man in a long flaring coat, his commanding jawline accentuated by a beard with no moustache. Curling waves of metal hair and incongruously glaring white eyeballs made him look deranged. An earlier visitor must've painted them with liquid paper – Starkey probably. The pupils were holes, one of them plugged with a marble.

Despite standing two metres tall, the man was dwarfed by a gargantuan bull whose rump his hand rested on. The bronze had darkened with time, but the bull's horns, snout and the ring that pierced it were gleaming like gold from all the hands that had rubbed them through the years.

'Hello, big fella!' I said, rubbing his snout.

A loud snort knocked me flat on my arse.

'HELLO!' he rumbled. 'MY NAME IS KING HENRY, THE FIRST THOROUGHBRED STUD IMPORTED BY JOSEPH MILLINGTON DRAKE IN EIGHTEEN NINETY-FIVE. OVER A DECADE I SIRED MORE CALVES THAN ANY OTHER BULL BEFORE ME, LAYING THE FOUNDATIONS FOR THE NATION'S SUPERIOR STOCK. AFTER WINNING THE BLUE RIBBON AT THE DUBBO AGRICULTURAL SHOW, MY MASTER DEEMED ME HIS FAVOURITE SON, MUCH TO THE AMUSEMENT OF HIS WIFE AND THREE BEAUTIFUL DAUGHTERS.'

I rubbed King Henry's snout once more to hear the spiel again. No wonder Millington Drake was proud of the beast. Beneath his right foot was a plaque detailing his measurements, right down to the twenty-eight-inch girth of his scrotum. I went behind the bull to check out his equipment. Sure enough his balls were enormous, and, like his snout and horns, were burnished gold by all the rubbing. I restrained myself, half-fearing he might come to life and kick out my teeth, or that I was being filmed.

On my way back out of The Labyrinth I scratched the hives again, only making them worse. And then I had a revelation: The Labyrinth *had* answered my question, in the form of the rash. That was how I would get out of swimming – by claiming an allergic reaction to the pool water!

I took a photo of my arm to present as fake evidence to Simmons. When I finally emerged, Jespersen tapped his watch. 'About time,' he said. 'I have to pick my wife up from yoga.'

Later I met Isa and Phoenix at International Velvet. They were sitting in the corner booth, still wearing sweats from their after-school dance class, sharing earphones as they watched a YouTube clip and practised the routine with their fingers. I ordered a macchiato at the counter and returned to hear them discussing David York and Heather Treadwell's budding relationship. Apparently the staunch atheist and the zealous Christian had hooked up.

'Sorry to state the obvious, but they epitomise incompatibility,' Phoenix said. 'They're complete opposites.'

'That's probably the attraction,' Isa said, then turned to me. 'How was your session with Dr Limberg, Lincoln?'

'Surprisingly productive,' I said.

Phoenix huffed. 'I don't trust the Cheeseburger. She always looks so perfect. Why did you have to see her, anyway? Do you have issues?'

'Don't embarrass him,' Isa said. 'It's probably confidential.'

'Don't pretend you've never gone through her files.'

'Ignore her,' Isa said. 'She thinks she's Velma from *Scooby-Doo*. Obsessed with conspiracy theories.'

'You have to admit I am a diligent investigator.'

'True.' Isa gave me a little shove. 'You won't believe what Phoenix dug up on our school's beloved founder.'

After the tour by Nigel Lethbridge, Phoenix had wanted to find out more about Joseph Millington Drake. There was almost nothing online, so she searched the school library catalogue and found a listing for a book he'd written called *On Building Tomorrow's Man*. The only problem was that instead of a shelf location, the book was labelled R.A. for restricted access. Mrs Deacon told her it was so old and fragile it could only be viewed under a teacher's supervision. Thinking it might contain something juicy or controversial, Phoenix passed on that and instead looked it up on the City of Sydney Library site. She found only one reference copy, listed at the Customs House branch.

'It was pretty much a white supremacist manifesto,' Phoenix said. 'I took photos of a couple of the pages. Given my family background, this one interested me the most.' She handed me her phone and the girls inserted their earphones to let me read.

The influx of Celestials on our goldfields was but a mere trifle. The hundreds of millions of China, like a sleeping giant, will soon awaken and arrive upon our unprotected shores as a formidable enemy. Though we may be small in number, we are superior to the Asiatic in physical strength, moral constitution and intelligence. We must populate our vast nation now, taking great care to remove any defective traits that may threaten to weaken it. To neglect this imperative would be akin to racial suicide. Man has always been attracted to beauty and woman to strength, but in the modern age we have interfered with this process of natural selection. In the name of charity, the weak, defective and undesirable have been overly protected and are now outbreeding their superiors.

For the sake of our nation, we must actively assist nature in what she already does. In selectively breeding cattle and the like, we seek to reproduce beneficial traits and remove the defective or weak. We must now do the same with our human population. The fit must be given incentive to breed and the unfit discouraged, or prevented from doing so.

No bloody wonder he had the statue of his prize bull King Henry erected in the centre of the school! I swiped across to the other photo Phoenix had taken of the book.

The Australian aborigine is a primitive race that will eventually disappear. The process may be expedited by allowing half-caste girls only to marry white men, thus diluting the coloured blood in future generations. And regardless of race, marriage restrictions must be applied to all peoples affected by tuberculosis, epilepsy, sex pervertism, insanity, alcoholism, pauperism and feeble-mindedness.

Of all the boys turned down by the selection committee of Crestfield Academy since its inception, 73 per cent had one or both parents who were imbeciles, dullards or tainted by alcoholism. My stringent selection methods have been criticised heavily by supposed do-gooders, but nurturing the weak will only serve to increase their number until they become an unmanageable burden on society.

It is negligent to allow the unfortunates to replicate themselves. For the health and purity of our nation, they must be segregated and undergo full or partial sterilisation. Only when our most noble values are exalted will we become a great people. Crestfield Academy was established in the true spirit of progress, with the highest hope of raising a new brotherhood. Rigorous mental stimulation is merely the foundation. All boys must be strenuously trained and participate in every form of physical competition, not solely to produce medal-winning athletes, but for the development of the body and the improvement of the national physique.

'That's some seriously crazy shit,' I said.

Isa and Phoenix took out their earphones, nodding at me.

'Millington Drake was a member of the Eugenics Association,' Phoenix said. 'He wanted to create a master race before the Nazis got hold of the baton.'

'That doesn't make him a Nazi.'

'Only because they hadn't invented themselves yet.'

'A lot of other people probably had similar ideas, though,' I said, playing devil's advocate.

'It was more than an idea for Millington Drake,' Isa said. 'He founded our school on those principles.'

'There was a chapter on the selection test,' Phoenix said. 'Every prospective student had to be measured, from their height right down to the length of their fingers. He had a formula to figure out the perfect proportions, and you had to fall within an acceptable range.'

'I had to be measured last year for the student profile,' I said.

'Back then, if you had blue eyes you got extra points. Forget about applying if your skin wasn't white – you lost fifty points immediately and stood no chance. Ever wondered why there are so few of us Asians at Crestfield?'

'Not really. It's about the same as my old school.'

'And that's on the insular peninsula,' Isa said.

She had a point. The demographic of my old school was more smoking pot than melting pot.

'Are you suggesting Crestfield still has a racist selection process?'

'It's called the panel interview,' Phoenix said. 'It allows them to consider a student's appearance. Who knows how much that influences their decision? At some other selective schools, the vast majority of students are Asian. Crestfield supposedly has an emphasis on its students being more well rounded, demonstrating an interest in sport and the arts. That's how I got in.' She performed a hand flourish.

'Crestfield is a business above all else,' Isa said. 'It's a brand.'

I already knew Isa was on a scholarship and that her mum paid minimal fees because of her high score on the entry test. But she explained that an opposite principle also applied, whereby rich parents could pay big bucks for their kid to attend even if they bombed the test. The school's academic record was protected by the Year 9 cull: students with the lowest results were asked to leave unless their parents forked out for the dubiously named Parallel Growth Program. Isa confirmed what Tibor had told me earlier, that Nads was on it.

'His father's company sponsors the sports department and practically built The Hive,' she said. 'Dashwood suspended Nads but he'd never expel him. Crestfield would lose a massive chunk of funding and the board would have Dashwood removed.'

'The cull is a deviously clever way of making money,' Phoenix said. 'No matter how high the Year 9 standard, there'll always be a bottom percentile. Only a few leave, and the following year the blow-ins take their place. That explains you,' she said to me with a smile.

'Yeah, cheers.'

Isa explained that Phoenix's research had inspired her idea of knitting the DNA chain, with the intention of displaying it in a prominent position to draw attention to the dodgy eugenicist foundations of the school. It was serendipitous that I'd just visited the statue of Joseph Millington Drake and King Henry in The Labyrinth. I held on to this little gem until both Isa and Phoenix had exhausted their cache of dark secrets. And then I said, 'I know the perfect place to hang our work.'

After school, I put my 'get out of squad' plan into action by calling Tibor Mintz. I reminded him of our conversation on the far side of Old Block and asked if he ever felt like fighting the system. He said he'd already started to, and with a bit of prodding revealed all. For no reason other than the challenge, Tibor Mintz had hacked The Owl. Using a combination of logic, psychology and probability, he'd figured out the password of a senior faculty member in less than an hour.

Fostering a new level of trust, I told Tibor exactly what the goons had done to me. He said Nads generally left him alone because he relied on him, but Starkey made his life hell whenever Nads wasn't around. He'd put banana peels, glue and dog shit in his satchel, broken his nose by slamming his face on the water fountain and stolen his wallet five times. Tibor completely understood my reason for wanting out of squad, and agreed to the favour I requested without hesitation.

CLOSE TO THE BONE

Over breakfast on Saturday, Mum told us that a plastics manufacturer had begun fabricating the Venus shell and the giant inflatable pool.

'I saw Vienna on the videowall at Westfield,' I said. 'She's exceedingly fit.'

'I think we chose the perfect Venus.'

'You remember how I came up with a solution to your shell dilemma? Would I be able to help out at the event and see her in person?'

'It's possible,' Mum said. 'Let me think about it.'

Joy glowed in my heart for two minutes, before Mum pulled the plug and drained it away down the sink: 'I forgot to mention Grant's coming for lunch.'

'Grant who?'

'Grant Marsh, the fellow I've been seeing.'

'I'm so not hanging around for that.'

'Yes, you are,' Venn said. 'You can't abandon me.'

'It's very important for me that you both meet him,' Mum said.

Grant Marsh arrived at midday in a cloud of fragrance so obnoxiously musky it made Oscar run away. He was wearing a bright-pink Versace polo with a popped collar, and turquoise shorts that exposed calves knotted with varicose veins. A blue-bezelled Rolex Yacht-Master® on his wrist completed the picture. Even his hair looked purchased.

During lunch, Grant praised Mum's baked salmon, the earrings he bought her at the markets and her golfing form. Having been starved of compliments by Dad for so long, she lapped it up. Grant pretended to be interested in my life for roughly thirty seconds before banging on about the Chinese economy and moving on to his love of the great outdoors.

'Grant's quite the athlete,' Mum said. 'He cycles to West Head and back every morning.'

'That explains those magnificent calves,' I said.

Mum glared at me and said, 'I think we should all go for a lovely bushwalk this afternoon.'

'Sorry, I can't,' Venn said. 'I'm going to yoga with Jessie.'

'I have to finish reading *Frankenstein*,' I said, thinking on the spot. 'And my book's at Dad's.'

According to Mr Field, even the most unlikeable characters in literature often possess some sort of redemptive quality. The most impressive thing Grant Marsh possessed was the Ferrari I saw parked in our drive as I was leaving. And the fact he owned one made him an even bigger twanger.

On the bus home, I read *My One Redeeming Affliction*. I was up to the part where the spinster Althea starts driving a wedge between Walter and his daughter Esther – who he'd banned from seeing William.

Althea Beauclare's increasing presence at Fernleigh stuck in Esther's craw. She'd never trusted the woman's constant ebullience, nor considered her conspicuous acts of charity anything more than a ploy to inveigle her way into Walter's life. Always the essence of kindness in front of him, Althea hectored the servants behind his back, reserving particular disdain for Dora Hinkley, the housekeeper.

Inevitably, Walter became engaged to Althea, and shortly after they'd made the announcement, Walter gave Mrs Hinkley a month's notice. Dora had given twenty-one years of her life to the family, serving my grandmother Martha before Esther had been born. By yielding to Althea's wish to replace Mrs Hinkley with her own housekeeper, Walter severed the most reliable tie to the memory of his children's mother.

Esther recorded no details of the wedding in her diary, merely indicating the date with a sketch of a dark storm cloud. Immediately after the couple's return from a month's honeymoon in Tasmania, Althea set about redecorating Fernleigh. She employed a small army of carters to strip the living room of furniture. She removed all of the drapes and sold the Oriental fans, candelabra and vases to a dealer in one consignment. Esther pleaded with her father to intervene in the woman's ruthless mission, but he abnegated all responsibility.

The final item to go was a gold-plated Russian samovar that had been passed down from Esther's great-grandmother. Althea had promised to retain it, but on returning home from work late one evening, Esther noticed its absence from the sideboard and confronted her stepmother. Without even bothering to pretend to have an ounce of contrition, Althea stated that she'd donated it to the women of the Temperance Union for serving tea at their charity bazaar, to be auctioned at day's end. 'Instead of gathering dust,' she said, 'it will join the fight against the scourge of alcoholism currently plaguing this town!'

Esther hoped that a degree of forced civility might return now that Althea had removed every material trace of her mother's grace and style. But one night, in a stolen moment of reminiscence after a second snifter of cognac, Walter made the irreversible mistake of telling Esther she looked exactly like her mother had at the same age – in the presence of his new wife. Over the ensuing months, Althea made a determined effort to find a suitable husband for her stepdaughter, inviting possible suitors to monthly recitals. Having already entered into a clandestine courtship with William, Esther deeply resented the intrusion and would rarely perform for them. Walter urged her cooperation, failing to understand that the root of the problem was his new wife's jealousy – an all-consuming jealousy that would only be alleviated by Esther leaving Fernleigh forever.

*

That was all a bit intense, and got me worried about what would happen if things progressed between Mum and Grant Marsh. She'd asked me not to mention anything to Dad, which effectively tripled the mental burden of knowing.

My arrival at T H E E Y R I E was badly timed. Dad was blending a protein smoothie, which meant he had a date with Sergio.

'Back early?' he said. 'Great. You can join me for a workout.'

'I was thinking more a surf. Haven't been for ages.'

'I'll drive you down after.'

I reluctantly got changed, grabbed a towel and swallowed the last three human growth pills that Nads had given me.

'How's your mother?' Dad said in the lift down.

'She's good.'

'She's not seeing somebody, is she?'

'That's such a random question.'

Dad saluted Frank at his desk and resumed the enquiry as we stepped outside. 'I've been mulling over something Don Partridge said the other day. Apparently Maxine told him that your mother looked happier than she has in a long time.'

'Surely that's a positive?'

'She's seeing someone, isn't she?'

'You'd have to ask her.'

'I knew it! I had a feeling in my gut. No more questions, that wouldn't be fair.' But halfway down William Street and, mysteriously, right outside a prestige car dealership he said, 'Have you met the new Lothario?'

'Today at lunch. He's a complete and utter tool, and funnily enough he drives one of those,' I said, pointing at a Ferrari.

'You don't have to tell me anything else. I'll find out soon enough.' Three more steps. 'Bugger it. What's his name?'

'Grant Marsh.'

'Good God above! How could your mother do that to me?'

Sergio instantly sensed Dad's agitation when we arrived and asked where it was coming from. Without hesitation Dad told him about the home invader. 'Eight years I trusted him with my financial affairs. Now the bastard's managing his own personal affair with my wife.'

Sergio massaged Dad's shoulders. 'You're holding tension across your back, hips and buttocks. You must channel your anger into reps.'

Dad positioned himself into the squat machine and followed Sergio's advice until the grunting became so loud it prompted an announcement from the receptionist.

>IN CONSIDERATION OF OUR OTHER VALUED MEMBERS AND GUESTS, WOULD THE PERSON WHO'S GRUNTING PLEASE STOP IMMEDIATELY.<

Sergio removed four of the plates and said, 'Lincoln, you have chicken legs. Get on the machine.' The first set was a breeze so he doubled the load. The second was a struggle. 'Deeper, deeper,' he said, until my knees touched my chest. 'Feel the burn.'

I felt more than the burn. I felt something rupture at the base of my spine and groaned louder than Dad. 'ARRRRGH!'

'Good,' Sergio said. But it wasn't good at all. It was extremely bad. I got out of the machine and was unable to straighten my body. 'You need assistance?' he said.

Afraid that he'd try to unfold me himself, I said I was okay.

'Then we move on to leg extension.'

The initial sharpness of the pain was replaced by a pinching knot that crept up to the base of my skull. The veins in my temples throbbed to the beat of the dance music belting from the speakers. I didn't want watermelon quads like Sergio, but endured the pain of completing the workout to prevent him from investigating the source of my pain.

'Ready for that surf now?' Dad said as we fetched our bags.

'I wouldn't be able to zip up my wettie,' I said as we passed a bodybuilder whose excessive application of tiger balm punched right through his oniony body odour. My vision blurred and I walked straight into the glass door.

'I'm calling Dr Nixon, my new GP,' Dad said.

'Don't!' I said, a little too emphatically. 'I just need a good lie-down.'

Dad went to the beach without me. After a long nap, still in my sweaty clothing, I peeled it off and stepped into the shower. Normally I made minimal contact with the nub, but the incident demanded closer inspection. It was extremely tender to touch and even more swollen than before. Holding a hand mirror, I stood with my back to the full-length mirror and for the first time in weeks saw the thing in its entirety. Instantly the scales of denial fell from my eyes, and I was more shocked and repulsed than I can convey in words.

Perhaps I'd locked the truth away in some compartment of my brain and fooled myself into thinking the nub would remain nothing more than an inconvenient bump. The thing is that I now have—

The hairy nub had changed slowly, up until today when I'd over-exerted myself. 'Hairy nub' was a euphemism for something potentially hideous that I'd hoped would never come into being, but today it has.

The thing is that I have – I'm quite sure that I have . . .

a tail.

There, it's out.

Last year its development had been almost imperceptible. This year its metamorphosis must have been accelerated by pressure, friction, injury and possibly the human growth boosters that Nads gave me. Steroids can shrink your nuts and make you grow boobs – why not develop a tail if you already have the raw materials? Nads told me the pills weren't steroids but maybe they had their own side effects. I'd taken three before the gym today and something painfully decisive had happened during squats – the exertion must've popped the thing out into its 'proper' position.

The thing is a tail. TAIL TAIL TAIL.

Pas tous les singes ont des queues.

Not all monkeys have tails.

But some humans do.

The tail is covered in dark hair. It is vile. VILE is an anagram of EVIL. What if Nicole Parker's hunch was correct? Maybe I am the beast?

I measured the tail with a piece of string. Base to tip it was thirty-three millimetres – thirty-three millimetres too long.

Stirred by my acknowledgement of the full extent of my heinous deformity, Homunculus advised its immediate removal. He wouldn't allow me to see Dr Nixon or Finster or any other medical professional, so I agreed that self-excision was the only course of action.

I went into the kitchen, drew the titanium chef's knife from its block and sharpened it.

>fwssht/fwssht\fwssht/fwssht<

Conviction was building with each pass across the diamond-dusted rod.

>fwssht\fwssht/fwssht<

'The tail is a parasitic entity that needs to be eradicated,' Homunculus said, blithely unaware of the irony that I most often felt the same about him.

>fwssht<

'You need to kill it!'

After counting exactly a hundred passes, I pressed the knife's keen edge against the base of the tail. The thing retracted like a small, frightened animal as I drew the blade five or six millimetres across it. A thin red line screamed murder. The prospect of extreme pain almost evaporated my reckless and misguided courage.

'You'll need a serrated knife to cut through the bone or cartilage or whatever's in there,' Homunculus said.

'You can't be serious? I'd sever my spinal cord and become para-lysed – if I didn't first bleed to death or get carted off to a psychiatric hospital.'

'You're weak.'

'I don't have the training, experience or equipment to remove the tail, and you know it.' The logic of the statement shut him down momentarily. But as I was returning the knife to the kitchen he said, 'At least you could tidy it up a bit – make it less visibly abhorrent.'

So I moved operations to Dad's bathroom, shook up a can of Gillette® Foamy®, lathered the tail and shaved off the hair with his razor. Though infinitely less risky than a full tailectomy, I still managed to cut myself twice. Nonetheless, the sight of the hair-flecked raspberry-and-cream substance swirling down the sink bolstered my hope of an aesthetically acceptable result.

Using the double-mirror method again, I checked my handiwork and was mortified. The bald tail looked ten times worse than the hairy version, and the bleeding wasn't helping. I used half a roll of toilet paper to staunch the flow and flushed the evidence. I dabbed the cuts with a vicious and hopefully effective antiseptic, accepting the sting as punishment for my vain stupidity. I rinsed and returned my father's shaving equipment to the cabinet without changing the blade because there were no spares, further compounding my shame by choosing expedience over hygiene. Dad arrived home about ten minutes later.

Feeling ninety degrees less than average at dinner this evening, I had to fake a breezy mood to reassure Dad that I didn't need to see a doctor. I went to bed pretty early but, afraid of staining my sheets and unable to lie on my back, I didn't drop off till after 2 am. A bald man with glasses on the end of his nose appeared in a dream and began explaining the regions of a ceramic phrenology bust.

'Here is amativeness,' he said, pointing to the back of the skull. 'The aptitude for demonstrating romantic love. Currently non-existent in your life, but something you may discover in the not-too-distant future.'

'That's impossible,' I said. 'Nobody will ever be able to love me the way I am.'

'There's nothing wrong with you, young fellow.'

'Who are you?'

'Dr Martin Eisler, Professor of Phrenology and Mesmerism, at your service.' As he rotated the ceramic bust to show me his name on its chest, it slipped from the stand and shattered. The crash woke me at 3.15 am. Unable to discern between dream and reality, I reached behind me, hoping to find my problem had somehow vanished. But the bald, spiky, scabby, tender thing was still there.

SEE THE WORLD

Sunday morning I woke with my sheet in a bundle on the floor. I got up and turned to the page of the book where William had a session with the phrenologist to see if it matched the dream and found this:

'The organ of amativeness lies here beneath the occipital bone, and as it is highly pronounced, indicates proficiency in the art of love.'

My failure with Nicole Parker last year and romantic drought ever since confirmed my lack of proficiency in the art of love, but Dr Eisler's encouraging words about the possibility of love in the not-too-distant future produced a tiny bit of hope in me.

I was also burning with curiosity to discover if Bert's ceramic head had been made by Eisler. I showered, dressed and walked out the door before Dad could stop me. Then I skated down to Bert's house and rapped on the flyscreen door.

'Hold your horses!' he yelled, then had a coughing fit followed by a round of hoicking, spitting and toilet-flushing. 'Just clearing out the lungs – or whatever's left of 'em.' Eventually his hunched form manifested behind the mesh. 'If you're collecting for crippled kiddies, you're plum out of luck. I'm poor and crippled myself.'

'Bert, it's Lincoln from up the hill.'

'Come in, Lincoln from up the hill, but mind where you tread.' He led me down a hallway ravined by a vast assortment of treasures and junk. There was a glass cabinet filled with doll parts, a huge wooden letter B marquee light with empty sockets and a globe with America dented and burnt, as if struck by a meteorite.

Sitting on the kitchen table was a gleaming gold water-heating device replete with taps and spouts, and a teapot perched on top that could've been nicked from the Mad Hatter's tea party. Beside it was a rag and a bottle of Silvo® polish.

'What's that?' I said.

'A Russian samovar. Set you back two grand.'

'It's beautiful,' I said, then remembered I'd read about a samovar just yesterday.

'Don't expect me to fire it up. It's teabag or nothing.' He filled a chipped green ceramic kettle with water then plugged it in and turned it on.

'Where did you get all your stuff?'

'Auctions, dealers, deceased estates. Inherited some of it. Nothing off the back of a truck.'

'The samovar?'

'You'd have to ask Ruby. She had a yarn about every piece, and if she didn't know where it came from she'd get creative. Loved the samovar, would never sell it. Had it heating all day in winter – made tea for the customers.'

'Where did you meet Ruby?'

'I was a grease monkey at the Ampol garage. Worked on Jack Monodora's Lincoln Continental – most beautiful automobile in the entire world, it was. One day he asked me to be his personal driver and mechanic. Had nine cars to look after.'

The boiling kettle's whistling interrupted him. Bert yanked the plug from the socket and continued the story without making a move to brew the tea.

'Monodora ran the Continental Lounge up at the Cross. Fancy place it was, too. Nothing like the sleazy shitholes that popped up like toadstools afterwards. No strippers – none of that funny business. It was a swish supper club with a band and floorshow. Served liquor after hours – mind you, all them places did. Made a killing.'

'Did Ruby perform there?'

'You're a smart one. I'm working the bar one night when the chitter-chatter dies and a vision of loveliness appears on stage. Shimmering emerald gown and long gloves, hair like Veronica Lake's peekaboo, only red. She starts singing her first number and I swear she's eye-balling me. Every Joe in the joint is thinking the same, but I'm the only mug daft enough to do anything about it. Can't buy her a drink because they're on the house for the artiste. So I pay her a compli-ment – tell her she'd have made Billie Holiday proud.'

'Who's he?'

'She was a famous jazz singer.' Upstairs a clock chimed the hour, then another clock and another and another, until there must've been at least twenty sounding simultaneously. 'Here's some free advice for you. Never chase someone you don't count yourself worthy of. The jealousy will do your head in.' He paused. 'Now, follow me. It's time to visit Jack Tar.'

He led me further down the hallway to a door with a gold-lettered sign above that said DINING CAR. Inside was a row of retracted green leather seats facing a puppet theatre. Suspended from wooden crosses were three marionette puppets: a sea monster, a mermaid and a buck-toothed sailor in a little moth-eaten blue suit.

'Sit down. The show's about to start.'

I pulled down a seat and it released a musty odour. Bert sat on the other end of the row and stared at the puppets. With nobody pulling the strings, they hung limp. But then Bert narrated the action as if he was watching a performance. 'Jack Tar, face like a smashed crab, lured to the island by the beautiful mermaid's song. Falls head over heels in love and marries her. And then the jealous bastard stops her singing to the other lonely sailors. Thinks they're all pirates. Catches one stealing a glance and knocks the guy's teeth out. He loses all his mates, turns into a monster and frightens the mermaid away forever after.' Bert exploded with mad hoots of laughter and applause then said, 'The ending always gets me.'

'Nothing happened.'

'Of course it did. A long time ago.' He turned and fixed me with his good eye. 'May I enquire as to the purpose of your visitation?'

'I was wondering if I could have another look at the phrenology bust you showed me on Wednesday? I dreamt about it last night. Dr Eisler told me that amativeness means the ability to show romantic love.'

'Eisler? Wouldn't know him from Adam.'

'His name was written on the chest, and I wanted to see if it matches yours.'

'Sorry, no can do. Last night I got up and pissed a kidney stone. Hurt like the buggery. On me way back, I knocked the head off its stand. Smashed into a hundred pieces.'

'What time was it?'

'Who's watching the clock when they're pissin' blood?'

'Sorry.'

'Three-fifteen.' The same time it smashed in my dream.

Walking home, I speculated on whether Bert had actually ever seen that puppet show. Was he pulling my leg or trying to tell me something – or was he just completely mad? Maybe his mind's eye had developed more acutely to compensate for the real one that he'd lost.

As soon as I got back to the apartment, I resumed reading *My One Redeeming Affliction* in search of some answers to the increasing number of questions troubling my mind.

One fine February morning, a year after her father's wedding, Esther left the family home forever. Sitting on her suitcase at Woolloomooloo Wharf nursing a carpetbag filled with picnic supplies, she awaited her new husband's arrival on the *Phantom*. The day before, William had married Esther in the Registry Office with no relatives present, her father having forbidden all family members from involvement with the couple. Arthur and Samuel had promised to watch her departure this morning through binoculars from the ridge of Fernleigh's steeply gabled roof. As the *Phantom* pulled in, she turned to wave to the boys but couldn't make them out, her vision flooded with tears as the deckhand called, 'All aboard!'

The guilt and doubt Esther felt about leaving was mitigated by William's long embrace, a great relief after the scarce opportunity they'd had to be alone during their secret courtship. Halfway between the heads of the harbour, a blustery nor'-easter whipped off Esther's hat, lifting it high into the sky then dashing it directly before the threshing paddlewheel. Released from pins, her hair flicked about like a magnificent chestnut tail and whipped forward over her face. Instead of racing inside to fix it, she abandoned all hope of regaining decorum and laughed. Her decision to surrender to the natural elements by remaining outside with William was rewarded by a most wondrous spectacle – a pod of dolphins breached at the ship's bow and escorted them all the way to Manly.

Directly opposite the narrow wooden jetty, Henry Gilbert Smith's Pier Hotel gleamed like a white castle. The couple's room was situated next to the central turret, commanding glorious views of the harbour in front and bushland behind. After unpacking, they strolled down the Corso to the oceanfront and claimed a rare patch of new grass beneath a baby Norfolk pine. They feasted on cold cuts, Scotch eggs and fancy buns, watching the blue Pacific deliver her evenly spaced waves to the shore. Afterwards, they climbed Constitutional Hill to the camera obscura, an octagonal tower with no windows – the only light entering through a tiny hole. With a combination of lenses and mirrors, the surrounding landscape was projected onto a round table in the centre.

How strange to stand inside a dark chamber to view a mere reflection of the world outside. And yet the remoteness somehow offered a compelling new perspective of the location. Esther wrote later that day that for years she'd been locked in her own tower, observing life remotely, and in seeking to escape her father's restrictions she'd only subjected herself to the endless demands of Madame Zora instead. She wrote, 'Now, to my great relief, I've been rescued from miserable isolation and have finally tasted what it means to be truly alive. Could it be possible that this sense of elation is the responsibility of another? I would caution myself against attributing all of my new-found happiness to William – and yet it seems so. I am through with testing the waters. Casting all vestments aside, I shall let the waves crash over me, dive deep and yield myself to the rhythm of the sea.' Of course, she meant this in a strictly figurative sense, as public bathing was banned between six in the morning and eight at night.

On Monday, the couple headed north for Belgoolar by coach. The journey took a full day, as they stopped numerous times to swap passengers and twice to swap horses. Though the ride was hot and bumpy, the views were spectacular, with successive headlands revealing the golden crescents and turquoise waters that lay between. Whenever the road wove inland, the ocean's crash and settle remained in earshot. They crossed swampy mangrove flats and wooded hills, bidding farewell to their fellow travellers as they disembarked, until late in the afternoon when they sat alone with their driver.

He negotiated the final serpentine descent with consummate skill, keeping the horses well away from the road's crumbling edge. At last reaching the final bend he cried, 'Here's your bonny wee castle!' Perched on a grassy knoll and surrounded by palms, the weatherboard cottage featured a balcony facing the sea. After helping William offload the luggage, the driver let the horses slake their thirst, then drove them back up the hill before it swallowed the sun.

Days of blissful indolence, bushwalking and swimming unclothed as nature intended lulled Esther into imagining residing there permanently by the sea. Free now from obligation to her family or Madame Zora, she dreamt of returning to her first love – illustrating birds and other small creatures. Belgoolar's wildlife was magnificently diverse. Or perhaps William could open a fine-dining establishment in Manly? Heaven knew it was in dire need of one.

The weather remained fine until Friday, when the humidity rose dramatically, and late in the afternoon a storm front approached from the south-west – roiling clouds, dark and foreboding, being drawn up into the form of an enormous wave.

The couple observed the spectacle from the veranda – the lightning flashing white and purple over turbulent seas, until the clouds burst and the rain drove them indoors. Shortly after retiring for an early night, they heard a dog barking outside the cottage. Unable to remain in bed while the frightened creature was suffering beneath the storm, Esther went out and unlatched the little wooden gate at the bottom of the steps, allowing the chocolate-brown labrador up onto the veranda. William was annoyed at her indulgence, insisting that the dog would've found his way home soon enough if she'd ignored him. The veranda's protection was inadequate anyway, and the dog began barking again, so Esther let him into the cottage, placing a flatiron against the front door to keep it open.

My parents had their first heated argument that night. The dog had begun scratching at the bedroom door, desperate for the reassurance of company. My father refused to allow him in. My mother surrendered to my father, but was unable to adequately muffle her ears with her pillow against the poor creature's whimpering, which continued well into the night.

The next morning, the skies were still overcast and the atmosphere still humid. My mother's intuition told her that I had been conceived. But the brown labrador had disappeared. Decades later, in one of her rare lapses into irrational and superstitious musing, she expressed concern that the dog's presence that night, or her emotional response to his yelping, had somehow caused my affliction.

The return coach ride was hotter and bumpier than the trip out, and the couple were grateful to finally reach Manly and board the *Phantom*, as crowded as it was. Halfway across the harbour, my mother mentioned that she'd had a whimsical notion of residing somewhere far from the bustling city. My father initially dismissed the possibility, citing his need to be close to the restaurant. But further on, as the ferry passed the handsome villas on Kurrabeena Point at Mosman, he assured her that a pleasing compromise could be reached. Nine months later, I was born at Ambleside, the property closest to the water in Mosman, with the most beautiful grounds.

HOT OR NOT?

I entered The Hive on Monday morning with the forged medical note I was about to give Simmons burning in my pocket. Tibor had come through for me. I found the coach in his office, engaged in his favourite activity – reclining in his orange, yellow and brown tartan armchair, eating a sugar-dusted jam donut.

'Lincoln Locke,' he said, wiping his mouth. 'I hope you have a very good reason for disturbing my breakfast again.'

'Donut King, sir?'

'You wouldn't be stupid enough to offer nutritional advice?'

'No, sir. I came to tell you that I can't be in squad any longer. I've been diagnosed with a severe chlorine allergy. After swimming I break out in hives.'

He gave me a sceptical look. 'Let's go down to the water and you can show me.'

'Well, the thing is, the reaction happens eight or nine hours after exposure. Here's a photo of my arm.' I showed him the shot that I took in The Labyrinth and gave him the fake medical note, which he read as he chomped into his second jam donut.

'Hmm, Dr Torsten Mintz. Father of Tibor? Would you mind if I gave Dr Mintz a call to discuss the best way to manage the situation?'

217

'It's a bit early.'

'Not now, later.' He finished the donut then nailed me with his gaze. 'I'm very disappointed about this, Locke.'

'That makes two of us, sir. I'm devastated that I won't be able to represent Crestfield.'

'We can't have you missing out then. You can train in salt water, under the supervision of one of your parents or a designated guardian. They'd be fully aware that the selection committee's decision to offer you a place at Crestfield was significantly influenced by your swimming ability.'

Not the worst outcome, but far from the best. If Simmons called Tibor's father, I'd be toast. I went to the upstairs toilets and spent longer than necessary washing my hands. By the time I returned, the lanes were filled with splashing swimmers. I sat with Gelber and she grilled me on the allergy, then asked me to hand out the pull buoys. Nads was first out, heading my way to grab one. Asking if he enjoyed his break wouldn't go down well. Best to let him speak first. He snatched the pull buoy without saying a word. Mullows and Starkey followed, looking straight through me. Starkey's uncharacteristic restraint was unnerving.

Pericles came last and asked me why I wasn't in the pool. I told him the fake excuse and he called bullshit, so I fessed up.

'I have a problem that's way worse than some skin allergy.'

'Shit – it's not something fatal, is it?'

'Far from, but it's killing me with embarrassment and I can't talk about it right now. I got Tibor to write a fake medical note to get me out of squad.'

'For real? Tibor's a legend. Does that mean you're off the relay team for the Invitational, and I'm back on?'

'Simmons is making me train in salt water. Sorry, mate. I'm still on the team.'

'It's all good, bruh.' Pericles gave me a wet bear hug. 'I hope your embarrassment problem clears up soon.'

*

218

After school, Isa took me to her place, a narrow two-storey terrace in Erskineville, to work on our project. As we walked through the kitchen she called out to Delilah.

'She's helping with the weeding,' a voice replied. We went to the garden, where a woman in denim shorts and red singlet was kneeling on a pad, turning the soil. Delilah was pouncing on the weeds she flicked aside. Then, just like Oscar with new company, she trotted up to me and rubbed against my calf.

'I usually wait till I'm introduced before I do that,' the woman said to the cat.

'Terri, this is my friend Lincoln. We're collaborating on an art assignment.'

'Hello, Lincoln. I'm Terri, who's just picked some overripe tomatoes from the vine.' She tossed one to Isa. 'Stef's going to make a batch of passata.' Terri scratched Delilah's neck until her tail started snaking left and right, and I felt a sympathetic, irritated tingle in mine. Then the cat twisted around and clawed Terri's forearm. 'How quickly she turns.'

'Dinnertime for you.' Isa scooped up Delilah. The cat growled and writhed free, then ran and hid among the creepers. 'Wait till your mother gets home!' Isa said.

Back in the kitchen, she poured me some water and I asked if Terri lived with them.

'Terri and Mum have been friends forever. She and Stef have the upstairs. The garden's communal.'

'Is Terri a lesbian?'

'She's an antiques and vintage dealer.'

'No, seriously.'

'You'd have to ask her wife.'

'She doesn't look like a lesbian,' I said. Isa rolled her eyes. 'Sorry. Stupid comment.'

'Yeah, a bit. And before you ask, my mum's not in a polyamorous relationship with them and she's not a lesbian.'

'I wasn't going to.' There was an awkward pause.

'Some people think Phoenix and I are together, but we're not.

I love her to death but not in a sexual way. Phoenix says gender plays no part in who she's attracted to – it's the person that matters.'

'Do you think sexual orientation's genetic?'

'Probably, but I don't believe it's a binary thing anyway, not even a scale. I think we're all on a swirling sphere. What about you?'

I twisted my ear, hoping it might produce an answer – but nothing came, so I shrugged and said, 'Don't know.'

'It's complex,' Isa said. She rinsed the glasses, then turned back around and said, 'Talking of genetics, we should get started on the DNA. I've made a couple of base pairs.'

Isa pulled two knitted cigar shapes from a wicker box and tossed me a pink-and-green one. 'That represents guanine and cytosine. The yellow-and-blue is thymine and adenine. Make sure you stick to those combinations. Here's the chart,' she said, passing it to me. 'I've calculated we'll have to knit five hundred each.'

'Is that even possible?' I did a quick mental calculation. 'If it takes me an hour to knit one and I knit for two hours every day, it would take me eight months and that's not even taking the coils into consideration.'

'That's why we need a crew. Phoenix, Mum and Terri are on board, and your nana is a gun. It doesn't matter if it ends up a bit shorter than planned.'

We began knitting. After a while the conversation turned to fellow students and Isa suggested we play 'Hot or Not?' She mostly said 'hot' for the girls, whereas I never said 'hot' for any of the guys. After almost exhausting the Year 10 student body, Isa frowned and said, 'Are you trying to tell me there're no good-looking guys in our year?'

'You only chose three or four.'

'What about Pericles? Hot or not?'

'He's my friend. I don't see him in those terms.'

'He's my friend too and I think he's completely hot.'

'Okay, I concede he's good-looking.'

'Why can't you say "hot"?'

'If I said he was hot while knitting it would look indisputably gay, so I'm putting it down first.' I did so, then cleared my throat and said, 'Okay. Pericles Pappas is hot for a guy.'

We resumed knitting and worked till sometime after 8 pm, when Isa's mother arrived home. 'I don't smell cooking,' she said, walking down the hall.

'We were busy with the project.' Isa introduced me to Dee, an intensive-care nurse who looked as though she could've been Isa's older sister, and asked how her day had gone.

'Mr Charles didn't pull through, which was terribly sad, and I know you're thinking I've had a cigarette and you're correct and I'll start quitting again tomorrow. Lincoln, I hope you're staying for dinner? We're all vegetarian here. Do you eat meat?' I nodded. 'Of course you do,' she said with a wink. 'Hot or not?' She frisbeed an Indian delivery menu to Isa. 'Order whatever you like, darling, and something for the carnivore while I have a pee. And don't forget that naan we love, the potato one.'

I shared a dinner with Isa's family – Dee, Terri and Stef and Delilah – and observed her interacting with the women with warmth and humour. The single hiccup came when I asked for a cushion to go on my slatted wooden stool because it was aggravating the tail, and Terri hassled me for being the only princess in the room. I broke into a sweat and blamed the vindaloo, then Isa deftly took the heat off by passing me the raita. In a lively conversation after dinner, she held her own on topics that ranged from pop culture to literature to world affairs, and I internally conceded something that I'd suspected for some time: Isa Mountwinter was way smarter than me.

EVERYTHING TURNS

Two weeks passed and Sydney finally threw off its cloak of humidity for a snappy new autumn outfit. The days were bright and sparkling, sunny but cool. The sea was the only part of the city graciously holding on to its warmth. I'd started training at Bondi in the day and some nights in T H E E Y R I E's pool if there were no more than two other people in there. It was usually only Patricia from level twenty-nine – the lady with the daisy cap, who mostly swam breaststroke and kept her head above water. Anybody else and I'd have kept my board shorts on. The tail had become easy to spot in Speedos, but with the end of the swimming season approaching, the threat of exposure would soon be removed.

Our group of collaborators on the art project widened. Nana Locke and her friend Glenda both knitted five-metre coils, and I went to Isa's place three more times for knitting circles. Isa, Phoenix, Dee, Terri and I knitted while Stef looked after drinks, snacks and neck massages. Sometimes it was awkward being the 'only rooster in the hen house' – Dee's words, not mine – and I hardly spoke unless Stef said, 'Now let's hear from the voice of man', which made the pressure to represent without sounding sexist or anything-phobic a bit tricky. But the friendly needling, mostly figurative and sometimes literal, was a small price to pay. My friendship with Isa was advancing in leaps and bounds, and she invited me to her birthday at Luna Park.

Friday night, Dad arrived home and went straight to his room without saying hello. When he finally emerged, his face was swollen, lips puffy and teeth arctic white. Following my interrogation, he finally admitted to a couple of non-invasive rejuvenating procedures.

'The swelling should go down by tomorrow and nobody will notice the difference,' he said.

'What's the point of it then?'

'In a competitive environment like mine, looking fresh is equated with relevance. It's all about giving yourself an edge over your rivals.'

'So you can pick up younger women like Sophie?'

'I was talking about work, mate. I'm competing with cowboys ten, fifteen years younger than me. Steve and I share some interests, but his preference for younger women definitely isn't one of them. There's nothing happening with Sophie.'

I was tempted to confront him about Maëlle but I literally bit my tongue to stop myself. Seeing my father yield to whatever pressure he felt to look younger made my heart sink. Mum was often surrounded by tight-faced celebrities and pouty models but she'd never gone as far as cosmetic procedures. Despite her line of work, she maintained that beauty is within. I didn't fully believe that, though – from what I could tell, it was mostly physical and largely determined by genetics, and you could be beautiful even if you were a complete and utter turd. There were heaps of beautiful shits in the world.

On Saturday evening Isa, Dee, Phoenix, Pericles, Tibor and I met under the menacingly happy face of Luna Park. Darkness hadn't fallen but its crown was already flashing – its teeth glowing almost whiter than Dad's. In the interest of remaining unencumbered, Isa had insisted on no cards or presents so I complied, wishing her a happy birthday with just a peck on the cheek. Flouting the rule, Pericles gave her a Tiffany heart bracelet. The extravagance made Tibor and I look tighter than a pair of sardine's arseholes. Tibor filled the awkward void with trivia. 'The first Luna Park opened in Coney Island, New York, in nineteen hundred and three. Ours opened thirty-two years later, with a funhouse called Coney Island located inside the park.'

'Fascinating,' Phoenix said. 'Shall we go in now?'

Stumbling along the motorised shuffle boards of Coney Island's Wonky Walk, Tibor looked like Bambi on ice. Isa told me to stop laughing, but wasn't laughing the point? Once inside, we charged through the Barrels of Fun and rode hessian mats down the Giant Slides, which had shrunk since I was a kid. The Joy Wheel was still Coney's best feature. The girls claimed prime position on the slightly conical disk, linking arms back to back at the centre. As it started revolving, we all pressed in. Phoenix peeled Tibor's fingers off. He lost traction, tucked into a ball and rolled off, hitting the boundary's padding with a >BOOF!< that thrilled the spectators. Pericles wedged himself between Dee and Isa's legs, but Dee prised him away with her heel. Halfway down he grabbed my foot, and as he was whirling at five times my speed, the force was irresistible. We slipped and spun off like skydivers breaking formation, me on my stomach to avoid tail friction.

Pericles cuffed me. 'Why'd you let go, pussy? We could've taken them down.'

The operator cranked it to top speed but still couldn't budge the girls. They remained a unified force until the disk stopped spinning, then stood up and walked off with their fists in the air. 'Who runs the world?' Phoenix shouted.

From that moment, Pericles turned everything into a competition. At the dodgems I scored a clapped-out jalopy. Lap after lap Pericles rammed into my car then forced me into a corner, wedging me between two other stalled drivers. Before I could extricate myself from the jam, the bell rang – session over. Next was the Tango. Waiting in line, Pericles claimed shotgun and manoeuvred himself next to Isa. Phoenix chose Dee, leaving me with Tibor. As the ride turned, Tibor made a valiant attempt to stay on his side of the carriage but as we reached full throttle his strength failed and he slammed into me. Hurtling around the undulating track with AC/DC's 'T.N.T.' destroying the speakers and Tibor destroying my ribs was hilarious.

'So much fun,' Dee said afterwards. 'But I might've done a little wee. Perhaps we should have a break on something more gentle, like the Ferris wheel?' Together in one gondola we were lifted into the clear night sky, high above the park's flashing lights, and I felt happier than I'd been for a year. Tibor and Pericles discussed the ramifications of dropping a fifty-cent piece from the Harbour Bridge. Would it crack the skull of a tourist on a ferry gliding beneath or just give them a nasty fright and a permanent dent? Meanwhile, Isa and Dee admired Phoenix's manicure, indigo with glow-in-the-dark skulls.

'You like my nails?' she said, waggling them in front of Pericles. 'Remember when we painted yours?'

'No.' Pericles hid his hands.

'How could you forget? The colour was Flaming Flamingo.'

Dee rescued Pericles by cutting in. 'Next ride will have to be our last. Let's have a vote.'

The decision was unanimous: the ROTOR.

On a cream-coloured façade was a sign that read:

LUNA PARK
PRESENTS
PROFESSOR E. HOFFMEISTER'S
WORLD FAMOUS SCIENTIFIC THEATRE

and beneath, in glowing red letters:

ROTOR

Decorating the façade were comical paintings of women trying in vain to stop their skirts riding up and an upside-down sailor. 'Let's give it a go,' Pez whispered to me, as we climbed the narrow stairs. Isa and Dee continued up to the spectator gallery. Phoenix, Tibor, Pericles and I entered the rubber-lined barrel of what was ostensibly a giant washing machine. The operator issued instructions we ignored and the barrel began revolving.

'Look up!' Isa called from the gallery and took a photo. As we approached top speed, the floor dropped away from our feet, eliciting a squeal from the ROTOR virgins, despite us all being safely pinned against the wall. The spinning was nauseating until my brain readjusted, making me feel as if I was stationary and the spectator gallery above was revolving instead.

'Now!' Pez said, and began manoeuvring himself around. I followed his lead, wincing from the pain of my tail grinding against the black rubber as I turned.

'Don't back down now,' Homunculus said. 'Stay with him!'

Soon Pericles was completely upside down and I was ten degrees off vertical.

>RETURN TO THE UPRIGHT POSITION IMMEDJIATELY, OR THE RIDE WILL BE STOPPED AND YOU WILL BE ESCORTED FROM THE PARK!<

The vocalised 'J' of the operator's empty threat made us laugh, because if she stopped the ride 'immedjiately' we'd come crashing down on our heads. But we followed her order and edged ourselves back to the correct position. As the ride slowed, everybody began to slip, an aspect of the experience I'd forgotten to anticipate. The drag of the tail against the rubber produced a searing pain as if it were being torn from its roots, so I spread my arms and tried to dig my fingers into the wall to resist the pull of gravity. Isa and Dee called something from the gallery but my hearing and vision were fading.

And I blacked out.

Instead of the ROTOR, I was now riding a red-and-gold bike in a circle, chasing my father who was chasing Maëlle

chasing Mum
chasing Starkey
chasing Nads
chasing Tibor
chasing Mullows
chasing Phoenix

chasing Pericles

chasing Isa

chasing me. Our bikes were fixed on a huge revolving ring. The race was futile but still we pedalled faster and faster, until the pain from the narrow bike seat became unbearable and I shouted, 'LET ME OFF NOW!'

I opened my eyes and found myself back on the floor of the ROTOR with my friends around me, the circular platform having ascended to its starting position.

'It's okay, mate,' Pericles says. 'We're all getting off now.'

'How long was I out for?'

'I didn't realise you were.'

Nothing I'd read lately in *My One Redeeming Affliction* had grabbed my attention like the scene with the labrador in the storm. The chapter after that had mostly been about Edwin Stroud's supposedly perfect childhood days growing up at Ambleside in Mosman, and the arrival of his brother Thomas and sister Loula. But the passage I read tonight when I got home from Luna Park got my head spinning.

In my father's thirteenth year of operating his restaurant at Pemberton's Magnificent Emporium, the banking crisis struck and rates of visitation to the glittering palace of consumerism plummeted. Living by the adage that one has to spend money in order to make money, Pemberton spent a small fortune purchasing new attractions for the Market Carnival, hoping his confidence would inspire the masses to follow suit. Regardless of economic climate, people are irresistibly drawn to novelty, if only as a distraction from their woes, and George Pemberton was the undisputed king of innovation. His prized attraction, the Velocipede, was imported from France, and forty-two lucky people were invited to partake in the inaugural revolution, my family topping the list.

The mechanism looked similar to a merry-go-round, with red-and-gold cycles replacing the horses for men and two-seater carriages for the ladies – at least that was the order of things when operating in Paris. But on the ride's first run in Sydney, my mother put my sister

Loula and brother Thomas in a carriage and claimed the cycle behind them. My father took the cycle in front and allowed me to lead the charge, though as I was only eleven my feet barely reached the pedals. Pemberton delivered a welcome speech then nodded to a red-coated attendant, who tooted his whistle to set us pedalling.

The giant ring revolved slowly at first, but once momentum built we were whizzing around the banked metal track at a decent clip. The men and my mother – the only woman cycling – spurred each other on with high-spirited taunts. Faster and faster we pedalled, sending the carriage-riders into fits of laughter and squeals of terrified delight. Then, just as we hit top speed, Loula's hat was blown off, provoking a shriek high enough to shatter the crystal ornaments in the homewares department. We ceased pedalling and, when the ride eventually stopped, my mother lifted Loula bawling from the carriage.

'Here's a treat to cheer you up!' the avuncular Pemberton said, pulling a strap of liquorice from his sleeve. 'I think Her Majesty will take great pleasure in our new marionette theatre. And what jolly good fortune: the first performance is about to commence!'

We made our way to the theatre and settled in for the show. Sailor boy Jack Tar was lured to an island by a mermaid's singing, his boat destroyed on the reef. The mermaid promised to kiss him if he closed his eyes. When the hapless sailor puckered up, the mermaid switched places with a sea monster, who kissed the sailor passionately. Jack Tar recoiled from the sea monster's fishy breath and offered him a tin of Hooper's Cachou for breath correction. Mortally offended, the sea monster swallowed the sailor whole then writhed about with indigestion. Finally he released an enormous belch, expelling Jack Tar's tiny white bones – peppermint candies that Thomas, Loula and I scrambled to gather.

As the other guests were leaving, Pemberton invited my family to his quarters for a special private viewing. Before allowing us to enter, he gave an impromptu speech on the way forward for mankind. 'We must learn to embrace not only our neighbour but also the foreigner – the stranger on the other side of the globe who is our cousin, distant only geographically. Whether black or white, brown, yellow or red, we are one family.'

There was a hoot and screech followed by a bang from behind the door, which he ignored.

'Peace amongst the nations will surely only prevail when we all acknowledge our common ancestor.' Another, louder bang.

'What's that noise?' Thomas said.

'Mr Darwin postulated that all living things originated from a single source and, over millions of years, evolved in diverse ways. I have behind this wall one of our closest cousins who grew up in deepest Congo, blithely unaware of man's existence. I've been teaching him how to behave like a gentleman, but he will not be displayed until he's quite fit for the challenge. His name is Mr Whitby Pemberton. As long as you promise to keep his existence secret, you may now enter and make his acquaintance.'

My father, my siblings and I were all delighted by the caged chimpanzee. But I'll never forget the desolation on my mother's face when Whitby Pemberton soiled the trousers of his ill-fitting suit.

I was baffled by the fact that Edwin Stroud's description of the Velocipede matched the vision I'd experienced just hours earlier on the ROTOR. Even the colours of the cycles were the same – red and gold. The synchronicity was starting to spook me. At least the puppet show in the book wasn't much like the version that Bert had narrated. But still, the coincidences were uncanny. Had Bert read *My One Redeeming Affliction* at some point in his life and merely forgotten the details of the show? Or had he been trying to tell me a story of his own?

TERMINALLY DISCONNECTED

I swam a couple of lengths of Bondi Beach early this morning, without Dad. The Invitational is approaching and if I don't perform well in the relay the Gooch Gang won't be happy. Sitting on the promenade eating a smoky-bacon triple-fillet chicken burger, I noticed seven boats grouped near Ben Buckler Point. A humpback whale breached next to them, close enough for me to see its barnacles. Must've been the first whale of the season. I remembered that in the film *Pinocchio*, Monstro the whale swallowed Geppetto, Pinocchio, his cat Figaro and goldfish Cleo. The Bible has Jonah being swallowed by a whale. And in Edwin's account of the puppet show, the sailor was eaten by a sea monster. Maybe it was a common plot device, like Punch and Judy assaulting each other back in the day? After my freak-out last night, I reassured myself there were probably hundreds of sailor puppets, and Bert's just happened to be similar to the one in the book.

Riding the bus home, I recalled that Pinocchio's lies not only caused the nose action, he also grew a tail. What had triggered the growth of his humiliating appendage? I found the origin of the curse on a YouTube clip. On his way to Pleasure Island, Pinocchio was coaxed into smoking a cigar and drinking beer by a punk called

Lampwick. Partaking in those vices triggered his metamorphosis into donkey boy.

'You've been cursed for getting drunk at the party last year and swallowing those pills Nads gave you,' Homunculus said.

'Settle down, Jiminy Cricket. It started growing much earlier. Around the time I lied about the letter from Crestfield.'

'Bingo! You're Pinocchio Mark Two and Bert, with his collection of mangy puppets, is a bald, alcoholic and deranged Geppetto.'

Crazy old Bert – he'd looked so gaunt the last time I saw him, like he hadn't eaten for a week. A momentary surge of compassion jump-started my little wooden heart and led me to the Vietnamese bakery across the road to buy him a pie, sausage roll and pork banh mi. I walked down to his street, congratulating myself on my second kind act for the year, after having visited Nana Locke last month. But then I figured that neither act was entirely altruistic: I'd seen Nana Locke for a knitting lesson and today I was planning to finally ask Bert if he'd ever read *My One Redeeming Affliction*. Approaching the junkyard, I saw this sign posted outside his neighbour's house:

INTRODUCING PARADIGM
THE ELITE NEW LIFESTYLE PRECINCT
WITH STUDIOS, 1-, 2- AND 3-BEDROOM
OPPORTUNITIES
FOR SALE OFF THE PLAN NOW!
ULTRA-MODERN DESIGN WITH FLUID
INTERIORS, EXPANSIVE ENTERTAINING
OPTIONS AND STUNNING VERTICAL GARDENS
CREATING THE PERFECT SANCTUARY
IS OUR VISION
PARADIGM IS YOUR NEW REALITY
PRICES RANGE FROM $590,000 TO $3,500,000

Beneath the blurb was a web address and phone number to register interest.

Bert's house would be dwarfed by the development. It wasn't even included in the artist's impression.

There was now a locked chain on his gate. 1-2-3-4-5 seemed too obvious, but the lock fell open when I dialled the combination. Around the back, Bert was hunched on the crimson chair muttering away to Percy, three empty longnecks lined up on the ground. 'What are you doing here?' he said, his working eye fierce.

'I thought I might pop in to—'

'You've popped in and now you can pop out again.'

'I brought you something to eat.'

'Broke my lock, did ya?' He was fidgeting with a bunch of square-holed Chinese coins on a wire loop. 'You're a real regular Alan Turing.'

'It wasn't hard.'

'Only sequence I could remember.' He kicked a milk crate towards me, so I sat and tried to ignore the discomfort of the hard edges cutting into my tail. Bert was giving me a quizzical look. 'What's in your bag then?'

'A meat pie, sausage roll and Vietnamese roll, if you want them?'

'Lost me appetite.' He slid the coins along the wire as you would an abacus. 'Worry beads. Help me to mull things over.' He used one to prise the cap off his next bottle.

'I see you've got some new neighbours moving in.'

'Sanctuary, my arse! They're destroying my sanctuary, building that pile of shit smack-bang on top of me like a gravestone.'

'They can't do that. This is your home.'

'Not anymore. We got a little behind on the mortgage repayments – bank foreclosed on us. Have to be out in a month.'

'Not much warning.'

'Two years ago the developers came with their offers. Chickenfeed at first but went up. Neighbours dropped like flies. Took the cash and ran. I stuck to me guns. Just wanted to stay put. I was happy here. Then those young larrikins started giving me grief. Called the coppers on 'em a few times. Reported them to the principal.'

'How could I forget?'

'I'm no weatherman, but I'd say this is my last winter.'

'It's only just autumn.'

'The collector will be collected, terminally disconnected, thoroughly disinfected, rudimentally inspected, scientifically dissected, bagged and ejected.'

'Where will you go?'

'I'm banking on instantaneous obliteration. Never ascribed to the idea of eternal torment. Done that to myself for long enough. Poof!' He made a gesture like an explosion. 'I'm gone. No comeback tour.'

Bert chuckled himself into a violent coughing fit and waved me away but I couldn't just leave. Then he spat a gob of screamingly red phlegm onto the ground, turned to Percy and said, 'What are you laughing at, you little shit?' He ripped the bird off his perch and threw him at my chest. 'You can piss off now, the pair of you. And you can take these with you.' He threw the coins at my feet as if I was some sort of Judas. I picked up Percy but left the coins. 'You've got more worries ahead of you, boyo. Pick them up.'

I shook my head.

'PICK THEM UP!' he shouted.

So I picked up the coins.

'NOW GET OUT OF HERE! GO!'

I hightailed it out of the yard, leaving the food behind, and walked up to the apartment. Percy was looking even more ruffled than me, so when I got back to my room I wrapped him in tissue paper and put him in a small box. Then I lay on my bed, fiddling with the Chinese coins and worrying over what would become of Bert. Fearing that time was running out for him, and with it the opportunity to find answers to my gnawing questions, I read on.

My mother learnt of my father's addiction to gambling only after his untimely death. Ah To, a.k.a. Johnny, his friend of seventeen years, came to pay his respects and share his account of the last few hours of my father's life. Since their goldmining days, both men had been keen players of fan-tan, a devilishly simple game of chance wherein the operator inverts a bowl of coins on the table and the players bet on how many will remain after being divided into lots of four with a bamboo hook. Johnny and William's favourite venue was located on the top floor of a warehouse in Chinatown. One wet June night the operation was raided.

Spotting two policemen scaling the roof, Ah Jung, the lookout, raised the alarm. Sergeant Hale, walrus-like both in stature and appearance, got momentarily stuck in the skylight, affording the gamblers and operators precious time to hide the evidence. By the time he and the younger Constable Maclean stormed into the hall, most of the men had taken up books. Hale approached my father, the only Caucasian player, whose head was buried in a Chinese newspaper, and told him to read the headline.

'Rabid dog bites man on Liverpool-street,' my father replied, without missing a beat.

Walking across the room to examine a ceramic urn, Maclean trod on a loose floorboard and lifted it. He ferreted between the joists and discovered a gaming mat, then declared the entire company under arrest. But whether it was a case of racial prejudice or William being known to him, Sergeant Hale offered clemency to my father. 'You're surely not acquainted with these Oriental heathens?' he said. 'Stumbled in here to escape the rain, didn't you? I suggest you stumble back out quick smart, or your name won't be worth the stink of shit on my boot.'

My father gathered his jacket and hat and walked to the stairs, leaving Johnny at the table. But before descending he said, 'My apology for contradicting you, sergeant, but I do know one of these men very well.' He indicated his friend with a nod. 'Johnny is the hardest working, most honest man I've ever had the fortune to meet. If you'd kindly overlook this one indiscretion and allow him to accompany me, we would both be eternally grateful.'

Despite his subordinate's protest, Sergeant Hale permitted both men to leave without further questioning. Instead of demonstrating the sort of caution one might expect after a close call by heading straight home, my father and Johnny celebrated their exemption from arrest at the Light-house Hotel. After downing three pints, my father farewelled Johnny and rode a tram towards Bridge-street, intending to catch the last ferry from Circular Quay back to Mosman. But as the tram approached the terminus, with three pints of false confidence under his belt he leapt without looking, into the path of an oncoming engine. The south-bound tram smashed my father's spirit clear out of its physical home forever.

I felt an almost physical blow to my chest that knocked the wind out of me. I recalled that, earlier in the book, Edwin had written:

Bloody arrival to bloodier departure, my father William's life was punctuated by accidents – some grave, others fortuitous.

So I should've been in some way prepared for it. But William's sudden death by tram resonated heavily with Pop Locke's demise by 4WD. I'd only known William through the book, and yet reading the account of his death made me exceedingly sad. I threw off my quilt and hid Percy and the Chinese coins in the guest room, hoping that would prevent them from seeping into my dreams.

THE CRUELLEST WORDS

I expected Consumer Mathematics to bore the living shit out of me but as Mr Monaro began explaining the finer points of compound interest, credit cards, mortgages and loans I became engrossed. Not because I could see myself ever having any of those things, but because it helped me to understand Bert's dire situation. How could you get so old and still be paying off a mortgage? In French, Miss Moreau had taught us that *mort* means death. Appropriate. Bert couldn't make the payments and now he'd lost his place on Earth.

Fifteen minutes before lunch the electronic glockenspiel sounded and the Dash announced a special assembly for Years 10 to 12. Everyone filed into the auditorium buzzing with speculation, which turned to disappointment the second Heather Treadwell took the stage. 'Another recruitment drive for the debating team or God Squad,' Phoenix said.

But instead Heather started talking about Fergus Martin, the kid I'd seen on *Extreme Medical Intervention* who'd lost both legs after catching meningitis. An image of an older Fergus standing on pros-thetic legs was projected onto the screen behind her.

I nudged Isa and said, 'That's the guy I was telling you about.'

'I figured.'

'You might be feeling sorry for Fergus,' Heather said. 'But he needs something more practical than sympathy. An expert in advanced bio-mechanics has nominated Fergus as the perfect candidate for bionic legs with powered knee and ankle joints, but they cost over one hundred and thirty thousand dollars each. I thought Crestfield should do something to help and came up with a fun idea that involves every single one of you.'

'Here we go,' Phoenix said.

Heather announced a 'Dance for Fergus'. Tickets would be fifty bucks each, or eighty for a couple if you invited someone from outside Crestfield. Volunteers for the organising committee were asked to meet after the assembly.

'What a great idea,' Isa said on our way out. 'I hope everyone goes.'

'Doubtful,' Phoenix said. 'It'll be something ultra-nerdy like square dancing.'

'I don't think so,' Pez said. 'Have a look at who's joining the organising committee.'

At the foot of the stage Cheyenne Piper, the Petersen twins and two Year 12 girls were holding each other's hands and jumping up and down in a huddle around a glowing Heather.

This afternoon in English I learnt that Mary Shelley began writing *Frankenstein* when she was eighteen. What messed-up stuff was swimming around in that girl's head? Messed-up enough for her to release a monster that still lingers in our collective psyche 200 years later. I also learnt that the monster himself had no name. Frankenstein was the scientist who built him from a selection of body parts he'd gathered from the slaughterhouses – a little bit of everything thrown in, like the meat tray Nana Locke often wins at Dee Why RSL. When Mr Field called on me to explain what I thought the book was about, I said that when you're hell-bent on fulfilling a vision, you can easily lose perspective. Like Dr Frankenstein, your dream can turn into a nightmare that will eventually consume and destroy you.

Mr Field said, 'Very interesting, Mr Locke.'

'Very interesting, Mr Locke,' Starkey echoed twenty minutes later as I was unchaining my bike from the rack, before flicking his cigarette butt at me. 'Looks like you've become a Field mouse.'

'That's ripe coming from someone who looks like a rat.'

'You're coming very close to having your face smashed in.'

'Can I quote you on that?'

'Fucking squealer!'

'I didn't squeal. You copped the punishment you deserved for harassing a defenceless man. Why do you do that cruel shit anyway?'

'Are you talking about the Nang-Nang?'

'Starkey, there is no Nang-Nang. There's just a lonely old guy called Bert McGill.'

'You've gone there again.'

'No, I haven't.'

Starkey grabbed my collar and pulled my face towards his – eyes burning with hatred. 'Funny, I could've sworn I saw you there.' His rank breath hit me with force.

'Why do you care if I visit him? It's got nothing to do with you.'

'Oh yes it does, and this is your last warning. Stay away or you'll be the one needing someone to wipe your arse for you.'

Tuesday afternoon, I invited Isa to knit at my place instead of hers. Reaching level twenty-seven, I told her to stay in the hallway so I could tidy up a little. I ran to my bedroom, threw my stray undies in the drawer then ran back to let her in. 'Welcome to Locke Tower,' I said with a sweeping gesture.

'Is your dad, like, a billionaire or something?'

'Not even something. The bank owns it.' I gave her the grand tour and she couldn't resist touching surfaces: the engineered-stone kitchen bench, wooden coffee table, soft leather sofa. She knelt on the lounge-room floor and caressed the carpet. 'Grading the wool?' I said.

'I'm a very tactile person.'

'Oh, I can see that. Come and check out the view.' I led her out onto the balcony and instead of expressing awe she asked if I spied on the neighbours.

'Of course not.'

'I would,' she said, and gave me a wry grin. 'Show me your bedroom?'

'All right, but you can't touch anything.'

She walked in and said it looked like an IKEA showroom.

'Try out the POÄNG,' I said. 'It comes with a ten-year guarantee.'

Isa sat down and bounced. 'Why haven't you put up some pictures or anything?'

'I wasn't planning on staying long so I kept it devoid of personality.'

'Funny – that's exactly the impression you gave when you started at Crestfield. You never spoke to anybody and never smiled. I thought you were completely full of yourself.'

'Now that is funny,' I said, holding up a finger. 'Because I thought the same about you. You acted like you'd never seen me before when I was waiting to see Dr Limberg.'

'Point taken. That was unfair and I apologise. This is no excuse, but it was all about self-protection.' She went on to tell me about her experience doing school service, which was similar to Tibor's. Cheyenne Piper and her friends had started calling her Nurse Betty when she worked in Student Welfare, and Dawn Sparrowfart when serving in the café. Cheyenne would order ten things and keep changing her mind, then say she forgot her purse and walk away. Dee told Isa they were jealous because Isa had earnt her way into Crestfield while their parents had paid their way in. She suggested embracing the personas they'd foisted on her – make fun of herself before they could, to take their power away.

Isa and I talked and knitted for a couple of hours, both lowering our guards more than ever before. After a period of silence, she asked if I was going to the Dance for Fergus.

'Haven't thought about it,' I said. 'What about you?'

'I haven't stopped thinking about it. It's an honourable mission but could so easily turn pageant. Last year Tiffany Chaney wore a Prada gown to the Year 12 formal that cost three grand.'

'You made that name up.'

'Unfortunately her parents did.'

'So are you going?'

'Maybe, but the whole "who's going with who" performance annoys me. You can go alone of course, but it's not a good look. I hate feeling like I need a guy to validate me. If nobody asks me I might invite Phoenix.'

'And fuel the rumours?'

Isa looked to the ceiling and groaned. Then, without warning, she pounced onto my bed and started tickling me. 'Stop!' I said, unable to push her away with the knitting in my hands.

'Wee bit ticklish, are we?' Her fingers dug between my ribs and one of my needles dropped. She tickled my stomach, causing my tail to flick rapidly and my right leg to shake like Gus's used to.

'Please stop!'

'Sorry, I can't hear you.' Isa's nails were grazing me all over, driving me into a frenzy of involuntary laughter.

'Oh God, please stop! Think of the project.'

Isa was drunk with power, oblivious to my pleas – sadistic Nurse Betty, probing to discover my sensitive regions.

'What about here?' she said, yanking and twisting my earlobes. 'Or here?', fingers burrowing under my arms then behind my knees. The knitting was a lost cause – almost completely unhitched. Then she ran her fingers down my vertebrae.

I had a flashback of the fateful night with Nicole Parker, terrified Isa would touch my tail. 'NO!' I yelled and pushed her off.

'Whoa. Overreaction much?' she said, propping herself up. 'I thought we were having fun.'

'You were,' I said, but my tone was too harsh. Isa looked confused and hurt.

'I guess I should be going then?' she said, fixing her hair.

'You don't have to.'

'Said with such conviction.' She fetched her bag, slung it over her shoulder and walked to the door. I followed her.

'I'm really sorry that I snapped. It's just – it's just that I have this really stupid thing about people coming into my personal space and—'

'No need to explain.' She was almost at the front door when it flung open and Dad walked through.

'Oh – hello there,' he said. 'I'm Lance. I don't believe we've had the pleasure?'

'I'm Isa. Your son and I have been working on a project together and I was just leaving. Nice to meet you, Mr Locke.' And she was gone.

'Wowee!' Dad said, pulling a beer from the fridge. 'I knew you were knitting with a friend, but you didn't tell me what a stunner she is.' He opened the bottle and flicked the cap into the bin. 'You've been up to something, haven't you, eh? Son of a gun.' He tousled my hair. 'Just like your old man after all.'

'You mean creepy?'

'I beg your pardon?'

It probably wasn't the ideal time for a confrontation – there rarely is – but his comment about Isa had lit the fuse.

'Did you fool around with Maëlle Beauvais in your den on the night of Mum's fiftieth birthday?'

'Don't be ridiculous,' he said with a crooked smile.

'Venn showed me an email from Maëlle where she confessed that you'd kissed.'

Dad placed his beer on the bench too carefully, as if he was trying not to smash it, and looked directly into my eyes, defying me to continue. With a wavering voice I told him everything that I'd read in the email. He didn't flinch. He didn't speak. He just shook his head. Then he walked out to the balcony and back, slapped his palm on the seat of a stool and told me calmly, in an even voice, that she'd made it up.

'Bullshit,' I said. 'One of the other guests told Mum she'd seen you in the den with Maëlle.'

Dad fake-laughed and said, 'I'd invited her to come and sign the card. I told her I was stressed and she gave me a neck massage. Nothing more.'

'I know that you kissed her but I don't want to believe it. So if you keep denying this, it'll do my head in.' Tears welled in my eyes and my

241

voice wavered. 'The sad thing is that you've already done that to Mum. You made her feel like she was going mad.'

Instead of admitting his guilt, Dad reeled off a list of excuses for his behaviour. Mum had been remote for months, she was going through menopause, she was making him feel unwanted, he'd been stressed at work, he felt like a failure, Maëlle had seduced him. I stood there listening to it all, irritation bubbling inside me, and when he reached the point I feared he was heading for and used Pop Locke's death as an excuse, I lost all respect for him.

'As I told you, our last talk was an argument,' he said. 'We never had the chance to mend our relationship. The grief of losing my father was compounded by the bad timing. I felt like a lost and confused child.'

'Then imagine how ashamed he'd be of you right now,' I said. They were the cruellest words I've ever spoken to my father, and before my eyes he crumpled beneath the weight of them.

'You've broken me,' he said, chin quivering, holding back tears, leaning on the kitchen bench for support.

'No. You managed that all by yourself.'

I left him alone in the kitchen and hated myself for it. And hated even more that such a small moment between two people had caused so much harm for everybody.

ALL OF MY PROBLEMS ARE RELATIVE

We gave ourselves twenty-four hours to settle down. Then on Wednesday night Dad and I talked for hours about the Maëlle incident, covering territory that was painful for both of us. At the start it was difficult listening to him express the shame and humiliation he felt, as though he was a hapless victim of his own 'slip-up' or 'weakness' or whatever else he called his behaviour. But eventually he admitted full responsibility for his actions, and we were able to move on to the ramifications for the family. Finally he was able to express remorse, and committed to seeing a therapist. I should've charged him for *our* lengthy session.

Concerned that holding on to Percy and the Chinese coins was giving me bad juju, I walked down to Bert's on Thursday arvo to return them. Bert was sitting on his pink rubber ring on the armchair nutting out a crossword, and shushed me before I could speak. 'I'm concentrating,' he said. 'Sit on that.' He kicked the arse-cutting milk crate across and pinned me with his good eye.

'I brought Percy back.'

He snatched the bag and pulled the bird out. 'I missed you, little fella.' He scratched his chest then glared at me. 'You think I've got bats in the belfry. I know full well that he's stuffed.'

'My biology teacher told us that Governor Hunter sent a platypus pelt back to England and they were so confounded they thought it must be a duck and a mole sewn together.'

'Clever-dick poms thought he was a counterfeit, eh? I've got one of them down in the bunker.'

'An Englishman or a platypus?'

'Neither, smartarse. Two different creatures sewn together. Come down with me and we'll find him.'

'I'm claustrophobic.'

'Don't you worry about that. There's enough room to swing a cat and everything needed to skin one. Talk to the bird while I fetch a torch.'

The moment he was gone, Homunculus said, 'Don't go underground with the Nang-Nang. You won't come out alive.'

I blocked his fearmongering by gripping the milk crate – gripping so tightly it cut into my hands, the lattice base almost bisecting my tail. I took Bert's rubber ring and placed it under my butt. The donut shape nested my tail perfectly, way better than a regular cushion. Bert came out swinging an Eveready Dolphin® torch before I could jump off so I leant forward, trying to hide the ring with my forearms.

'Bit young to be suffering haemorrhoids,' he said and laughed. He banged the torch with the palm of his hand till it yielded a feeble glow. 'Should hold out for a minute or two.'

Bert led me to what I'd assumed was an old dunny shack, with a sloping corrugated-tin roof, then opened its creaky door. 'In you go. I'll hook it back to give us more light.'

Suppressing my sense of imminent danger, I obeyed and got only two steps down before taking a crack to the front of my head. The front – not the back. Though stunned, I realised I'd walked into a beam.

'Watch your noggin,' Bert said. 'Low clearance.'

'Thanks for the warning,' I said, rubbing my forehead. 'You'd better go first with the torch.'

He led me down wooden steps hardly substantial enough to feed a family of white ants. The air at the bottom was mouldy and gassy. 'Are you sure this is safe?'

'Safe, my arse.' Bert's laugh crackled with phlegm. The door above banged shut, snuffing out the last trace of daylight. Instead of guiding us, he waved the torch around, spotlighting random paraphernalia. Eventually the weak beam rested on a beastly snouted face with tusks and piggy eyes, decorated with shells and a thatch of black bristles sticking straight up. 'Sorry, old chum, didn't mean to disturb you,' Bert said to the thing. 'He's from Papua New Guinea. Made of wood and pig fat.'

'I've seen enough now, thanks. I'm going back up.'

'Don't have a conniption. I'm sure he's around the back here.' Just when I thought he'd made the whole thing up, his torch exposed a hideously mangy creature made of what looked like the head of a giant rat attached to the body of a rooster.

'What on Earth is that thing?'

'The only known example of a potorooster. Half-rooster. Half-potoroo. The species is now extinct.'

'No wonder, if people hunted them to make those ugly things.'

'Steady on. How would you feel if you were half-beast and someone spoke to you like that?' The question, though rhetorical, made my head spin.

'I feel terrible. I need to get out right now. I can't breathe.'

'Don't you want to see the mount of poker-playing rabbits? It's a hoot.'

'I have to get to work.'

The torch died and we inched our way back in the darkest darkness I'd ever known. At the top of the stairs, Bert struggled to push the door open until I added my desperate heft. It finally gave and we stumbled out, blinded by the glorious afternoon light. The potorooster was under his arm. Though I'd initially been frightened by the fugly thing, a golf ball of sadness lodged itself in my throat when I saw it in the light. It was a miniature animal version of Frankenstein's monster – the dignity of the original creatures stolen and the combination less than the sum of its parts. I thought of Esther making small mounts for Madame Zora, but that crossbreed would've been terrifying perched on somebody's head. 'Where did that little beast come from?' I said.

'Cabinet of Curiosities. I bought the whole menagerie in one lot at auction. He and the bunnies are the only ones left. He's yours if you want him.'

'Absolutely not.'

On my way out, I stopped to check the developer's sign again as an A380 flew overhead and noticed the contact number ended in 380. Not an amazing coincidence in itself – but then out of nowhere I remembered that they were also the last three digits of the angry man's phone number I'd called the week before. I checked my call history to confirm. So the guy I'd rung after midnight – the one who berated me and called me Chester Hunt – was also the agent for the Paradigm development.

CALL KEN BARNSDALE TO REGISTER YOUR INTEREST TODAY

I wouldn't be calling him again but I did take a photo of the sign, then hotfooted it to work.

Sam was arguing with Manos when I arrived at Give Me the Juice. Manos wanted him to finish his accounting degree but Sam only wanted to race V8s. Sam pushed past me and flung his apron to the floor. Manos chased him, swearing in Greek.

'They won't be back,' Pericles said. 'Could you work up front with me and then stay for close?'

'Sure. What's up with the twins?'

'They want to knock off a bit earlier tonight. Synchronised periods. Full moon makes it worse.'

Later it seemed the moon must've been affecting some of my customers as well. One of them asked for a carrot, apple and beetroot juice, then complained it was red. I made them a replacement and they asked where the beetroot was. The twins stayed up the back and never resurfaced from the doldrums. At 8.45 they left Pez and I to clean up.

Rinsing the dispenser units, I told him about my discovery of the matching phone number and showed him the photo.

'Do you reckon the real-estate agent put the tongue in your bag?'

'I think Starkey did it then used Barnsdale's phone to send the text so I wouldn't know it was him. No idea how he got it, though.'

'He could just be some random who left his phone lying around?'

'Doubt it. It's no coincidence that Ken Barnsdale is involved with the apartment development and Starkey warned me to stay away from there. I'm not liking this at all.'

'Me neither, man. It's really fricking creepy. I could get my cousin Angelo to carry out some surveillance – find out if there's a connection. He wants to be a private investigator.' We began wiping down the benches.

'Nah, I can do it myself. I've got Barnsdale's website address.'

'That won't help. You should call the number from a different phone with a fake voice, pretending you're interested in buying one of the apartments. Ask him if there are any good schools in the area and see if he mentions Crestfield.'

'I couldn't pull it off.'

'You know, Isa's an expert at playing characters.'

'There's no way I'd get her involved.'

'Speaking of'—Pericles laid his cloth over the tap—'are you asking Isa to the dance?'

'Where'd that come from?'

'It's obvious you've got the hots for her.'

I denied it, perhaps too defensively. But after pushing her away on Tuesday night, I'd lost any hope of starting something with Isa. Without probing further, Pericles turned off the lights, set the alarm and locked the sliding glass door, then we walked to the station.

'Thanks for staying back,' he said. 'I didn't mean to hassle you about Isa. We're mates and you can be totally open with me.'

'A hundred per cent.'

'I really think you should ask her.'

247

'We've become a bit closer working on the project, but nothing more than friends. I definitely won't be asking her to the dance.'

'Sweet. I just needed to check.'

'What does that mean?'

'You're both my friends and I want my friends to be happy.'

I got home at 10 pm, chatted to Dad about nothing intense, ate leftovers and knitted till midnight. Too late to start reading, but I did anyway.

The shock of my father's sudden death was compounded by three successive blows for my poor mother. The first came when she visited the bank to withdraw cash for funeral expenses and was told there were insufficient funds. Later, in the office of my father's accountant, she discovered that he'd mortgaged Ambleside, our home in Mosman. The accountant advised her to sell my father's remaining share of the business to his partner. The following day she almost collapsed when Dimitrios told her that he already held ninety per cent. Over the years my father had sold portions of his share to cover gambling debts, and the remaining ten per cent was still less than what was owed his friend.

The funeral was a bitter formality lashed by rains that kept most of my father's former acquaintances away. I struggled to maintain my composure throughout the service, no mean feat at the age of twelve with Loula tugging at my coat-tail, demanding to know when our father would return. The one saving grace was the heartfelt eulogy delivered by his friend and mentor George Pemberton, who'd covered the cost of burying him. My mother visited him a week after the event to reassure him that everything would be repaid in full.

'Will you return to Fernleigh?' Pemberton said.

'No. My father has shown no contrition for rejecting William since his passing. We will find a small and cheery place of our own.'

'How will you provide for your family?'

'I was hoping you might be able to offer me some form of employment?'

'Sadly, there is nothing befitting your station,' he said.

'I have no station and would do virtually anything, no matter how lowly, to save my family from destitution.'

Pemberton poured them each a glass of whisky and revealed the details of his new plan. The Waxworks and Hall of Mirrors were to be replaced by the Cabinet of Curiosities – no mere chest, but an entire pavilion full of wondrous objects: crystals, skeletons, a Roman coin embedded in lava, an Egyptian mummy and a dragon's egg. The ceiling would feature a tromp l'oeil of clouds parting to reveal a glimpse of Heaven, while the floor would be splitting open to reveal the Earth's fiery bowels. And the pièce de résistance, the Hybrid Menagerie, would display fantastical combinations of diverse creatures. Pemberton offered Esther the job of manufacturing them.

'Forgive my candour,' she said, 'but your scheme sounds slightly deceptive.'

'Fooling someone in order to create a sense of wonderment is a noble pursuit in these gloomy times.'

'My father would be mortified to discover I was responsible for creating something so unnatural with the skills he taught me.'

'Are you still beholden to his opinion, even in your estrangement? I'd pay handsomely to exploit those skills. I already have many fine mounts, including a potoroo and rooster. Conjoined, we would make a potorooster! Imagine the delight on children's faces when they see it?'

'Or the horror.'

Or the horror on my face when those words wrapped themselves around me and pulled me back down into that dark subterranean place.

'Even better,' Pemberton said. He told her that new creatures would be required monthly to retain the public's interest, and guaranteed my mother at least two years' employment creating them in the old millinery studio. Despite my mother's distaste for the proposal, concern for our survival prevailed and she accepted Pemberton's offer.

She wrote of that moment in her diary, 'It was most unnerving when shaking the hand of my saviour to feel a chill run through my entire being, as if I'd just made a pact with the devil.'

Most unnerving? Boy, that was an understatement. Reading that Esther had been employed to create the hybrid creatures and had probably made the potorooster that Bert had found in his underground storage facility gave me more than a chill. Was Bert connected to all of this to a greater degree than he was letting on? Or was I slowly losing my grip on reality?

On Friday afternoon I went down to Bondi to train. The sky was uniformly grey and the ocean was rough, so I walked around to Bronte Baths instead. I lowered myself into the shallow water, wearing board shorts, and swam. With an incoming tide, waves were breaking over the wall and the spume was invigorating. I swam harder and further than ever before. Not because I wanted to win at the Invitational, but to wash the troubles from my mind – or at least make sense of them. Climbing out two hours later, I saw a dad wrapping his shivering son in a towel. The kid was a miniature version of his father. I thought again about the possibility of my tail being a genetic endowment. There was no way of researching my father's family history, but maybe, just maybe, it could've come from Mum's side.

Saturday mid-morning, I walked into the kitchen of the Signal Bay residence to find Grant Marsh operating the espresso machine that had once been Dad's sole domain. 'Good morning, Lachlan,' he said. 'Would you like a coffee?' No, I didn't want a coffee, and I didn't correct him because allowing him to continue misnaming me would be a more effective way of allowing the dickhead to shine. 'We've been apartment-hunting in Dee Why,' he said.

'Are you and my mother moving in together?'

'God, no!' He laughed. 'Helping your sister on the hunt.'

I found Venn in the lounge room playing with Oscar. 'Are you moving out?' I said.

'If Jessie and I ever find a place.'

'Are you taking the cat?'

'I'll have to. Mum's selling the house.'

Angered at having been left out of the loop yet again, I went upstairs and barged into Mum's room. She was wearing new orange, yellow and brown tartan golf pants and pretending to putt in front of the mirror. 'What do you think?' she said.

'I think you're about to sell the house.'

'The place is far too big for one person, darling.'

'That man in the kitchen is orchestrating this.'

'Nonsense. Your father and I decided to sell the house and divide the assets last year, well before I started seeing Grant. And, for the record, I won't be moving in with him or any other man. I'm looking at buying a small place in Paddington or Surry Hills. Closer to work . . . and you.'

I ignored her plastic olive branch. 'The pants? They look exactly like Coach Simmons' chair.'

I went back down and told Venn I'd confronted Dad about Maëlle, and that after coming up with a hundred excuses he'd shown signs of remorse.

'Did he try to get your sympathy by trotting out the whole adoption story?'

'How do you know about that?'

'He told me on the phone. Personally I think face-to-face would've been more appropriate.'

'Except that you wouldn't agree to see him.'

'Please don't start defending him now.'

'I'm not, but I can understand how badly Pop Locke's death affected him.'

'Yeah, look at how many times he's come to visit Nana since. She wants to stay in the flat but she's going to need a bit more help occasionally. That's why Jessie and I have been looking for a place somewhere in Dee Why.'

'That's really kind.' And it gave me the perfect opening to talk about Bert. 'There's an old guy in my neighbourhood who wants to stay in his place too, but developers are forcing him out. He's been there forty years.' I told Venn all about Bert's massive antique, vintage and junk collection and about the unlikely friendship we'd forged. 'Some kids at my school have been harassing him and I suspect one of them might be connected to the developers.' I explained my plan to get someone to call Barnsdale posing as potential buyer and asked if she could be that someone. With a little arm-twisting she agreed. I knew she wouldn't be able to turn down a chance to defend a frail and elderly David against those arrogant sons of Goliath.

After Mum and Grant left for golf, I gave Venn the number and went upstairs to listen on the other phone. Sounding scarily like Mum, well spoken and insistent, she easily convinced Barnsdale that she was a legit buyer and he suggested she come in for a virtual-reality walkthrough. There was a moment of silence where I feared she might hang up. But then she said, 'Before we do that, I have a question you might be able to answer. Our eleven-year-old son has received an offer from Crestfield Academy and I've heard varying reports. Have you had any personal experience with the school?'

'It just so happens that my nephew attends Crestfield and loves it there. They have a magnificent pool and gymnasium. Does your boy enjoy sports?'

'He's more the academic type.'

'Evan tells me that his teachers are all very dedicated, going the extra mile to ensure optimal results. If you choose Crestfield for your lad, the Paradigm Apartments are very close. Give me your details and I'll send you the prospectus.'

>CLACK!< Venn hung up.

I bolted down to the living room. Venn's face was glistening, her neck red. 'Oh my God!' she said. 'That was so nerve-wracking. I didn't know what to say and I panicked.'

'No, you totally nailed it.'

So Kenny Barnsdale is Starkey's uncle. The plot was getting thicker, and harder to swallow than a bowl of cold porridge.

*

Before heading back to the city on Sunday, I asked Mum what she knew of her ancestry. 'Why the sudden interest?' she said.

'If you don't know where you came from you can't know where you're going.'

'Very true. My Aunty Dot was the family historian. Lovely lady, she died about five years ago. But she drew up our family tree and sent everybody a copy. I'll see if I can find it.'

A few minutes later Mum returned and handed me a piece of yellowed paper. On it was a big tree with roots that went back to my eight great-great-grandfathers all born in the 1860s and 70s, but no further. There was Harrison, Cornelius, Theodore, Edmund, Johnathon, Gideon, Festus and Floyd. There was no Edwin. Edmund was close, but his surname was Snook not Stroud. The disappointment outweighed the relief.

Back on the eastside I went for a final training session in the building's pool before the Invitational on Wednesday. Mulling over the Starkey–Barnsdale family connection while I swam, I wondered if Starkey and the goons' dedication to the task meant Barnsdale had paid them. One way or another, I was determined to untangle the cords of their involvement in the sinister operation.

WHO RULES THE POOL?

Monday morning, the goons swaggered into the squad briefing session with freshly shaved heads. Their commitment to gaining even the slightest edge over their opponents won applause from everybody except Pericles and me. The look almost suited Nads, but Mullows looked bereft without his ginger mullony and Starkey resembled a newborn ferret. Simmons read the final list of contenders for each event, with Pez in the individual butterfly and me to swim fly in the relay – Crestfield's glory event.

'I'm sure your delicate skin can handle thirty-odd seconds of chlorine exposure,' Simmons said. 'There'll be a medical officer present if you have a reaction.'

Nads drew the relay team aside and said to me, 'Your bullshit scam to get out of training doesn't cut it. If you don't show on Wednesday, I guarantee your life won't be worth living.'

'Nothing like boosting team morale.'

'WHAT!?' He slammed my shoulder with his palm. But instead of intimidating me, it gave me a measure of stupid courage.

'Look at you three bald clowns. I bet Simmons would be interested to find out what really gives you the edge.'

'Who do you think supplies them to us, arsehole?'

254

Deb Gelber came over carrying a pile of blue-and-gold kits. 'What's going on here?'

'Nothing, miss. We're just firing each other up.' Nads grabbed Mullows' shoulders and shook him roughly, then slapped his face like a boxing trainer would. 'C'mon, c'mon, C'MOOON!'

'Enough of that,' Gelber said. 'I want full focus. No shenanigans on Wednesday. Remember, you're representing the school.' She handed each of us a Crestfield tracksuit and a pair of Speedos that were blue at the front and yellow at the back. The perfect colour for making the tail really pop. No way could I wear them.

During Art on Tuesday, Isa asked what was bothering me. I wasn't about to confess that I was terrified of being humiliated by a crowd of people seeing a lump in the wrong side of my Speedos, so I told her I was worried about Bert – which was true. She kept probing until I revealed the Starkey–Barnsdale connection and my suspicion about what was going on.

'Oh my God!' she said. 'That's seriously heavy. Do you realise they've committed a criminal offence?'

'Maybe – but I don't know what to do about it.'

'Tell. The. Police,' she said, tapping the table with each word.

'Can you even imagine the trouble that would cause? The damage has already been done. Bert's sold his place and they've backed off.'

'What about that Barnsdale creep?'

'There's no way of proving he got them to harass Bert.'

She gave me a look that suggested I hadn't explored all my options.

After school I tried on the official Crestfield Speedos and the exposure of the tail was worse than feared. The single thin yellow nylon layer failed to hide the tail's dark hair even with the costume dry – wet, it looked obscene. If I shaved it again tonight, the spikes would be sticking through by morning and the bulge would still be visible, and if I nicked myself shaving tomorrow it could be disastrous. I tried wearing a second blue pair underneath, but it made the yellow look green. So I went into the city and bought a pair of baggy blue-and-yellow board shorts from Lowes, hoping they'd do the trick.

I woke early on Wednesday and had three-and-a-half bouts of exceptionally violent diarrhoea before breakfast. Only the dread of further retribution from Nads stopped me from calling the school to say I couldn't swim.

On the bus to the Eastside Aquatic Centre, Nads began a chant:
'WHO IS THE SCHOOL THAT RULES THE POOL?
'CRESTFIELD! CRESTFIELD! CRESTFIELD!'

It got louder and louder till Starkey, possessed by hysteria, leapt from his seat and performed a dance down the aisle.
'WHO IS THE SCHOOL THAT RULES THE POOL?
'CRESTFIELD! CRESTFIELD! CRESTFIELD!'

A car cut in front of our bus and Jespersen stamped the brake pedal, slamming Starkey onto the front windscreen. 'Sit down, you stupid little bastard!' Jespersen shouted. 'You almost killed us all.'

The individual events were swam in the morning. Nads and Mullows won their races convincingly and got out of the pool without showing any sort of excitement – as if coming first was the only possible outcome. In the hundred-metre fly, Pericles led all the way but was pipped at the finish by a guy from St Eugene's with massive lats and feet like flippers. Oddly, Pez didn't seem too disappointed when he got back to the stands.

'It's all about steady progress,' he said philosophically.

The medleys and long-distance events were scheduled after lunch. As each race was contested and the medley relay drew closer, the knots in my stomach tightened. The plan to protect my modesty with board shorts was far from foolproof.

At 2 pm all competitors in relay events were called to the marshalling area.

'That's you,' Pericles said. 'Get down there and show those bastards what you're really made of. Smash it, bro.'

We fist-bumped. We man-hugged.

Simmons rallied the team before our race. My brain, buzzing with thoughts of impending humiliation, scrambled his pep talk. The goons peeled off their Crestfield tracksuits while I removed only the top. Nads and Starkey followed a marshal to the other end of the pool, and I stayed with Mullows.

'Good luck, mate,' he said, with a pat and a glint of something approximating camaraderie in his eyes. He dropped into the pool, adjusted his reflective goggles and gripped the bar. The whistle blew and he steadied himself.

'On your mark!'

The photograph from the Hallway of Champions – Mullows the snarling backstroker – came into my mind.

>BEEP!<

He catapulted backwards and surged down the pool.

I peeled off my pants and left the board shorts on, hoping Simmons and Gelber had their gaze fixed on Starkey. Evan Starkey, teen reprobate, was now breaststroking towards me – his movements lopsided from hurting his shoulder when he hit the bus windscreen – trailing the competition. I mounted the block and shook myself out. Starkey was swimming through treacle. Time divided into milliseconds – nanoseconds. Starkey was close – closer – so close – almost there – only a metre away – a reach – two hands. *GO!*

I was a submarine.

Homunculus was my captain, controlling every limb and digit, every fibre of every muscle. 'Rigid, rigid and release!' he commanded.

My black metal hull dissolved.

I morphed to amphibian, exhaled and surfaced.

'Ignite the furnace!' Homunculus commanded. Fire blazed across my back, chest and arms. Energy rippled through my entire body as I rose and plunged, driven by my tiny extension – guided like a ship by a rudder.

There was no drag at all.

'Have I lost my shorts?'

'Focus on the end of the line.'

'What if they've slipped off?'

'Finish butt-naked.'

'God, please no!'

>FWOOSHKA!<

>FWOOSHKA!<

>FWOOSHKA!<

I slammed the pad with both hands.

Nads dived over the top of me. The other freestylers followed.

We were in the lead. I felt for my board shorts. Still on, thank God.

Nads was overtaken by a guy from Clovelly College and we were beaten by 0.34 seconds. My time was a personal best, Starkey's probably his worst, but Simmons directed his anger at me when he met us poolside.

'What the hell are you wearing those for?' he shouted. I wrapped my towel around my waist. 'You were issued with regulation Crestfield Speedos.'

'But these are the right colours still, sir.'

'Don't be a smartarse, Locke. Just tell me why.'

'I couldn't find my swimmers this morning. I left them at Avalon, sir.'

'We have spares. You should've told us.'

'You cost us the relay,' Nads said. With veins pulsing in his shiny bullet-head he'd never looked more menacing.

'Naylor's right. You cost us the relay and the points we might need to win the meet.'

'But I took us into the lead.'

'You would've dropped three or four seconds without the drag of those shorts.'

'But—'

'Don't "but" me. You have piss-all regard for the team and you won't be swimming at zones. As of this moment you can consider yourself thrown out of squad.'

'Thank you, sir.'

'Oh, don't thank me. Because you won't be swapping to another sport. You'll be on garbage patrol for the rest of term under

Mr Jespersen's constant supervision, and you'll do whatever he requires. Do you understand?'

'Yes, sir.'

'Now get out of my sight, worm!'

THINGS THAT BIND US

Being thrown out of squad was the best thing that could've happened, and if that meant being asked to leave Crestfield altogether, then bring it on. The idea of Simmons supplying his star swimmers with human-growth boosters, which Nads had implied, was hardcore fraudulent.

I should've learnt by now that reading the book would provide no form of escape from my troubles, but tonight as I read in my bedroom, the distance between Edwin's past and my present was obliterated as our stories came crashing together.

Driven by financial necessity, my mother uprooted us from the fragrant gardens and bushland of Ambleside to replant us in the industrial centre of Sydney. Pyrmont was two short ferry rides from Mosman but could've been on the other side of the world for all its stark differences. Towering chimney stacks outnumbered trees, puffing their smoke into an atmosphere redolent of the abattoir and tanneries. The ubiquitous woolstores had a distinct odour, greasy and oppressive, but tolerable compared to the constant stench emanating from the cesspits. Our dark-brick terrace was squeezed like a narrow book between six others on Harris Street. Bereft of distinguishing features, their façades gave no indication of the stories held inside.

On arrival, our family was treated with a mix of curiosity and suspicion by the locals, who must've wondered what grim circumstance had blown us into their midst. My mother had retained some of her favourite pieces of furniture, which arrived on three carts, drawing urchins as to a circus parade. The carters scattered pennies to stop the grubby children pawing the fine upholstery. Thomas, Loula and I watched from the top window as the penny-scramble evolved into an all-out brawl. My mother called us away, drew the moth-eaten curtains and reminded us of how fortunate we were to be sleeping in our own beds. The next morning, we woke covered in rashes. She investigated our mattresses and bedclothes to no avail then, examining the walls, discovered a colony of bed bugs beneath the peeling paper. Ignoring our pleas, she sent us off to our new schools, stripped the wallpaper and had the dwelling fumigated.

The newcomer always faces challenges, and being covered head-to-toe in an angry rash certainly didn't win me any friends on that first day. But as the weeks rolled on, we three children proved our resilience and found ourselves enveloped by a tight-knit community that always looked out for one another. Whenever my mother was held back late working for Pemberton, Mrs Budd next door would send her daughter Deidre over with a pot of stew. And as Pemberton had promised, there was ample work for my mother to create hybrid mounts for his Cabinet of Curiosities. She toiled on those strange little monsters till the bones in her hands ached. It seemed patently unfair that I should continue at school while she struggled alone under an insurmountable burden of debt, so at thirteen I left to join Sampson's Sawdust Company. Initially my mother was vexed by my decision, but later came to appreciate the relief an extra source of income brought – as meagre as it was.

My job entailed helping old Neville Sampson and his arthritic horse Thunder collect sawdust from the timber mills for delivery to butchers and furniture-packers across town. The prospect of advancement was commensurate with the level of skill required to perform the job – nil – but it paid slightly more than streetsweeping.

My one respite every other day was picking Thomas up after work for a swim at the baths. Men's days were ruled by Sid Whitfield, a barrel-chested lifeguard who kept watch from a wooden throne, blowing his whistle at the first sign of horseplay. But the moment he abandoned his post to relieve his notoriously weak bladder, cannonballs, dunking and wrestling always broke out. Sometimes we ventured outside the baths to catch a yabbie or squid, which we'd trade for a piece of Mrs Stefanides' exotic syrup cake at the corner store. It's funny now to think that my greatest achievement back in those days was swimming two full lengths of the baths underwater – a feat that won the respect of all the lads except Reg McGuffin, whose record I'd broken.

Older than the other boys, McGuffin's physique had guaranteed his position as their leader. In the middle of my sixteenth year, my body went through a series of changes that had quite the opposite effect. I became unusually hirsute, which caused a degree of self-consciousness I'd not known before. Then one month shy of my sixteenth birthday, a strange protuberance developed at the end of my spine. I expected it to go away on its own, but instead it grew and sprouted coarse dark hair. Desperate to keep this strange and ugly affliction a secret, I stopped swimming at the Pyrmont Baths – bad news for Thomas. And after young Arthur Carter dived into a submerged rock and suffered a fatal spinal injury, my mother forbade Thomas from swimming alone. She resisted his pleading till late in February when the city, gripped by a heatwave, hit one hundred and thirteen degrees. At her wit's end she ordered me to take him to the baths, whether I wanted to join him in the water or not.

I'd read many books where I felt a strong connection to the author, but nothing like this – this mingling of lives with somebody who was no longer around. The revelation felt heavy and incomprehensible. I dozed off and dreamt.

I was standing by the edge of a tidal pool. Two boys were trying to climb from the murky water but a group of scrawny thugs were blocking their exit. The boys swam to the other ladder but the ruffians followed and kicked them back into the water. A whistle lacerated the air. I turned and saw a sunburnt, white-haired guy in a singlet.

'That's enough from you, Reg McGuffin!' he yelled at the only boy with well-developed muscles. 'Let them out.' The two boys emerged in old-fashioned swimsuits, their short-and-singlet combinations sagging with water. The taller one was holding his hands behind his lower back.

'Watch out!' McGuffin said. 'He's got a jelly!' He and another punk tugged the boy's arms away, but there was nothing in his hands. The boy threw wild punches at McGuffin that failed to make contact.

The lifeguard whistled again. 'There'll be no fisticuffs on my watch!' he yelled. 'Not like you to be causing trouble, Edwin Stroud. Get out of here and don't come back until you've learnt to control that temper.'

As the boys walked away, I felt the kid's pain – the dead weight of injustice. And then, still dreaming, I remembered the photograph from the exhibition. The boy sitting on the edge of the pool, apart from the others. Edwin Stroud. I watched the two brothers walk up the hot road with their heads low. The younger one, Thomas, put his arm around Edwin's shoulders. Edwin shook it off.

Then I saw the small protrusion at the base of his spine. The thing we share. The tail. The shock woke me up in a cold sweat, my pulse racing from panic that had gripped me like a fever. And I read on.

One chilly April morning I woke with such pain in my lower back I was barely able to move. Against my wishes, Thomas was sent to request Dr Fletcher visit me on his afternoon rounds. At midday, Diddy Budd rapped on the back door and let herself in. 'Edwin, poor lamb, it's me!' she called on her way up the stairs. She opened the bedroom door and poked her head in. 'Your mother said you might be running a fever, and judging by your trembling I think she's right. Here, I've brought a damp cloth to lay on your forehead.'

'Please don't touch me,' I said. 'Stay back!'

'Oh dear. The fever's gripped your mind.'

'Get out! I'm begging you.' I pulled the sheet over my head.

'I brought some vegetable-and-barley soup to heat up later if you're able to eat. I'll be downstairs praying for you until the doctor arrives.'

263

'No prayers! No doctor! Please don't let him see me this way.'

'Your fevered state demands his urgent attention.'

Diddy left me alone, but every half-hour she returned to observe me and I pretended to be asleep. Later, she sent the doctor up. He had plastered-down black hair and a defiantly ginger moustache that hardly inspired confidence.

'Awfully stuffy in here,' he said, forcing the sash window up with a screech. 'The most important ingredient for a speedy recovery is fresh air, a rare commodity in this neighbourhood.' He checked my vital signs then palpated the glands in my neck and under my arms. 'Everything normal,' he said, sounding annoyed that it was. 'Your brother told me you were suffering a fever that had rendered you immobile.'

'My back was crook. That's all.'

'Playing possum, were we? Idle hands are the devil's workshop, young fellow.' Without warning he ripped away my sheet and blanket. 'Turn yourself over.'

Deserved or not, the physician carries an authority above the average mortal's. And so I turned over, exposing the protuberance. After an interval of hemming and hawing, Dr Fletcher said, 'I now see your reason for wanting to keep that thing hidden. I've read of similar cases but never seen anything quite like it.' He seemed fascinated and repelled in equal measure, but thankfully didn't resort to touching the thing. Instead he fired a barrage of questions. Was I eating fresh fruit and vegetables, or meat only? Did I recall any disturbing experiences involving an animal when I was a child? Had I recently acquired any unsavoury habits that may have caused the thing to develop? The humiliating enquiry finally came to an end with the restoration of my bedclothes.

'Never fear, young man. I have exactly what you need to eradicate or at least diminish your unfortunate growth.' From his enormous black bag he pulled a small ceramic pot labelled 'Centaur Embrocation' and gave me instructions for its application. As soon as he left, I opened the jar and smelt the unguent. The camphorous assault to my nostrils seemed a promising sign. I applied a small dab to the protuberance and felt nothing, so I scooped two fingerfuls and smothered the thing. When the ointment penetrated my skin, the sensation was so exquisitely painful I chewed through two knuckles to stop myself howling.

The mere use of the word 'camphorous' had me dry-retching with memories of Pop Locke displayed in his coffin, Nigel Lethbridge's jacket and the hedges of The Labyrinth. I felt a sympathetic burning on my tail, just like the time I applied too much Dencorub Extra Strength Heat Gel® to my glutes and accidentally hit the spot in the middle. Any thought of ever returning to see Dr Finster completely evaporated.

ONE MAN'S TRASH

On Thursday afternoon, our final day of school before the Easter break, my free period was commandeered by Mr Jespersen for garbage patrol induction. He issued me with a high-vis vest emblazoned with the word TRASH, just in case any other students were wondering who I was, along with a yellow plastic sack and a pincer-pole so I didn't have to bend over or handle the garbage – beneficial for both posture and hygiene. I pincered 192 items, including thirty-three cigarette butts and twelve dried-up turds, despite the fact dogs aren't allowed to smoke on school grounds.

As I was finishing up, >PLINK!< a text arrived.

Isa: Hey Bin Boy! Nice vest. You missed a Twisties packet.
Me: How do you know?
Isa: I can see you from the drama studio. Turn around.

I turned and saw Isa waving from a third-floor window of New Block.

Isa: Meet me at International Velvet at 4. I've got an idea.

As soon as we sat down with our coffees, Isa grilled me on the goons' persecution of Bert and the extent of Barnsdale's involvement.

'Whatever part he played, it's not right,' she said. 'I believe in the process of justice, and they should all be made accountable.'

'It's too late. They've won.'

'Maybe so. But there's still a way we can help Bert out. You know how Terri's an antiques and vintage dealer? She might be interested in helping sell his stuff if he has things worth selling. He has to live somewhere, and it'll be more bearable if he has a bit of money. Why don't you take me down to meet him?'

We walked down to Bert's lane and I showed her the Paradigm sign.

'I can't believe they're knocking down these beautiful old homes to build that monstrosity,' Isa said.

'See that schmuck with the hair? That's what Starkey will look like in thirty years. It's his Uncle Kenny.'

I noticed that Bert had ramped up his security, with a chunky padlock and two more warning signs. Beneath BEWARE VICIOUS DOG were

DANGER
ELECTRIC FENCE
KEEP OFF – KEEP AWAY

and

DANGER
HAZARDOUS MATERIAL STORAGE AREA

'This is probably not such a great idea after all,' I said.

'Don't be silly. You're his friend. Hellooo!' she called out. 'Anybody home?'

The door scraped open and Bert appeared with a scowl that evaporated the second he laid his good eye on Isa.

'Hello there, lovely lady,' Bert said, removing the padlock.

'Hello, Bert. I'm Lincoln's friend Isa.'

'Isa, Isa, why's a tidy lass like yourself knocking around with this chancer?'

'He has some good points,' she said, patting my shoulder.

'I'll make you a nice cup of tea and you can tell me what they are.'

We followed Bert down the hall, Isa marvelling at the columns of newspapers and magazines stacked just shy of the ceiling, me at his unusual demonstration of hospitality. Sitting on the kitchen table was half a chocolate sponge roll being dismantled by a two-way line of ants. Bert flicked them off and plugged in the green kettle.

'Thanks, Bert, but we've just had afternoon tea,' Isa said. 'Is that a Russian samovar up there?'

'Gold-plated. Comes with six cups.'

'You have some amazing pieces here. My housemate Terri is an antiques dealer, so I know a little bit about old things.'

'Would you like a free tour then?'

'That would be wonderful.'

'I'll take you somewhere this one's never been,' he said with a nod towards me, 'the Carnival Room.'

Abandoning tea service, Bert led us upstairs and knocked on a red-and-yellow door then turned its brass knob. Inside was a mad circus of bug-eyed creatures made of papier-mâché and fibreglass. A giraffe, pelican and Betty Boop knock-off were among them, all looking delighted to meet us. And suffocating in dusty plastic bags hanging from a rail near the ceiling were five giant Kewpie dolls, beneath them a row of old amusement machines.

'It's just like Coney Island,' Isa said.

'Well spotted, missy. Half of it came from there.'

'Look at that one,' she said, pointing at an upright machine with two metal handles. Its vertical glass panel was decorated with two columns of love hearts beneath the word PASH-O-METER.

'Measures the electrical flow between lovebirds,' Bert said. 'Why don't we give it a burl, eh? I'll go around the back and plug it in. You two hold the handles.'

'I'll give it a miss.'

'Don't be a spoilsport,' Isa said.

'You heard the lady – nobody likes a wet blanket.' Bert plugged in the machine. 'Now grab the handle and hold tightly.'

'Just to keep you both quiet.' I took hold of the handle and the hearts on my side glowed dimly, pulsated a few times then died. 'Wow, that was impressive,' I said.

'You're supposed to be holding hands, Casanova. Don't be afraid, she won't bite.'

'I'm not afraid,' I said, my overly defensive tone betraying the fact that I was petrified. I took Isa's hand. We'd never actually held hands before, and doing it in front of Bert was awkward and my sweaty palm failed to increase conductivity. 'Still nothing happening.'

'Stop your jabbering and give her a chance to warm up.' A couple of seconds later both of our bottom hearts lit up at COLD FISH. 'Hold tighter,' Bert said. I squeezed Isa's hand and her heart ascended.

COLD FISH > ALL TALK > HARMLESS > MILD > LOVEABLE >

It hovered there for a while, then continued to NAUGHTY and stopped on PASSIONATE! Mine remained on COLD FISH the whole time.

'Dodgy machine,' I said, and let go.

'It's not finished yet. You have to wait for the card.'

'Really?' I said frowning. I took Isa's hand again and my heart started rising.

COLD FISH > ALL TALK > HARMLESS > MILD > LOVEABLE > NAUGHTY > PASSIONATE! > HOT STUFF!! > **ANIMAL!!!**

The top heart flashed, and the machine buzzed and rattled. I burnt with shame, imagining for a moment that the machine had exposed my secret, but Isa and Bert were laughing. A small pink card appeared from a slot at the bottom. Isa pulled it out.

'Ninety-seven per cent compatible,' she said. 'Do you mind if I keep it?'

'All yours,' I said.

'Real regular Romeo.' Bert cuffed my head. 'The Love Tester never tells a lie. Your father better keep an eye out for this one, missy.'

Isa ignored the comment and walked away to explore the room.

'She's cute as a bug's ear with a dash of the sauce,' Bert whispered. 'Nothing to be scared of, though. I've got something over here you might be interested in.' He opened a cupboard and pulled out a moulded metal hen on a nest. She was all black except for her red wattle and comb.

'Does she do anything?'

'Used to lay an egg with a surprise inside for the youngsters. Lolly or handkerchief. Pemberton's famous mechanical hen – Ethel. She's over a hundred and twenty-five years old.'

Isa returned and patted the chicken. 'She's stopped working. It makes me sad.'

I looked at my watch. 'I have to get to work.'

'You wait downstairs for the little lady,' Bert said. 'I've got a small present to give her.' I hesitated because I didn't fully trust him and saw no reason to be excluded, but Isa nodded her assent.

'Scoot!' Bert said. 'We won't be a minute.'

Whatever he gave her must have been small because she came down empty-handed. We said goodbye to Bert and walked towards the station. Instead of giving her the satisfaction of me trying to find out what her present was, I asked her why the chicken had saddened her.

'She reminded me of my father. Mum told me that he died when he was just a boy, really. Only two years older than you.'

'Sorry,' I said, wondering if a real chicken was somehow involved. But not wanting to sound insensitive by asking, I said, 'I'm missing the connection.'

'The hen reminded me of him because she held a novelty inside. The only physical evidence of my father's existence, besides me, is a novelty that came in a plastic capsule from a vending machine.'

'I should mind my own business. You don't have to tell me any more.'

'I want to.' Isa took a deep breath and told me the story of her origin.

Dee had been a young nurse working in the intensive care unit of the Royal Adelaide Hospital. There, she cared for a young patient called Paul who'd previously had part of a brain tumour removed. The surgeon had gone back in for a look and discovered it had grown much larger and was inoperable. Paul was only eighteen. One night he confessed to Dee that he'd never done anything more than kiss a girl, and was going to die without knowing what it was like to make love. Dee didn't have a boyfriend at the time and figured there was one thing she could do to bring him some happiness. They made love right there in the hospital bed.

Paul died at his home just one week later. Dee realised she was pregnant and sought her parents' advice. Her father was a strict Catholic and gave her two options: leave the city for nine months then have the child adopted, or leave permanently if she wanted to keep it. Paul's family were Adelaide establishment so she never told them. She moved to Sydney with Terri, who was nursing with her, and eight months later Isa was born.

'It must be strange having no connection with your father's side of the family,' I said. 'Not being able to see photos of him and stuff like that.'

'This is the only thing we have.' She pulled out a ring attached to a chain around her neck. 'My father bought it from a vending machine at the hospital kiosk and slipped it on Mum's finger. It's a mood ring but doesn't change colour anymore. It stays blue.'

We'd reached Kings Cross Station. Isa was waiting for some kind of response from me, but the story was so hefty I didn't know what to say without sounding stupid or trite. She broke the silence by asking if I'd made any progress on finding a date for the dance.

'I'm still thinking about it. What about you?'

'I'm going with Pericles.'

My heart was torpedoed. Struggling to maintain composure as it sank, I said, 'What about Phoenix?'

'She's going with a Year 11 guy, Kirk Shepard. I was wondering if you wanted to come in the stretch Hummer with us. The more the merrier.'

'And the cheaper it works out for you.' The words broke into our conversation with an unrestrained petulance.

'I just thought it might be fun all going together. Tibor and his cousin Ziska are coming.'

'I can arrange my own transport, thanks.' This time I sounded snarky, and Isa looked hurt, which was understandable considering she'd just opened up about her father and I was acting like a tool.

'Well, thanks for taking me to meet Bert. His stuff was amazing and I really liked him. He wasn't half as mad as you made him out to be.'

'You know me. Always exaggerating.' Third strike of misjudged responses.

Isa glanced at the departure screen and said goodbye.

Working with Pericles this afternoon was tricky because neither of us brought up the dance. He hadn't cut my grass, because from his point of view I wasn't cultivating the lawn. He'd asked me point blank if I liked Isa and I'd denied it. He'd encouraged me to invite her and I'd declared zero interest. Why was I so jealous of them both? Later, I lay in bed fantasising about exacting some form of spiteful revenge on my friends for an imagined wrong. It wasn't helping me get to sleep, so I returned to my book.

One stormy night in May, I lay awake counting the intervals between lightning and thunder. Focusing on the task was sending me back to sleep until a cold drop fell on my face, then another. I went downstairs to get a pail and found my mother warming milk. In our five years at Pyrmont she'd met every obstacle with a defiant optimism, but when I told her about the hole she broke down and wept.

'Don't cry,' I said. 'I'll fix it tomorrow.'

'If only my predicament could be fixed so easily,' she said, and recomposed herself. 'My work for Pemberton is coming to an end. The hybrid creatures have lost their appeal and he plans to replace them with live acts.'

'A circus?'

'An exhibition of human performers burdened with extreme proportions, alongside a few animals.'

'A freak show?'

'He used the term "prodigies". Do you remember Whitby the chimpanzee? He's been training him and the other apes to mimic human behaviour. He plans to have them perform in miniature domestic settings dressed in children's clothing, purportedly to demonstrate their similarity to humans. Like Darwin, he believes them to be our ancestors.'

'Don't you agree with him?' I asked.

'His primary goal is profit, not enlightening the masses. The poor creatures will be terrified by the bright lights and howls of laughter. Anybody who believes in Darwin's theory should be treating animals with greater dignity, not less.' My mother let out a deep sigh. 'I compromised my belief in the integrity of nature by creating those deceptive hybrid animals. Compromise is sometimes necessary for survival. But I told Mr Pemberton I couldn't abide the inhumanity of his new venture, and so he's looking for somebody who's free from such scruples.'

'I'll press old Sampson for more hours.'

'Collecting sawdust is no job for someone like you. Your mind is being wasted at the mills.'

'Then tomorrow I'll begin searching for other work.'

Six months later, Pemberton's Theatre of Scientific Wonders opened to a packed house. The well-received ape-and-monkey show was followed by a succession of human acts from all over the colonies and abroad, among them Leona the Lion Lady, Otto Zeep the Armless Violinist from Austria, Lottie the Largest Woman in the World and her twin sister, Lena the Living Skeleton.

Advertising was key to the venture's success – Pemberton had employed a small army of lads, including me, to plaster every square inch of the city with eye-catching and sometimes bawdy posters promoting upcoming acts.

My mother was in two minds over my involvement. The income certainly helped, but she wasn't thrilled about my promoting Pemberton's circus. His latest and most outlandish publicity stunt had all of Sydney abuzz with excitement:

GEORGE PEMBERTON, ESQUIRE
ISSUES A CHALLENGE TO THE WORLD!
TO PRODUCE INCONTROVERTIBLE
AND LIVING EVIDENCE
OF DARWIN'S MISSING LINK
IF THE CREATURE WILL REMAIN ON PUBLIC DISPLAY
FOR THE TERM OF ONE FULL MONTH
ITS DISCOVERER WILL BE REWARDED WITH
THE SUM OF
£100
NOTE! IF, HOWEVER, THE LIVING SPECIMEN
IS PROVEN TO BE FALSE
BY ANY MEMBER OF THE GENERAL PUBLIC
£100 WILL BE GIVEN TO ANY NOMINATED
CHARITABLE ORGANISATION

I googled how much the reward was worth now: $15,000. I figured that was going to be the 'redeeming' part of Edwin's 'one redeeming affliction'.

'Edwin Stroud is going to show off his arse on stage for fifteen grand,' Homunculus said. 'You could do the same and call yourself Missing Lincoln.'

FILTHY LUCRE

'They started selling these ten days after Christmas this year,' Dad said, between mouthfuls of hot cross bun. 'Pop would've blown a gasket. He only ever sold them on the Thursday. Never opened on Good Friday.'

I thought about all the Easter long weekends our family had spent with the Partridges over on Mackerel Beach. Kids in the water, oblivious to summer ending; adults boozing on the decks, oblivious to the kids. On Good Fridays, Pop Locke would expound on the true meaning of Easter, hoping a moment of reverence would save us from total hedonistic abandon. On Sunday, locals and blow-ins alike would get together and organise a massive chocolate egg hunt where all that mattered was filling your basket with the most eggs.

This morning, the memory of those days dissolved my contempt towards Dad. Things weren't exactly humming with the rest of my life and I needed some equilibrium. I forgave him for all the shitty things he'd done last year and then asked his forgiveness for saying Pop Locke would've been ashamed of him. 'Pop Locke often told me how proud he was of your success. He just couldn't find the way to tell you himself.'

'Come here,' Dad said, and hugged me for the first time this year.

*

On Saturday morning, rolling along on the B1 past Collaroy's apartment blocks, takeaway joints and surf shops, I calculated that in two weeks I'd have saved enough money to buy my new board. I just had to mooch eighty bucks off Mum to cover the tickets for the dance. So later, when she asked me to prepare the barbecue for dinner, I went straight out the back, wiped the grill down with newspaper, fired it up and returned for the prawns, behaving like the perfect son.

'You can relax now,' she said. 'I'll cook them.'

'Barbecuing's a man's job.' I picked up the bowl but she pulled it away, spilling the skewered crusties onto the kitchen floor.

'Shit!' she said, and bent down to pick them up. 'Thanks for helping, darling. But go and say hello to your sister or something.'

I went up to Venn's bedroom and found her studying plant diagrams. 'Why's Mum so crabby?' I said.

'Grant Marsh is seeing other women. Last night Maxine caught him playing tennis with Sue Perch.'

'You can't catch people playing tennis unless they're doing it in the nude. Were they nude?'

'That's so puerile. Have a little bit of sympathy.'

'Why? That guy's less authentic than seafood extender. He got my name wrong three times.'

'It's not all about you.'

'Exactly. It's about Mum, and I'm glad she found out for herself what a total arse-hat Grant Marsh is before it progressed any further. The possibility of being in a blended family didn't thrill me, and I bet you weren't too keen on three insta-siblings?'

Venn grimaced.

Mum called us for dinner. The prawns were chewy – overcooked. As if further evidence of Mum's dark mood was required.

'Perfectly done!' I said, before moving in for the kill. 'Do you think you could spot me eighty bucks for the school dance?'

'Eighty dollars for a social? That's a bit steep.'

'It's a fundraiser for a guy called Fergus who lost both legs and now has a dream of competing in the Paralympics. Eighty bucks is for two. Tickets, not legs. I already ordered them, although I don't have anybody to take.'

'I'm sure Venn would be more than happy to step in.'

'Absolutely not!' she said. 'That's wrong on so many levels. Why don't you ask Penny from Mum's work?'

'She's a bit old,' I objected.

'She's only eighteen,' Venn said.

'Cougar to a sixteen-year-old.'

'Don't be ridiculous,' Mum said, offering me more prawns, which I declined. 'You'd have a ball with Penny. She's always been fond of you and she's been mooning about ever since breaking up with Curtis. It might do her some good.'

Age discrepancy was obviously not a big deal for Mum – understandable considering she'd chosen a fifteen-year-old model to flog the magic youth elixir to older women.

'Do you think she'd consider coming with me if I approached it from the charity angle?'

'Who's the charity?' Venn said. 'Her or you?'

'Fergus, the guy who needs the legs.'

'I can't see why not,' Mum said. 'Why don't I give her a call?'

'It's probably best if I do that.' With her stunning looks, cracking banter and height advantage, Penny Button was well out of my league, which made her the perfect candidate to make Isa jealous. 'Give me her number and I'll think about it.'

On Easter Sunday, Mum gave me a packet of Cadbury Creme Eggs®. I told Venn that Jesus would be okay with Creme Eggs® because they have a yolk fondant inside, like a real egg, to symbolise new life. Then I testified to the transforming power of forgiveness, citing the recent lightness I'd experienced after forgiving Dad, and encouraged her to do the same. 'Sister, can you find it in your withering heart to extend the mercy of forgiveness to your own father?'

'How can you forgive somebody when they're not even sorry?' she said. 'Besides, if you do a little research you'll discover that Easter was adapted from some pagan fertility festival.'

'Who cares?' I said. 'The power of love and forgiveness transcends religion.'

'Preach it, brother.'

Back at T H E E Y R I E tonight, I was pacing the balcony, phone in pocket like a slab of kryptonite, afraid that if I asked Penny to the dance she might say no; almost equally afraid of her saying yes. Dad came out and gave me a pep talk. 'Take a few deep breaths and calm yourself down. Act casual, almost nonchalant. Women don't like desperados.'

I went to my room and called Penny's number. She answered the phone before it rang, which caught me off guard, so I quit the call. Dad poked his nose in and asked if I'd done the deed.

'I hung up when she answered.'

'That was too nonchalant. Get straight back on the horse. She'll think you're a stalker if you don't call back and actually speak.' My phone rang before he left the room. It was Penny.

'Hello?' she said. 'Who is this?'

'Oh, hi Penny. It's me, Lincoln Locke.'

'Lincoln? Did you just call me a moment ago?'

'Yeah, sorry, I dropped my phone.' I waved Dad out. 'Sorry for bothering you on a Sunday night – Happy Easter! . . . No, there is something else. It's really short notice, but I was wondering if you'd like to come to an event next Saturday night to raise money for a guy called Fergus who needs bionic legs. I've already bought an extra ticket and the drinks are on me . . . No, just mocktails, but you won't have to spend a cent.'

'Is it a dance?'

'It's a retro thing. "Double O Dance for Fergus – Hits from the Noughties". But we don't have to dance if you don't want to.'

'I love dancing. But don't you think I'm a bit old?'

'You're the same age as some of the Year 12 kids. My friend Tibor is taking his cousin Ziska and she's twenty-one. Now that could be awkward.'

'Gee, you sure know how to make a girl feel like a princess.'

'If Your Highness would be pleased to accept my humble invitation, there is a dress code – black and gold.'

'I love playing dress-ups. You're on.'

Even though the dance was six days away and Penny was only coming as an act of kindness, I felt a sudden surge of self-confidence when she said yes. Not ten minutes later it was replaced by a trickle of doom scenarios from Homunculus. At first I diverted them with reasoning and logic, but then they came faster, building into a steady stream of imagined gaffes and social blunders. Fearing I'd be swept away in a flood of panic, I picked up the dark-blue leather-bound book, *My One Redeeming Affliction*. The simple act of holding it calmed me down enough to read.

Public reaction in Sydney to the news of Nellie Bly's solo journey around the globe in seventy-two days paled in comparison to the excitement generated by George Pemberton's announcement that the 'missing link' he'd challenged the world to find on his advertising bills had been discovered and would soon be exhibited. Newspaper articles speculated on whether it would be closer to man or beast. Church ministers warned parishioners against attending. Arguments broke out among both friends and strangers. But nowhere was it more eagerly discussed than at our kitchen table. Pemberton had given me work as a stagehand, so my siblings were constantly badgering me to reveal what the creature looked like, unaware he was living among them.

One morning over porridge, Loula said, 'I bet he's an ugly, hairy monster with a squashed-up nose and sharp, sharp teeth.'

'I promise he's not that awful. Dressed in a suit, he could walk about town without raising an eyebrow.'

'Do they let him out on the streets?' Thomas said.

'Only every second night, to prowl for food.'

'Eeeeek!' Loula squealed.

'Enough about Pemberton's latest ruse,' my mother said. 'You're still employed at the mill and Mr Sampson will be waiting.'

'Who cares about Sampson? I've got half a mind to tell the old fart he can get stuffed with his own sawdust.' Thomas's and Loula's jaws dropped at my rare display of audacity. 'Pemberton pays me three times more.'

'Even so, I dread to imagine what sort of behaviour you're being exposed to by those theatrical types if your language is any indication.'

'There's nothing to be afraid of. Mr Pemberton sent you an invitation to the opening night so you can make up your own mind.'

'You seem to forget I was employed by him to manufacture those hideous oddities.'

'On the contrary, I'm trying to help us all by following your example. Only now I promise everything on show will be alive, and authentic.'

The Theatre of Scientific Wonders was breathtaking in its illusory splendour. Pink-and-cream walls held a lofty cobalt ceiling sparkling with several thousand gold stars. Glowing shrines along the walls housed Greek deities purchased from Dimitrios for a song when the Ionian had closed. And flanked by enormous columns, the half-moon stage jutted into the audience. I spied my mother occupying the best seat in the house. Perhaps most qualified for detecting stage trickery, she'd come hoping to claim the prize money for proving Taloo the Missing Link to be a fake.

The show opened with Whitby the chimpanzee, dressed as a caretaker and sweeping the stage, before the orchestra played a rousing overture and the curtains lifted. The ape-and-monkey act was followed by Otto Zeep, the armless violin virtuoso. Using one foot for fingering and the other for drawing the bow, he played 'Bach's Violin Concerto in A Minor' and received a standing ovation. Conjoined twins Evelyn and Josephine Hart, speaking synchronously, regaled the audience with humorous tales of their European tour. Then Evelyn sung a touching version of 'Where Corals Lie', accompanied by Josephine on the recorder.

Watching the acts from the wings, I became increasingly self-conscious of my lack of performance skills as my grand finale approached. Thankfully Pemberton had employed an actor playing a fictitious explorer, 'Professor Whittleworth', to plump out what was little more than my act of indecent exposure.

Dressed in safari suit and pith helmet, the 'Professor' delivered a 'scientific lecture' on his recent trip to Tambullubuku, a tiny island northwest of New Guinea, where he had supposedly discovered the most primitive version of mankind in existence. He returned to England with a young member of the tribe called Taloo. Subsequently examined by scientists and doctors at the Royal College of Physicians in London, the man/beast was declared the missing link. The orchestra swelled and the curtain rose to reveal me, Edwin Stroud, standing centre stage: arms akimbo, body painted nut-brown, wearing a lap-lap, bone necklace, feathered eyemask and curly black wig. I remained frozen as he resumed his patter.

'Though happily ignorant of our civilised, industrialised world, the Tambullubukan has adapted perfectly for surviving in his native environment, possessing a sense of smell a hundredfold more acute than yours or mine.'

Ten audience volunteers were given numbered paddles then instructed to approach me so that I could sniff them. I was blindfolded and the volunteers were reordered in a line fifteen yards away. In turn they took two steps closer and I identified each correctly by personal odour alone. The fevered whispering of the crowd indicated to me their astonishment. Then Professor Whittleworth returned for the big reveal.

'Ladies and gentlemen, you are about to witness something so confounding it may challenge your assumptions on the very origin of mankind. If you fear being offended by the exposure of an intimate part of Taloo's anatomy, I invite you to leave the theatre immediately and a refund will be afforded you in the foyer.' Three or four delicate souls took advantage of the offer. Once they'd left, the houselights dimmed and I walked, hunched over, to the edge of the extended stage. Illuminated only by footlights, I moved through a series of dramatic simian poses. Then Whittleworth said, 'Without screen, smoke or any form of obfuscation, Taloo will now reveal the unique vestige of evolution that proves him the missing link!'

Returning to centre stage, I climbed onto a plinth beneath the limelight. I turned my back and partially rolled down the lap-lap. Even from the stage, I heard a few more patrons leaving the theatre. But I rolled it down further, fully exposing the hairy tail between my bared buttocks. There was absolute silence as the audience held its collective breath. And then Whittleworth, wielding a wooden pointer, explained that the appendage not only contained blood vessels and nerves, but also the extra vertebrae that normally dissolve in the womb before birth.

'Initially I was unable to ascertain its function,' he said. 'But later, during some sort of fertility ritual, I saw their tails adorned with feathers, leaves and flowers, and concluded they were celebrated as indicators of virility.'

'Make it move, then!' a sceptic yelled.

'The tail isn't prehensile. Rather, more like the domesticated cat or dog, its movement is determined by the mood of its owner.'

'Codswallop!'

Whittleworth promised to eradicate any doubt of authenticity, and on cue a stagehand delivered a platter bearing a glistening roast leg of lamb, its sweet rosemary-infused aroma causing my tail to wag furiously. Speaking in my contrived native language, Whittleworth invited me to come down and feast. I seized the lamb, turned to the audience and tore flesh from bone like a starving wolf.

Caught up in the performance, I failed to notice a fellow approaching the stage until he hoisted himself onto it. The ginger moustache instantly identified its owner: Dr Melvin Fletcher.

'Godless charlatans!' he cried, charging at Whittleworth and knocking him down. I wielded the leg of lamb like a club but he seized it from me and flung it into the orchestra pit, where it crashed into a cymbal. Before I could escape, Fletcher tore off both my mask and wig and announced to the audience, 'This scoundrel is one of my patients, Edwin Stroud of Pyrmont. And these shysters are agents of the devil, making filthy lucre and attempting to destroy your faith with this abominable act!'

*

Everything suddenly irritated me intensely – my scratchy sheets and pillow, my itchy arms and legs, and most of all the prickly tail. I got up and went out onto the balcony wearing only boxers. I ran three circles in the cold night and returned to my bed, where I lay twitching sporadically until I fell into a troubled sleep.

RICH WHITE KIDS
PRETENDING
THEY'RE NOT

Saturday evening I showered, sprayed my pits and chest with Lynx Gold Temptation®, brushed my teeth twice, gargled Listerine® and put on my newest underpants, a black t-shirt with gold lightning bolt, black jeans and bowler hat from an op shop on Crown Street.

'Where are you off to?' Dad said.

'The Dance for Fergus.'

'The guy with no legs?'

'That guy. What do you think of my outfit?' I spun around on the spot. 'The theme's black and gold. I don't want to look like I tried too hard.'

'You've certainly achieved that.'

'Could I use some aftershave?'

'On my dressing table, champ. Don't go overboard – less is more with fragrance.'

The cabbie said 'Woof!' when I got in and he lowered every window – a bit dramatic, considering the interior was already ripe with tobacco and arse sweat. Mercifully for both of us, the ride to Penny's place in Surry Hills was short. She came out looking a million bucks in a dress made of tiny sparkling gold disks.

'Wow! I'm unworthy.'

'Tan's not too dark?'

'Not at all.' The fake nutty brown set off the gold perfectly.

On the trip to Crestfield, I gave Penny the lowdown on my friends and suggested we invent a code word in case either of us needed to get away from an awkward sitch.

'What about "ukulele"?' she said.

'Random but perfect.'

'I miss my high school days.'

As I was paying the driver, a black stretch Hummer pulled up in front. A door opened and the chorus of 'Don't Cha' by the Pussycat Dolls spilt out, along with Phoenix in a slinky black catsuit, gold belt and super-long fake ponytail. 'Over here!' a photographer called from the pavement. Phoenix obliged with a series of feline poses, swishing her hair extension to max effect. Her date, Kirk Shepard, stepped out, shielding his face. 'Don't be like that,' the photographer said. Phoenix pulled Kirk close and the photographer snapped away.

'That's enough now, Dad,' Kirk said.

Next out was Tibor in a gold jacket with padded shoulders and his cousin Ziska in an eighties gold puffball dress. The photographer took a perfunctory single shot of them.

The song ended and Isa emerged in a long black sheath dress with a gold halter neck. Hair pulled back. Gold hoop earrings. She had a corsage of black flowers tied around her left wrist, which Pericles must've bought. He was wearing a sharp black suit, thin black tie and suede winklepickers. Hair sculpted into a high fifties Elvis pomp.

'Ohmygod,' Penny said. 'They look like movie stars. Are you going to introduce me?'

'Maybe later. The ukulele player's about to perform his set.'

Penny scrunched her nose. 'I'm not mad about the ukulele.'

'Remember the code word?' I said. 'Let's go in.'

Heather's team had transformed the auditorium into a glittering party palace, with all the decorations donated for the night by local businesses. Black foam stalactites hung from the ceiling between gold polyhedrons reflecting lasers in a thousand directions. Behind the DJ booth was a massive revolving cog, shafts of gold light strobing between its spokes. And on either side of the stage were video screens. Across the dance floor I spotted the pop-up mocktail bar that Manos had agreed to let Helena and Christina run – all proceeds going to the cause.

'Wow! Interesting look,' Christina said as we approached. 'Dressed by San Vincenzo de' Paoli?'

'Close,' I said. 'Christina, this is my friend Penny.'

'Hi, Penny. Love the dress. You look so expensive standing next to him. What would you like?'

Penny examined the specials board. 'The Pash-and-Dash sounds exciting.'

'Make that two,' I said.

Penny excused herself to go and freshen up her make-up. Christina leant forward and said, 'Ohmygod, Lincoln. She is drop-dead gorgeous. Pericles told me you were going stag.'

'Seems he was mistaken.'

'Have you seen his hair? Took me an hour and a half. He's so fussy. But don't they make the perfect couple?' she said, looking over at him and Isa. The word 'couple' hit me like a stone in the eye.

Helena returned with drinks garnished with pineapple spikes. 'Specially for you,' she said.

Wearing a surprisingly daring and constrictive dress that appeared to be made of gold latex, and with her hair in a gold-sprayed beehive, Heather Treadwell waddled onto the stage and delivered the official welcome, making a very dubious connection between Fergus Martin's bravery in learning to walk again and being unafraid to make a fool of yourself on the dance floor. 'I suppose that I should lead by example,' she said. 'SO LET'S GET THIS PARTY STARTED!'

On cue, the DJ started playing the old Pink banger. Heather came down and danced around David York like a duck snapping at the heels of a gazelle.

'That's seriously painful to watch,' I said to Penny. 'I'm sorry for dragging you along to this.'

'Don't be silly. I'm having a great time.'

'You're being charitable.'

'I think we should both be charitable and help them out.' So we joined Heather and David on the dance floor. Penny was a very expressive mover and when I complimented her, she explained that she'd taken salsa and belly-dancing classes. To be honest, she could've made the Chicken Dance look sensual. We danced for almost an hour, me trying with limited success to emulate her, and gently steering her away whenever Pericles and Isa were in close proximity.

Heading to the entrance for some fresh air, we saw Nads, Mullows and Starkey arrive with Cheyenne Piper and the Petersen twins. The guys were in black sweats, reversed baseball caps and fake gold chains. The girls wore gold crop tops, black hotpants and thigh-length boots.

I bought Penny a Don't Let Your Man-go at the mocktail bar and she told me all about how much she missed Curtis and how she'd thought he was the one even though they'd been together for a grand total of six weeks. Again she asked me if I had the Cupid she gave to me ages ago and I confessed I'd defaced him in solidarity, which made her laugh. At that exact moment, 'Single Ladies' started playing. Penny said 'That's me!' and pulled me back onto the floor. Liliana Petersen and Cheyenne Piper suddenly flanked her, and the unexpected trio matched the moves of Beyoncé and her two dancers on the giant video screens as if they'd spent a week practising the choreography. A crowd including Nads and Mullows gathered to watch.

Feeling less needed than a fridge in Siberia, I surreptitiously tried to shuffle into the background. But Penny wouldn't let me go so easily, and started dropping and fanning and twerking against me. Terrified she might inadvertently touch the tail and freak out like Nicole Parker had – but this time with spectators there to witness the destruction of my last skerrick of dignity – I excused myself for a pee.

All of the men's cubicles were occupied and Starkey was leaning on the wall, so I turned to leave.

'Can't you piss in the urinal?' he said, with scant whiskers twitching like those of a sewer rat sniffing an opportunity for trouble.

'I like my privacy.'

'Did you come in here for a tug or a slug?'

'Neither.'

'Loosen up, man – try this.' He thrust a silver flask at my face and hit my teeth. 'Fuck, sorry about that.'

'I'm fine.' I tried to get past but he grabbed my arm.

'Not so fast.' His breath was sour and smoky. 'Where did you find the hottie? You're punching above your weight with that one.'

'She works with my mum.'

'You got your mother to pimp for ya? I was expecting you to make some faggy statement by turning up with your boyfriend Pappas. You must be shat off that he stole the bitch you've been spading despite Nads warning you to stay away?'

There was no way I could pee in peace with Starkey there, but I was still aching for a leak so I headed for Old Block. Walking through grass that hadn't been cut over the break, I felt the dew soak into the cuffs of my jeans and a breeze chill the sweat on my neck. Crickets stopped chirping as I approached Old Block, and a fruit bat swept low enough for me to smell its fecundity – the moon revealing the veins in its membranous wings.

The Old Block toilets were locked and there was nowhere else to go, so I walked down to the roped-off Port Jackson fig, trusting its girth would protect me from view. In its upper reaches a hundred or more of the bat's friends were hanging upside down, conducting their own social event, eating figs, chattering and screeching. It was the first time tonight that I'd felt like I actually belonged. But the second my stream of piss hit the trunk of the fig, every dark and furry creature took flight, wings buffeting the air, making it thrum and shudder. It was the most terrifying wee I'd ever taken.

On my way back towards the auditorium I spied two figures cosy on a bench but couldn't make them out. 'Locke!' Pericles called. 'Leave those bats alone and come over here.' As I approached him and Isa, I felt the tail shift into a new position, almost vertical, and begin vibrating, which I assumed indicated a perceived threat. But instead of jumping onto Pericles and sinking my teeth into his throat, which would have been a very literal example of overkill, I said, 'Oh, it's you two! Great night, eh? Heather and her crew really pulled it off. Just came out for some fresh air. I'll leave you to it then.'

'Wait,' Isa said. 'Why have you been avoiding us all night?'

'Penny, the girl I brought – chronically shy.'

'She didn't look shy on the dance floor,' Pericles said.

'She's okay with dancing but doesn't speak English very well. It'd be unfair talking to my friends when she can't join in.'

'Where's she from?' Isa said.

'Croatia.'

'I went to Croatia in Year 7. All the students there learn English. Bring her to the afterparty so we can talk.'

'She has to get home before midnight. Anyway, I'd better get back.' I walked away as quickly as possible, trying to look like I wasn't.

I found Penny where I'd left her. She was now dancing with my Maths teacher and a cluster of students. Monaro was popping and locking to Daft Punk's 'Harder, Better, Faster, Stronger', and everybody else was trying to copy his moves. 'Show us your Lawnmower!' Penny shouted. Monaro robotically mimed pulling the starter cord and pushing a mower along. I really wanted to disappear but Monaro pointed at me and shouted, 'Robot Packing Boxes!'

'What?' I shrugged.

'Like this!' With stiff arms and a jerky pivoting motion, Monaro actually resembled an automated production-line worker, removing any doubt that he was the most massive tool in the faculty's shed. Penny was clearly enjoying herself, though, and it would've been rude to pull her away, so I joined in and played Follow the Leader until we'd virtually exhausted all the animals, occupations, sports and famous people we could think of.

Mercifully there was no slow song to finish. Heather took the stage, golden beehive deflated and tilting, and introduced a short video of Fergus expressing his gratitude. She announced that $17,000 had been raised tonight, and >BOOM!< glitter cannons shot out golden hearts that fluttered down upon us all.

'How beautiful!' Penny said. 'I've had the best night ever. Is there an afterparty?' But I saw Pericles and Isa approaching, so I told Penny I had a headache.

'I've got some Panadol in my purse. Let's get you a cup of water.'

Pericles and Isa were almost upon us. The tail went fully vertical again, rigid and prickling.

'I've got ukulele lessons in the morning,' I said.

'Right,' Penny said. 'Let's blow this joint.'

On the cab ride to Surry Hills, Penny asked me why I'd been so edgy around my friends and I confessed that I'd wanted to ask Isa to the dance but was too insecure.

'Take it from me, there's no reason to be,' she said. 'You're handsome and charming and any girl would be lucky to have you for a boyfriend.'

'Thank you so much for coming with me,' I said as the cab pulled up to the kerb.

'My pleasure,' she said, and kissed me on the cheek. 'Anything for Fergus, eh?'

BETTER OUT THAN IN

Sunday morning I walked to Centennial Park and sat by the Duck Pond, mulling over the level of anger and jealousy I'd felt seeing Pericles with Isa. Then I called him to say I couldn't work at Give Me the Juice anymore. He forced me to admit it was because of Isa. I accused him of cutting my grass and he reminded me that I'd been emphatic about not liking her that way.

'You still knew that I liked her. Why didn't you tell me you wanted to ask her? Because you're Shady McShitball.'

'I can't believe you just called me Shady McShitball. I'm the one who really needs a friend right now.'

'You should've considered that before the dog act.'

'You're not listening to anything I say.'

'Because your mouth's dribbling shit.'

Hanging up on Pericles was quite a rush. But rushes by definition don't last long, and as I walked home I felt terrible about losing a friend over the stance I'd taken. I called him back three times before he answered.

'What do you want now?' he said.

'I've been thinking about what happened and I'm willing to forgive you.'

291

'That's really special but I don't want your forgiveness. A friendship should be built on honesty. I tried to be open and you cut me off. I wanted to tell you something important because I value our friendship. Now I think it might destroy what's left of it – if there is anything.'

'This had better be good.'

'There's nothing good about it. You may hate me even more when you hear the truth.'

'I don't hate you now.'

'Can we meet somewhere? I can come over your way.'

'Sure. Meet me at International Velvet. Do you know it?'

'I've been there once or twice. I'll be there at eleven.'

Pericles beat me to the café. He was sitting on the lips sofa, acting busy with his phone. All the outside tables were occupied by Sunday brunchers and their miniature dogs.

'Thanks for coming,' he said. 'I ordered you a macchiato.'

'How did you know?'

'Isa talks about you nonstop.'

I slid in next to him and a waitress with a bleached pixie cut and Bambi eyes set our coffees on the knock-off Brillo® box. 'Thanks, Candy,' Pez said.

'You know her?'

'Isa and I used to come here all the time. That was our table under the Edie Sedgwick photo – my favourite Warhol superstar.' He nodded towards the large framed print. 'Now that couple in matching Gucci tracksuits have taken over.' He paused. 'You've got a coffee moustache.'

'Always happens. What did you want to tell me?'

'Where do I start? Isa and I clicked the first day we met back in Year 7, and we've been tight ever since. Never anything more than friends though. Last year Nads was hounding her and one day followed us to her place. I told him to back off and it turned into a fight. It got me thinking there might be something more between us after all.'

292

'I knew it!' I said and whapped the sofa, drawing stink eye from the tracksuit couple. 'Sorry, that was a bit much. You should've told me from the start.'

'Hold on, let me finish.' Pericles delivered a padded-out story about how much everybody in his family loved Isa, especially his father, who assumed they were together. It was the one thing that made him proud but it wasn't true. When Pez convinced him that he and Isa were just friends, his father told him it was time to man up and ask her out. So he did.

'She laughed and said I'd caught her off guard and needed time to think about it. Two days later she said no, because there was a huge obstacle in the way.' Pericles was pouring a sachet of sugar onto the glass on the Brillo® box and shaping the granules into a circle. 'She told me I was gay.'

'That's stupid.'

'She reckons she knew.'

'You can't tell somebody else what they are. Gaydar's bullshit.'

Pericles grinned crookedly and swept the sugar crystals into a serviette. 'Promise me you won't tell anybody this?'

'People have asked me that a few times lately. Yeah, okay I promise. But no pinky.'

Pez took a deep breath, turning his gaze to the framed photo. 'Isa was right,' he said to Edie Sedgwick, then turned back to me. 'I bat for the other team. Well, I haven't really batted yet, except on my own.' He half-smiled. 'But I am gay.'

'You're stitching me up?'

'I wish I was, but it's true. I've been attracted to guys for as long as I can remember but had fooled myself into thinking I could have something romantic with Isa and it would change me. She knew me better than I knew myself. I'm a legit fag.'

'Don't even use that word.'

'Legit? Sorry.' He mimicked the screaming-in-fear emoji. 'I'm just a fag. And you know what?' he said with a theatrical hand flourish. 'It's liberating to own the word after being called it so many times by people who had no idea I was one.' Pericles had raised his voice and I could see other customers registering the conversation. 'I am a fag. F-A-G fag! Hello, everybody. I, Pericles Pappas, am a legit homosexual.'

The tracksuit couple fairy-clapped. I asked why he'd chosen this moment to come out to me.

'Because you lost your shit about Isa. The only reason I'd asked her was because she was upset you hadn't. That's why I spoke to you first – to give you a nudge. I don't want to lose our friendship, but I'm giving you the chance to distance yourself before it's all out in the open.'

'Give me some credit. Why would I do that?'

'So people don't think you're a poof by association.'

'Now you're talking mad shit again.'

Pericles looked around the room, buried his face in his hands and pressed his fingers into his eyes, as if preparing to pluck them out.

'There's more,' he said. 'You're going to hate me for this and I don't blame you.'

'I won't hate you. Keep going.'

'I was in the library messaging Isa when Starkey swiped my phone and locked himself in a toilet cubicle to read through our conversation. There was a part where she was talking about being jealous of your and my friendship, and wondering if you were gay too. I told her I hoped so and made a stupid joke about her being a fag-magnet.'

'Shit, Pericles!'

'I'm not attracted to you. I was being smartarsey because I was jealous of Isa spending more time with you. It's all good now because you like each other. God – I completely hate myself right now though. I want to melt and disappear through the cracks in the floor.'

'Don't beat yourself up. Things must've been really difficult for you in ways that I can hardly imagine. But I can relate to how you feel because I've felt that way as well. I've got a problem that I'm disgusted by, and it means I'll never be able to date Isa, or any other girl.'

'What is it? You have to tell now.'

And just like that I'd reached the point of no return. I took Pericles through a similar build-up, swearing him to secrecy and making him promise that he wouldn't laugh at me. Dr Finster and Nicole Parker were the only people who knew about my unnatural extension – assuming that Nicole hadn't told anybody, that is. 'Unnatural extension' was the term I used instead of tail, and I could see Pericles struggling to keep a straight face. But instead of being repelled he seemed fascinated, which made me feel a small degree less uncomfortable. I finished my tale of woe by saying, 'It's been quite a mission to keep it hidden. And I want to keep it that way – but your coming-out will probably make you feel freer than you've ever felt before.'

I leant over and hugged Pericles on the lips sofa, then felt him shuddering in my arms. 'Love you, bruh,' I said, and hugged tighter. The waterworks fully opened. The Gucci couple were staring, so I blew them a kiss over his shoulder and they went back to their eggs. After calming down, Pez told me it was the best day of his life, which made me think the rest had been one extended stay in Shitsville. Turns out Starkey had been blackmailing him. Against my wishes, Pez had confronted him about his uncle. He'd asked him directly if Ken Barnsdale had paid him to harass Bert. Starkey initially denied everything but then contradicted himself by revealing he'd taken screenshots of Pericles' messaging session with Isa, and threatening to out him if he told anybody about Barnsdale.

'Everything will be okay.' I went to pay the bill. On our way out I said, 'Our generation's way more accepting than our parents'.'

'That's who I'm afraid of. I don't want them to find out about me from somebody else.'

'There's only one way of preventing it.'

'I could tell Mum. But it would kill my father.' His eyes widened. 'Unless he actually kills me first.'

'You might be surprised.'

'And I might be thrown out.'

'I'm sure that won't happen – and you can stay with me if it does.' I gripped his shoulders.

'Serious?'

'I've got your back, no matter what.'

'Same.'

Once we'd parted ways, I walked up Bayswater Road, kicking the orange and brown leaves, happy that I'd patched things up with Pericles and even happier that I might be able to do a little patchwork with Isa as well.

GOODBYE, PARADISE

Instead of going to Signal Bay this afternoon, under Mum's direction I took the L90 to Palm Beach Wharf, then caught the little ferry *Myra* across to Mackerel Beach via Bonnie Doon and The Basin. Venn was waiting on the sofa in the jetty's shelter, reading *The Wonders of Lichen,* which she'd picked up from the community library there. 'Hello, stranger,' she said. 'Mind if I finish this first?'

'That's a brick. What are you up to?'

'Second page.' She laughed and slid the book back onto the shelf. Walking along the shore to Amphitrite, the Partridges' sculptural black-steel, glass-fronted 'beach shack', we reminisced about a game we used to play called Fifty Steps. Standing back-to-back on the beach, each holding a stone, we'd take fifty steps away. Then we'd turn and, with eyes closed, take fifty steps back towards one another and lay our stones on the sand. Their proximity was supposedly the measure of our connection. Often the stones were less than one metre apart, but strangely, we'd never bumped into each other.

'I hope you're up for a Rummikub marathon tonight!' Maxine called from the deck as we approached. The Partridges had hosted us at Amphitrite through ten Easters, most nights involving three or four rounds of the tile-based game, followed by Dad and Don's whisky-fuelled philosophy hour. This afternoon Mum and Maxine were on the champagne. 'Glass of bubbly, sweets?' Maxine said as we joined them.

'Just this once,' Mum answered for me.

'Goodie,' Maxine said. 'We'll have to open another one. Could you do the honours, darling?'

In the kitchen, I saw two empty Pol Roger bottles on the bench. I returned with a third, popped its cork, filled our glasses and asked Mum what we were celebrating.

'Maxine's thirtieth wedding anniversary,' she said.

'Cheers, Max. Where's Don?'

'Out woop woop, location-scouting for his next film. I'd rather he was here, but at least he came through with the goods,' she said, bunching the pearls around her neck.

'I'm also celebrating,' Venn said. 'Jessie and I found a place at North Curly, one street from the beach.'

'Well done. Can you see the greenish shade of envy on my face?'

Venn smiled and passed me the nuts. 'Do you think you could help me move on Tuesday?'

'Of course he can,' Mum said. 'He's a man of leisure for another week. How was the dance? Did Penny enjoy herself?'

'Naturally.'

'I heard you like cougars?' Maxine said with a wink.

'I only asked her because there was nobody else who—'

'Why do you men have such a difficult time making us women feel special?' she said. Fuelled by booze, the women listed the major and minor disappointments with the men in their lives. My youth and lack of experience disqualified me from offering any sort of defence – not that I even wanted to.

Rather than boring us all by ragging out Dad again, Mum turned to her most recent dismissal. 'I have to concede that Grant was always very attentive,' she said. 'But it turned out that he was being attentive to other women at the same time.'

'You cracked him off so quickly,' Maxine said. 'After all, it was only a friendly game of tennis with the Perch.'

'Says the amateur sleuth who called to report the sighting.'

'Just looking out for you, darling. Thought you should be informed.'

'Exactly what you said last year when you caught Lance. And that turned out well.'

'What?' I said to Maxine. 'It was you who busted Dad?'

'Hardly "busted", sweetheart. After a great deal of hand-wringing, I shared some concerns I had with my dearest friend.' She banged on about the agony of being caught in a moral dilemma. 'Don hadn't wanted me to say anything, and if I'd kept quiet, everyone might still be playing happy families.' She threw the remaining champagne down her throat.

During dinner, the conversation revolved around Maxine's submission for Sculpture by the Sea and Mum's launch of the E-Radiata Serum™. She'd arranged for me to help out next week, so I asked if I could bring a friend.

'As long as you both stay well away from the bar area,' she said.

When Maxine called for the game of Rummikub, I excused myself and went up to my room. Lying on my bed, I fell under the hypnotic spell of Barrenjoey Lighthouse. An image came to mind – the last family photo taken at Mackerel. It was the picnic shot with Maëlle feeding a goanna – the shot with Maëlle crossed out in Mum's office.

On Saturday morning, before the others had risen, Venn and I walked to the northern end of the beach then climbed the track towards West Head. Reaching the plateau, we sat beneath a scribbly gum and broke out the trail mix. Venn pointed to an impressive tattoo on the tree's trunk, created by the movement of moth larvae between the layers of bark. 'It could be a map of our lives,' she said.

'Which one's you?'

'This one,' she said, tracing a line that zigzagged away from the others.

'There's a difference between being a free spirit and isolating yourself,' I said. 'You're always talking about healing and harmony, but you can't even forgive Dad. You think that somehow frees you from what happened, but you're actually the most bound up.'

'I can't get over the betrayal.'

'Everybody experienced that in some way.'

'Mine was different because it was double.'

Descending the stairs above Resolute Beach, Venn's words continued to gnaw at me – her assertion that she'd suffered most because she'd been let down by both her father and her friend. She'd maintained the judgemental stance of the faultless, conveniently forgetting she'd once betrayed me. So, on reaching a section of the track that weaves between a cluster of grass trees, I drip-fed her a dose of home truth. 'Do you remember when you first hooked up with Elliot Grobecker?'

'Of course I do. The rest of the family had gone home.'

'Do you remember what happened the day before?'

'He snapped off the tallest spike,' she said.

'It was that one,' I said, pointing to the plant that was now the shortest.

Back then Venn had said nothing because she was smitten by the idiot, even though she knew the grass tree could've been over a hundred years old. Elliot kept prodding me in the back with the spike until we reached the sandy delta and I ran away. He chased me and hurled the spike at me, yelling out at the last second. I turned and the spear hit my right eye. They made me wash away the blood in the sea, and when we got back, Venn told all the parents that I'd copped the black eye and swollen nose from walking into a branch. The next day my eye was infected, so Mum and Dad took me home early to see Dr Finster. Venn was allowed to stay on at Mackerel with the Partridges, and that was when she got with Elliot.

'Your relationship began with a betrayal,' I said. 'You broke our allegiance to impress that little turd, and the gang of three became two.'

Venn hung her head and didn't speak until we reached the other end of the beach. I thought she must've been formulating an apology – but no. As we were brushing the sand off our feet she said, 'You know, I used to open my eyes in Fifty Steps.'

Venn's confession was punishment for my digging up and spreading historical shit. So I swallowed everything I wanted to say and shrugged as if not freshly wounded. For the rest of the afternoon we moved around each other with unusual caution. At 6.30 pm, the four of us, including Maxine, caught the last ferry home. As the *Myra* skipped across the gentle waters, Maxine told us that she and Don had put Amphitrite on the market. We'd just spent our final day there.

'Everybody's downsizing,' she said. 'Goodbye, paradise.'

On Tuesday, Venn borrowed Jessie's boyfriend Nate's ute to transport her prized possessions to the Curl Curl flat and some unwanted household stuff to Vinnies. Halfway through packing she got stuck vacillating between keeping or dumping her boxes of thirteen years of schoolwork.

'Just leave it here with Mum,' I said, bristling with annoyance that I had to help Venn on my holidays and she didn't seem very grateful.

'The last thing Mum needs is more junk when she's trying to sell the house. Could you please take them to the recycling bin for me? I can't deal right now.'

'Whatever you want.' I carried the boxes to the garage and riffled through the contents for anything important-looking. Her reports reminded me of how much smarter and more diligent my sister was than me, having topped just about every subject. Surely she wouldn't want me to trash them? Fifteen minutes later, though, she came down to find me. 'Just dump them,' she said. 'We need to return the ute by midday.'

'Perhaps you should keep a few of these?' I handed her a drawing she'd done in Year 3. Our family was a line of stick figures holding hands, descending in height: Dad, Mum, Venn, me and then Gus, who was a little black ball. Nana and Pop Locke were waving from the top of a rectangle in the background – the Dee Why apartment they'd just moved into. We both laughed, which relieved the tension. Venn's face softened.

'I wish everything was back the way it used to be,' she said, getting teary.

'It can't be. But things will improve.'

'Hey, I'm sorry about everything I've said, everything I've done, eh? I'm not trying to make excuses, but last year was so hard losing my grandfather, then my friend, then my boyfriend, then my dad.'

'I don't think you've lost Dad, though. I don't think you could ever lose him, no matter how hard you tried.'

'I've been thinking about what you said. I want to repair my relationship with him. It was unbelievably difficult having all of that business going on while I was studying for the HSC. The exams were gruelling. But I know I need to move past that.'

'And as bad as it all was, you still fully smashed it and got into law.'

'You know I've only deferred? I just wasn't ready for it this year. Environmental Law is postgrad, so it's going to take a while. But that's where my heart is. I'd study for a hundred years to make restitution for that grass tree.'

We drove to the flat in Curly. Carrying in the first box, I understood why Venn had been so ruthless in the culling process. The apartment only had one bedroom, so her domain would be the tiny sunroom. The living-room carpet was smelly and the walls were apricot, but it had a balcony and you could hear the crash of the surf. Perfect.

After filling practically the entire space with Venn's stuff alone, we delivered some old but functional kitchen appliances, sporting equipment and clothing to Vinnies and returned Nate's ute to his workplace in Dee Why. Then we bought some grilled fish, calamari and chips, and walked to Nana Locke's unit for lunch.

When we arrived Tippi went ballistic with excitement, running between us and pawing at our knees. Nana insisted on making a salad to 'liven things up' and while she was in the kitchen with Venn, I looked at her collection on the sideboard and mantelpiece – the strange little plastic dolls in the national dress of countries she'd never visited, the crystal sherry glasses and miniature family photo gallery. Nothing much had moved position in the ten years she'd lived there.

Over lunch, Venn seemed determined to gain a better understanding of Dad by asking Nana Locke a bunch of questions about what he'd been like in his youth. Nana confirmed what he'd told me about busting his nuts to please Pop Locke. 'Your grandfather was a little on the sterner side of virtuous back then,' she said. 'A good man, but very hard to please. Wanted the best for your father, or his idea of what that was. Proud as punch of everything your dad did, but didn't often tell him. Things were different back in those days.'

'Why did Dad take so long to tell us he was adopted?' Venn said.

'He struggled with it in his later teen years. Not the "being adopted" part, but being deprived of the opportunity to discover who his birth parents were. Sometimes he used to mutter away to himself in his room. One night I listened behind the door as he asked his mother why she'd abandoned him. Heartbreaking. Later, when he became a little reckless, he blamed his behaviour on character traits he thought he'd inherited from his birth father. In his mind, that man was the opposite of Pop Locke – more the scoundrel type.'

It seemed that Dad's imagination had got the better of him, and he'd reached a point where he had to accept that Nana and Pop were the only parents he would ever know. Until Nana Locke explained it to me, I hadn't thought about the fact that Venn was the first blood connection Dad had known, and I'd been the second.

'Pop adored each of you from the moment you were born. He softened almost overnight and spoilt you rotten when you were little. I think your father kept his own beginnings secret for Pop's sake somehow. And I think it was also partly his way of building a safe and secure world for you.'

'Ironic that he ended up blowing it apart,' Venn said.

'He was very foolish and he knows that. I hope you can find it in your heart to forgive him. It's in the heart that connections are made and broken. It's all about connections, which reminds me – Lincoln, darling, close your eyes because I've got a surprise for you.'

She left to fetch something from her bedroom then returned and asked me to stand back-to-back with Venn, who was also told to close her eyes. I heard the sound of something being pulled from a plastic bag then felt myself being bound to my sister with Nana Locke's knitting. We both laughed as she wound from our legs up. She hushed us and told us to keep our eyes closed, which was close to impossible because Tippi was yapping with all the excitement and nipping at the loose ends.

'One, two, three – open!' Nana said.

She'd bound herself in the knitting as well, with a bridge of wool connecting us. 'And now I've finally passed my DNA onto you,' she said. There were metres and metres of the pink-and-green and yellow-and-blue double helix. 'And some of Glenda's for good measure.' The madness of Nana out-ritualising Venn sent the three of us into hysterics.

Then Nana Locke dealt us another surprise. 'I hope it's enough, darling,' she said to me, 'because I won't be knitting anymore. Clarry from six-oh-five is taking me and Glenda and this little one for a trip to Tathra on the Sapphire Coast. It was Pop's favourite holiday spot and he wanted his ashes scattered over the ocean.'

The Jack Russell–Chihuaha yapped once. Nana scooped her up and held her close.

'I'm glad Tippi's going along to keep an eye on things,' I said.

Nana smiled at me and winked.

PINK ELEPHANT

Pestered by a smidge of guilt that Nana Locke's contribution to the DNA project would be far greater than mine, on Wednesday I signed up for a VIP card at Spotlight and purchased twenty balls of the cheapest synthetic yarn. I hadn't spoken to Isa since the dance and the confession session with Pericles at International Velvet. His belief that she liked me wasn't exactly a green light – more a tentative amber. So for the next four days, between catch-ups with my schoolwork, I knitted alone. On Saturday, which was Anzac Day, I went down to visit Bert but he wasn't home. Maybe he'd gone to the dawn service and hadn't returned. Perhaps he'd served in the armed forces and lost his eye in battle. Who knew?

Back at school on Monday, I showed Isa a photo of Nana Locke and Glenda's 12.3-metre stretch of double helix and the four metres I'd completed. She gripped my shoulders and shook me. 'This is going to be beyond incredible,' she said. 'Are you excited? I'm excited.' Those green eyes. Splinters of golden light in rainforest. Though we hadn't discussed the school dance or my talk with Pericles, something between us had shifted.

Ms Tarasek requested that the collaboration pairs write a description and creative rationale for our work, along with display preferences.

As our work was a guerrilla operation, neither Isa nor I had anticipated having to reveal its meaning before installing it – that would have defeated the purpose. 'I'd thought we'd get Mr Jespersen to let us into The Labyrinth late one afternoon before security arrived,' I said. 'Now it seems we'll have to go through official channels.'

'Ms Tarasek won't have a problem, but Dashwood probably wouldn't approve of an artwork about the school being founded on eugenic ideals being wrapped around the nutbag who came up with them.'

'We could omit the specific reference to eugenics and use some irony. Say it's about Millington Drake's dedication to the advancement of science for the betterment of humanity.'

'I think we should be completely honest with Ms Tarasek.'

'That puts the onus on her,' I said. 'This way we take responsibility for our own work. Once it's up, we can tell people what it's really about.'

'I see your point. You're as passionate about this as me now, aren't you?'

'After all the work we've put into it – yes.'

'So we agree. We have to make sure it goes up.'

Together we wrote out a description of the knitted DNA that sounded more eulogy than indictment of Joseph Millington Drake. We submitted it, cautiously optimistic.

At lunchtime I met Isa, Phoenix and Pericles in the grove. Phoenix was explaining why she'd already ditched Kirk Shepard. 'He was a terrible kisser. Too much pokey snake tongue.'

'Maybe you could train him,' Isa said.

'What am I, a charity?'

'Send him to me for a lesson,' Pericles said. Then to the girls, 'Don't worry. I've told Lincoln.'

'At long last,' Phoenix said. 'It was becoming such a hassle keeping it secret. Starkey's already telling people anyway, and you'll be the pink elephant in the classroom if you don't come out soon.'

'That's a helpful way of putting it,' Isa said.

'It's the truth. Nathan Trammel asked me if you were Pez's beard.'

'What's that?' I said.

'The fake girlfriend or wife of a gay guy to make people think he's straight. Big in Hollywood apparently. Even Heather Treadwell came up and asked me if it was true. She wanted to know so that she could pray for you, Pericles.'

'Shit! Why is this even an issue?' he said. 'What am I supposed to do, call a special assembly? "Yes, it's true. I am gay. That is all."'

'Maybe you should start with your family?' Phoenix said.

'Are you running for president of the Crestfield Gay and Lesbian Acceptance Group or something?'

'No. But I do believe our school would benefit from more diversity. And I'd do anything to support you. We all would.'

'Okay, then. You're right – I'm sick of keeping it a secret.' He took a deep breath. 'I'm telling my parents tonight.'

'Do you really think it's the right time?' I said.

'There is no right time.'

At the end of the day, Starkey manifested like a tormenting spirit at the racks again, cigarette glowing on his lip. He blew smoke in my face and said, 'How's your bum chum going, trashman?'

'Get lost.'

'Little bit tetchy, are we? Had a lovers' tiff?'

'Piss off!' I turned my back to him as I dialled the lock's code.

'Trying to hide the combination? Don't wet your pants – I wouldn't be seen dead on that thing. It's gay, like you and your boyfriend. I've got proof on my phone.'

All of a sudden I smelt burning rubber. Starkey was bent down, melting the sole of my shoe with his cigarette lighter.

'What are you doing, you psychopath?'

'Seeing how long it would take you to notice.'

'Whatever. I feel sorry for you.'

'Not as sorry as you'll feel when I tell everyone about you and Pooficles Poparse.'

I bit my tongue and pushed my bike up the embankment.

Tonight after dinner I received a text from Pericles.

I've been kicked out of home. Can I stay at yours?

Things had gone as bad as he'd predicted. I explained the situation to Dad and asked if Pericles could stay with us. Dad didn't hesitate. His only question was whether Pericles needed to be picked up.

Pez declined and caught the train to Kings Cross like thousands of outcasts before – only his shelter was a luxury apartment on the twenty-seventh floor.

'Thank you for letting me stay, M-M-Mr Locke,' Pericles stammered when Dad met him at the door. Dad took him in his arms and hugged him till he started sobbing, then held him even tighter. He looked over his shoulder and winked at me. The hug we'd shared on Good Friday had been the first in ages, and I felt Dad's love for me again as he embraced my friend. On release, Pez apologised repeatedly for being an inconvenience and disturbing our night. Dad made him a cup of tea and eventually he calmed down and shared his story.

He'd only intended to tell his mother. She cried then was struck mute for fifteen minutes. The first word she uttered was 'Why?', which was difficult for Pericles to answer because it seemed more aimed at God than him. When she finally composed herself, she hugged Pericles and told him that she'd love him no matter what, and that nothing could ever change that. It was probably unnecessary to add, 'Even if you murder somebody' – but she had.

Pez took some comfort from his mother's allegiance, until his father's car appeared in the driveway and she said, 'You'll have to tell your father now. I won't be able to hide this from him.' He begged her not to, but before Mr Pappas even had a chance to sit down she said, 'Our son has something he'd like to tell you.' There was no escape. He'd wanted to do it by degrees, but his mother had decided differently.

'I'm gay,' he said to his father.

Mr Pappas walked away without saying a word. Pericles followed him to the vegetable patch, where he was supposedly checking the progress of his eggplants. He turned and exploded in Greek. Pez understood nothing but the swearing. Then in English his father said, 'This is your mother's fault for letting your sisters dress you like a girl.'

'That has nothing to do with it. I'm a man. I like being a man. I like other men.'

'You're wrong,' Mr Pappas said. 'This is a weakness you must overcome.'

The argument raged for an hour. Mrs Pappas, who'd forced the issue, desperately tried to placate her husband. But he was acting like a bull whose left testicle had been sliced off. He told Pericles that he wouldn't permit 'filthy behaviour' with other boys under his roof. Interpreting this as an ultimatum, Pericles had thrown some clothes in a bag and come to ours.

Dad left Pez and me to talk, and we sat on the balcony watching the lights of the city. 'Your father's awesome,' he said.

'Trust me. He's far from perfect.'

'It was good of him to let me stay here with you. Even though the coming-out backfired, I'm glad Phoenix pushed me. It was like cutting open a festering boil. Not just my father, but heaps of other people have said homophobic stuff over the years without really meaning it, assuming I was straight. It probably slides off if you are. I thought it was sliding off me because I was in denial. But this tiny voice in my head would keep repeating words like "poof" and "faggot" over and over. It was killing me.'

'It's tough when the little man inside your mind is against you.'

'Leave me out of this,' Homunculus said to me.

'I thought if I denigrated myself enough it would go away, like it was an ugly part of me I could get rid of. I thought it was so small and insignificant it would disappear if I kept it hidden. Now I've realised it's not a separate thing. It's part of who I am. The worst thing had been my father's ignorance of how much he was hurting me. Now at least I'll know that he means everything he says.'

'You've been thinking about this for a long time,' I said. 'For years. And most of that time you've been fighting it. Your dad's only just found out and his immediate reaction was to fight as well. But when he's had a few days or weeks to think about it he'll probably come around.'

'More like months or years – if he ever changes his mind.'

'You can stay with us for as long as you need to.'

'That means a lot to me, but I don't want to be a burden to your father.'

309

'You're not a burden and I can tell that he likes you already.'

'Are you sure that you're okay with having me here?'

'Shut up,' I said, giving him a playful punch on the shoulder. 'I always wanted a brother.'

I showed Pericles where everything was and made up the bed in the guest room. After saying goodnight I went to the bathroom to brush my teeth and heard him talking to Christina on the phone. The fallout had been huge – his father had dumped a tonne of shame on him. Shame seemed to be the flavour of the month. It felt like the right time to return to the book and discover what had happened to Edwin after being outed on stage by his doctor.

Hoping to receive some measure of consolation from my mother on returning home, I was cut to the quick when she expressed mortification at having witnessed my 'indecent behaviour' on the stage. Assuming she was talking about the exposure of my deformity, I argued that my sole purpose had been to rescue us from poverty.

'You misunderstood me,' she said. 'I was referring to the deceitful impersonation.'

'It was done only to protect my dignity.'

'And instead destroyed it. There is no virtue in masquerading as a dark-skinned man and behaving in an animalistic fashion to suggest he's inferior to ourselves. That sort of degrading act appeals to an ignorant audience.'

The following week I was ridiculed, spat on and several times beaten by Reg McGuffin and his gang, many of whom I'd once counted as friends. Their cruel blows were endurable but when they egged our home and pounded my brother Thomas black and blue on his way home from school, the weight of my responsibility was too much to bear.

When I thought matters couldn't possibly worsen, I learnt that George Pemberton had been forced to pay Dr Melvin Fletcher one hundred pounds for proving me a fake. Pemberton invited me to his office on Monday and I feared he would demand compensation. On entering his sanctum sanctorum, I found he had company.

'Edwin, thank you for coming in the midst of all the brouhaha,' he said. 'Allow me to introduce one of the world's greatest showmen, Irving Melinkoff.' The impresario was shorter and stockier than he'd appeared in the newspaper illustrations I'd seen. He was sporting an elegant green-and-silver-striped suit, a jewelled cane and a large mole above his lip, which was difficult to avert one's eyes from. 'Mr Melinkoff owns four theatrical establishments in America that by comparison make our humble operation resemble a flea circus.'

Pemberton invited me to sit on an Oriental chaise flanked by a moulded-tin foxhound flocked with tiny hairs. The dog's wagging tail matched the rhythm of the seconds ticking away on a clock built into its side.

'I found him while touring Germany,' Melinkoff said. 'Presented him to George as a small token of my appreciation for organising this meeting.'

'Mr Melinkoff may well have the solution to our present troubles. Dr Fletcher has already donated the one hundred pounds to the Home for Destitute and Crippled Children. And while there's no worthier recipient, it was galling that he'd claimed the prize, knowing full well your condition is authentic. Our only "ruse" was fabricating a more exotic identity for you.'

'I must apologise, sir. I never expected him to come to the show.'

'Don't fret, son. Every setback is an opportunity in disguise. Three reporters were present when I handed over the cheque to Fletcher, and there's nothing more effective than a magnanimous gesture to restore one's reputation.'

'Or to cover a multitude of sins,' Melinkoff said with a wink. 'But your reputation may be more difficult to recover.' He turned and fixed his gaze upon me. 'I've heard your neighbours have been downright unneighbourly.'

'I'd run and hide ten thousand miles away to escape, but that would only be abandoning my family.'

'Not necessarily.' Melinkoff's smile was all gold. 'George here tells me you swim like a fish?'

'I haven't been to the baths in months for shame of my growth, sir.'

'That wondrous anomaly will be your ticket to fame and fortune, my boy. I've got big plans for an aquatic show in a giant glass tank at Coney Island. I plan to have high-divers, mermaids, feats of endurance. Can you hold your breath for two minutes? Of course you can. Let's time you.'

I filled my lungs with air, then closed my mouth and pinched my nose. After ninety-five wags of the tail, each more agonising than the last, I surrendered, gasping for air.

'Not bad at all. I'll have you doing three, four minutes with some training. You must come with me to Coney Island, son.'

'With all due respect, sir, I couldn't desert my mother.'

'With the fortune we'll make together, leaving your family for a while would be the kindest thing you could do. How does thirty pounds sound to you?'

'Thirty pounds a month?'

'A week – plus fifty right now if you sign on the spot. And one hundred to compensate my friend George here.'

After a few moments weighing my mother's rebuke against Melinkoff's undisguised eagerness, I said, 'I'd be honoured to accept the offer, on condition that I'm not required to blacken my face.'

'It's a deal!' He pumped my hand and slapped my back.

Thirty minutes later, alone on George Street, I realised what I'd done. The excitement of the offer soured quickly as I thought of the people I'd be leaving behind. I went straight to Lassetter's and used half my first payment to buy a solid gold brooch: a dove flying through a diamond-studded heart. The accompanying letter I wrote to Diddy Budd is printed here with her permission.

My dearest Diddy,

If you're reading this letter close to seven in the evening, my faithful brother Thomas has performed his commission with expedience. I imagine myself now standing on the stern deck of the S.S. Oceania *as it passes between those rocky sentinels, North and South Head, looking back at the lights of the city and thinking of all the dear people I won't see for at least a year, possibly longer.*

As you're aware, I've brought great shame on my family. How stupid I was to assume Dr Fletcher's confidence! It would grieve me tremendously if you felt in any way to blame for what transpired by having allowed him up to my room that day. You have only ever shown my family the greatest kindness, for which I am truly thankful.

Taking yet another great risk now by leaving for America, I hope to earn enough money to clear my late father's debt. Yet I remain the lowest form of coward, slipping away without expressing my true affection towards you in person. You see, it would break my heart beyond repair if ever I caught a look of revulsion in your eyes at the sight of me. You must have wondered why I'd backed away from you over the past few months. At least you now know the reason.

I once thought the problem would go away of its own accord, but that hasn't eventuated. Pardon my arrogant assumption, but if you have any feelings for me then you must let them go. I've chosen never to marry, because the thought of passing this affliction on to some innocent offspring is unconscionable. As deeply as it pains me to write this, you must open your kind heart to another who is more deserving. Though initially painful, it will be easier for us both if we correspond no further. I have no right to ask this, but it would please me greatly if you maintained your friendship with my family, as they all adore you.

Finally, please accept this small token of my deep affection and gratitude for your unwavering kindness. Fly free and find great love, little bird.

Yours sincerely,
Edwin Stroud

*

Having experienced the look of revulsion from Nicole Parker last year, I fully empathised with Edwin's fear of rejection from Diddy Budd. Both he and Pericles, for different reasons, had demonstrated a huge amount of courage by exposing themselves. In both instances their decisions had pretty much backfired – especially in the immediate fallout for their families. Their demonstration of courage had a price. One that I wasn't prepared to pay.

THE CHURCH OF TIME

Wednesday morning before Art, I gave Isa the skinny on Pericles. To my surprise, she took my hands and squeezed them. 'I'm so proud of you for looking after him. You probably saved his life.'

'Don't know about that,' I said, not quite sure how to deal with her admiration. 'Just being a friend.'

Eager to know what Ms Tarasek thought of our proposal for the DNA piece, we went into the studio, but she hadn't arrived, and everyone was arsing around. A hush came over the room as Dashwood walked in and ordered us to our seats.

'Year 10, I have some serious news.' He smoothed his hair and licked his lips. 'Due to unforeseen circumstances, Ms Tarasek will not be returning to teach this year.'

He read a message from her, the gist of it being that she'd loved our enthusiasm and was sad to be leaving, but had faith we'd continue to thrive under her replacement. She said just knowing we were thinking of her would help her get through a difficult situation, but asked that we respect her need for privacy.

Dashwood left to fetch the new teacher, and wild speculation about the reasons for Ms Tarasek's departure abounded – from eloping to pregnancy to witness protection and alien abduction. This last theory,

315

proposed by Ashleigh Robinson, seemed the most implausible, until the Dash returned with Miss Timms – whose tiny nose and mouth made her pale-blue eyes appear massive. She looked as though she was taking mental photographs of everything before reporting back to the mothership. I was hardly the person to be critiquing anybody else's unusual appearance, but you'd have been hard-pressed to find anybody who looked more like an alien attempting to pass as an earthling.

After Dashwood left, Miss Timms repeated what he'd said verbatim then added, 'I've heard nothing but praise for the work Ms Tarasek has done here, especially in regard to the YOU ARE HERE! exhibition. You are all still here, but unfortunately Ms Tarasek isn't, so Mr Dashwood has postponed the show.'

At lunch we met up with Phoenix and Pez, who'd already heard the news and formulated their own conspiracy theories.

'She was obviously forced to resign,' Phoenix said.

'And the reason would be?'

'You two, of course. The subversive nature of your proposed DNA installation probably freaked out the Dash. Remember Lethbridge, the school historian? He's also on the school board and was supposed to be opening the show. As if Dashwood would allow a knitted chain of DNA to be tied around the neck of Crestfield's founder, exposing him as a eugenics enthusiast and white supremacist. The board would give Dashwood the chop.'

'He could've just told Ms Tarasek that our piece was inappropriate.'

'Singling it out would've drawn more attention.'

'Why not just cancel the exhibition?' I said. 'He didn't have to force Ms Tarasek to resign.'

'Maybe he didn't. Maybe he voiced his disapproval to Tarasek and she argued for freedom of expression. Then he gave her an ultimatum.'

'This is nuts!' Isa said. 'You've been reading too many thrillers.'

'Actually, I've just visited the library,' Phoenix said. 'I wanted to check if Millington Drake's wacky manifesto was still on the digital catalogue. "*On Building Tomorrow's Man*,"' she said with air quotes. 'And guess what? It's not.'

While it seemed unlikely that the school board had any involvement in Ms Tarasek's sudden departure, I recalled Liliana Petersen bragging in class last term that her mother was a board member and threatening the teacher with removal for shredding our assignments, so who knew? The possibility that Isa and I were even remotely responsible for our favourite, most radical teacher being exiled from Crestfield was heavy shit to contemplate.

After school on Thursday I showed Pericles *My One Redeeming Affliction* – the book, not the actual tail. I read him the passages about the phrenology bust, the samovar, the oyster knife and the puppets, and told him I believed Bert owned those very objects.

'That's probably the Baader-Meinhof phenomenon,' he said. 'You read about something unfamiliar or new and then start seeing it everywhere. Think about it – there are probably hundreds of objects mentioned in the book that you haven't seen, right? And the ones you have noticed might just be similar to the description. Anyway, there's only one way to find out. Show the old dude the book and ask him directly.'

'Do you want to come with me?'

'One hundred per cent.'

On our way down the backstreets and lanes of Darlinghurst, I told Pericles something I'd been pondering for weeks now as I'd been reading the book. I felt connected to Edwin Stroud in some way beyond sharing the affliction – in fact, there were so many weird coincidences between our lives that I thought we could actually be related. I said it was maybe far-fetched and ridiculous, but I couldn't shake the feeling. Anyway, Edwin hadn't appeared on my mother's side of the family tree and I'd probably never know Dad's ancestry because he was abandoned without a clue.

'That doesn't mean you're not related,' Pericles said, unfazed by my theory.

'Apparently, when he was about my age, Dad really struggled over having no way of exploring his family history. I want to discover why I sprouted an extra appendage and who I might've inherited the special little feature from. The answer might be close, but I feel like it's slipping away.'

Walking through Bert's now unpadlocked gate, we found him out the front, snipping a rosebush with secateurs. 'Don't bloom if you don't prune,' he said to me. 'Who's your chum?'

'This is Pericles. Pericles, Bert.'

'Never trust a Greek bearing gifts,' he said, eyeing the book.

'Don't worry, it belongs to the library.' I held out the book but he didn't take it. 'I was just wondering if you'd read it.'

'Can't read anything without my monocle, and I don't own one.'

'There's a bunch of things I've read about in here that I've seen at your place. There's even a cockatiel called Percy.'

'Well, that's a little bit spooky, isn't it? A very strange coinky-dinky, I'll give you that much. Come inside and I'll show you something.'

He led us to one of his bookcases and pulled out three fat nineteenth-century catalogues for department stores – Anthony Hordern's, Frederic Lassetter's and George Pemberton's – which he handed to me. I flipped through and saw illustrations of everything from carriages and farm machinery to piano accordions and croquet sets.

'Despite the fancy name, the Magnificent Emporium was the smallest of the three,' he said. 'Lassetter's was enormous, took up four city blocks on George Street. I've probably got a few thousand items from Lassetter's here. Business went down the gurgler in twenty-nine.'

'So you know of George Pemberton? I was wondering if you had any personal connection to him, or maybe Edwin Stroud, the author of this book.'

'Curious little bugger, aren't you? Everything will be revealed in perfect time, and time will reveal everything perfectly.' He looked at his watch, heightening the dramatic effect of his cryptic comment. 'Now it's time to go upstairs.'

He took us up to a blue door opposite what he'd earlier described as the Carnival Room and made us close our eyes before opening it. He guided us in and I heard a sound like a thousand eggs hatching, then opened my eyes and saw clocks – hundreds of them. Grandfather clocks, cuckoo clocks, wall clocks, clocks with thermometers and barometers and a glass cabinet full of fobs and wristwatches. Most of them running close to the correct time – 3.55 pm.

'Check these out!' Pericles said, pointing to a collection of animal clocks. Holding pride of place among them was a life-sized dog with a timepiece stuck in his side. I'd read about him last night – the mechanical foxhound that Melinkoff gave Pemberton! He still had a few defiant patches of hair remaining on his legs, but his head and back were barren, presumably from years of patting. The clock had stopped at 3.15.

Bert shuffled over and said, 'His tail used to mark the seconds.'

'Must be hard maintaining all your clocks,' I said.

'Once took pride in keeping everything tickety-boo. Time is a great teacher but eventually it kills all its pupils.'

'Maybe you should think about selling some of your stuff.'

'You were the first person to buy something from me in years, young fella. Cocky little bastard you were, too, demanding that bike. Mind you, repairing it gave me a new lease of life. Started tinkering with other things.'

'Our friend Isa, who you've met, thought you could have a garage sale. You'd have less stuff to move and more money to live on.'

'You think letting a few nosy neighbours poke through my junk will make a couple of hundred bob?'

'This stuff must be worth tens of thousands,' I said. 'At least.'

Bert tapped his watch and shushed me.

>TICK<tick>TICK<tick>TICK<

A cuckoo sprang from his little house and cuckooed four times. One of the grandfather clocks chimed and the rest of the clocks followed, marking the hour in their unique ways. Cuckoos, chimes, bells and dinky digital riffs, all together in a shambolic orchestra. I stroked the dog, and the tempo of my internal clock – my heart – accelerated with the conviction that the three of us, Bert, Pericles and me, were together in the Church of Time.

I looked at Pericles. His eyes were closed in reverence as the last of the clocks made its late claim. And then, again, there was only ticking.

We talked further about having a sale. Bert liked the idea but wasn't keen on haggling with strangers. I reminded him that Isa's housemate Terri was an antiques dealer with a wide network and could bring heaps of people, even run things on the day. Bert's enthusiasm seemed to rise.

'I'd like to keep a few special things,' he said.

'You could put a red sticker on them and label what you want to sell with a recommended price.'

'Sounds like you've planned the whole thing already.'

'Now that you've explained where they came from, some of these things have a special meaning to me too, and I hope they go to good people who might look after them. And I want you to be okay.'

'You're a good egg. And to demonstrate my appreciation, I'd like you to have something special.' He went into the Carnival Room and returned with a small wooden box and the mechanical chicken.

'No, I don't deserve that,' I said.

'You deserve a good clip over the ear for annoying me. As sure as eggs is eggs, Ethel is going to you. Leave her with me for now and I'll see if I can't get her cackling again.'

'It's ten past,' Pericles said. 'We'd better get to work.'

'Just a minute, there's a gift for the Greek as well,' Bert said. He took a large gold coin from the box and pressed it into Pericles' hand. 'Guard this with your life. You never know when it might come in handy.'

'Thanks, Bert.' Beaming like a five-year-old on Christmas morning, Pez showed me the coin. One side was embossed with a sailor looking through a telescope and the words, DISCOVER NEW WORLDS . . . On the other, it said, AT PEMBERTON'S MAGNIFICENT EMPORIUM, beneath the profile of a bearded man, presumably Pemberton himself.

'What about the sale?' I said.

'Let me do a stocktake first,' Bert said, which we took as our signal to leave.

*

When we arrived at Give Me the Juice, Helena and Christina raced up and sandwiched Pericles in a hug. 'Settle down,' he said, wriggling free.

'Where's the love?' Christina said. 'We haven't seen you for two days, little brother.'

'How did you manage without me?'

'Not funny. Dad's gone apeshit.'

'So what's new?'

'He's taking it out on us.'

'He wants you to come home,' Helena said. 'Even the neighbours were asking where you were.'

'I hope he went over there and explained it's because he's disgusted by the sight of me.'

'Don't speak like that.'

'It's the truth.'

Sam was looking through the hatch, bristling with anger because we were running late. He came out and spun Pericles by the shoulder. 'Listen, malaka, I personally don't care if you're a pillowbiter, arse-bandit, or the Christmas tree fairy, but you're not George Michael and we still need to make money. There's customers waiting to be served, so start serving them, yeah?'

'You know what? Fuck you!' Pericles gave him the finger and walked out. I went to follow but Sam seized my arm.

'Don't even think about it. You'll make it twice as bad. Dad will want to know why the takings were shit and I'll have to explain why we were two staff down, and then he'll tell Uncle Con.'

'Tell your dad he was sick,' I said.

'Yeah, like sick in the head. This is a business, mate, not a counselling service.'

'Please stay,' the twins said, 'for our sake.' So I stayed and it was pretty bloody infuriating because I had to work out the back with Sam, who I'd used to think was a decent bloke but now thought was a king-sized homophobic prick.

There were ten minutes of itchy silence before I spoke up.

'You could've shown him some sympathy.'

'Why?'

'Remember when your dad got on your case the other week?'

'That was about working on cars, mate, not prancing around at poofter clubs.' Apparently people reckoned society was more accepting of gay people these days. Well, all of this was making me think it must've been pretty fucking horrible before.

During my break I called Pericles to see if he was okay. He told me he was watching waves crash on Ben Buckler.

'Don't do anything rash,' I said.

'I'm not at The Gap, bud. It's just that sometimes I wish I could cut off parts of myself.'

'Don't even try. Believe me – it gets very messy.'

On our way back home, having met up with Pericles, I told him about my failed attempt to remove the tail. He winced in sympathy, but then laughed when I told him I'd settled for shaving it. Hair removal for him was a weekly necessity. We talked for ages about how, in our own ways, we both felt like freaks.

I said goodnight and went to my room to read, eager to see how Edwin would fare in America. I caught up with him and Melinkoff on board the S.S. *Oceania*.

Irving Melinkoff spent most of his evenings in the Neptune Lounge, puffing on Cuban cigars and sipping cognac, discussing the latest ventures of the Vanderbilts and Rockefellers as if intimately acquainted. He'd introduced me to our fellow passengers as his nephew, and every night I was required to wait until the last of our company had retired before descending to our tiny cabin three decks beneath theirs. This usually occurred in the wee hours, as Melinkoff was a flamboyant raconteur and his accounts of exotic adventures and daring escapades were loaded with embellishment and diversion. The stories often contradicted one another, yet his audience never seemed concerned with their veracity, content to be distracted from the monotony of the voyage.

I, on the other hand, had entrusted a year of my life to him, and if gross fabrication came so easily to Melinkoff, I wondered how he could be trusted to deliver the promised financial rewards. My niggling doubts, exacerbated by long stretches without sight of land and a harrowing four-day storm, evolved into an unshakeable dread of never being able to return home. Setting foot on solid ground in Honolulu brought such great relief that I considered giving Melinkoff the slip and not re-embarking for the final leg. Only the shame of returning to Sydney with empty pockets vanquished the idea.

On arrival to San Francisco, the port was shrouded in a thick fog and low cloud, and not a single feature of the city was visible as the tugs, horns tooting, guided us to the wharf. But shortly after disembarking, the fog lifted and with it my despondency. Immediately after checking in to our room at the Royal Hotel – a great improvement on the cabin – we visited the offices of the *San Francisco Examiner*, where Melinkoff placed an advertisement appealing for 'freaks and prodigies of all shapes and sizes, articulate, athletic and able to entertain'. The following Wednesday, a hundred and sixty hopefuls, less than one quarter of whom fitted the description, queued outside the hall of the Quilters' Guild, awaiting their chance to impress the showman.

The first to succeed was Ruthie Davis. Expelled from ballet academy for growing too tall, she'd sought comfort in the consumption of fancy pastries and dramatically expanded her girth. Melinkoff renamed her Baby Cakes the Living Doll, and ordered a childlike dress to be sewn up for her costume. The muscled torso of Roy Lister the Human Globe was tattooed with a map of the world, and he could make the oceans ripple by undulating his stomach. Melvina Wellington suffered from hypertrichosis, but bearded ladies were a common feature on the circuit, so Melinkoff came up with the idea of having her five-year-old son, Leopold, don a fake beard to appear alongside his parents as the first Fully Bearded Family. Fire-breathing sword-swallower Milton Banks, a.k.a. the Whispering Flame, was married to Serpentina, who, with her diamond python Octavius, had earnt the dubious distinction of being the most risqué act on the West Coast – woman and snake becoming so entwined in the finale it was impossible to tell them apart. The only other animal act was Samson and Delilah, two magnificent white leopards, and their trainer, Lloyd Farbridge.

The last person to join our troupe had never before set foot in a theatre. Paulo Esposito was born with phocomelia, a genetic disorder that had prevented his limbs from developing properly while in the womb. The upper sections of both arms and legs were missing, and the lower sections were very short, which made his hands and feet appear to be directly connected to his torso. All of his fingers were fused, giving his hands a flipper-like appearance. Heedless of the fact that he'd been taunted by the name since childhood, Melinkoff reinstated the moniker Paulo Penguino.

While the rest of the troupe spent the following week in rehearsals, I was employed constructing props, collecting costumes, organising photography sessions and printing thousands of posters, handbills and pitch cards. Initially I revelled in the excitement of traversing the restless and hilly city by cable car and the independence that came with Melinkoff's preoccupation with the other performers. But by week's end, vexed over the lack of attention he'd given me, I felt it judicious to remind him of my extremely brief time on stage and the matter of the glass tank, which hadn't been mentioned since we'd left Australia.

'Transporting a glass tank by rail would be too risky,' he said. 'It will be constructed on arrival in New York. In the meantime we'll have to invent a suitable persona for you.' He paused for a brief moment. 'I have it! Instead of a Pacific Islander, we'll make you an Australian native – a simple matter of blacking up and wearing as little as you can get away with. No need for feathers and masks here.' He produced a newspaper clipping dated July 1883, advertising the showman Robert Cunningham's first troupe. Beneath the headline 'AUSTRALIAN CANNIBALS' was an illustration of shipwreck survivors being pursued, killed and eaten by Aboriginal people.

'With respect, sir, I only agreed to this venture on condition that I wouldn't be required to impersonate a dark-skinned fellow.'

'How then can we convince the public that you represent the intermediate stage of man's ascension from beastly form? A skinny white lad with an unfortunate deformation is hardly exotic enough. We'll have to compromise. The spiel is coming to me . . . Take this down!'

Introducing for the first time ever
THE ASTOUNDING BOUNDING
KANGAROO BOY!

HAROLD HOPKINS, a mere babe of one month,
SOLE SURVIVOR of a **TRAGIC SHIPWRECK** on a remote
Australian island.
DISCOVERED by a kangaroo and **ADOPTED** as one of her own!
SUCKLED on her milk, he developed **BESTIAL** characteristics!
SPEARED by fierce Aboriginal hunters, his mother was
killed and eaten.
Resisting their **CANNIBALISTIC** urges, the savages
spared the strange child.

He was **PADDLED** to the mainland on bark canoe and
DELIVERED into the caring arms of Christian missionaries.

Intrepid explorer and theatrical impresario **IRVING MELINKOFF**
has searched the darkest corners of the Earth
to find this **REMARKABLE** and **GROTESQUE** specimen,
the likes of which **YOU WILL NEVER** have the chance
to witness again!

Spared from performing the artless mimicry that my mother considered denigrating to my fellow man, I was initially pleased with Melinkoff's solution. Later, though, I realised that my relief and instinct for self-preservation had blinded me to the destructive nature of the myths I'd be perpetuating. At the time I justified my acquiescence by imagining that the vast distance between our continents somehow absolved me from any responsibility to my countrymen. But that stance required a wilful ignorance of the plight of the American Indian and indeed coloured folk in America – slavery having ended only thirty-four years earlier.

*

325

I googled Robert Cunningham. He'd 'procured' nine Aboriginal performers from Palm and Hinchinbrook islands and had taken them on tour with P. T. Barnum's Ethnological Congress of Strange and Savage Tribes. Afterwards, he toured them separately on the American dime museum circuit and then across Europe. Most of them became sick and died while on tour, never making it back to their home. Twice more he 'acquired' Indigenous performers and worked them to the point of exhaustion and death. He obviously believed that 'the show must go on' at all cost – even human.

MOST BEAUTIFUL

The staging for the launch of E-Radiata Serum™ at Farm Cove was a design and engineering marvel that I'd contributed to in a small way. The runway emerged from between two enormous screens, intersecting a traverse stage and extending ten metres before encircling the pool. Viewed from the top of Fleet Steps, the whole stage resembled an elongated female/Venus symbol. The Venus shell was concealed behind a black curtain studded with Swarovski crystals that formed the logo for $KiNT, the designer who was involved with the launch. Pez and I, stoked to be given the ushering gig and a chance of meeting Vienna Voronova, had arrived early and joined the briefing session.

'Absolutely no seating changes,' Mum said. 'I don't care if it's somebody's third cousin twice removed or Anna Wintour herself – seating allocations are not transferable. Now, here are your shirts in requested sizes,' she said, handing them out. 'No modifications please.' SANCTUS MINERALIS was written on the back and $KiNT on the front. Mum confirmed everyone's duties then introduced $KiNT, who I instantly recognised from BigTown Gym™.

'Thank you, Charis and Morgan, for a truly stunning set.' He blew them kisses. 'All models are now in hair and make-up. Our story today is dreamboats and shipwrecks, and I've instructed the models to move languidly – as if underwater. Please carry that into whatever you're doing because you're all part of the show, yeah?' He demonstrated the desired motion. 'Float and glide, people.'

'$KiNT is showing thirty-five looks,' Morgan said. 'The show will run for exactly twenty-three minutes, including finale. Vienna will be concealed inside the shell ten minutes before start, over half an hour total. There's no chance of suffocation, but I don't want her in there a second longer than necessary, so stick to timings.' He pointed to his very expensive watch.

Penny took orders for coffee and then came over. 'Hi Elvis!' she said to Pericles. 'I saw you at the dance but this one kept steering me away.'

'Penny Button, meet my buddy Pericles Pappas,' I said.

'Could you two please help me deliver the coffees?'

Waiting at the catering tent for the baristas to load our cardboard trays, I asked Penny if she'd seen Vienna yet.

'I picked her up from the hotel this morning.'

'What's the most beautiful woman in the world like in person?'

'No idea because she wouldn't talk. Her mother said she must rest her face before an appearance. Lucky her directions don't call for smiling.'

'Where is she now?'

'Make-up trailer. But don't you dare go sniffing around. Charis wants you in position.'

After delivering the coffees we went sniffing around the make-up trailer and got sprung by Morgan. 'Time to get to your post,' he said, tapping his TAG®.

We went to the top of Fleet Steps to greet and direct guests. They all looked either important or beautiful, but Pericles and I recognised nobody until two famous swimmers turned up. Interesting, considering their job description didn't actually involve clothing. Next was an NRL player and his model girlfriend followed by some exposure-starved ex-reality-show contestants, including Kimberly Romaine. She was on the very thick, brown, tattooed arm of Dad's personal trainer Sergio, who was wearing a black shirt unbuttoned to his navel, a tonne of gold chainage around his neck and massive sunglasses perched on his forehead. 'Hello, Lincoln,' he said. 'What a little world. Why are you here?'

'My mum's calling the show. And you?'

'$KiNT is my partner and this is Kimberly. She wears one of his designs.' He twirled her around. 'You like?'

'It makes tomorrow look like yesterday.' I looked at my clipboard with the seating plan. 'You're in the second row on the garden side.'

'Not in front?'

'Seating allocations are final, but I don't think anybody could stand in your way.'

'I joke.' He gave me a playful chest poke and walked down.

'How do you know him?' Pez said.

'He's my dad's trainer.'

'He's built – but what a tosser.'

'Spot on.'

Ten minutes before showtime we went to our second position, backstage, which was brilliant because we could check out the models. They were all wearing kaftans and most had frizzed hair, some matted with flotsam and jetsam. The dressers were adorning them with multiple strings of fake pearls, tarnished costume jewellery and plastic crabs.

'I was expecting this to be glamorous,' Pericles said. 'But it's already exceeded my wildest expectations.'

We were only five minutes behind schedule, despite the chaos of last-minute adjustments, when one of the model's necklaces broke and plastic pearls went pinging all over the runway and into the water. Morgan slapped his forehead.

'Boys, I need every single one of them retrieved,' he said. Pericles and I jumped into action and Morgan radioed Jules to bring Vienna Voronova.

A few minutes later, a golf buggy arrived. Vienna stepped off and an assistant removed her robe. It wouldn't be stretching the truth to say that Botticelli's Venus came to life before our eyes, even more beautiful than in the painting. Her modesty was only protected by long golden hair extensions sewn onto flesh-coloured bands of sheer fabric. Morgan held Vienna's forearm to help her across to the shell but she shrugged him off and said, 'Don't touch me.'

Everything would've turned out differently if Vienna had accepted his assistance – but she hadn't. And when she slipped on the single plastic pearl left on the runway, she fell face-first onto the edge of the shell, making a loud and sickening crack, then slid into the pool. Morgan jumped in fully clothed to rescue her. Penny and Jules grabbed towels. Pez and I ran for first aid and when we returned with the officer, Vienna was sitting up with her bloody hand over her bloody mouth, surrounded by bloody people holding wads of bloody paper towels.

'Hi, my name's Norman,' the first-aid officer said to her. 'Everything will be okay now. Take your hand away and let me see.'

Vienna dropped her hand and tried to smile.

Both her front teeth were missing. Exactly like in my dream.

Perfection – so fragile and transient. And even though Vienna's teeth were both retrieved and would hopefully be reinserted, I couldn't take pleasure from her misfortune. No schadenfreude. Losing a key part of her identity, her beautiful smile – albeit temporarily – would've been deeply traumatic for someone as vain as Vienna Voronova.

Tonight I was lying in bed contemplating this and other more serious matters, like the imminent demolition of Bert's house.

'The door of opportunity is closing soon,' Homunculus said. 'There'll be no more fascinating objects to discover. No more spurious connections to make. No profound meaning to extract from any of it. You'd better crack on with the book before it's all gone.'

Melinkoff's Astonishing Assembly of Freaks opened at San Francisco's Palisade Theatre to a packed house, largely due to Serpentina's scintillating preview performance with python Octavius outside on the bally stage. Following the act, a team of shills posing as ticket-buyers had stormed the box office, prompting the masses to follow. When every inch of standing room had been sold, a bell signalled the show's commencement and I hid behind the wings.

The instant Ruthie Davis stepped onto the stage, the limelight transformed her into Baby Cakes the Living Doll. She recited 'Ode to a Pudding', skipped about while shaking a giant rattle, then performed a ribbon dance. Though the act hinged on the basic visual gag of a large woman dressed as an infant, Ruthie was nobody's fool. The wiseacres cocky enough to heckle her with vulgar suggestions were shrivelled by her withering retorts. Roy Lister the Human Globe appeared next, moving through a series of poses that showed off his finely sculpted physique, then he performed a set of vertical rope stunts that culminated in a death-defying slack drop with his nose stopping barely an inch from the floor.

Each successive act exacerbated my concern that I'd developed no special talent since leaving Sydney. Even Paulo Penguino, the penultimate performer, had been trained in circus skills over the previous weeks. When he balanced a spinning ball on the tip of his nose, the enthusiastic applause was my cue to take to the stage, but as I looked down at my ridiculous costume, comprising scraps of cowhide sewn onto a flesh-coloured bodysuit, I was paralysed with fear. Worsening matters, the smell of leaking gas induced a flashback of my ignominious unmasking by Melvin Fletcher, which deafened me to Paulo's coaxing as I gripped onto a wall ladder. A second of inactivity on the stage is a minute of tedium for the audience, so Roy Lister peeled my fingers away and threw me to the proverbial lions. The audience began a slow clap. 'Hop!' Roy called, so I hopped. I hopped and hopped in a mad circle around the stage, matching the tempo of the crowd until it broke into a crescendo of cheering and stamping.

When the applause died away, Melinkoff delivered the lecture and I played along, miming the actions of a feral child raised by kangaroos. It was highly improbable that anybody in the audience had ever seen one of the creatures, and they seemed convinced as I licked the back of my hand and groomed myself, gnawing at imaginary ticks. Melinkoff added unrehearsed and ludicrous details to his spiel, which I feared would only lead to a very disappointing reveal as my tail, though unique, was a tiny thing compared to the apparatus of a kangaroo. So I turned my back expecting laughter and derision – but there was silence, and when I unbuttoned the flap and let it drop, the tail drew a collective gasp. With great concentration I made it move, and the crowd roared their approval. And for the briefest moment, I believed that, like the rest of the performers, I too had undergone a metamorphosis of sorts. No longer Edwin Stroud the sawdust collector from Pyrmont, but Harold Hopkins, Kangaroo Boy.

I rolled onto my stomach and, with great concentration and trepidation, tried to make my tail move. I fooled myself into thinking something was going on back there until I realised that I was only squeezing my butt cheeks or tightening my ring. After a moment of relief at having no volition over the tail's movement – that it only responded to emotional or external stimuli – I almost felt disappointed.

The Astonishing Assembly of Freaks had a rolling stock of six rail cars – paltry compared to P. T. Barnum's sixty, but as the engine hauled our garishly painted carriages out of San Francisco, I felt part of something inconceivably grand. The journey to Sacramento was shorter than the ensuing walking tour that Paulo Esposito gave me of his hometown. A decade earlier, sections of footpath and many of the city's fine brick buildings with arched and shuttered windows had been jacked up nine-and-a-quarter feet from their original placement to protect against future flooding. We visited Paulo's humble family home, where he introduced me to his mother and eight brothers. His father had been killed two years earlier in a wheat-silo accident. When I shared the story of my own father's demise he made a formal declaration that we would be friends for life.

We played three shows every day for a fortnight in Sacramento then rolled on to Denver, Colorado. The glory days of silver and gold were long gone and Denver had moved on to growing carnations. The ubiquitous pink bloom remains one of my fondest memories of the place, second only to the view of the majestic Rocky Mountains to the west. In Denver I found myself enjoying the thrill of performing, and surrendered to the role. I trained myself to squeeze out tears when

Melinkoff reached the point in the story of my parents drowning in the shipwreck. Envisaging myself as the helpless infant, I felt the comfort of my adoptive mother's pouch and the warm droplets of blood on my forehead each time she was speared by the native hunters. Motivated by the need for money, I'd calculated that the greater my engagement with the audience, the more photos and biography booklets I was able to sell after the show. And to my shame, I smothered any scruples I once held about the misrepresentation of my Aboriginal countrymen.

Omaha, Nebraska, in America's heartland boasted some lovely boulevards yet seemed plagued by packs of wild dogs and quack physicians offering miracle cures. A representative from one shonky institute approached Paulo, offering to cure his deformed limbs using a program of cold baths and electromagnetism. Paulo's unique form was his meal ticket, so he politely refused. On our third night in the city, great misfortune struck when Farbridge's leopards escaped their unlocked cages. Samson mauled a stray hog and was shot dead by its owner, who was later quoted in the *Omaha Herald* saying, 'He got off light compared to Joseph Coe.' Joseph Coe had been a Negro man executed by a bloodthirsty mob and hanged from a trolley car wire only a few years earlier in Omaha. One could only speculate as to whether the farmer had been among them.

The troupe was restored to its original complement in Milwaukee with the addition of Hilda Groot, a young barmaid at Schlitz Park, the most popular beer garden in the city and our venue for a week. It boasted a three-level pagoda with views to Lake Michigan and a bowling alley – the first I'd ever seen. The mighty Schlitz Brewery itself occupied two city blocks and produced over half a million barrels of beer every year. I can still recall the posters I saw plastered all over the place: 'Schlitz – THE BEER THAT MADE MILWAUKEE FAMOUS'. And, I should add, the beer that made Irving Melinkoff exceedingly drunk. Hilda had caught his eye in our merchandise tent and, like hundreds before her, shared with him her dream of joining the circus. Dazzled by her physical charm, he invited her to be his Circassian Beauty. She accepted on the spot and was renamed Zerodia Nashko.

*

I did some more googling, this time about 'Circassian Beauties'. Apparently, women from the Caucasus region near the Black Sea were considered by some the 'purest' example of 'white beauty' and favoured by the Sultan of the Ottoman Empire for his harem. Then later the cosmetic industry latched onto the concept as a marketing ploy. In 1864, while the American Civil War was being fought over slavery, good old P. T. Barnum exhibited the first 'Circassian Beauty' – a white woman with a high-volume hairstyle like an afro – and all the fake Circassian Beauties that followed, like Hilda Groot, copied the look.

Interesting that a 'beauty' was displayed among all the 'freaks'. Perhaps the contrast exaggerated the features of both. Perhaps my perception of my own ugliness had made me obsessed by Vienna Voronova – someone society deemed perfect. She'd been chosen for the campaign because she was flawless, to make women feel they were somehow lacking something, that they needed to buy the product to make themselves more like her. And really, I knew that was how the whole sorry thing worked.

LOVE YOU, BRO

Neil Armstrong was the first man to walk on the moon, but Buzz Aldrin was the first to pee on it – or at least pee while he was standing on it. Pericles, Tibor and I were discussing who had better bragging rights when Starkey swaggered over and said, 'Is this a meeting of Poofters Anonymous?'

'It certainly is,' I said. 'And there's always room for new members in our friendly circle.'

'Fuck you!' He smacked the chicken baguette from my hands.

'That wasn't very friendly,' Tibor said as I salvaged my lunch.

'I'm no friend of filthy knob jockeys,' Starkey said. 'Why are you hanging out with these two confirmed faggots?'

Pericles squared off with Starkey. 'For the record, I'm the only faggot here. Unless you've got something to get off your chest?'

'Oh yeah, you've discovered my dark little secret, Pappas. And right now I can hardly stop myself from kissing you.'

Evan Starkey did not kiss Pericles Pappas. He leant back a little then slammed his forehead into the bridge of Pericles' nose. Pez swayed and collapsed. Starkey walked away, wiping his hands. I tried to rouse Pericles but he was out cold – blood dripping from his nose onto the dirt.

'Cunt,' Tibor said through his teeth, eyes burning with rage. I watched with shock and admiration as he raised his fists, contracting all the muscles in his body till he began shaking, as if opening the vault where the hurt from years of bullying had been stored. Then he sprang up and charged after Starkey, pounced like a panther onto his back and knocked him over the embankment. They rolled down, entangled, Tibor's arms flapping about. Starkey got to his feet before Tibor could push himself onto his knees and kicked him in the arse twice, and hard. He spat on him and swaggered back to the playground. Tibor hobbled over to us, sore but proud. 'I just took on Evan Starkey and lost,' he said.

'You were legendary.'

Pericles half-emerged from his stupor and said, 'I don't know what just happened, but thank you.' He spat five or six times then ran a finger along his teeth. 'I thought there was grit in my mouth but they were chips from my teeth.'

I tried to convince him to report Starkey, because in a perfect world there would be justice, but the Dash would ask him what the fight was over and Pericles didn't want to talk about it. So instead of going to Student Welfare, we cleaned him up in the toilets.

At the end of the day we met up to walk home. Pez's nose resembled a baby eggplant, matching his purple left eye. We'd hardly left the gates when Mullows caught up with us.

'So, Starkey told me what happened and—'

'You came to check out his handiwork?' Pez said.

'No, I came to tell you I think it was a total dick act. He beat you up for being gay and I'm not down with that.'

'Great,' Pericles said. 'Thanks for the support. See ya.'

But Mullows persisted. 'I don't think you can help being who you are. It's not your fault you turned out that way and I personally don't have a problem with it.'

'Gee, thanks – that's incredibly open-minded and tolerant of you.'

'Nads and Starkey have done some crazy shit lately and I'm through with it.'

'Defecting from Clown Town?' I said.

'Nah. Nads and his family have been good to me ever since I moved here from the bush. But I won't let either of them lay a finger on Pericles again.'

'You know what?' Pez said. 'I can look after myself.'

'Yeah, sure looks that way. Anyway, I'm sorry about what happened.' He reached out and squeezed Pez's shoulder, holding it for a bit longer than comfortable, probably expecting some expression of gratitude that he didn't get.

'That was awkward,' Pez said when Mullows had walked away.

'Yeah, just a bit.'

I didn't understand why Pericles refused to tell Dad what had happened, but I agreed to back up his story of being hit by a cricket ball – after all, I'd once used a similar fake explanation. Before we started dinner, Pez delivered grace – unprecedented in the apartment – which incorporated thanking my earthly father for taking him in.

'It's been a pleasure having you,' Dad said, raising his glass. 'Here's to the three amigos.' As we began eating, Pez's phone rang with the danger alert tone. He declined.

'Who was that?' Dad said.

'Nobody important.' His phone rang again so he turned it off.

A few minutes later, the home phone rang and Dad answered. He put his hand over the receiver and said, 'Your father wants to talk to you, Pericles.'

'Tell him I'm not here.'

'He knows you are.'

'Please tell him that I don't want to speak with him.'

Dad shrugged and told Mr Pappas that Pericles was currently unavailable. We could hear Con's garbled response from the dining table. Dad replaced the receiver.

'He's on his way over. We've enjoyed having you, buddy, and you're welcome to stay for as long you need. But I can't stand between you and your father.'

'He can't force me to go with him.'

'Of course not, but—'

'Thanks for having me, Mr Locke,' Pericles said, defeat tugging down on the corners of his polite smile. I'll pack my stuff and get out of here before he arrives.'

I followed Pericles but Dad stopped me.

'Let me talk to him,' he said.

Dad somehow persuaded Pez to stay and at least speak to his father, but he couldn't eat his dinner, and when Mr Pappas buzzed the intercom he flipped out and went to the bathroom. Dad greeted Con at the door. Short and stocky like Manos, he was carrying a box of vegetables under his arm, which he presented to Dad.

'There's a fine-looking specimen,' Dad said, lifting a bunch of silverbeet for me to see. 'Are you a greengrocer, Con?'

'Nah, that's my brother. I work in airport operations. Potter around in the garden for stress relief. I hope Pericles hasn't been any trouble?'

'It's been a pleasure having him. Lincoln, could you go get him?'

'Lincoln?' Con said. 'You're the boy who knocked him out of the relay team?'

'I guess.'

'Good job. It might put a bit of fire back into his belly.'

'He doesn't need it,' I said without bothering to add that I'd already been kicked out of squad. I went and knocked on the bathroom door. Pericles told me to come in, and I found him sitting on the toilet with the seat down.

'I think you should come out,' I said. 'Your father seems in a good mood.'

'He'll be laying on the charm offensive.'

Dad and Con were on the sofa with beers when we returned to the lounge room. Con's jaw practically disengaged when he saw his son's bruised face. 'Pericles, have you been in a fight?'

'No. I just got beaten up for being a poofter.'

'Don't speak like that in front of these nice people.'

'Are you suddenly trying to be politically correct now?'

'No. You've misunderstood me because you don't listen properly. I don't have a problem with you being a homosexual, but this is what happens when you wave it about in people's faces.'

Pericles closed his eyes and took a deep breath.

I jumped in. 'Pericles was standing up for me and our friend Tibor against a homophobic bully.'

Con looked confused. 'Is there a whole group of you at the school?'

'I'm not gay, Mr Pappas. Pericles and Tibor were the only people who made me feel welcome when I started at Crestfield. Pericles lent me his goggles and taught me how to swim butterfly properly.'

'That's commendable, son.'

'Then why are you always so disappointed in me?' Pericles said.

'I'm only disappointed that you're choosing this lifestyle.'

'Don't start that again in front of everybody. I need some air.' Pericles walked out to the balcony. Dad left me with Con to fetch another couple of beers. Con immediately dropped his attempt at the nice-guy façade and pointed his finger at me.

'I hope you're not secretly his boyfriend.'

'Afraid not, Mr Pappas.'

Dad returned with the beers and a bowl of unshelled pistachios. Something about the way Con opened them with his teeth instead of his fingers and then chomped away caused my tail to rise and prickle. I wanted to knock the bowl out of his hands and tell him to eat with his mouth closed.

Pericles came in and sat a distance away from us, backwards on a dining chair.

'Sit properly,' Con said, 'or you'll break the good people's furniture.' Pericles turned the chair around and sat stiffly with his hands clasped in his lap, silently mocking Con's directive. 'A man's home is his castle, Pericles. And the castle has rules. When you come home you'll follow my rules until you turn eighteen and then you can run around and do whatever you like. That's reasonable. I'm sure Mr Locke would agree with me.' He looked at Dad for backup.

Dad looked at me and raised his eyebrows. 'Yes, Con, it's true. Every family has rules, spoken and unspoken. But I'd be the worst kind of hypocrite if I sat here pretending that I hadn't broken one of the most fundamental ones. Because I already lied about it more than once and lost the trust of my family in the process. This isn't my castle, Con. It's just where I live after my wife threw me out.'

'No need to elaborate,' he said and walked over to Pericles, gripped his shoulders and shook him twice. 'All I ever want is the best for you, Perilakimu. Will you come home with me now? Your mother's been sick with worry.'

Pericles surrendered himself with a small nod. I followed him to the guest room to get his stuff.

'That was his best behaviour you saw tonight. He'll start yelling at me the moment we get in the car.' Pericles lowered his head, pinching the bridge of his nose. 'Sorry about all the drama I've caused, Lincoln.' He looked up. 'And thank you for letting me stay here. You saved my life.'

'Now you're being dramatic.'

'No, fully literal. I was teetering on the brink for a while. I was really fucking hating on myself and lost hope of ever feeling different. But something inside me has changed, even if my father hasn't. I used to be terrified of him and now I'm not. It's because I'm not afraid of who I am anymore.'

'That's good. You know I've always got your back.'

'Same.'

'It was a short stay but I'm going to miss having you here. Dad will too.'

I hugged Pericles hard – square on, not just right shoulder to shoulder. No pat-pat-patting on the back. And I told him that I loved him.

He said, 'A hundred per cent.'

After Pericles and Con left, Dad and I pulled apart everything that had just happened. 'Con's a hardarse,' I said. 'But at least his visit tonight has made you seem not so bad in comparison.'

'That's lavish praise.'

'Seriously, that was huge when you spoke so honestly about yourself. You didn't have to, but it shut Con up.'

340

'Thanks, mate. One day when you're a parent you'll come to understand how difficult it is raising a family. And how wonderful.'

'I don't want to have children. The idea doesn't appeal to me.'

'Not right now, but the time will come when you've settled down with the right person.'

'Maybe.'

I'd barely started coming to terms with the tail, and wasn't thrilled about the idea of reproducing that part of myself. Maybe Edwin had? I said goodnight to Dad and returned to the book.

In Chicago, I took the world's longest elevator to the rooftop of the Auditorium building, where I caught a glimpse of Lake Michigan through the smog. After playing Pittsburgh and Cleveland, we reached our final destination, New York City. America's largest town seemed no better than Sydney in its planning or sanitary arrangements. Everywhere squalor nipped at the heels of extravagance. Immigrant factory workers were packed into four- and five-storey tenement buildings with no gaps between, yet not a quarter-mile away were grand apartment buildings, elegant theatres and department stores with marble flooring that made Pemberton's Emporium seem hardly magnificent at all. There were fancy dining establishments that my father would've loved, and just down the street, food carts in their hundreds selling fried potato knishes, baked pretzels, pickles and clams, nuts and sweet pies.

The population was a heaving mass of almost three million people, each seemingly intent on getting somewhere fast, seizing the opportunity to make a new life for themselves by working around the clock. And when they stopped for just a moment of relief, there were two places they visited: the green of Central Park or the blue seaside pleasure resort of Coney Island, Brooklyn.

Coney Island was the birthplace of the manufactured dream and there was no greater dream-maker in those early days than the Fearless Frogman, Paul Boyton. After performing countless aquatic feats around the globe and touring with P. T. Barnum, he'd capitalised on his fame by opening Sea Lion Park, the first enclosed outdoor amusement park in America. Built around an artificial lagoon, it featured a water flume ride and the world's first looping roller-coaster. Unfortunately, the loop's diameter was only twenty-five feet and the sudden transition into the thrilling climax gave so many riders whiplash the ride was permanently closed. The sea lion shows proved more successful, especially when Boyton joined the performance. He loved challenging the visitors to swimming races and, with the advantage of a rubber buoyancy suit, he always won.

By the park's third season, the novelty-hungry public had seen just about every conceivable act that could be performed on the water's surface. Hungry for a piece of Boyton's pie, Irving Melinkoff had purchased a small plot of land close by and come up with a brilliant point of difference – he would allow the audience to see underwater! He had an enormous glass tank built, three-quarters of it underground. It was surrounded by two curving stairways descending to a cavernous viewing area. Electric light bulbs were installed behind the tank, illuminating the walls with magnified ripples, and there was an air pump at the bottom that released flurries of bubbles.

Melinkoff planned to open the Underwater Grotto with The Battle of the Atlantis Brothers, starring Hilda Groot as the mermaid princess, with Paulo and I fighting for her affection. He began promoting the show before even bothering to ask if Paulo could swim, assuming that with webbed fingers and toes he'd be a natural. But Paulo had never been in anything deeper than a bath and I was given just one week to train him. Though his limbs were extremely short, his torso was powerful, so I taught him the rippling motion of the dolphin kick and soon he was gliding through the water as if born to it. Hilda had grown up on Lake Michigan, and with the addition of a rubber tail easily outclassed both of us. Advertising bills featuring a photo of Hilda in the tank, flanked by Paulo and me brandishing tridents, were pasted up all over Coney Island and drew a crowd at least five times the venue's capacity.

Never before had the public had an opportunity to view bodies underwater – bodies barely concealed by clinging suits, magnified into god or monster-like proportion by thick glass. Never before had they been able to scrutinise so closely such strange forms as those belonging to Paulo and me. And just as Pemberton's display of authentic artefacts had lent credibility to the fake hybrid creatures surrounding them, so Paulo's and my abnormalities lent plausibility to Hilda's tail. A *New York Times* reporter, so impressed by the illusion, wrote a tongue-in-cheek article espousing the existence of mermaids, and Hilda Groot became famous almost overnight.

Hilda's sudden rise to stardom, and corresponding earning capacity, made her even more desirable to Melinkoff. He took her to restaurants and shows, and lavished her with flowers, chocolates and jewellery. She accepted the gifts but resisted his passes. This strange dance continued for weeks until one day she returned every gift that hadn't perished or been consumed. Melinkoff suspected she'd found a lover, but his imagination failed when it came to airing his conjectures of who that could be. Then, one night, he spied them together down near the Elephant Hotel: Hilda Groot and Paulo Esposito, ravishing one another in public view, beneath an almost full moon.

Delirious with jealousy, but lacking the dignity to confront his rival directly, Melinkoff worked his revenge into the plot of the aquatic drama. He switched Paulo's character from ill-fated hero to a lecherous villain whose appearance was the result of an unnatural coupling. Seven times every day Melinkoff would stir the latent prejudice of the audience with his melodramatic narration, whipping them into a jeering chorus. Seven times Hilda was forced to revile the man she loved. And seven times Paulo would be strangled by me, his truest friend. Of course, up until that point we were only acting, but in the dying moments of the new, more violent finale, Melinkoff would delay the killing of the lights. Paulo, exhausted by the struggle, would be forced to lie motionless on the tank's floor, sometimes blacking out before the lights.

I recalled the photo I'd seen at the exhibition on my birthday, the one of Edwin and Paulo with their tridents on either side of Hilda. With stunted limbs, Paulo couldn't have been more than a metre tall and yet Hilda Groot, the beautiful mermaid princess, had fallen in love with him. What was Paulo's secret?

The thick glass tank would have enabled the audience to ogle the performers' bodies in their 'clinging suits', and to see Paulo's and Edwin's unusual features magnified. The possibility of anybody spotting mine in the pool had terrified me. I gained a new respect for these so-called freaks, who for the sake of their families had put themselves on display for the world to see. Maybe it was Paulo's courage that had won Hilda's heart?

LADY IN WHITE

Saturday morning I went down to visit Bert. The gate was unlocked so I walked around the back. Crimson chair empty, no pink rubber ring. I called through the flyscreen and got no reply, so let myself into the kitchen. All of the objects were neatly arranged on the shelves, with different coloured stickers attached. The kitchen was immaculately clean and smelling of lemon Jif™ – not usually the scent of trouble, but today it was.

A woman's voice came from upstairs. Nothing more said than a casual 'shit', as if somebody had asked her what cows do besides eat grass and make milk. Bert had never mentioned friends – not a high priority for a hermit. And I knew that, statistically, burglars were mostly men in a hurry. Maybe it was a mental-health outreach worker, or a volunteer from Meals on Wheels?

I sneaked back out and rang the cowbell. There were footsteps coming down the stairs. A silhouette behind the flyscreen.

'What do you want?'

'I'm here to help Bert get things ready for the antiques and vintage sale.'

'Which school do you attend?'

'Crestfield Academy.'

'I'm not aware of any arrangement to donate articles for a sale.'

'It's not for school. Bert's having a garage sale before he moves.'

She withered me with her eyes. 'I've heard troubling stories about Crestfield boys. Please go away now.' She closed the door, but I knocked until she reopened it.

'Your presence here is unwanted.'

'I just want to see Bert. He's a friend of mine.'

The woman clicked her tongue and shook her head. She walked away then returned, dusting something off her shoulder. 'Very well. You'd better come in.' She opened the door and directed me to sit. She had short black hair with a jagged fringe that made her eyes look impossibly blue. 'I'm sorry to tell you this, but Bert had a seizure. They say it happened three days ago.'

'Oh no. Poor Bert. I knew he wasn't very well. Lucky St Vincent's is so close. If you're picking up some stuff you should probably take Percy, his cockatiel.'

The woman's mask cracked, like a sheet of white ice breaking from an iceberg and sliding into the blue sea. And I floated somewhere safer above, watching a stupid schoolkid being told bad news by a woman in a sharp white suit. Her lips were moving but the kid couldn't understand what she was saying.

'What?' The kid was me but younger, smaller and naïve. 'What?' His mind tried to push the words back out of his ears. 'What?' Before they could take root. 'What?' he said, again and again, because he couldn't think of anything else.

The woman took a deep breath. Cleared her throat. Recomposed herself and lifted her head with the mask firmly back in place.

This incongruity – this dizzy chasm between the terrible news and the forced poise of the messenger – induced vertigo. The kitchen tilted and revolved like the automatic toilet the time old Bert had come charging up on Miss Daisy to rescue me. I closed my eyes and almost heard him yelling at Nads, Mullows and Starkey, scaring them away again. Bert was outside waiting for me. DOOR OPENING.

I opened my eyes. The woman with precision-jagged black hair was sitting opposite me in Bert's kitchen but there was no Bert anywhere. She touched my knee. 'Are you okay?'

'Where's Bert? Can I see him?'

'I'm afraid that won't be possible.' She poured me a glass of water. It seemed a kind gesture but as I drank she tapped her fingernails on the Formica, and the dark alchemy of impatience turned the water bitterly metallic in my mouth. 'The funeral service is on Wednesday,' she said. 'But I'm afraid it's family only.'

Bert is dead.

Who appointed her to inform me? What was she doing in Bert's house? In her white pants and white jacket, in Bert's house? I asked if she was the white lady from White Lady Funerals.

'No.' She almost smiled. 'My name is Lana. I'm Bert's daughter.'

'Bert never . . . You didn't visit much?'

'We live in Melbourne. I used to make the effort so that my daughter could get to know her grandfather – but over time we stopped coming.'

'Why?'

'My father had become a very bitter man and he made our visits difficult. In fact, over time, unbearable. My mother left him a very long time ago – nineteen seventy-nine.'

'Ruby?'

'Yes, Ruby.' She waved her arm around. 'All of this was her dream and she left it behind when she walked out on him, took nothing but me and the car. She was a brave woman.'

'What about your brother?'

'I was an only child.'

'Bert talked about someone called Johnny.'

'Did he? Well, there you go – his memory was very disordered.' Without missing a beat, she said, 'Please excuse me now. I have a lot to do.'

'He talked about Johnny and fighting. Was your father a soldier?'

Lana looked at the ceiling and drew a deep breath. 'Johnny Drinkwater and my father were best mates from the age of five. At school they made a pact to join the army. Thirteen years later Johnny enlisted but my father didn't pass the medical. Some spinal issue. Johnny went off to fight in the Korean War and was very badly injured. My father believed it wouldn't have happened if he'd been by his side.'

347

'He felt guilty?'

'Ten years later, in the sixties, Johnny took his own life. My father turned to the bottle.'

'Is that why your mother left?'

'Among other things. My mother was a cabaret singer when they met. She was very beautiful and my father was insecure. He wouldn't let her perform after they married – wouldn't even let her drive the car. He was suspicious because of his own philandering. One night she confronted him and he hit her, then went out and drank himself into a stupor. She took his keys and we headed west out of town.'

'Could she drive?'

'Hardly. The police pulled her over on the outskirts for running red lights. She charmed them and they let her go with a warning. Driving away she said, "At least I didn't get my hair set for nothing." Strange, the things you remember. What most upset me was us leaving town without my bike. It was an orange bike, a dragster that my father had found dumped somewhere. At first I'd refused to ride it because it was a boy's bike. So Dad attached plastic streamers to the handlebars and a little basket to the front.'

Before I could speak, a girl's voice came from the top of the stairs: 'You won't believe what I've just found!' She appeared at the doorway – nineteen or twenty, with strawberry-blonde hair tied back from her pale freckled face with a green ribbon. The mechanical hen was in her arms.

'Hello?' she said to me, frowning.

'April, this young man knew your grandfather.'

'Oh, right.' She laid the hen on the table, and looked to Lana. 'Isn't she wonderful? Do you think I could keep her?'

'I can't imagine anyone else wanting it.'

I chewed the inside of my cheek. Bert had wanted me to have the hen. 'Say something!' Homunculus said. I couldn't because I knew it would have been obnoxious and insensitive to make a claim, even though I was probably Bert's only friend in the world. Sure, it sounded like he was a bitter and mean old turd who'd done some truly heinous shit, but right near the end of his life I'd somehow managed to break through his hardened shell. Not from some altruistic motivation,

I had to admit – I'd wanted that bike so badly, the bike that had once belonged to his daughter.

Lana pushed on and told me the details of how Bert was found and I wished she hadn't. A jogger running past the junkyard late Wednesday night had noticed an awful smell and contacted the police. Her clinical report of the grim discovery was too much to bear.

Grief settled on my chest and dug its bony claws into my throat.

I was about to excuse myself when April said, 'Oh, I found this tied around the hen's neck. No idea what it means.' She handed her mother a small tag on a piece of string and Lana read it out.

'Good egg for a good egg – Lincoln from up the hill.'

Dad was mixing a pre-workout drink for a training session with Sergio when I walked into the kitchen with the mechanical chicken under my arm. 'Good God!' he said and turned off the blender. 'Where did you get that thing?'

'Bert gave it to me.'

'Who's Bert?'

'The guy who sold us the bike.'

'I thought I made it clear that you were never to visit him again?'

'You did.'

'And here you are with another piece of his junk! He's not a well man, Lincoln. I would even use the word "deranged".'

'I promise you that I'll never see him again.'

'You told me that before.'

'Dad, he's dead now.'

'Oh, the poor old bugger,' Dad said. 'He *really* wasn't well.'

I gave a brief account of what had happened and then Dad tried to comfort me – at least I wasn't close to Bert, etc., etc. I couldn't tell him that his death was hitting me almost as hard as Pop's.

On Sunday I caught the bus to Signal Bay and, seeing a furniture rental truck parked outside our house, I knew that hoping for any form of sympathy from Mum would be like expecting honey from a hornet.

When I walked into the living room I was confronted by a completely different interior. Mum was buzzing about with a stylist and a photographer, creating perfect pictures for property magazines and websites. Our furniture had gone to storage, replaced by a white leather lounge, coffee table, prints, plants and a massive fake flat screen – all rented by the stylist for the shoot and open house. There was no hint of the lives we'd lived there and I felt like a stranger in my own home.

The photographer asked me to step out of frame.

So I did. Then I walked back out the front door.

Mum caught me outside and apologised for being preoccupied. I asked her why she hadn't warned me before I came.

'Your room hasn't been touched,' she said.

'Everything else has gone.'

'Imagine how difficult it's been for me doing it alone. Getting emotional is a luxury I can't afford right now.'

'But why so fast?'

'I need this one thing dealt with to clear some mental space for other issues. The outfall from Vienna's accident has been an unmitigated PR disaster. The client expects compensation for her failure to appear, and Vienna's management are now threatening to sue even though her teeth were restored. It's a perfect shitstorm.'

I knew that Mum, teetering on the brink, wouldn't have been receptive to hearing news of the death of a stranger so I hugged her instead. 'I have complete faith in you.'

'That means the world to me. Why don't you go and visit Venn now that she's settled in? She'd love to see you.'

I caught the bus to the North Curly flat. Venn and Jessie had ripped out the smelly carpet, painted the apricot walls white and hung new blinds. Jessie was out surfing. Venn made me a cup of tea and we went out to the sunny balconette. I told her about Bert's death and thanked her for trying to help me save his home. 'In the end, nothing could save him,' I said. 'We were too late.' Venn scrunched up her face, which sent a tear rolling down my cheek. 'He was the opposite of Pop Locke. Pretty mean to me at first,' I said, 'but I'm already missing him.'

'You obviously shared a strong connection. Whether directly or through a million different lines and junctions, everybody's connected somehow.'

'True – Pop wasn't our biological grandfather and it made no difference to me. But it does mean we can't explore Dad's side of the family. Which means I'll never understand half of where I came from. There was something about Bert . . . He often seemed completely nutty, but he taught me things about myself that I can't explain without sounding equally mad. One thing I know even more strongly now is that life runs out and all we have is the present.'

'I've been thinking the same. Life's too short to hold grudges. They turn into monuments that you can't stop circling, like being trapped in your own museum of bitterness.'

'That was legit poetic, sis. A perfect metaphor.'

'I smashed my own museum of bitterness this morning, thanks in no small part to you. I called Dad and invited him over next weekend. He'll be our first official dinner guest.'

'That's comforting to hear in my moment of gloom.'

'Let's try something out. Stay still and close your eyes,' Venn said, as she stood and placed one hand on my chest and one between my shoulderblades.

'What are you doing?'

'Shh! I'm performing a solemn restoration.'

Warmth radiated from both of Venn's hands and built inside me until I felt almost hot and broke into a sweat. 'I think it's done.' I'm not really sure exactly what the ritual achieved, but I know that Venn extending the olive branch to Dad somehow instantly brought the two of us to a much better place.

Back home in the city tonight, I was confronted by a dilemma. Longing to know what happened to Edwin Stroud, I wanted to read the final chapter of his book – but doing so would bring the story to end.

Another ending was the last thing I needed, given Bert's death and the imminent demolition of his home. Fearing being left with nothing more to discover, I compromised by allowing myself to read half the chapter.

Early one morning, when the yellowing leaves were signalling the approach of autumn, Paulo and Hilda eloped, forsaking the significant sum of money still owed them by Melinkoff. The scrawled note Paulo left on our washstand made it clear their decision had been sudden – but still, I wondered, how could they have left without telling me? Paulo and I had become brothers on our journey across America, sharing everything we owned, both intent on saving money for our families back home. I'd been something of an accomplice to him in his budding romance, encouraging him to make his feelings known, and later taking late-night strolls along the boardwalk so he could entertain his sweetheart privately in our room. The fact he hadn't revealed to me his intention to elope belied the strong bond of trust between us and, feeling horribly abandoned, I screwed up his note and threw it into the fire.

Then, like a bubble in oil, a memory floated into my consciousness. I too had run away from a dear friend without warning, leaving only a letter and trinket. In doing so, I'd stolen Diddy Budd's chance to say goodbye, to reveal her true feelings. I realised I'd been afraid of what she might say – and even more afraid that she might have tried to stop me leaving. This memory of my furtive departure brought cold comfort. At least Paulo and Hilda had run away for love, whereas I'd run to escape its possible consequences. If the couple had made their plans known to me earlier, I might have dropped to my knees and begged them not to leave me alone with Melinkoff.

The showman was dead silent when I told him of the elopement, his face darkening as he absorbed the news. The object of his longing had been spirited away by someone he considered in all ways inferior to himself – a stealth assault on his once unassailable pride. More pressingly, they'd left him without a show. His hands trembled as he cut and lit a cigar, then paced the Turkish rug in his hotel suite without saying a word – just puffing, puffing. He poured and swallowed a snifter of brandy then lifted the glass balloon to the light. He turned it in his fingers, admiring its craftsmanship, then drew back his arm. I cowered, anticipating the missile whistling past my head and smashing against the mirrored wall. Melinkoff laughed and placed it on a coaster, then in a measured tone accused me of collusion.

I pleaded ignorance, deeply regretting having incinerated Paulo's note. Melinkoff lashed me with a torrent of obscenities, poking my chest repeatedly in the way that weak, anger-possessed men do to make themselves heard. He savaged Paulo's appearance, denigrating the physical features he'd exploited to make himself a fortune. I held my tongue even after he'd finished. Irritated and unnerved by my silence, he demanded I speak in my friend's defence. With unwavering clarity, I told him that Paulo Esposito had been the truest, most loyal and kind-hearted man I'd ever known and deserved every chance of happiness in life.

Without warning Melinkoff whirled around and struck the side of my head with such force it destroyed the hearing in my left ear.

My own left ear popped and rang in sympathy as I read those words. An intense painful needling deep inside my ear canal destroyed my last tiny bit of resolve to maintain a degree of distance, to remain rational, and I cried for this man who seemed so close to me yet so far away in time. I cried because I would never know him.

FAMILY TIES

Back at school on Monday I told the crew about Bert's death. Isa and Pericles had only met him once but were both more upset by the news than I'd expected them to be. I think it was the dying-with-nobody-around element that got to them. Phoenix broke through the heaviness of the situation with a cheering platitude: 'When your time's up, your time's up.' As obvious and unhelpful as the statement was, it got me thinking about Bert taking us into his Church of Time – the clock room. Maybe he'd heard his final call, and that was his way of letting us know?

'So there won't be any junkyard sale,' I said, saddened by the thought that none of Bert's instructions would be followed – except in the case of Ethel.

'Such a shame,' Isa said. 'Terri was on board and ready to go.'

'Initially Bert wasn't keen. But when I visited on Saturday there were heaps of coloured stickers on his stuff. He must've spent days pricing everything. The mechanical hen had a note attached that said "Lincoln from up the hill".'

'Did he get her working again?' Pericles said.

'I don't know. I haven't tried yet.'

Bert probably stopped moving before he'd had a chance to make Ethel start. That's all death is – you stop moving. Forever.

When I got home from school I stared into Ethel's painted eyes. Permanently gleeful, they got me wondering if there wasn't still a spark of life left in the old girl. She was well over a hundred years old, though, and would probably need a penny or a shilling to get her started, which I didn't have. So I dropped a twenty-cent piece in the slot. Nothing happened. I turned her over and shook. The coin rattled around but stayed in there.

On Tuesday I ate lunch alone near The Labyrinth, recalling the day Dr Limberg had sent me in there and I'd met King Henry the prize bull. I remembered how he'd started talking to me when I rubbed his snout. Bert was always talking to little Percy, and often acted as if he could hear Percy speaking to him. While I didn't believe that lifeless objects could converse, I did believe they had stories to tell. And I had a hunch that Ethel had something important to tell me. It was only a matter of figuring out how to make that happen.

When I got home from school, I stroked Ethel's metal wings and whispered into the spot her ears might be, 'How do I make you work again?'

I stilled my thoughts and waited at least ten minutes for an answer. There was no audible voice, no omen or the slightest inkling. I tried again before going to bed, but nothing. Defeated, I brushed my teeth, crawled into my cocoon and pulled the doona over my head.

On the verge of falling asleep, golden phosphenes danced across the dark screen of my closed eyes and a possible solution came to me. Bert had given Pericles a gold token and told him to guard it with his life. He'd said, 'You never know when it might come in handy.'

On Wednesday morning as soon as I got to school I found Pericles and asked if I could borrow the coin.

'Sure.' He shrugged and unzipped his wallet. 'Oh no . . . it's not there!'

'Have you lost it?'

'No, no, no.' He squeezed his eyes then looked up. 'I think it's still at your place. I wanted to escape before my father arrived and couldn't decide between crashing at Isa's or running away, so I flipped the coin. It rolled under the bed and as I was reaching for it, your dad came in and persuaded me to stay. I'm so sorry. With all the shit that was going down I totally forgot to retrieve it. It must be under the bed.'

When the electronic glockenspiel sounded at the end of the day, I tore home on my bike and dived under the bed. The gold token *was* there against the wall. *Eureka!* I dropped it into the hen's slot.

Nothing happened. It got trapped in there with the twenty-cent piece.

Early the next morning, halfway through breakfast, I heard my father's bedroom door open and someone coming out. Judging by the footfall, it wasn't Dad. It had to be the light step of a woman.

I leant back on my stool and, peering down the hallway, caught the door closing again. The person must've seen me first and ducked back in. Ten minutes later, Dad came out in boxers and ruffled my hair. 'You're up early this morning, champ.'

'Couldn't sleep.'

'You've got two hours before school. Why don't you hop back into bed?'

'Things to do.'

Dad ground some coffee beans and set the machine for two cups. I told him I didn't want one, but he said he was having a double shot. Then he complained that the milk was sour and asked me to nip down to the shop to get a fresh carton.

'Anybody would think you were trying to get rid of me. If I took a stab, I'd say you brought somebody home last night and you don't want her to know you have a teenage son.'

'Nonsense.'

'I heard you both coming in.' I hadn't heard them but I wanted to force a confession.

'All right. You got me. Guilty as charged. But she already knows about you. She's painfully shy and you're making this very awkward. How about you duck back into your room for ten, fifteen minutes and give her a little space to leave?'

'If you're playing Secret Squirrel because you're worried I'll tell Mum, you can relax. I'm good at keeping secrets.'

'Thank you for being so considerate, but your mother already knows.'

Dad went down the hall, knocked on his bedroom door and said, 'The gig's up. The kid won't budge.' A middle-aged woman emerged and walked down the hallway wearing one of my mother's black dresses. She even bore an uncanny resemblance to my mother.

'Who's cooking the eggs?' she said. 'Both of you should've had enough practice by now.' She turned to me. 'Why the look of horror, darling?'

'Sorry, but nobody expects their father's one-night stand to be their mother. There's something so heinously wrong about it.'

'Honey, we're your parents. We've been doing it for more than twenty years. There's nothing more natural.'

'Not when you can't stand each other.'

'Here's some news for you,' Mum said. 'Sex isn't always about love. People have needs.'

'Way too much information.'

After their initial awkwardness at being sprung, my parents turned the tables and enjoyed making me squirm, which sucked considering I was the only one in the group with an ounce of discretion. I'd only recently forgiven Dad for all that he'd done, and only just come to accept that I'd never move back home because soon it wouldn't be ours. Now here they were – the two people who'd caused untold upheaval in my life, having sexual congress right under my nose. It was too much.

'So are you two back together now or what?' I said.

'No, we're not back together,' Dad said. 'But if you require some sort of definition, I suppose you could call us friends with benefits.' He slipped his arm around Mum's waist.

'Steady on, tiger,' she said, removing his arm. 'I haven't said anything about being friends. And the jury's still out on the benefits. Lincoln, yesterday afternoon I went to the funeral of a distant relative.

He'd been estranged from his family for years and nobody was there when he died. Ghastly affair. I only went out of obligation to my cousin Lana. We got a bit drunk afterwards so I stayed here last night instead of going all the way back home. There's nothing more to it.'

'Whose funeral was it?'

'My Uncle Albert. You never met him.'

'What was the funeral like?'

'Mercifully one of the shortest I've been to. The minister either knew nothing about him or was very diplomatic. Albert was far from squeaky clean. He was a driver for one of Sydney's biggest underworld figures in the fifties and sixties – Jack Monodora. Never convicted of anything, but I'm sure he made the occasional special delivery.'

'I can't believe it,' I said. The dawning realisation was like being with Mum in the car sliding backwards down the driveway at Signal Bay all over again. Hearing the names Lana and Jack Monodora hit me like an airbag, knocking the wind out of me.

I drew up the family tree in my head.

Bert was my great-uncle.

'What's the matter?' Mum said. 'You look like you've seen a ghost.'

'Just surprised to learn our family has a few dark secrets.'

'All families have their colourful characters,' Dad said, failing to make the connection.

'That's euphemistic, Lance. He was a volatile alcoholic and Lana hadn't seen him in a decade. You can try to sever the ties, but family is family. Albert was still her father and she was a howling mess at the funeral.'

Mum's words became background noise as I thought through the consequences of being related to Bert. I remembered what Lana had said about him not passing the medical because of a 'spinal issue'. Was Bert's spinal issue a tail? He'd blamed himself for Johnny's death, and the shame had destroyed his life. I needed time to sort a few things out before I could tell anybody anything. Fortunately Mum had reached the end of her story.

'Skip the coffee,' she said. 'I have to dash.'

*

The day at school dragged on and on. Bert's death and the subsequent revelation that he was family had raised even more questions and I desperately wanted to finish the book to find some answers, but after school I had to work at Give Me the Juice with Pericles.

In my half-hour break I raced down to Sushi Train® and claimed one of the two vacant stools. Three purple plates of raw tuna later, a lady in a brown coat excused herself and sat on the stool next to me. Devoid of make-up and colourful clothing, Ms Tarasek looked nothing like her usual flamboyant self and I might've left without recognising her if she hadn't said my name.

She asked how Art was progressing with the replacement teacher, and I said that Miss Timms was all about the theory and very little practical work.

'Is the exhibition going ahead?'

'Postponed, which I think means cancelled.'

'I am not surprised. I had resistance from Mr Dashwood.' She lowered her voice. 'He said that your piece and two others were too controversial for display. I argued that they must be shown. Otherwise what is the point of art?'

'Is that why you left?'

'No. I would never back down so easily. My father is terminally ill. So I will soon return to Poland to be by his side.' She took a bowl of edamame off the belt, popped a couple and began eating the beans separately with chopsticks. After expressing my condolences, I told her that Isa and I had discussed installing the knitted double helix unofficially.

'You must choose your fights carefully,' she said. 'Be aware of the possible repercussions and be willing to face them. Two generations of my family have suffered terribly for their art.' She didn't elaborate further and it didn't feel the right time to probe. Imagining it probably involved confiscation, burning, imprisonment or execution, I figured Isa's and my effort was likely to seem trivial in comparison.

'The worst they can do to us is cut it down before anybody has a chance to see it,' I said.

'I am proud of your courage,' she said. 'Teachers are not supposed to have favourite students, but we all do. You and Isa were mine.

Such passion and dedication. Will you take my email address and let me know what happens?'

'It would be an honour,' I said. I put it into my phone then dashed back to work.

After all that had happened today, explaining to every third customer that we were out of bananas took all the patience I could muster. Sam continued to hassle Pericles but now he brushed it off or silenced him with much wittier retorts. As the clock approached nine, he could see that I was exhausted, and didn't ask me to stay back and help him close. I left a hundred per cent confident that he wouldn't allow Sam to get under his skin again.

I caught the train back to the Cross and rain began falling the moment I stepped out of the station. One minute later I entered our lobby saturated. 'Cats and dogs out there,' Frank said as I passed the desk. Home at last, I showered and climbed into bed, then turned to the final pages of *My One Redeeming Affliction*.

Bitterly cold winds hastened the termination of the park's season, but Irving Melinkoff, unwilling to forfeit a single penny, refused to cancel the show. Instead, he forced me to perform increasingly difficult and sometimes life-threatening underwater stunts to entice the park's dwindling visitors. In Hilda's absence, the mermaid princess was played by a submerged mannequin whose single moving feature was her hair. Neglect of the tank's maintenance turned the water cloudy, and a vibrant green film of algae spread over the mannequin's skin, terrifying and delighting the younger members of the audience in equal measure. The fouled water infected both my good and bad ears, and provoked a severe case of dermatitis that blistered and became fiercely itchy.

Where once I'd enjoyed astonishing the audience with my fellow performers, I now dreaded being the sickly object of their leering gaze. Each night, after seven exhausting performances, returning to my lodgings brought little comfort. Bereft of my friend Paulo and his belongings, the small room seemed cavernous. And in the oppressive silence, my thoughts returned to my family and Deidre Budd. For more than a year I'd maintained my vow not to write to her, and with no photographic portrait to cherish, my mental picture, conjured too many times, had irretrievably faded.

One evening the landlord delivered a letter from my sister, Loula. Following the usual pleasantries came some troubling news: Deidre Budd was being courted by one of the local Pyrmont lads. The blow of discovering the suitor's identity on the next page struck harder than a prize-fighter's uppercut to the jaw. How could she have fallen for someone as low as my tormentor, Reg McGuffin? McGuffin, the pug-nosed thug who'd stirred the Pyrmont lads against myself and Thomas. Surely the heartless ruffian who'd hurled a rock through the window of our family home hadn't reformed sufficiently to merit her affection?

Hoping to expunge all thoughts of Diddy from my mind in the revels of the racing crowd, I washed and shaved, dressed in my finest suit and headed for the New Brighton Hotel. Having hardly partaken of spirituous liquor since leaving Australia, I expected a whisky might loosen me sufficiently to enjoy the company of strangers. But my hearing loss made it difficult to follow conversation, and impossible to contribute – the raucous singing and laughter only mocking my desperate loneliness.

After downing my third drink, I found my way to a dive bar in an area fittingly coined The Gut, where nobody would bother to interrupt a man's solitary descent into delirium and stupor. There I threw back shots until my vision blurred and veins knotted my temples. Yet still the blaring torment of being condemned to live alone forever continued. I drank one more for the road, lurched outside and witnessed the modern miracle of a million electric light bulbs spinning above me.

Even in my miserable state, the tawdry beauty of the place wasn't lost on me as I attempted to gather myself on a bench. And where there is any form of beauty, there is life. If only I could manage to find my way home, I thought, everything might somehow be all right. But the address of my lodgings and the ability to walk there had abandoned me. I needed someone who could point me in the right direction. Instead, a raven-haired woman wrapped in fox fur took my arm and pulled me east towards the Elephant Hotel, where a room could be paid for by the hour. On reaching the boardwalk I seized a pole and refused to continue. She drew close and traced a line down my back, her breath hot in my ear, whispering her desire to see the thing I was famous for – to touch it. She began to unbutton my fly, and I burnt with the shame of inexperience and unwanted arousal.

'Don't be shy,' she said. 'You wouldn't be my first animal act.'

Her forced interest in my abhorrent feature for the sake of money filled me with loathing and self-loathing. I asked her to stop, but she dug her nails into my arm and said, 'What's the matter? You don't like girls?'

I shook her off and staggered away but she followed, unrelenting in her taunting solicitation. I pulled the remaining bills from my wallet and pushed them into her hand, then walked towards the sea. The woman remained on the boardwalk and yelled, 'I don't need your lousy change!'

I reached the lapping waves. Water seeped into my shoes.

'I've met some crazies in my time, mister. But you sure take the cake!'

Fully clothed, I walked into the inky sea, lights dancing on its surface. I hardly registered the chill until it reached my aching ears, and cut off the woman's voice.

My toes curled with a chill of recognition that ran its way up my entire body, setting me shivering convulsively. When it reached the top of my head, I remembered properly for the first time how I'd walked inebriated and fully clothed into the sea, wanting to die from the shame of Nicole Parker discovering my ugly secret.

Exceedingly intoxicated, I'd convinced myself that I'd never find love and happiness, and attempted to drown myself. Only by the grace of God did I fail. My father had always told me never to give up the fight, and at that crucial moment his words returned to me. I saw the faces of my dear family longing for my return, a revelation of their great love for me, and I chose life. I allowed the waves to wash me ashore and crawled up the sand. The cold bite of the ocean had restored enough sense in me to find my way back to my lodgings. I built a roaring fire and spent the night beside it, thawing my frozen body and planning my return to Australia.

There I would fulfil my goal of setting my family free from their bondage of debt with the money I'd earnt from putting myself on display. Touring with the Astonishing Assembly of splendid performers had opened my eyes to variances in human anatomy and appearance, and given me an interest in studying medicine. I would eventually establish a practice that provided comfort and assistance to people suffering from any condition that made them feel isolated from society. And by accomplishing this, my own affliction would at last be redeemed.

Edwin Stroud's story finished happily enough, but the abrupt end of the journey left me feeling flatter than three-day-old roadkill. I lifted Ethel off the shelf and asked her if there was anything more to know, and if there was any way of finding out. I waited for five minutes then, putting her back onto the shelf and feeling utterly defeated, I noticed a tiny hole at the left side of her base – a keyhole.

'Of course! You need to be wound,' I said. 'But where is your key?'

Calling Isa after midnight was impulsive and perhaps selfish, but I desperately needed to slow my speeding thoughts. After she'd expressed her sleepy incredulity at the hour of my call, I asked what Bert had given her. She said it was a tiny brass key.

I gasped, stopped breathing momentarily.

'Are you still there?' she said. 'Speak or I'm hanging up.'

'I'm still here. Could I please borrow the key?'

'What for?'

'I can't divulge that right now – maybe later. Could you please bring it to school tomorrow?'

'Sure. Goodnight.'

THE KEY TO
UNDERSTANDING

Friday was cold and half the students had switched to the drab winter uniform. Isa was one of them. And she'd forgotten to bring the key. Unable to maintain a rational and objective view of the world, I accused her of doing it intentionally to annoy me.

'It makes me sad if you really think that,' she said. 'I might've remembered if you'd bothered to tell me why you wanted it after waking me up in the middle of the night. I'll bring it on Monday.'

'Can I come to your place after school instead?'

'If you insist.'

After my longest day in living memory, we caught a train to Erskineville. Isa said I'd been acting remote, bristly and dismissive.

'I've got stuff going on that you couldn't imagine,' I said.

'Newsflash! You're not the only one. Everybody has stuff going on all of the time. That's what life is – stuff going on. You don't realise that other people are struggling with shit because you're so focused on your own.'

'Well, excuse me for thinking that I might actually be going insane.'

'Calm down. People who are really mad are totally unaware of it.'

'That is complete and utter bullshit!'

'Shh . . . We're in the quiet carriage and you're disturbing the other passengers.'

'SORRY, FELLOW PASSENGERS! I am not completely crazy. You all just think I am because I'm talking loudly.'

Isa put her hand over my mouth. 'The only crazy person on this train is me, because I actually used to like you. I liked you a lot, if you want to know the truth. But I'm struggling to remember why. Because right now I don't like you very much at all.'

'Great, because I feel exactly the same way about myself.'

We got off the train at Erskineville Station and walked up the stairs.

'Lincoln, what's going on with you?'

'Yesterday I found out stuff that has me questioning the origin of my existence.'

'You've completely lost me.'

'I really hope not.'

'What do you mean?' Isa stopped walking.

'Nothing. I just thought you were one of the few people who got me.'

Knowing that I hadn't come for conversation or refreshment, Isa offered me neither when we got to her place. She made me wait at the bottom of the stairs while she fetched the key. Delilah must've picked up on the tense vibe, because when I reached down to pat her she clawed the back of my hand then pissed off into the back garden. Isa returned and dropped a charm bracelet into my hand. 'There you go,' she said. 'Take extremely good care of it.'

Attached to the chain, along with the little brass key, was the mood ring Isa's dying father had given her mother, and a dove flying through a gold heart studded with diamonds – the brooch Edwin had given to Diddy Budd. Two love tokens.

'Don't you want to take those off first?'

'No. Because against all current evidence telling me not to, I trust you one hundred per cent.'

'And there's the little key.'

'There's the key. Bert told me you might come looking for it. He said, "Make sure the little bugger gets it. But don't make it too easy for him."'

'You've done your job well.'

'Is it for winding the mechanical hen?'

'I hope it's for the hen. Bert left a tag around her neck that said, "Good egg for a good egg – Lincoln from up the hill." This is going to sound completely mad, but I think there's something inside the hen that's for me.'

Isa smiled and touched the lapels of my blazer. 'You know, you really are a good egg,' she said. Then she crinkled her nose and kissed me on the cheek. 'Good luck.'

As the elevator ascended to level twenty-seven, I prayed that the hen would recognise her key. I paced the balcony before going to my room. I took Ethel off the shelf and said to her, 'I think I've got what we need to get you going.' I removed the key from Isa's charm bracelet and guided it into the keyhole in Ethel's base. It fitted perfectly but there was resistance when I turned it – an unhealthy grinding. Instead of forcing it, I found a tiny plastic bottle of hair-clipper oil in Dad's bathroom and squeezed three drops into the hole. After waiting a minute, I tried the key again and it turned, no resistance, until the hen was fully wound. I removed the key and set Ethel on the table. I waited and waited, but she remained still. I figured she needed the token, but it was already trapped inside.

Then I noticed a tiny hole under the base. I poked in Dad's smallest screwdriver. A hatch fell open, releasing the gold token and the twenty-cent piece.

I kissed the charms on Isa's bracelet. I picked up the coin, and I kissed the sailor and I kissed George Pemberton. Then I dropped the golden coin into the slot. Immediately something inside Ethel whirred and vibrated. Her head turned from side to side, surveying her new home. She winked at me and nodded three times. There was more whirring, and the sound of something shifting inside. Her whole body lifted slightly then she lowered herself back onto the nest and shook her tail feathers. I bit my lip to stop myself laughing, concerned it might disturb the ritual. Ethel trembled, both metal wings ruffling as much as metal wings can, and she bobbed up and down. She clucked and cackled, scratchy at first then louder and clearer, igniting an intense feeling of joy deep in my soul. The irrepressible joy burnt through my chest and up my throat, erupting as laughter, squeezing tears from the corners of my eyes. Ethel was going completely berserk. Good to his promise, Bert had got her working again.

She quietened down and became still.

I held my breath and waited.

She clucked intermittently, then again came the whirring and shifting of gears.

Then nothing – nothing at all.

My heart sank. I recalled my dog Gus's valiant last attempt to stand – how hard my loyal friend had tried to please me.

I said to the little hen, 'Don't worry about it, Ethel, you gave it your best shot. You can let go now.'

She clucked one last time and she did let go.

She let go of a golden egg, which came rolling down the little chute. The cool, smooth metal warmed quickly in my hand. The egg had a seam like the wooden ball. I peeled off the sticky tape around the seam and unscrewed the egg. It contained neither of the things Bert mentioned, no lolly or handkerchief. But there was something much more promising – a scroll tied with a tiny blue bow. I slid off the ribbon and, fearing the scroll might disintegrate or tear, uncurled it just enough to see perfectly formed but miniature writing – as if penned with the aid of a magnifying glass. I squinted, but it was still impossible to read.

I searched everywhere for a magnifying glass without luck. I went to the chemist on Darlinghurst Road but they didn't sell them, so I tried the newsagency. There was one left, the size of a bread plate with a super-thick lens – sure to work. I waited behind a guy who was having his lotto ticket checked. He won fifteen bucks. It was a good omen. I congratulated him and bought the magnifying glass, then ran past Frank at the concierge desk, holding it up to my eye for comic effect. Caught the lift up to level twenty-seven. Uncurled the scroll and held it in place between a metal ruler and my mouse.

I read these words:

Dear friend,

In faith I trust that you are the intended recipient of this missive, and am heartened it has finally reached you. Yet I'm also saddened that your possession of it means you bear an affliction that I am in part responsible for passing on. For, if all instructions have been executed as prescribed, then you are my descendant, and alone will be able to determine exactly how many generations apart we are. Not only do I seek to convey my deepest sympathy and most humble apology, but I also hope to express the type of encouragement only possible from one who has shared your peculiar condition.

Where to begin? Perhaps at the very beginning of life itself. All humans in the embryonic stage possess extra vertebrae that are somehow absorbed before they're delivered screaming and bawling into this world – yes, each and every one of us. But a very few are born with vestigial evidence of this formation intact. I was born with no obvious abnormality, the discolouration not becoming a protuberance until my adolescent years. Initially it was small and easily ignored, but over a period of months it grew to a little over three inches in length.

Recently I completed an autobiographical account of the early portion of my life, which I hope has also found its way into your hands. Some names were changed to enable me to tell my story as candidly as possible while protecting the privacy of those close to me. My real name is Theodore Stonehouse. Edwin Stroud is the alias I used from my first performance in Sydney to my final one in New York. The story ends with my decision to return to Australia after fifteen months performing in the United States of America. The next chapter of my life, described briefly below, is intended for your edification only.

Reuniting with my family was one of the greatest joys of my life. Especially as I'd returned with enough money to pay off all our debts and buy a modest stone cottage in Balmain for us to inhabit. Many things had changed in my absence, but the impact of Federation seemed insignificant compared to matters of a personal nature.

368

My beloved Daisy Blythe, Deidre (Diddy) Budd in my memoir, had fallen pregnant to Reginald McGuffin, who demonstrated his true colours by abandoning her the day after she told him. It was the most dire of predicaments for Daisy, but for me it was an oddly fortuitous turn of events. I'd ruled out the possibility of ever marrying and having children, for fear of passing on my affliction. Here was the perfect solution for both of us! I'd never stopped loving Daisy, and without hesitation I proposed to her. We married quietly and lived with my family in the cottage. I hired a tutor and finished my secondary education around the time our son Otto was born. He is now a fine young lad, exhibiting the kind and serene nature of his mother and none of the malignant traits of his biological father.

Immersed in my later study of medicine at the University of Sydney, I was content with our small family, but women can be persuasive creatures. Shortly after my graduation, Daisy's belly began to swell a second time and with it my anxiety that something might go awry. My fears proved unfounded when Alice arrived in the world perfect in every way. However, it was only on reaching sixteen that my problem manifested, and the same may yet happen to her. Even if Alice develops no malformation, she may carry the trait to future descendants, which is my reason for writing.

Three years ago, our dear friend George Pemberton passed away and in his will left Ethel the mechanical hen to me. On completing this letter I shall seal it within her egg. Alice will be given charge of the hen on her sixteenth birthday, along with the key and golden token required to set her in motion. If blessed with children of her own, she will pass Ethel on to them and so on down the family line, with instructions to be activated by the person who manifests the strange affliction. That person, my dear descendant, is you.

I hope that you're living in a kinder and gentler world than the one I currently inhabit. A world where difference is tolerated, if not celebrated – a world where men and women are treated equally and a person is never denigrated or shown prejudice because of their physical bearing, colour of their skin, religion or creed.

369

On my return to this land, I learnt that our newly formed Federal Government had not recognised Aboriginal people properly in the constitution. It seemed a perpetuation of the barbarous treatment they've been subjected to for the past hundred-odd years. And it shames me deeply that while my short performing career earnt enough money to rescue my family from debt, my early act was rife with a pernicious form of humour that condoned bigotry. I must live with this and many other contradictions and failings. There is no possible means of calculating the extent of the historical harms I have caused. So I continue moving forward, seeking to address and oppose ignorance in its various guises, in the hope of a more enlightened future.

Some poor souls are bound and paralysed by their secrets. In my medical practice I often see patients afflicted by what others might consider insignificant, and yet they remain oppressed by their inability to bring them to the light. Once I considered myself too hideous for a woman to love. It took a long time to realise how wrong I was. It is only through accepting our faults and imperfections that we can accept others and love them as they truly are. So I hope that, knowing my failings, you're still able to feel some sort of bond with me, even though I am probably no longer of this world, and you are not yet in it as I write. I hope that my story gives you strength to prevail against any adversity you face.

Finally, possessing a tail may be an inconvenience, absurd and at times embarrassing. But it really is a tiny problem in relation to the multitude of challenges some people face every day of their existence. Lacking a sense of the ridiculous is a far worse plight – one of the most terrible incapacities a man can suffer from. So never forget to laugh at yourself. The tail is, after all, quite funny.

Yours most lovingly,
Theodore Stonehouse, a.k.a. Edwin Stroud

REDEEMING MY
AFFLICTION

I ran through the full-moon night to Bert's place, hoping for one last look before the bulldozers arrived. I was too late. The property was wrapped in mesh screens printed with the words PARADIGM — YOUR NEW SANCTUARY, over and over. What a bitter irony to swallow, like a fat green pickle in a glass of sour milk. I crawled under the mesh where the gate was and forced my way in. The plane tree and the fake totem pole were the only things standing. Bert's house had been demolished.

I sat in the rubble and told old Bert about finding the message and what it said, even though I knew it was too late. Too late because I'm pretty sure that Bert had already opened the egg, read the message and resealed it – sticky tape wasn't invented till 1930. Too late because Bert died more than a week ago. And yet the broken pipes and piles of bricks conveyed a finality I hadn't fully comprehended when Lana had broken the news to me. I never had the chance to talk to Bert about being related. He must've been too ashamed of the feature we shared and the way he'd treated his own family. At least I'd told him I was glad that I'd found him.

I got up and searched through the debris, scouring the area like a volunteer rescue worker, stupidly hoping to discover a trace of a life lived there before construction began.

And then I found Percy. Flattened and dirty. Both eyes missing.

I brought the little guy home and laid him next to Ethel, then went out onto the balcony. Twenty-seven levels above the ground. The night was still and cold, the air sharp, city lights unblinking and the moon high.

One hundred and twenty years ago, my great-great-great-grandfather ventured across the world to save his family by putting himself on show, exploiting the thing that had made him feel ugly. The thing we have in common. I remembered seeing Edwin's real name, Theodore Stonehouse, on Mum's family tree. Knowing where it came from and who had gone before me, I wasn't so ashamed.

This tail is in my genetic make-up. Its appearance was inevitable – my predetermined legacy. I don't believe that everything happens for a reason. But everything has a cause. Knowing the cause of the tail has liberated me from the search for its meaning. The only meaning is the one that I choose to attach to it. If Theodore Stonehouse had fronted up to the physical examination for Crestfield Academy 125 years ago, Joseph Millington Drake would have been disgusted by what he saw and rejected him as the progeny of depraved parents. Maybe I should've whipped mine out at the interview? Theodore was right. The tail is, after all, quite funny. And laughing at it was one way of redeeming my affliction. The other would be daring something worthy.

HERE IS THE END

The early morning sky was gold on the horizon, then blue, with barely a transition. The Crestfield colours. It was ten degrees and still an hour before sunrise, which meant an hour before the opening of International Velvet. Isa had brought a thermos of coffee, which she poured as we sat on the backpacks we'd stuffed to bursting with the knitted DNA.

'Your hands are shaking,' she said as I took the cup. 'Are you nervous?'

'Just cold,' I said, even though I was scared shitless on at least two counts. Isa had figured out I'd been faking my appreciation of the macchiato, which was a huge relief, and she'd made the coffee sweet and milky but strong enough to provide a much-needed surge of courage and determination.

I took out her charm bracelet and held up the little key. 'It worked,' I said. 'Last night I wound the mechanical hen, and when I dropped in Pericles' token, Ethel started clucking.'

A smile lit up Isa's face, and her eyes widened.

'She laid a little golden egg with a message inside. A message to me, and Bert as well. A secret about our shared ancestry.'

'I don't understand?'

I gave her a smile. 'It's a long and crazy story, so I'll save it for after we get this thing up.'

Walking through Crestfield's rear gates with the weight of hundreds of hours of knitting on our backs, I figured we'd be easily spotted on the security footage. 'Let's hope nobody's watching the live broadcast,' I said. 'It would suck if this thing got cut down by a security guard before anybody else had a chance of seeing it.'

'No chance of that happening,' Isa said. We reached The Labyrinth and dropped our packs. 'I'm going to record the installation and post it on The Owlet.'

'Serious?'

'Last night I wrote this blurb to go with it.' On her phone she showed me a rationale of our work more explicit and detailed than the one we'd submitted to Ms Tarasek. It was followed by a call to action, urging the students to sign a petition demanding that the faculty, administration and board commission plaques outlining Joseph Millington Drake's involvement with the eugenics movement and his establishment of a racist and discriminatory selection process. The plaques would be attached to the statue and the auditorium bearing his name.

Why not have the statue and references to Millington Drake removed altogether? 'Whitewashing,' Isa said. 'What he did should be talked about. Not forgotten.'

Isa climbed over The Labyrinth gate first. I heaved over the backpacks then followed. We walked to the centre in silence, contemplating the magnitude of what we were doing. Isa had never entered The Labyrinth before, and she laughed when she saw Millington Drake with his hand on King Henry's rump. 'Pompous git,' she said, and reached for the bull's snout.

'Don't! If you touch him he talks, and it might set something else off.'

We unpacked the two massive lengths of DNA. Isa stitched them together then filmed us wrapping one end around Joseph Millington Drake's neck. We trailed the coil almost halfway back to the entrance, at which point it ran out, then tied on a single thread that we laid the rest of the way to the gate. Isa attached a small disk to the end that said YOU ARE HERE! We climbed back over the gate, then hid our empty backpacks behind the recycling bins and found a spot in the grove that was catching the first rays of sun.

Beginning with the discovery of my connection to Edwin Stroud, a.k.a. Theodore Stonehouse, I told Isa all about myself. I told her about the strange discoloured patch that had become a nub, which grew into a tail. I told her of my fear of it being exposed and the shame that had controlled me. She was incredulous, astonished, perplexed then curious, but never once showed any sign of being repelled. She hardly spoke until I'd finished and asked what she was thinking.

'It must've been a huge thing for you to deal with. Especially trying to work through all of the possible causes. But maybe now you've shared it, you'll realise that it's actually a really small thing.'

'It's almost five centimetres.'

'Okay. Well, out of all the afflictions that anybody could have, it's still far from the worst.'

'You don't think I'm a complete freak?'

'It makes you unique, which is a good thing. We should embrace the unusual. And like Theodore wrote, it is a little bit funny.'

'Remember when we were at my dad's apartment and I pushed you away?'

'How could I forget?' She rolled her eyes. 'It almost killed me.'

'Same. But now you know the reason.'

The sun had risen high enough to provide a little warmth and give Isa a beautiful golden glow. 'Would you push me away now?' she said.

I shook my head and Isa moved in close. Right on the verge of something exceptionally amazing happening, Pericles appeared in the corner of my eye. With zero sensitivity for the moment, he yelled out and came gambolling down. 'Did it work?' he said.

Unsure if he meant the key in the chicken or the art project or telling Isa everything, I said, 'It worked!' and he pulled us into a three-way hug.

*

375

During Maths, Isa sat with Phoenix and I sat next to Pericles and none of us gave Monaro a second of our attention. The air was electric with anticipation. Tibor poked me in the back and asked what was going on. Considering his vital role in devising the DNA pattern for Isa, I passed him a note saying that we'd installed it this morning. He sent one back saying, 'May the Force be with you.'

Second period, Isa and Phoenix had Dance, and Pericles had Woodwork, leaving me alone with free study in the library – almost an hour to speculate on the possible scenarios that might play out. Though initially I'd hated going to Crestfield, I now had a tight crew of good friends and was worried we might be broken up. But I figured that expelling Isa and me would only bring unfavourable attention to the school and its troubling foundations.

For the final five minutes I stared at the library clock, willing the second hand to move faster. And when the electronic glockenspiel finally sounded, it wasn't the regular signal for recess but the call to special assembly. Adrenaline spread like poison through my vascular system. My heart raced and the tail folded in on itself.

I took the catwalk to the Joseph Millington Drake Auditorium, calling and texting Isa on the way, but there was no response. I lingered near the entrance, asking other Year 10 students if they'd seen her. Cheyenne Piper said Isa had gone in already so I made my way up the stairs. And just as I was about to enter alone, there was a tug on my blazer. 'Shh!' Isa said as she took my hand then led me back down the stairs and around the side of the building. 'Word on the street is that two meddling kids have tampered with the statue of our beloved founder and his bull.' She opened her laptop and got onto The Owlet. The clip of us wrapping the DNA around Millington Drake's neck was ready to post. 'I think it's time,' she said, and tapped SUBMIT, sending the footage, exposé and petition to every exceedingly gifted and dangerously privileged student enrolled at Crestfield Academy.

'You're the bravest person around,' I said. 'No matter what happens next, we're in this together.'

'There's nobody in the world I'd rather get into serious trouble with,' Isa Mountwinter said. And then she kissed me.

ACKNOWLEDGEMENTS

Thank you, Mum and Dad. I wouldn't be here without your love and unwavering support.

To Belinda Bolliger and Mark Macleod for first showing faith in me and this story a long time ago.

To my early readers: Beth Gallate for thinking the first draft was already perfect at one thousand pages, and Jason Gallate for other superlatives I didn't deserve but kept repeating to myself. To Drusilla Modjeska, for telling me I had a voice. You opened your door and invited me into another world. And to Martha Bentley, for getting me the moment we met, falling in love with Lincoln Locke and starting the Secret Middles twenty-four-hour support group. To dedicated members Maggie MacKellar, thank you for words that live between Earth and Heaven, and Our Kate Gordon for your constant buoyancy. #BeLikeTaffy.

To my publisher, Nikki Christer, for picking up something I feared was irredeemably broken and believing it could be rebuilt better, faster, stronger. To Celine for drafting a plan. To my lovely editors Catherine Hill and Tom Langshaw for your kindness, dedication, craftsmanship and perspective. You made this thing so much more than it was in my hands alone. To Alex Ross for your plucky cover design and to

Mike Windle for your banter while snapping me. And thank you to all the other good people at Penguin Random House who I haven't yet met but helped get this book out there.

Thank you to my agent, Jane Novak, for taking me on and keeping it real.

Special thanks to Louise McLeod Tabouis for booking me on a tour of the Musée des Art Forains in Paris. Riding the magnificent vélocipède changed everything. Thank you, Douglas Channing, for granting me conversations without time limits. To my colleagues over the years who've endured me banging on about this book and wondered if it would ever materialise – here it is! Thank you to all my dear friends for your encouragement and understanding why I was doing the hermit thing. To the real Bert and Percy, thank you for lending me your names. And to Coco for trotting into the pages as Tippi and performing your own rescue.

To everybody else in my family: George, Tanja, Xanthe, Zachary, Zoe, Angela, Che and Solomon. Thank you for the unconditional love.

Steven Berkoff's stage adaptation of Franz Kafka's *The Metamorphosis* at the Nimrod Theatre blew my mind and reshaped my thinking when I was thirteen years old. And these brilliant books among many others helped me to build a world for my characters to inhabit and provided me with many missing pieces of the puzzle: *Cole of the Book Arcade* by Cole Turnley; *Professional Savages: Captive Lives and Western Spectacle* by Roslyn Poignant; *The Showman and the Slave* by Benjamin Reiss; *War Against the Weak: Eugenics and America's Campaign to Create a Master Race* by Edwin Black; *Freak Show* by Robert Bogdan; *Prelude to Christopher* by Eleanor Dark.

Finally, to you, dear reader, thank you for coming all this way with me. Knowing you would one day be holding this in your hands kept me going.

ABOUT THE AUTHOR

Bernard Gallate began his professional life in the animation industry with Hanna-Barbera, later working for Walt Disney and a multimedia agency. After studying acting, he ran climbing tours of the Sydney Harbour Bridge for six years while writing and illustrating books for younger readers. Bernard currently teaches programs on early Sydney life and archaeology at historical sites across the city. *The Origin of Me* is his first novel.